This book is dedicated to Paul, my loving husband, critique partner, and scene enhancer, and to my father. Without him, consistently placing fantasy books in my hands, my love for fantasy and sci-fi would never have grown.

THE BEGINNING OF THE END

Chronicles of Atlantis
Book 1

Self-Published by
Sarah M. Wasson

FANTASTICAL REALM
PUBLISHING

Fantastical Realm Publishing
Book List
Author Sarah M. Wasson

Chronicles of Atlantis
The Beginning of the End – Book 1
The Journey Continues – Book 2
The End of Atlantis – Book 3 – releasing 2025
Royal Line – The Search – a Chronicles of Atlantis Short Story

A Prophecy Foretold Novel
Twins of Fate – Book 1
Wizard's Hat – Book 2
Infinite Medallion – Book 3 - forthcoming

Short Stories
To Train a Falcon

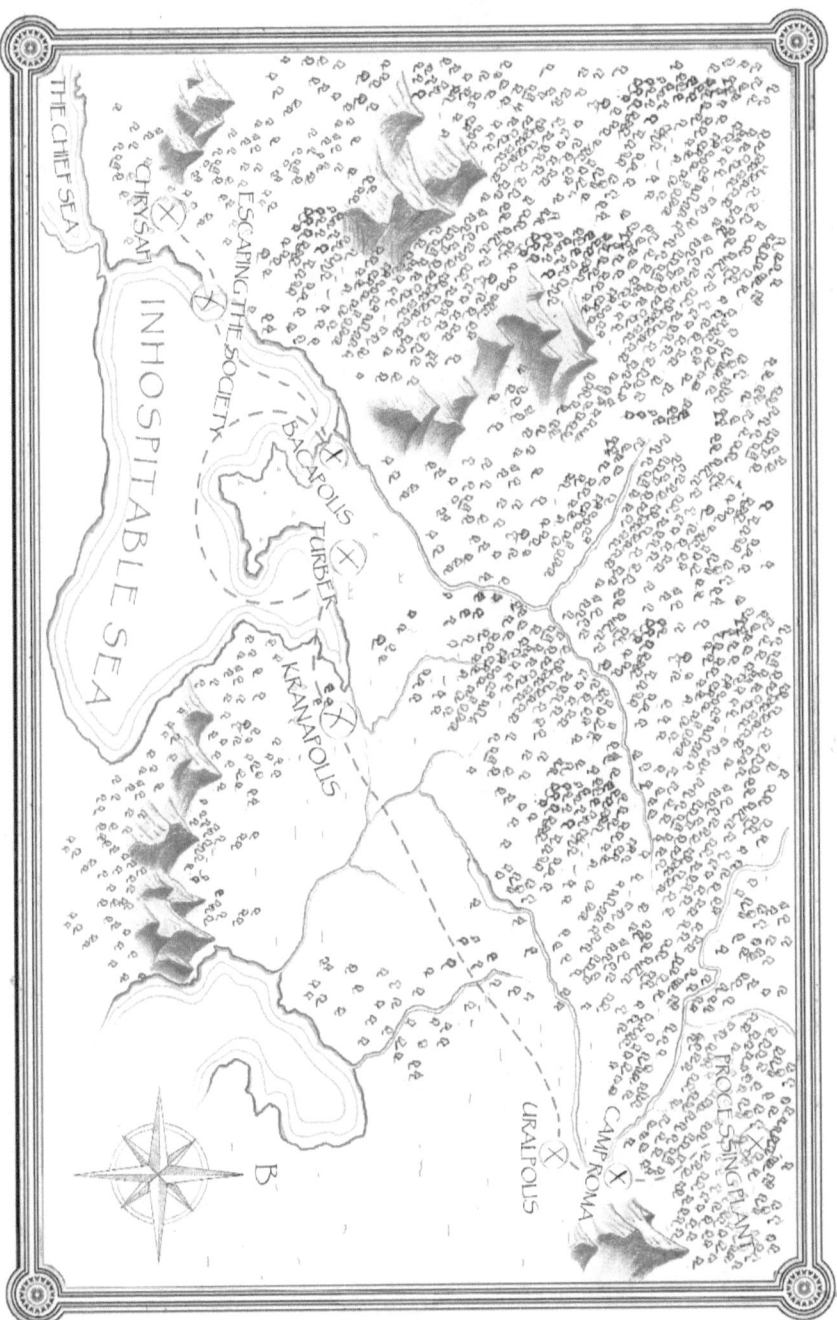

∞ PROLOGUE ∞

"**WE** found it, sire! We found it!" an old man said, rushing into the conference room carrying a large stack of papers and star maps.

King Sil sat up straighter in his chair. "You found a suitable planet?"

"Yes, sire. After searching the known galaxies, we finally found a planet that has not been claimed yet."

"Where is it?" King Sil jumped to his feet and helped the Star Finder lay out his maps.

"This planet here is the one that we feel will work best." The Star Finder pointed to a map of a nine-planet solar system. "This is the only one that meets our needs. The research team arrived last night. Their commander will be here shortly with his report, but I don't think we will find a better planet."

Sil looked at the map, then reached for another one. He looked up and walked to the west wall of the conference room. The entire wall was a star map of every solar system they had explored. "Show me where this planet is."

The Star Finder walked over to the wall and pointed to a small spiral solar system at the far end of the map.

"So far away. How long has the research team been gone?" King Sil asked.

"They were the first ones who left. The ones we thought were lost, sire."

King Sil staggered back to the table in the middle of the room. "They left over a decade ago." Sil shook his head and racked his fingers through his hair.

"Thirteen years ago, my liege," a new voice said from the entrance.

King Sil looked up to see a familiar face, now over ten years older than when he had last seen him. "Adamo, my friend. I thought I would never see you again." Sil's face broke into a smile.

Adamo smiled in return as he walked across the room. "There was a time when I thought I would never see my home again. It's great to be back."

"What can you tell me about this planet?" Sil asked, gesturing to the seat beside him.

"It's quite small, but the air is breathable, and the atmosphere is tolerable."

"You walked on the planet?" Sil asked, his eyes widening.

"Yes, my friend," Adamo said, taking the offered seat. "I will tell you all about the planet, which I have named Krill."

"Krill? Truly, you couldn't think of a better name than that?" Sil rolled his eyes.

"Did I hear someone say my name?" a woman asked, entering the room.

Sil and Adamo looked toward the rear of the room. A panel was open, and a slender woman emerged from the secret passageway into the conference room.

"That is not your name, dear sister," Sil said with a chuckle.

"Just a nickname I haven't heard in ages."

"Trillenna, it is so good to see you. Those were the days, were they not? Sneaking out of the palace and riding into the countryside without our guards," Adamo said, embracing Trillenna.

"Taking on silly names, thinking it would fool everyone we met." Trillenna laughed.

"And not considering that our horses and clothing would be recognized," Sil added. They sat in silence, reminiscing for a moment.

"When did you return, cousin?" Trillenna asked.

"Only moments ago. I was just about to tell your brother about the planet I've found. It will be perfect for our penal colony: it's outside any trade routes, hasn't been claimed, and is far from any other inhabited solar system."

"Sounds almost too perfect," Trillenna said.

Sil looked at Adamo, waiting for his response.

"Well, there are primitive people on the planet currently, but from our initial findings, they shouldn't cause any problems. There aren't many of them, and they have only mastered stone tools and weapons. With the new memory sweep, which I've heard many good things about, we'll be able to utilize this planet for generations."

"Memory sweep? You aren't really thinking of doing that, are you?" Trillenna asked, horrified.

"It is the most humane solution we can think of. We will sweep their minds of most of their memories and let them live out the rest of their lives as they see fit. With no knowledge of where they came from or who they were, they can turn over a new leaf, as it were," Sil explained. "The alternative is something I know you would object to."

Trillenna crossed her arms. "We are not bringing executions back; I will not budge on that topic."

"Cousin, dear," Adamo started. "What would you have us do then? Lock them in a cage for the rest of their lives, feeding and clothing them but never being able to release them?" "We have tried rehabilitating some of them. Don't get me wrong; it works for most. But…" He held his hands out. "It doesn't work for all. Those who have committed the most heinous crimes must be dealt with."

Trillenna frowned. "I know. Okay, I see no alternative. How soon before we send the first… um… shipment?"

"Shipment? Now that sounds horrible," Sil said mockingly. "We will send the first subjects within the month."

∞ 1 ∞
EVERYTHING CHANGES

NEIAPHI sat alone in her quarters, lost in thought. She gazed out the window at the sky, a soft blend of light green and blue.

A chime resonated through the complex. Neiaphi hung her head, letting her long brown hair cascade over her shoulders. She swept her hair back and groaned. Standing up, she gathered her silk teal robe and tablet before leaving her quarters.

She walked down the glass-enclosed corridor, her pale reflection and blue eyes staring back at her. She stopped at a doorway and looked out at the garden. Brightly colored flowers were in bloom, as was the cherry tree in the center. A small creek flowed from the central fountain, its shimmering green water disturbed only by the occasional rock or flick of a fish's tail. She stepped into the garden and tilted her head to the sky, which was a greenish-blue at this time of year, with pale pink clouds becoming more numerous. As the suns neared their highest point in the sky, their warmth radiated down on the city and warmed her skin. She closed her eyes and imagined a Pegasus frolicking among the clouds. What a sight it would be to see a flying horse—so white, so beautiful. But sadly, the Pegasus had disappeared long before she was born. As the second chime echoed through the corridor, she snapped out of her daydream and started to run; she was going to be late for class. Skidding to a halt at the classroom door, she hastily smoothed her hair and adjusted her dress. She glanced around the deserted corridor and cursed under her breath—she was the last to arrive. Slowly, she opened the door and hurried to her seat at the back of the room, trying to avoid her teacher's glare.

Pi, the elderly teacher with grey hair pulled into a tight bun on top of her head, walked purposefully up and down the rows of students. "Now that everyone has finally arrived," she said, fixing her gaze squarely on Neiaphi. "I have an announcement," she said, addressing the entire class from the front of the room. "Several of your fellow students will leave within the moon cycle with their families, as the Krill Colonies need additional guards. This also means that more officials will be needed."

Neiaphi groaned—perhaps a bit too loudly. The entire class turned to look at her.

"Come now, Neiaphi, you can't tell me you're not looking forward to moving to the colony. What an experience that will be! You'll get to see an elephant and a deer up close. I know those are your two favorite animals from our studies. This is a once-in-a-lifetime opportunity, and few will get to experience it."

"I know I should be happy and looking forward to it, but I don't know. I've never left the city, not even for a ride in the mounds. Everything will be so different: the sky, the terrain, the primitive Krillians, and the Apemen. I don't even want to think about them. They look like us but are so different," Neiaphi said, shuddering at the mental image of their dark skin, dark hair, and shorter stature.

"Now, Neiaphi, it's not polite to call them primitive or use that other term. You know that. They may not have the benefits of our technology, but most are quite civilized, from what we've been told. And remember, they call themselves The People. They have feelings, too, so keep that in mind while you are there."

"That's why I don't want to go," she whined. "Here, I don't have to remember that and can call them whatever I want. I can't imagine a Citizen mating with them. Yuk." The class burst into laughter.

"Alright, everyone. That's enough," Pi said, struggling to hide her laughter.

"Let's continue where we left off the last time we met. We were about to discuss The People," Pi emphasized the word People and glanced at Neiaphi with a grin. "And how they came to be. Now, who can tell me when we first encountered the ancestors of the present-day People?" Pi looked around the room. No hands were raised, and every head was bowed. "Cret, how about you? You'll need to know this, especially since you'll also be living there."

Cret looked up and cleared his throat. "Well, I think it was during the time of King Sil if I remember correctly. King Sil faced a problem with housing criminals and began exploring nearby planets to establish a colony. He discovered a strikingly blue planet in the Krill System that orbited a single sun. It seemed well-suited for human habitation. King Sil sent a research team to the planet, and when they returned, they reported that it would be suitable. King Sil inquired about the local life forms on the planet. The team reported that there was a species resembling humans but with more ape-like features. They informed King Sil that interbreeding would not be possible. King Sil announced to the populace that all criminals convicted of major offenses would be sent to this new colony." Cret immediately looked down at his hands in his lap.

"If I remember correctly? Know it all."

"Hepluosis, that will be enough," Pi said sternly.

"That's correct, Cret. Very good. For many solar cycles, all criminals convicted of major offenses were sent to the Krill Colony. They were left there to do as they pleased. We stripped them of all their possessions and clothing and essentially set them free. We established no guard posts and had no control over them. As a precaution, King Sil had their minds erased of all knowledge. They would be unable to mount any attacks when future shipments arrived. After some time, King Sil's great-great-great-grandson sent a research team to the colony to check on things. To their great horror, the team discovered that the criminals were, in fact, interbreeding with the locals. This new species resembled citizens, but most specimens had darker features, with some being very dark.

Yes, I know some citizens have a darker complexion, but they have white hair, not black. Blonde, brunette, and red hair were also observed, but these individuals had darker features than ours."

"When the team reported their findings to King Silsi, he was horrified. He immediately assembled a team to send to the colony to get things under control. The team was led by Poseidie, a distinguished leader and nobleman, who brought his ten sons with him. Poseidie discovered an uninhabited island and began constructing a great city."

"In case the locals and criminals mounted an attack, he wanted his city to be well fortified. He built three rings of canals, with two land masses between them and an island at the center. At the very center of the island, he built his quarters."

One of the students raised her hand. "Yes, Phylas?"

"How did Poseidie get to his quarters with a ring of water around it?" the petite girl asked shyly.

"He brought six Pegasus stallions to pull his golden chariot. King Silsi permitted this, only to later realize that the Pegasus population would soon decline. Now, where was I? Ah, yes. Poseidie had no wife, so he found a local maiden to care for his sons. He named her Cleito. They rounded up all the full citizens they could find and brought them to Poseidie's quarters, which were now called Atlantis, named after his eldest son, Atlas. Those of mixed descent were left where they were found but continued to be monitored by the guards. Poseidie's next hurdle was organizing the criminals and setting up several guard posts across the planet. He decided that religion would be the easiest way to achieve this and settled on a multi-god system. King Silsi was established as the supreme god, but the name needed to be changed. Even with their minds erased, their memories could resurface if triggered. He chose the name Zeus but then changed it to something more powerful: Poseidon, the God of the Sea. He instructed a few team members to develop the details and model this religion after our society, but with different names. He wanted the criminals to embrace the religion willingly, with something that felt natural.

"Atlas took over where his father left off, with the help of his nine brothers, and the religion grew, becoming widely accepted in the region. Other religions emerged in different regions but were allowed to develop on their own. Every few solar cycles, more criminals arrived, and new guards and officials were sent to replace those already stationed there. Most citizens, it seems, chose to remain on the planet and continued to serve the King. Interbreeding continued until only one species was found outside the guard posts. The People, as they called themselves, even started to govern themselves with the rules set forth by Poseidon and Atlas. Everything remained peaceful for many cycles.

"There have been some uprisings recently, which is why additional guards and officials are being sent there. Yet do not worry; peace will prevail there as it has here.

"Everyone, take out your tablets, and we'll continue with today's written lessons."

Several fingers of time passed, and Neiaphi struggled to concentrate on her lessons. At last, the dismissal chime rang through the classroom.

"Okay, everyone may go. Some of you need to prepare for a long trip. Good luck." Pi stood near the door, collecting the completed tablets and distributing new ones. She gave the five departing for Krill quick hugs and pats on the back.

Neiaphi left the room feeling even more worried. She would be leaving the only home she had ever known to enter a troubled world where more guards were needed to maintain the peace. How selfish of her parents to make her join them. They should have allowed her to stay with her paternal grandparents. Yes, that's it—she would tell them they should have done that. "After all, Father said we would only be there for a few solar cycles," she murmured as she walked back to her quarters.

As Neiaphi neared the garden by her quarters, she let out a loud sigh. She paused and took another look at the tranquil setting, feeling she wasn't ready to face her parents just yet. She stepped outside and followed the creek past the fountain to the market square. At this time of day, the market was bustling with activity. Merchants shouted over one another to draw attention to their wares. Silk, jewels, fruit, artwork, and an assortment of everyday items were displayed everywhere she looked. *What a wonderful place to live*, Neiaphi thought. Everything she could ever want was here in the city. Neiaphi turned up a side street and walked down a narrow alley. She passed a tavern window and overheard several men discussing the Krill Colony. She crouched beneath the window, glancing around nervously. It wasn't polite to eavesdrop, but she couldn't help herself.

"When was the last time we sent anyone to the colony, criminals or citizens alike?" a man with a nasal voice asked.

"None have been sent in my lifetime that I've heard of," another man replied in a deep voice.

"Then why are they in need of more guards and officials if we haven't sent any more criminals?" the first man asked.

"There have been reports of uprisings near Atlantis."

"Uprisings? Can't the citizens already there handle it? They should have plenty of armaments."

"Armament isn't the problem; it's trained personnel."

"Have they forgotten how to train personnel? I'm sure there are enough able-bodied individuals there to handle it."

"Well, I'm not sure if they're talking about guards," the first man said. "All I know is that a report came several moon cycles ago requesting more guards and officials. They said that the number of full citizens is declining and that some of The People are being given higher positions."

"King Titern is concerned that if these people rise too high in power, they might discover their origins, and our control could be lost."

"Might I ask a question or two?" a younger man asked.

"Yes, yes, my young pupil. What can I answer for you?" the man with the deep voice replied.

"We set up the criminal colony almost an eon ago and sent countless citizens to live there. We haven't sent anyone new since the time of King Titern's father, King Titanis. We don't need to send anyone new; our way of life has been so peaceful and tranquil, with very little crime occurring."

"The original criminals sent to the Krill Colony have long passed; all that's left are their descendants. Why do we keep them there without knowing where they came from? It is not their fault who their ancestors were. We should allow them to come home."

"Good question, young Crils. Long ago, it was believed that a truly evil person would pass that trait to their offspring. To this day, some citizens still believe this is true because, looking at us now, no crime has occurred, and everyone lives in harmony. Others say this may not be true, though. For cycles, Atlantis has reported peace.

"Unfortunately, the citizens I first mentioned make up the majority of our populace. They believe that all the descendants of the criminals will be just as evil, if not more so. However, I do not believe this is true. I believe that most citizens are good at heart, and only a few go bad."

There was a moment of silence before Crils continued, "Why don't we petition King Titern to conduct a study to see if some of those citizens can return home?"

"Well, the problem we face now is that there may be no full citizens left among the criminal population. They have mixed with the locals. Since the criminals could not remember who they were or where they came from, why would they mate purely with their own kind? They wouldn't know the difference. Furthermore, the guards and officials have been there for so long without replacements that full citizens might also find it difficult to locate them. If we don't send more soon, we may lose our hold forever, and the colony will be lost..."

The voices trailed off as the men departed. Neiaphi stood there, reflecting on everything she had heard. Crils raised questions that Neiaphi had been pondering herself. After a few moments, she continued down the alley, made her way up to the next street, and soon arrived at her favorite stand. She sat at a vacant table and pulled out a tablet her mother had given her. It contained a list of items she needed to gather to help her family prepare for the move. A woman, twice Neiaphi's age, approached and asked her what she would like. "I think I'll have a Cherry Bloom today."

"Very good," the woman replied and walked away. A few moments later, she returned with a tall, skinny glass and set it on the table. Neiaphi placed two coins down, and the woman smiled before leaving. Neiaphi took a sip of her drink. The smooth, sweet, and velvety texture touched her tongue, drawing a smile to her face. The cool liquid slid down her throat, leaving her feeling comforted and refreshed. She would miss her afternoon stops here, but she planned to visit every chance she got before she had to leave.

She sat for a while, studying her tablet. As the air cooled with the setting of Plexus, the largest of the two suns, she decided to head home, though she would take the long way.

Neiaphi wandered through the city, taking in the beauty of the buildings. Every structure was clean and orderly, and every citizen she passed seemed content with their lives. She smiled and nodded at several women tending to very young children. As she began to think about everything her family would be leaving behind, she found some comfort in the fact that her little brother was too young to remember their life here. She knew she needed to be assertive when speaking with her parents that evening. She had never stood her ground with them before and hadn't imagined she would ever need to. But this was her life as well, and she needed to have a say in the matter. She rehearsed in her mind how she would present her concerns to them. So engrossed in thought, Neiaphi nearly ran into her door.

By the time she reached the door, she had worked herself into such a frenzy about her parents' perceived selfishness that she flung it open, ready to shout. But her anger dissolved into surprise upon seeing her mother crying on her father's shoulder. Neiaphi froze, her mouth hanging open and her fists clenched. It took her a moment to regain her composure. With a deep breath, she walked over to her frail-looking parents, her anger replaced by growing concern. "Mother, Father, what's wrong?" she asked, her voice trembling. Her mother, already in tears, burst into more sobs and fled from the room. Her father sank heavily into a chair, opening his arms in a gesture of helplessness. Neiaphi went to him and sat next to him. Her father wrapped his arms around her and held her tightly. "Father, you're worrying me," she said. What's going on?"

"Your brother was in the court garden with your mother when I called her inside. She only left him for a moment, but in that short time, a wolver jumped the barricade and... and we were too late. Your brother was killed."

Neiaphi sat there stunned, her mind struggling to process her father's words. Her little brother was always in the way and full of questions, and more than once, she had told him she wished she didn't have a brother. But she never meant it—not like this.

Neiaphi collapsed into her father's arms and cried for the little brother she would never see again, realizing just how deeply she cared for him. Her tears were also for herself because she knew she couldn't leave her parents now, nor could she share her true feelings about the move. She had to be strong—stronger than she ever knew she could be.

∞ 2 ∞
CRET

CRET lingered by the classroom door, his eyes following Neiaphi as she rushed down the corridor. Her tense posture and hurried pace indicated that something was wrong, but whatever it was would have to wait. With a sigh, he turned away and made his way outside, the unanswered questions about her weighing on his mind. As Cret walked past the school's exercise yard, he noticed a group of students intently observing a teacher demonstrating swordplay. The teacher's movements were precise, the blade flashing as he executed strikes and blocks with a shield. Cret spared the scene only a glance before continuing, his steps leading him into the stable.

The stable greeted him with a rich blend of aromas: sweet hay, the earthy musk of straw bedding, and the warm, familiar scent of the animals. Most of the stalls were filled with horses, but a few housed more exotic mounts, each with its own unique presence. As Cret walked by, several horses snorted or nickered in recognition, their breath misting in the cool air. Cret paused to scratch a bay mare behind the ear, eliciting a contented nicker, before making his way to his family's stall. Inside, their griffin, Bol, greeted him with a low rumble. Cret gently patted the creature's beak, feeling the warm, smooth surface beneath his hand. He then inspected the saddle and bridle the stable hand had already secured on Bol, ensuring everything was perfectly in place for the journey ahead. Cret led Bol out of his stall and used a mounting block to swing onto the griffin's back easily. With a gentle nudge, he guided Bol out of the stables. Bol was an impressive sight, towering over most other mounts. His sharp, golden eyes and sleek feathers adorned an eagle's head and neck, while his powerful body, covered in tawny fur, was that of a lion, making him one of the largest and most formidable of his kind.

As soon as they were outside, Bol spread his wings wide and released a piercing screech that echoed through the air. It had been too long since he'd had the space to fully extend his massive wings. Cret tightened his grip, pressing his legs firmly against Bol's sides. The griffin began with a steady jog, quickly building momentum until he was racing across the ground, his powerful wings beating in rhythm. With a mighty leap, Bol launched into the sky, soaring above the stable and exercise yard below.

Once airborne, Cret guided Bol westward, urging him to greater speeds. The wind whipped through his short brown hair, and tears streamed from his eyes as the thrill of flight overtook him. Despite the sting, a wide smile spread across his face, and he couldn't help but let out a joyous shout lost in the rush of the wind.

They soared over the city, leaving its bustling streets behind as they ventured into the quiet countryside. This was Cret's last visit to his maternal grandparents before his family departed for Atlantis, a farewell he wasn't ready to face.

Cret had always cherished these solo visits to his grandparents. His grandmother's sweet treats and the peaceful atmosphere had made their home a sanctuary for him. But this time, as the familiar landscape came into view, a heavy sadness settled over him, knowing this would be their final time together before the journey that lay ahead. Since they couldn't bring Bol along to Atlantis, Cret's grandparents had kindly agreed to look after him. The flight to their home had been quick, but the return journey over the mounds on horseback would be far more arduous.

In no time, Bol and Cret landed smoothly at the grandparents' farm. Cret's grandfather was already outside, eagerly waiting for them. He quickly offered assistance, helping Cret settle Bol into their well-kept stable and ensuring the griffin was comfortably housed before Cret embarked on the long ride back.

"Goodbye, Bol. Be a good boy, and I'll see you in a few cycles," Cret said softly, wrapping his arms around the griffin's eagle-like neck for a quick, affectionate hug. He gave Bol's lion-like flank a reassuring pat before stepping out of the stall.

"Rest assured, Cret, I'll take excellent care of him," his grandfather said warmly. "It'll be as if you never left."

Cret's grandfather wrapped an arm around his shoulders, guiding him toward the house with a comforting presence. As they walked, Cret took in the sprawling estate, his eyes wide with awe. He was aware of his grandparents' wealth, but the sheer expanse of their land still amazed him, stretching out farther than he had ever imagined. The house stood proudly as a two-story structure framed by a vibrant garden brimming with colorful flowers and neatly tended vegetables. The perimeter fencing soared nearly three times Cret's height, a testament to its original purpose. When his grandfather built the estate, a high fence was necessary to keep out the numerous wolvers that roamed the area. Now that the wolver population was under control, the main gate was often left open, welcoming visitors to the estate's serene grounds.

"Cret, do you understand the magnitude of the opportunity before you?" his grandfather asked, settling into his private study. "When I was your age, I dreamed of being selected to go to the Colony. It's an extraordinary chance, one that I would have cherished."

"Grandfather, I've heard that we'll only be in the Colony for a few cycles, but I don't quite understand. It's been ages since anyone was sent there, and it seems so uncertain. What about the citizens already there?" Cret asked, his brow furrowing with concern. "Why haven't any of them returned, and why haven't replacements been sent? We're not supposed to be replacing anyone who comes home."

Just then, Cret's grandmother entered the room with a warm smile, carrying a plate of sweet rolls. She set them down on the table, gave Cret a cheerful kiss on the cheek, and then quietly stepped out, leaving the two men to their conversation.

Cret's grandfather cleared his throat, carefully considering his response. "Those are indeed complex questions. According to the official reports from the Colonies, the Citizens there are content and do not seek to return. They're dedicated to their service and are eager to continue supporting the kingdom. Additionally, their children are trained to manage their responsibilities, so replacements have not been needed." Cret's grandfather continued, his tone growing more serious. "The Colonies are now struggling with uprisings. Without new perspectives and fresh reinforcements, the children of the original citizens have become complacent. They find it difficult to manage the unrest because they relate too closely to the people they are supposed to govern—they've never experienced life on our home planet and lack the distance needed to maintain order. So, your father and the others will be sent there to take charge and restore order," his grandfather explained. "Their experience and fresh perspectives are meant to revitalize the Colony and ensure things run as they should."

Cret pondered his grandfather's words while savoring a bite of the sweet roll. The warm, tender dough practically melted on his tongue, releasing a comforting sweetness that reminded him of home. His grandmother's baking was unmatched; her skills in the kitchen were a source of pride and joy for him. Just as Cret was about to ask another question, a knock sounded at the door. He and his grandfather fell silent as his grandmother rose to answer it, her footsteps echoing softly across the room.

"Cret, dear, come here," his grandmother called out. Cret stepped into the front room and saw Chi, a centaur colt, standing on the entry landing with a friendly smile.

"It's been ages since I last saw you, Chi," Cret said with a warm grin. "How have you been?"

"I'm doing well. It's great to see you again, Cret," Chi said warmly. Chi's honey-blonde hair, tail, and golden hide gleamed in the light. Cret recalled the first time he had met Chi, marveling at how much the young centaur had grown since then.

The first time Cret saw a centaur, it had been a startling surprise. He was very young then and hadn't been prepared for such an encounter. The first time Cret saw a centaur, he mistook it for a large horse from behind. When it turned around, revealing its human torso, Cret panicked and shouted to his mother that a horse was eating a citizen. Fortunately, Chi's mother, a close friend of his grandparents, took the incident in stride, understanding that Cret was just a small child. Still, it was a close call that could have been quite embarrassing for his mother.

When it turned around, revealing its human torso, Cret panicked and shouted to his mother that a horse was eating a citizen. Fortunately, Chi's mother, a close friend of his grandparents, took the incident in stride, understanding that Cret was just a small child. Still, it was a close call that could have been quite embarrassing for his mother.

"What brings you here today?" Cret asked with a friendly smile.

"I saw you and Bol arrive earlier and thought it would be nice to catch up," Chi replied. "Would you like to come outside and hang out for a bit?"

"May I go, Grandmother?"

"Of course, but make sure you're back before dark," she cautioned. "That's when the wolvers come out."

"Thanks, Grandmother. I'll be careful," Cret promised. With a burst of energy, he ran out of the house, Chi at his side.

"Hop on, Cret. My father wants to meet with you," Chi said, patting his back.

"Your father, the King of the Centaurs?" Cret asked, his voice tinged with nervousness. "I've never met him before. What does he want with me?"

"I'm not sure why, but he was very specific that I should bring you along," Chi said.

Cret glanced at his friend, noting that Chi was nearly as tall as his grandfather's horses. With that size, he thought, riding on Chi's back would be no trouble at all. Hesitantly, Cret climbed onto Chi's back. With a powerful surge, Chi sprinted into motion. Though he wasn't as fast as Bol, he outpaced any horse Cret had ever ridden. Chi guided him through the forest, eventually reaching a secluded clearing where the Centaur Council convened. The clearing was nestled within a dense thicket of broad-leafed trees, accessible only by a narrow, winding path. The clearing would be nearly invisible to anyone unfamiliar with the area, concealed by the thick foliage surrounding it.

Cret carefully dismounted and bowed deeply before the King of the Centaurs.

"Rise, Citizen Cret, and step forward," King Rees commanded in a deep, resonant voice.

Nervously, Cret obeyed, his hands trembling with anticipation. What could the King possibly want from him? King Rees was an impressive figure, towering even among Centaurs. His coat was a striking pure white, contrasted by his blonde hair and tail, while his torso bore a rich, sunbaked tan.

"Cret, I asked my son to bring you here to share a tale and seek your help," King Rees said.

"What could someone like me do to help you?" Cret asked.

"Come with me, and I'll explain. Chi, you may go. I'll call you when it's time for Cret to return." With that, King Rees and Cret walked into the forest.

"Listen carefully, Cret. What I'm about to tell you may be difficult to grasp, but it's crucial that you remember everything," King Rees said.

"I will, sir," Cret replied, standing straighter despite the lump forming in his throat.

"You know the story of the first settlement in the Krill Colony from the citizen's perspective," King Rees began. "Now, I'll share a different story, one that's been kept from you. When King Silsi sent Poseidon to Krill, he also sent many of our creatures—giants, centaurs, griffins, Pegasi, and others. He intended to use the new planet as a penal colony and establish settlements to expand our reach.

"For many cycles, the Krill Colony thrived and was brought under control. However, when the first replacements arrived to relieve the original settlers, they found that those settlers had aged much more than expected. The accelerated aging process was anticipated, but its extent was shocking. While non-citizens aged more slowly than citizens, the difference was still so profound that no one could return home for fear of not surviving the journey back.

"When you travel to the Krill Colony, you'll be in stasis for five solar cycles to conserve food. On the single moon colony, they measure time by the movement of their single sun, which they refer to as years. Their years are equivalent to five of our cycles.

"King Silsi had promised the first settlers they would be away for a total of fifteen solar cycles. When the replacements arrived, they were alarmed and convened a meeting with the children and descendants of the original settlers. These settlers believed they had been forgotten and did not realize they were aging much faster than their families back home. It turns out time is relative to where you are.

"The original settlers expressed that their lives were fulfilling, and even if replacements had arrived sooner, neither they nor their parents would have wanted to leave. The new planet offered so many wonders to explore. The replacements were astonished to learn that the settlers had no desire to return home.

"Although the settlers lived in primitive conditions, they appeared to be in good health. The replacements spent one Krill year at the colony, assessing the situation and providing assistance. When it was time for them to depart, some chose to remain behind.

"When the ship landed, King Silsi personally met the returning replacements. He was stunned to learn that the round trip had taken ten solar cycles and that the replacements had spent only a short time on the surface. Furious, he decreed that all information about the mission be kept secret. King Silsi wanted to retain the option to send more citizens to the planet without them knowing they would be unable to return."

Cret's face showed confusion and concern. "If the King ordered everyone to stay silent, how do you know this?"

"The centaurs don't obey the orders of Citizens," King Rees explained. "Our representatives informed King Ril, who then issued a gag order to prevent the truth from reaching the citizens—that the centaurs had ignored King Silsi's commands. It could have sparked a war between our people. King Ril only shared the truth with his successor, who then passed it down. I am the sole centaur aware of this dark secret and will eventually pass this knowledge to my son. This is why no centaur has visited the planet since the first two trips. Over time, as Citizen Kings sent fewer non-citizens, our absence went unnoticed. Now, only a few centaurs and other creatures remain on Krill. Lacking sufficient numbers, they are gradually being exterminated by The People, who act out of fear and attack before understanding what they fear."

"How do you know this if no one has returned to tell you?"

"The returning settlers established a transmission station before they left. Those who stayed on Krill contact me every ten Krill years when our planets are closest. However, I didn't receive the expected signal during the last solar cycle. I'm worried about my brethren. That's why I need your help. I can't trust just anyone with this information.

"My son vouches for your trustworthiness, and I trust his judgment. I need you to locate any remaining centaurs and report back to me on their situation. I'll provide you with a portable transmitter that you can use only once. Do you understand?"

"Yes, King Rees."

King Rees handed Cret a flute. "To transmit, speak your message into the flute, play a single note, and throw it into a large body of water. The transmission will occur only once, capturing the last thing it hears. Use the flute if necessary, but ensure you complete the mission, no matter how long it takes to find a centaur."

Cret examined the flute and pocketed it. "I'll follow your instructions, but I'm feeling quite nervous now. I had looked forward to this, but this is my home, and I may never return."

"Cret, you must remain strong. From the reports I've received, the Krill Colony has many positive aspects, and all citizens sent there have adapted well. They are more attractive, physically fit, and intelligent compared to The People. While these traits appear in mix-bloods, they are more pronounced in full citizens. You will be respected and revered, even at your young age.

"Your father and the others were selected because they are average or slightly above average for our planet and would not reach their full potential here. On Krill, they will be among the wisest and will play a crucial role in advancing the colony.

"What you're doing will benefit everyone involved. Your fellow travelers will rely on your help and guidance once they discover the truth. They'll face greater challenges than you, as they won't learn the full truth until they are already stranded. Now, it's time to return."

King Rees escorted Cret back to the clearing. Cret, deep in thought, was surprised to see Chi waiting for him. He was grateful for Chi's silence as they made their way back to his grandparents' house.

That evening, Cret barely spoke and ate little. When he asked his grandparents if he could retire early, they exchanged worried glances but said nothing.

Cret awoke in a cold sweat in the middle of the night, haunted by a nightmare of a fire-breathing giant about to devour him. Though he knew the creature was only a figment of his imagination, it did nothing to lessen his fear. He eventually drifted back to sleep, only to be stirred awake by the first light of dawn, its faint glow creeping over the distant horizon.

Cret quietly slipped out the back door before his grandparents awoke and made his way to the stable. He led Bol out of his stall and mounted him, but instead of taking to the skies, he walked slowly around the grounds, savoring the sights he knew he would never see again. A deep sadness washed over him at the thought of leaving Bol behind, though he held out hope of finding another griffin near Atlantis. He shook his head, pondering how he would manage to comfort the other citizens. As he gazed at the clouds drifting by, he realized he needed to find his peace before he could offer comfort to others. He resolved to do his best once he had found solace within himself.

Only after both suns were high in the sky did Cret return to the house. His grandmother had prepared a lavish spread for lunch, filled with all the treats his mother would have disapproved of. She greeted him with her usual warm, beaming smile. Overcome with emotion, Cret rushed to her and embraced her tightly. "I'm going to miss you so much."

"Oh, Cret, don't be so sad. We'll see each other again sooner than you think."

Cret took a deep breath and stepped back. "I know, I know. But where's Grandfather? He can't miss out on this feast."

"He'll be in shortly with a surprise for you," his grandmother said. Cret sat at the table and waited for his grandparents to join him before he started eating. After lunch, they all went outside to see the surprise: a magnificent black horse stood proudly in the garden. "My great-great-great-grandfather was among the first to be sent to Atlantis but returned quickly because too many were sent. He brought back two stallions and ten mares. My uncle has since been raising them, ensuring they remain pure Krillian. He has gifted me this stallion for you to take with you."

Cret gazed at the magnificent horse and then at his grandfather. "But we're not allowed to take animals with us."

"Your great-uncle secured special permission from the King. Since this horse's ancestors originated from Krill and no crossbreeding with local horses has occurred, it's allowed. He is yours. You'd better get packed; you'll be heading back to your parents' first thing in the morning. The journey will take most of the day." Cret thanked his grandparents and then led his new horse into the stable.

Early the next morning, with his horse and belongings prepared, Cret grabbed a quick breakfast and set out. His grandmother had packed him a lunch and a snack. If he traveled directly, he should make it home by supper.

He named his horse Rees in honor of King Rees, who had entrusted him with a special secret mission. Cret checked his pocket to ensure the flute was still with him. Rees was a splendid steed, covering the ground effortlessly. Cret estimated he would reach home well before supper.

By the time he reached the outer city walls, Cret had come to terms with his fate. He felt a surge of pride at the thought of helping the Centaurs and wondered what the future might hold. Everything in his life was now left to chance. In Romota, his future had been meticulously planned, even down to his choice of spouse. In Atlantis, he hoped to find a life of his own making.

∞ **3** ∞
DEPARTURE

THE moon's cycle passed in a whirlwind of activity. Neiaphi had never imagined there would be so much to handle. Though she was excused from her schooling, she would have preferred that over the endless list of chores now on her plate. The night before their departure, Neiaphi's father held one final family meeting with her and her mother. Afterward, they went to the Common Hall to join the other families preparing to leave.

As a mid-level official, Neiluios was swamped with last-minute orders and details from his team.

Neiaphi stayed close to her father, trying to avoid getting in the way amid the bustling activity of the Hall. She struggled to remember everything being discussed, retaining only fragments of the information. Despite the chaos, she admired her father for his composure.

Neiaphi's mother, Altesse, fell into a daze whenever she wasn't occupied with a task. Neiaphi felt a deep sympathy for her but felt powerless to help. She even tried to provoke her mother to snap her out of it, but this only frustrated her father, and her mother remained oblivious.

Neiaphi spent most of her time with her father, who seemed pleased to have her around and even tried to involve her in his tasks.

As she scanned the room, she spotted her friend, Cret, approaching. She left her father's side and went to meet him halfway.

"Hi, Neiaphi," Cret said with a wide grin. "Isn't this exciting? I can't wait to get started."

"What are you two talking about?" Hepluosis interjected, shoving Cret aside.

"None of your business, Hepluosis," Neiaphi snapped back.

"Well, I can't wait to leave this dull planet behind."

"On Atlantis, my father's talents will finally be recognized, and he'll get the promotion he deserves," Hepluosis boasted.

"How would you know what he deserves? You're just parroting what he tells your mother," Cret retorted.

"Well, so what? I'm sure he's right—he's the smartest man on the planet, even smarter than your father, Neiaphi."

"I can't say whether that's true or not, Hep," Neiaphi replied calmly. "But since your father is a low-level official and mine is a mid-level official, I have to trust the King and his advisors on these matters."

"Just because your father is the youngest to hold his position doesn't make you a princess," Hepluosis snapped before storming off.

"What a spoiled little..." Cret muttered, his words trailing off.

"Hi, Cret. Sorry about that," Neiaphi said, nodding toward Hepluosis's retreating figure. "Why are you so eager to leave in the morning?"

"Why wouldn't I be? It's going to be incredible to experience a new planet firsthand instead of just seeing it on a screen."

"You know the planet is quite primitive, and we'll be without most of the comforts we're used to. It'll be like when we camped out in the garden near your quarters and stayed outside all night, but this time it'll be for several solar cycles."

"Is that what's bothering you, or is it that you're the only girl your age going? The next girl close to your age is either much younger or older."

"Well, that's part of it, but there are other things I'd rather not discuss right now," she replied. "Do you know how long the trip will take?"

"I... I'm not sure. I just know we'll be asleep for most of it," Cret stammered.

"What's wrong? Do you know something you're not telling me?" Neiaphi asked, grasping Cret's shoulders tightly. He pulled away, shrugging off her grip.

"No, I don't know anything more than you do. How could I?" He glanced down, nervously kicking at the ground.

"I don't believe you, but I need to get back. I'll see you before we board the ship. Bye." Neiaphi turned to leave.

"It'll be alright, Neiaphi. Bye," Cret said. Neiaphi glanced back at him as she walked toward her father, who was still watching her. She gave him a final smile and a small wave before he turned his attention back to his family.

"Neiaphi, there you are. We still have a lot to do tonight," Neiluios called out to his daughter. Neiaphi followed her parents as they left the Common Hall.

On the morning of their departure, everyone woke early to ensure nothing was forgotten. Neiaphi's friend, Phylas, stopped by to wish her luck and to take care of her pet, Rosk. Neiaphi was heartbroken that she couldn't bring Rosk with her, as only native animals were allowed in the colony.

Rosk resembled a squirrel she had seen in pictures from the colony, but that didn't change the fact that he wasn't allowed to go. Neiaphi was comforted by the knowledge that Phylas would take good care of him. After a tearful embrace, Phylas took Rosk and hurried back to her quarters.

Neiluios took one last look at their home before shutting the door behind them for the last time. When they returned in a few cycles, they would be assigned different quarters, as only three of them would be coming back.

Neiluios took Altesse's and Neiaphi's hands, leading them solemnly to the launch site.

They were the first to arrive, followed shortly by Cret and his family. Excitedly, Cret showed Neiaphi his new horse, sharing the story of how he had acquired it and promising her a ride once they landed.

After everyone arrived, the ship's crew guided them onto the transport craft and showed them to their family cabins. The journey would be long, with most of it spent asleep. They would awaken just in time to see their final approach to Krill. Neiaphi and Cret, each in their own cabins, looked out the small porthole windows one last time at the planet they both knew in their hearts they might never see again.

Neiluios embraced his wife and daughter one last time before activating the sleep pods. As the lids closed, they drifted into a deep slumber, knowing that when they awoke, they would be far from home in a distant world unlike anything they had ever known.

∞ 4 ∞
The Voyage

NEIAPHI clung desperately to a narrow ledge on the sheer cliff face. A fierce wind whipped her hair across her face, threatening to tear her from her precarious perch. Her hands, blistered and bleeding, clutched the crumbling rock, while her slippers were reduced to tatters. Inch by inch, she inched along every movement a battle against the elements.

"How did I get here?" she mumbled to herself. Suddenly, the ledge came to an abrupt end. Her right foot slipped off the rock, dangling in midair. Desperately, she scrambled to secure her grip, her palms slick with sweat and blood, her fingers cramping from the effort. Summoning a sliver of resolve, she clung on with all her strength, trapped and unable to move forward or retreat. Her throat was parched and raw, making swallowing impossible, and tears streamed down her cheeks. Suddenly, a massive Roc swooped down toward her. She raised one arm in a futile attempt to shield her face from the giant bird, but her grip faltered, and she began to fall. A scream tore from her throat as she plummeted, descending rapidly into the abyss below.

Neiaphi abruptly found herself on a path leading toward a vast expanse of sea or ocean. The sky above was a bright blue, sharply contrasting with the deep blue of the water below. Clouds drifted in a blend of white and gray, and the sun, a blazing yellow orb, was so intense it stung her eyes to look directly at it. Everything felt alien and unfamiliar. The path curved around a colossal tree, unlike any she had ever seen before. As she rounded the bend, she encountered a man *several cycles her senior. He seemed as astonished to see her as she was to see him.*

"Who are you?" she asked, but the man merely glanced at her before continuing up the trail. He cast a single backward look as he walked away. How rude, Neiaphi thought to herself. She settled onto a large rock beside the path, pondering the curious appearance of the stranger.

He had very dark hair and gray eyes, with a complexion deeper than hers—though not quite brown, just a shade darker. His features were undeniably pleasing, and she felt a blush rise at the thought. Her mouth fell open in shock. That must have been one of The People, and she found him attractive. Overwhelmed by the realization, she let out a scream.

The scene shifted once more, and she found herself riding a Pegasus through the pink clouds of her home planet. The exhilaration of riding this majestic creature was indescribable as the Pegasus soared and glided in graceful arcs. Summoning her courage, Neiaphi stretched her hands out to either side, then upwards. Her fingertips brushed against a fluffy cloud, a moment of pure, fleeting magic. The scenery began to shimmer and waver as a voice drifted towards her— it was her mother's voice, calling her to wake. Reluctantly, Neiaphi realized she wasn't ready to leave this enchanting place.

"Neiaphi, dear, wake up. Neiaphi, you must wake up," Altesse pleaded, her voice breaking with distress. "Oh, please, not you too. Neiluios, do something. I can't lose both of my children." Altesse sobbed as she shook Neiaphi. Neiluios came to his wife's side and gently took her hands in his. Altesse stopped shaking their daughter and grasped Neiluios's hand. He knelt beside the pallet where their daughter lay, her expression serene and beautiful—her soft, delicate features a mirror of her mother's.

"Neiaphi, my child, it's time to wake," he whispered gently into her ear. He took out a small vial and held it under her nose. Neiaphi jolted awake, gasping and choking.

Altesse quickly handed her a glass of water. "Drink it all. You'll need plenty of water over the next few days." Neiaphi took the glass, struggling to sip without choking, feeling sick and lightheaded. Altesse sat beside her, tears glistening in her eyes.

"Mother, why are you crying?" Neiaphi asked, catching her breath.

"I was so afraid you wouldn't wake," Altesse confessed, her voice trembling. "I've been a terrible mother these past moons, mourning one child while neglecting the needs of the other. I'm so sorry, Neiaphi. I promise I'll be a better mother from now on. You'll see."

Neiaphi turned and embraced her mother. "Mother, please don't blame yourself. The past few moons have been difficult for all of us. It wasn't your fault." After a moment, Altesse released Neiaphi from her embrace, wiped her face, and gave her daughter a broad grin—a sight Neiaphi hadn't seen in a long time.

When Neiaphi felt steady enough to stand, she walked to the cabin window and gazed at the stars streaking by. The motion made her feel dizzy, so she closed her eyes briefly to regain her balance before making her way back to her pallet.

"Can I just lie here for a while?" she asked softly.

"It would be best for today," Neiluios replied. Neiaphi settled onto her pallet and soon drifted into a peaceful, dreamless sleep.

The next morning, everyone was allowed to leave their cabins. Neiaphi chose a seat by a window in the Common Hall, located at the front of the ship beneath the bridge. From there, she had the best vantage point to view their approach to the Krill Colony. Almost everyone was mingling and chatting. Hepluosis stood near his father, engaged in conversation with two senior officials. He glanced her way, but to her relief, he did not approach. Cret and his family then entered the room. Neiaphi waved in Cret's direction to catch his attention.

Cret exchanged a few words with his parents and then approached her, with his little sister Sareen trailing behind. "Hi, Neiaphi. How did you sleep?" he asked.

Before she could respond, Sareen chimed in with barely a pause, "I slept great. Isn't this exciting? I can't wait until we land. Do you think it will feel strange with just one sun and one moon?"

"Sareen, one question at a time," Cret said, gently trying to cover his sister's mouth. "Sorry, Neiaphi. She's just really excited."

"That's okay, Cret. Let me see... I slept okay. I'm not sure yet if this will be great, but I'm definitely excited to see the landscape," Neiaphi replied, giving Sareen a friendly pat on the head.

The little girl flashed Neiaphi a wide smile. "How did you sleep, Cret?" Neiaphi asked.

"Okay, I suppose. I had some weird dreams."

"Me too," Neiaphi added, her expression turning serious. "Some of them were terrifying."

"Really? I'm sorry to hear that," Cret replied, his concern evident. "Being trapped in a bad dream and not able to wake up sounds awful."

"At least when the dream became too overwhelming, it would shift to another one," Neiaphi said. "I never want to go through that again."

"Don't worry, you won't have to," Cret replied, his tone laced with sorrow.

"What do you mean by that? What aren't you telling me?" Neiaphi asked, her concern deepening.

"Oh, it's nothing. I have to go now. I'll see you in a bit," Cret said, trying to brush it off as he and Sareen started to leave. But Neiaphi quickly stepped in front of him, blocking his path.

"No, wait a moment," she insisted. "You can't say something like that and then just walk away. You know something you haven't shared with anyone else. What did you learn at your grandparents' place? You need to tell me," Neiaphi pressed, her voice firm with urgency. "I can sense that something is very wrong with us being here. You must tell me."

Cret placed a hand on Neiaphi's shoulder, giving it a reassuring squeeze. "I promise I'll tell you everything I know when the time is right. This isn't the place to discuss it. I'll find you before we land. Everyone will learn soon enough, but I want you to hear it from me first. Please, don't mention this to anyone else."

"I don't know what I would say," Neiaphi replied, but Cret's intense look made her flinch. "I won't say a word."

Cret leaned in and kissed Neiaphi on the cheek. "It will be alright. You'll see." He and Sareen then walked back to his parents. Neiaphi touched her cheek, a rush of unfamiliar emotions flooding her senses. Her heart raced, and her breath quickened.

She sat back down, trying to compose herself, and turned her face toward the window to hide her flushed cheeks. The stars streaked past the ship so quickly that they merged into a blur. Lost in thought, Neiaphi stayed by the window, watching the blurry scene until her mother found her and gently announced, "It's time for dinner."

Later that evening, back in their cabin, Neiaphi and her parents began preparing for the next day. By midday, they would get their first glimpse of the Blue Planet, where the Krill Colony was situated.

A knock on the door startled them all.

"Hello, Cret. How are your parents?" Altesse asked as she opened the door.

"Just fine, Ma'am. May Neiaphi come out for a while?"

"I don't see why not. But don't be gone long, dear." Altesse patted Neiaphi on the head.

"Thanks, Mother. Bye, Father," Neiaphi said as she followed Cret out.

Cret and Neiaphi walked down a long corridor to the ship's cargo hold. Cret had already found a small opening behind some crates that led into a large cavern behind some crates.

"Neiaphi, you must not breathe a word of what I'm about to tell you to anyone," Cret said, his tone serious. "Technically, I'm not supposed to tell you either, but I can't handle this on my own. You have to promise me."

"I promise, Cret. Now, what's going on?" Neiaphi asked, her gaze fixed on him.

Cret began recounting his last journey on Bol to his grandparents' place. He described meeting King Rees and their private discussion. Neiaphi listened in stunned silence, her eyes wide with amazement. "How could such a conspiracy have been kept a secret for so long?" Neiaphi wondered aloud. Then, she recalled the conversation she had overheard in the tavern. She shared this with Cret, recounting the details of the discussion.

"How could anyone be so cruel, sending us here without telling us what was to become of us?" Neiaphi said, shaking her head and pacing back and forth in the hidden cavern. Cret watched her, searching for a way to calm his friend. If he could help Neiaphi, who had been anxious about the trip from the start, he felt confident he could assist everyone else as well.

"Neiaphi, please sit down," Cret said gently. "We need to stay strong. Consider the opportunity we've been given by being chosen for this mission. We're here to help our fellow Citizens regain control.

"If control isn't regained, all will be lost," Cret continued, shaking his head sadly. "But more importantly, we're being given the chance to shape our own future. Have your parents told you what your fate will be?"

"No, I'm still too young to know," Neiaphi replied.

"How could anyone be so cruel, sending us here without telling us what was to become of us?" Neiaphi said, shaking her head and pacing back and forth in the hidden cavern. Cret watched her, searching for a way to calm his friend. If he could help Neiaphi, who had been anxious about the trip from the start, he felt confident he could also assist everyone else.

"My parents decided to tell me several moons ago," Cret continued. "I'm set to follow in my father's footsteps. In one solar cycle, I'll begin as an apprentice official. If I work hard, I might advance to a low-level official position. They've said I'll be given quarters next to theirs and will marry within a solar cycle of taking office.

"I asked them who I would be marrying, and they said they were negotiating with several promising girls with decent dowries," Cret continued. "I told my parents I'd prefer to assist my great uncle with horse breeding. He has no sons to help him, and there are already enough young men to fill the official positions.

"They both smiled and said it wasn't my choice, that I would come to enjoy the life they had planned for me," Cret added with a resigned sigh. "They are the parents, and I am the child; they believe they know what's best for me. Well, now that life is behind me, new traditions can begin," he said, a hint of optimism in his voice.

"But how can you be so sure they won't make choices for you here?" Neiaphi asked. "How do you know they haven't already picked a bride for you, someone who might also be here? How can you be so certain that our lives will be better here?" Cret looked at his friend thoughtfully, considering her concerns.

"Well, I hadn't considered that," Cret admitted. "I just assumed things would be different. The customs here in Atlantis should be distinct from our own."

"Maybe not," Neiaphi replied. "Citizens established Atlantis, so they might have brought our customs with them. Things could be different, as you said, but they might also be very similar to what we left behind." Cret glanced down at his hands, then looked up into Neiaphi's deep blue eyes. For the first time, he truly saw her—and realized how beautiful she had become. He shook his head, trying to dismiss the thought.

"No, I won't let others determine my life," Cret said with resolve. "Things in Atlantis and the surrounding Krill Colonies will be different; I'm sure of it." He stood and looked down at Neiaphi. "I've been entrusted with a very important mission, and I need your help to complete it. I can't do it alone."

Neiaphi sighed, looking up at Cret. "I'll do everything I can to help you. When do you think the others will find out?"

"I'm not sure," Cret replied. "I'm guessing it will be after we land. If they told us while we're still in flight, there's a chance we might try to overpower the ship and return home."

Neiaphi's eyes filled with tears. Cret sat beside her and wrapped an arm around her shoulders. She leaned into him, finding solace in his embrace. They sat together for a while, offering each other support. Once Neiaphi had cried herself out, she looked up at Cret and asked, "How did you come to terms with this? You seemed so excited about coming."

"When I left my grandparents on my horse, Rees, I felt a whirlwind of emotions—sadness, fear, anger," Cret said. "But I eventually realized that if I ever wanted to choose my future, it had to be on Atlantis. You've raised a good point," Cret acknowledged, "but I figure that if my parents still insist on controlling my future, I'll simply leave Atlantis and explore the planet. Surely, The People don't follow these customs."

"I never saw having my future chosen for me as a bad thing before," Neiaphi said. "My parents have always known what's best for me, so I never questioned that they might make a mistake about my future. With my father's status, I have a substantial dowry and wouldn't need to work. My husband would handle that, while I would take care of our children. I've never even considered what kind of job I might like."

"Why should they choose for us?" Cret asked frustration in his voice. "If our parents believe we're old enough to start our own families and decide our children's futures, then why can't we choose for ourselves? Just because my parents bore and cared for me doesn't mean they know what's best for my life."

"That's a good point. I've never thought of it that way," Neiaphi admitted. She sat in silence for a moment, reflecting. "Now, back to our present situation. How do you plan to ease the fears of the others when they find out?" she asked, shifting the conversation back to the immediate problem.

"I'm not sure yet," Cret said. "We'll see The Blue Planet tomorrow at midday. I'll think about it, and you should do the same. We can discuss our thoughts in the Common Hall."

"Okay," Neiaphi replied. "I'm not sure if I'll come up with anything, but I'll do my best."

Cret walked Neiaphi back to her cabin, kissed her on the cheek once more, and wished her good night. Neiaphi watched him walk away, shook her head with a smile, and then headed inside.

"My goodness, child, have you been running? Your cheeks are all red," Neiluios remarked as she entered. Neiaphi covered her cheeks with her hands and smiled.

"Yes, Father. Uh, Cret wanted to race, and he won."

"That's not very ladylike, little lady," Neiluios said with a grin. "But at least you let him win."

"Stop teasing her," Altesse interjected, giving Neiaphi a knowing look. "It's time for bed. Tomorrow will be a busy day."

Neiaphi prepared for bed and fell asleep more quickly than she expected. That night, her dreams were a mix of peaceful moments and terrifying visions. She woke up in a cold sweat several times. During one of these moments, she found her mother at her side, gently placing a damp cloth on her forehead.

"It's okay, dear. It was just a dream. Go back to sleep. I won't leave your side," Altesse said soothingly, kissing Neiaphi's nose gently. Once Neiaphi had drifted back to sleep, Altesse walked over to Neiluios. "I'm worried, dear," she said quietly. "That makes five bad dreams in a row, or maybe it's the same one continuing," Altesse whispered. "I know she didn't want to go to Atlantis, but I thought she would accept our decision and be okay."

"I'm worried, too," Neiluios replied. "She's a strong-willed girl, always trying to put on a brave face to hide her true feelings. It's not healthy. I planned to talk to her after we land."

"I think you should speak with her sooner," Altesse urged. "I'm afraid for her health."

Neiluios paused, considering. "No, I'll talk to her as soon as we're settled in Atlantis. Come back to bed."

"I'll sit with her for a while," Altesse said softly. "Don't let it keep you up. You'll have more to handle than we will tomorrow."

The next morning, Neiaphi woke to find her mother sitting on the floor, her head resting on Neiaphi's pallet. "Mother, wake up! It's morning. Why are you sleeping there?"

Altesse blinked, rubbing the sleep from her eyes. "Oh! I didn't mean to fall asleep. I was just trying to comfort you."

"I had some horrible dreams last night," Neiaphi admitted.

"Can you remember any of them?" her mother asked gently.

"No," Neiaphi lied. She remembered every terrifying detail but couldn't bring herself to tell her parents—not yet, anyway. "Well, maybe that's for the best," her mother replied softly. "Come on, let's get ready. We should get to the Common Hall early to grab a good seat for the approach."

Neiluios had quietly left his two sleeping beauties earlier that morning; his day promised to be a busy one. His task was to inventory the entire cargo hold, ensuring that everything ordered had made it onto the ship as planned. While Neiluios believed the inventory should have been completed before departure, he didn't question his superiors. Fortunately, he was assisted by two others: Crelian and Japster, both low-level officials. Crelian was Cret's father, and Japster was Hepluosis's father—each with children around Neiaphi's age.

Crelian was already in the cargo hold when Neiluios arrived, right on time, as usual, displaying his characteristic diligence. Japster, however, arrived a few minutes late, mumbling a weak excuse about getting lost in the corridors and then running into Addident, the mission leader. Neiluios had briefly encountered Addident before heading to the cargo hold for a last-minute adjustment and knew that Addident would remain in his cabin until just before their approach. But Neiluios wasn't ready to deal with Japster's excuse just yet. There was too much work to be done if they were to join their families by midday.

Neiluios and Crelian handled the bulk of the work, while Japster dragged his feet, doing just enough to appear busy. Neiluios mentally noted Japster's actions—or lack thereof—aware that he would need to write a performance report later. With both Japster and Crelian being considered for promotion, Neiluios was determined to provide a thorough and accurate assessment. Crelian was set to receive very high marks, and Neiluios planned to request that he be assigned to his team. Japster, on the other hand, was performing so poorly that he barely warranted a mention, even in a negative light. Neiluios cast one last glance at Japster, shaking his head in disapproval. Crelian, catching the look, shook his head too, though with a half-smile.

Time slipped by faster than the work progressed, with midday approaching and just under half the crates still left to inventory. Japster muttered complaints under his breath about potentially missing the approach, blaming his colleagues for not working quickly enough. Neiluios sighed, then walked over to Crelian. "How's it coming?" he asked.

"Well, based on what we've processed so far, it looks like we're missing about half of what we ordered. I didn't expect we'd be this short. However, I've discovered some intriguing finds—items our great-grandfathers wouldn't have used. I can't understand why we have these ancient artifacts but not the modern equipment we're accustomed to." Crelian held up a rudimentary writing tablet.

Neiluios took the tablet from Crelian. It was crafted from a coarse, fiber-like material. As he rummaged through the crate, he found a quill and an ink well—items he had only seen in pictures or museums. He had never imagined he would need to use such antiquated tools.

"Atlantis and the Krill Colony are more primitive compared to our home planet," Neiluios explained. "To the People, a modern electric tablet would seem out of place. They probably use this, so we'll have to adapt and use it too."

The door to the cargo hold opened, and Addident entered.

"Good day, Neiluios. Have you made any progress?" Addident asked as he approached, shaking hands with Neiluios and then Crelian. When Japster extended his hand, Addident ignored it, prompting Japster to withdraw awkwardly. Crelian, unfazed, turned back to his work, continuing in silence.

"We've got a little less than half left to inventory, sir," Neiluios reported.

Addident shifted his attention from Japster. "Don't you have work to do?"

"Ah, yes, sir," Japster muttered, shuffling back to his crate, his grumbling barely audible. Addident, appearing unconcerned, continued his inspection.

"That's about twenty-five percent more than I expected. Well done, Neiluios. Finish up in the morning, and you can join your families in the Common Hall."

"Thank you, sir. We'll be back right after the first chime." Neiluios gave a nod of appreciation. Addident returned the gesture before exiting the cargo hold.

Japster moved to close the lid on the crate in front of him. "Not so fast, Japster," Neiluios said firmly. "You need to finish that box before you go. Once you're done, meet me in the Common Hall with all your tally sheets." He glanced over at Crelian. "That goes for you too, Crelian. I'll be randomly inspecting some of the crates you've worked on. Both of you are up for promotion, and it's my job to write the recommendation."

"What? Shouldn't you have told us that before we started?" Japster exclaimed, his frustration evident.

"What fun would that have been?" Neiluios replied with a smirk. "I needed to see your real work, not just a performance."

"I just finished with this container, and here are my tally sheets." Crelian handed Neiluios a large stack of papers.

"Very good. You may leave now. I'll see you after the first chime tomorrow," Neiluios said. "And I'll see you shortly, Japster."

Crelian and Neiluios left the cargo hold and headed straight to the Common Hall.

Japster glared at the half-empty crate in front of him. With a look of disgust, he picked up a stone shovel and tossed it into the transfer container. After recording the shovel on his tally sheet, he reached back into the crate to retrieve the next item.

He needed to figure out how to win Neiluios's favor if he had any hope of securing the promotion he felt was overdue after years of service. Crelian, several cycles younger and in the same position, was also being considered for promotion at the same time.

He made everyone he worked with look inept, completing every task in nearly half the time it took others— except Neiluios. That's why Neiluios held such a high position despite his youth.

Japster grumbled under his breath as he pulled another object from the crate. He finished just as the midday chime rang. Quickly closing the crate lid, he grabbed his tally sheets and dashed out of the cargo hold, not wanting to be the only one to miss the entire approach.

He arrived at the Common Hall just in time. The windows were still blacked out, as they wanted to wait until everyone had arrived. This was a significant moment—the only chance they would have to see the planet from space.

The Common Hall was packed with people. Although many citizens were aboard the ship, they had never all been gathered in one place before.

The officials and guards usually kept to themselves, but now they were all packed together. With thirty officials and their families, plus around eighty guards and their families, the Common Hall was standing-room only. Children were allowed to move to the front for a better view, but even so, it was difficult to get a clear sight.

The lights in the Hall dimmed, and the windows gradually became transparent. Before them lay a blue planet, adorned with white and gray clouds and vast landmasses. The view was breathtaking. Although the planet was much smaller than their home world, what stood out even more was the sun—remarkably close to the planet and intensely bright. Neiaphi thought to herself that the surface temperatures must be unbearably hot. Back home, their suns were much farther away.

No one spoke for several moments. Then, some of the children began to cheer, and soon, the entire room erupted into laughter and conversation.

Neiaphi and Cret exchanged glances, both wondering how long this happiness would last once the reality of their situation set in.

Cret gestured for Neiaphi to follow him to a quiet corner of the Hall. "Have you figured out how to help everyone?" he asked.

"No, not yet. I think the best approach is to wait and see how everyone reacts and if Addident takes control. It will be easier if the adults support each other and the parents look after their children. I don't think anyone would listen to us anyway."

"You're probably right. But I still need to help if I can."

"You have a good heart, Cret. One day, the citizens will look to you for guidance. You'll be a great leader." Neiaphi gently touched Cret's cheek with her fingertips before heading toward the front door.

Cret watched her until she disappeared into the crowd.

∞ 5 ∞
Prepare for Landing

"**Everyone**, please return to your cabins and prepare for landing," Addident called out, his voice loud but measured.

Slowly, the crowd began to disperse, making their way out of the Hall and toward their cabins. The children, still laughing and cheering, filled the air with their joyful noise.

While the high-level officials worked to keep the crowd moving smoothly, a fight suddenly broke out near the front of the room. Two guards, shouting at each other with fists clenched, were ready to strike. The larger guard threw the first punch, landing a solid hit on the other's cheek.

The struck guard stumbled back into the crowd but quickly regained his balance and lunged at his opponent. Before the fight could escalate further, Addident and a massive guard stepped in to break it up. The guard commander, an imposing figure, towered over everyone. While all guards were large due to the rigorous training they began at a young age, the commander stood at least a head taller than any man in the room.

With ease, he grabbed both men by the scruffs of their necks and knocked their heads together. The two guards collapsed in a heap, the fight instantly over.

"Nothing more to see, folks. Please return to your cabins," Captain Heu bellowed. "We'll be landing tomorrow evening, and everything in your cabins needs to be packed and ready for disembarking."

The rest of the crowd slowly dispersed until only Addident, Captain Heu, and the high- and mid-level officials remained in the room.

Altesse had returned to their cabin, assuming Neiaphi had done the same. But Neiaphi, curious about what would be discussed, was hiding behind a chair near the door, listening intently.

Addident walked to the window and gazed out at the blue planet. "What I'm about to say will be difficult to hear, but you're all in your current positions because you're level-headed and know when to follow orders without question." He turned to face the others in the room. "We will not be returning to our home—ever again. The planet you see behind me will be your home and your family's home from this day forward." He paused as Grueo's expression tensed. "Please, Grueo, let me finish. I'll answer all your questions once I'm done.

"When Poseidie and his team were sent to establish control on Krill, they were supposed to be gone for fifteen cycles before being relieved. However, something unexpected occurred. When the replacements arrived, they discovered that the original team had aged far more than anticipated.

"We knew they would age faster, but not to that extent. The original team had no idea they were aging more quickly than those back home and were just as shocked to learn the truth. On Atlantis and in the surrounding Krill Colonies, what they call a cycle is equivalent to five years."

Everyone in the room gasped.

"So, as you can calculate, the original team was gone for seventy-five years. No members of the original team remained, but they trained their children and grandchildren to manage everything. While most tried to maintain the old ways, the whims of the heart sometimes led them astray. That's one reason we're being sent here—to bring new blood. Arranged marriages haven't worked well in this environment but are still attempted.

"All of you were chosen for your skills, your obedience, your age, and the ages of your children. I first learned of this through a dispatch that I wasn't permitted to open until I awoke. Aside from the King and his heir, you and my family are the only ones who know this distressing truth.

"The replacements assisted the colony for one Krill year before returning home. Despite knowing they would never come back, most chose to stay. King Silsi ordered the returning replacements to remain silent, and they've kept the secret well. It will be your responsibility first to calm your family and help soothe the rest.

"Captain, I'll leave it to you to decide how to break this news to your men—you know them better than I do." The captain, looking grim, nodded in acknowledgment. "Our primary mission here is to assist the local Citizens in regaining control over The People and to support them in any way they need.

"We will receive further instructions after we land. Our secondary mission is to ensure that our children either marry someone from our mission or a full citizen of Atlantis, if possible. So far, we have already been away for five cycles. That's all I know. Are there any questions?"

"How could they, or the King, or whoever, do this to us?" Grueo asked.

"Kings have their reasons; I do not question them," Addident replied.

"The secret wasn't kept all that well. I'm not the only one who has overheard conspiracy talks in dark corners. Citizens suspected something was wrong, but no one spoke out, and as time passed, the stories grew. We will do what we must for our families," Neiluios stated.

"Very well put, Neiluios," Addident said with approval. "Everyone, please return to your families. I will contact you all before the last chime. Neiluios, stay for a moment."

As the others left the Hall, they spoke quietly in small groups of two or three.

Addident gestured for Neiluios to join him at the window. Neiaphi, still hiding, had to strain to catch their conversation. "I asked you to stay to inform you that I am appointing you as my First Agent," Addident said.

"But, Sir, that position should go to someone with more years of service and experience," Neiluios replied

"You mean a higher position. I understand it's customary to choose someone from the high-level ranks, but you're the most level-headed individual I've encountered in many cycles. I need you as my second-in-command. I don't know what awaits us when we land or if I'll even remain in command. I need someone strong by my side."

"Thank you, Sir. I'm honored. I'll do everything in my power to assist you," Neiluios responded.

"Thank you, Neiluios. You may return to your family now. We'll talk again this evening." Neiluios gave a short bow and began to head for the door.

"Don't forget to bring your daughter with you," Addident added.

Addident kept his back to the door, a smile playing on his lips. He remembered how his wife had once shared stories of following her father to secret meetings. Those experiences had served her well, enabling her to marry for love rather than status or dowry—a choice that had pleased him greatly. If it hadn't been for her blackmailing his father, their marriage might never have been allowed. Addident had seen Neiaphi slip into her hiding place during the commotion of the fight but had chosen to let her remain there. He sighed and shook his head, reflecting on how times were changing—and hoping they were changing for the better.

Neiluios grabbed his daughter by the scruff of her neck and pushed her in front of him. Neiaphi feared she had angered him; he had never been so rough with her before. About halfway back to their cabin, Neiluios grasped her shoulder and turned her to face him.

He picked her up and hugged her fiercely, and she returned the embrace with equal warmth. After setting her back on the ground, he asked, "Did you hear everything?"

"Yes, Father, I did. Congratulations on the promotion. Mother will be so proud."

"Thank you, daughter, but that's not what I was referring to," Neiluios said, his concern evident. He looked at her, wondering if she was already trying to suppress her grief. She was a strong child, but her lack of visible sorrow troubled him. Neiaphi sighed and stepped into a conference room they had stopped in front of. Neiluios followed her inside, and she closed the door behind him. She struggled with revealing that she already knew about their situation without disclosing what Cret had told her. It seemed inevitable; soon, everyone would know. She took a seat at the table, and Neiluios settled down beside her.

"When Cret visited his grandparents before we left, King Rees of the Centaurs told him a story," Neiaphi began. She recounted everything Cret had shared with her, omitting only his secret mission.

"Why would King Rees confide such information to a child?" Neiluios asked.

"He said he needed someone he could trust to keep the secret until the ship had departed. He didn't want King Titern to know the Centaurs were aware of it. The original Centaurs who returned with the replacements had defied King Silsi," Neiaphi explained.

"That could have led to a war. I understand now. I'm glad you already know; I'll need your help reassuring your mother." They left the conference room and returned to their cabin to share the grim and somewhat hopeful news with Altesse.

The corridors remained quiet for the rest of the day. With all high- and mid-level officials consoling their families, only low-level officials were visible. Just before the final chime, an announcement echoed through the ship, summoning all high- and mid-level officials to the main conference room. Neiluios instructed Neiaphi to stay with her mother, assuring her he wouldn't be gone long.

Neiluios was the first to arrive, shortly followed by Addident. Addident greeted him with a smile and a handshake. "I'll announce that you are my First Agent once everyone arrives. You'll need to choose an assistant for yourself. It can be anyone from the mid or low levels."

"I choose Crelian, Sir," Neiluios said.

"Good choice, from what I've heard. He's a hard worker. After we adjourn, you can go inform him and, while you're at it, share the news with his family about our future."

"Yes, Sir, I will." A few moments later, the rest of the officials began to arrive.

"Now that everyone is here, I'd like to announce my First Agent. Neiluios, please come up here," Addident said, motioning for Neiluios to step forward. "If I'm unavailable for any reason, you may confide all information to him; it will be delivered to me. How did your families take the news?"

"Tears and frustration," one official replied. The others nodded in agreement.

"That is to be expected," Addident said. "Tomorrow, we will make our final approach after midday. We've contacted those on the surface, and they eagerly await our arrival. Please complete any unfinished tasks and then adjourn to your cabins. I need five volunteers to help inform the other officials tomorrow." Five hands went up in response. Neiluios took note of their names. "You may return to your families now. I'll see you all after we land. The next few days will be challenging for all of us, and we need to stay strong and united for everyone's sake. Thank you, and have a good evening."

Addident nodded to Neiluios. "As soon as the meeting with the low-level officials ends, please come to my cabin."

"Yes, Sir," Neiluios replied. He left the conference room and made his way to Crelian's cabin. Once there, he paused in front of the door, uncertain how to break the news. He decided to speak with Crelian first and then inform the rest of the family. From what Neiaphi had told him, Cret had not yet informed his parents; he had only confided in her for support. It was good to have friends you could rely on. Neiluios cleared his throat and knocked on the cabin door.

Crelian answered, "Good evening, Neiluios. Can I help you?"

"I need to speak with you privately," Neiluios said.

"Of course. Dear, I'll be back shortly," Crelian said, addressing his spouse.

They walked in silence down the corridor toward the cargo hold. Neiluios wanted anyone who saw them to assume they were discussing the inventory project, which was likely what Crelian thought as well. Once inside the cargo hold, Neiluios folded his hands behind his back and cleared his throat.

"Addident has chosen me to be his First Agent," Neiluios began.

"Congratulations, Sir. No one deserves it more than you if you don't mind me saying," Crelian replied.

"Thank you, Crelian. As First Agent, I'm permitted to select an assistant. I've chosen you. In Romota, this would mean an increase in your pay to that of a first-cycle high-level official. However, I'm unsure what the compensation will be in Atlantis."

"Oh, thank you, Sir. This is the happiest day of my life," Crelian said, shaking Neiluios's hand.

"It will also be one of the saddest days of your life, I'm afraid."

"I don't understand."

Neiluios paced back and forth, his hands clasped behind his back. "Earlier today, after the first sighting, Addident informed all the high and mid-level officials about a briefing he received before we left Romota. He was instructed not to read it until after we had awoken. It revealed more about our mission. We will never return to Romota," Neiluios continued, recounting the entire story as Addident had explained it, including the details Cret had shared with Neiaphi. Crelian sat on a crate, struggling to absorb the gravity of what he had just heard.

"How did my son keep this from me? We have such a close relationship," Crelian said, visibly distressed.

"A king instructed him. He knows how to follow orders, just like any good official. He'll climb the ranks as quickly as you have. He's just like you."

"Thanks for that. Breaking this news to my family will be hard," Crelian said pensively. "When will everyone else find out?"

"Tomorrow, before landing. You, Japster, and I must finish inventorying the cargo hold before that meeting. You'll attend it by my side. Addident has left the task of informing everyone to me and five others."

"Would you like my help in telling your family?" Neiluios asked.

"No, I think it's something they should hear directly from me. At least Cret knows. That makes it a bit easier."

Yes, with Neiaphi already knowing, she was able to help me calm Altesse down."

"I don't know how Sephi will take the news. I hope she remains strong for the sake of our children," Crelian said, his voice filled with concern. Neiluios patted him on the back, and they left the cargo hold together.

The following morning, Crelian and Neiluios were in the cargo hold well before the first chime. Neither had managed to sleep. Crelian mentioned that his family had taken the news relatively well but expressed concern that they might be in denial.

Japster finally arrived a little after the second chime, as usual. Neiluios handed him new sheets and pointed out which crates still needed to be inventoried. Japster seemed unusually cheerful this morning, which made Neiluios uneasy.

"What's got you so cheerful this morning, Japster?" Neiluios asked, eyeing him warily.

"Why wouldn't I be?" Japster replied with a grin. "We're landing today and finally getting off this ship. I'm looking forward to breathing some fresh air."

"That's something to look forward to," Neiluios said. "But we need to finish up quickly this morning. There's a meeting in the main conference room before we make our final approach."

"Why couldn't we have had this meeting yesterday?" Japster complained. "I want to be with my family when we land."

"You will have a chance to be with your family," Neiluios said. "But some important news that needs to be shared before we land has come to our attention."

"What's the news? Just tell me now so I don't have to attend the meeting."

"I'm not at liberty to disclose it beforehand."

"Will you be at the meeting?"

"Yes."

"Then you don't know either. That's good; everyone should learn at the same time." Japster whistled to himself and started on his first crate. Neiluios decided to let him hold on to his delusion for now. They had work to do.

They finished the inventory just in time for the meeting and walked there together. Haimontor stood at the head of the elliptical table, with Neiluios and Crelian to his right and Vanlios, Kamkrates, Nestor, and Amplios to his left. The seventeen lower-level officials took their seats around the table.

"First, I'd like to announce that Addident has appointed Neiluios as his First Agent. As always, you can seek help and guidance from any high- or mid-level official, but for matters involving Addident, you must go through Neiluios. He will be very busy, and Neiluios will filter out unimportant matters. Neiluios has chosen Crelian as his assistant, so Crelian will also handle important matters.

"Secondly, you are here to hear the news we discovered just yesterday. Amplios, please take it from here," Haimontor said.

Amplios cast a grim glance at Haimontor, who remained oblivious. "When the first replacements returned to Romota, they met with King Silsi. They informed him that the original guards and officials sent to establish Atlantis had aged and would not be able to return home. This will be our fate as well. We are destined to spend the rest of our lives on this planet."

The room erupted into chaos as everyone shouted questions simultaneously. Kamkrates grabbed a large bowl and slammed it onto the table. The loud crack silenced the room. "Now that we have quieted down, we will address your questions one at a time," he announced.

Japster raised his hand. "Yes, Japster?" Kamkrates asked.

"What do you mean we cannot return home? How much have they aged?"

"On Krill, a cycle is equivalent to a year, but each cycle represents five Earth years. While we live on this planet, a year will feel like a cycle to us, so time will seem normal from our perspective. However, those we left behind will be aging much more slowly."

"While we've been asleep on this ship, five cycles have already passed back home," Vanlios clarified.

"When did Addident first learn about this?" another official asked. Neiluios couldn't identify who had spoken.

"He learned from a briefing he wasn't allowed to open until after we awoke. He was just as unaware as you were. We were all selected for this mission because each of us has something unique to contribute," Haimontor explained.

"Oh, we were chosen all right—because we were either too insignificant or too troublesome in Romota. King Titern got rid of us: the unwanted, the thorns in his side. Some of us he probably feared, and others he simply despised," Japster shouted.

"Japster, that's enough," Nestor said firmly but calmly. "King Titern remains your King until you're told otherwise, and you must maintain respect in the presence of others. We are all officials, regardless of rank. We need to keep a level head. How can our families cope if we cannot? Show some self-control. I apologize to Haimontor and Neiluios for lecturing on self-control while losing my own. Please forgive me."

"You are justified in your actions, Nestor. This is a stressful time for all of us. You are responsible for informing your families. Since you are the last to hear this news, you are free to discuss it with anyone you wish. We will make our final approach soon and land well after dark.

"We will undoubtedly be briefed on the situation once we're on the planet. Until then, you are to remain in your cabins. No one may leave the ship until instructed. Is that understood?" Everyone in the room nodded in agreement. "You are dismissed."

The seven officials at the front of the room remained behind.

"Well, I think that went about as well as could be expected," Neiluios remarked.

"That Japster irritates me," Vanlios said with frustration. "I'll ensure I don't get stuck with him on my team."

"That's fine. I'll request that he be assigned to my team, and he'll earn every task I give him," Haimontor said.

"If you gentlemen will excuse me, I must report to Addident. Crelian, would you please join me?"

"Good day, Neiluios," Haimontor said, offering a slight bow.

Neiluios was taken aback by the gesture, not expecting a high-level official to bow to him. Shaking his head in mild disbelief, he and Crelian continued down the corridor until they reached Addident's cabin and knocked on the door.

Addident's eldest daughter, Nidora, answered. She was a striking young woman with light blue, silver-shimmering eyes and blonde hair. Her mother's smile softened her features, but she carried her father's calculating gaze.

"I'm here to see Addident," Neiluios said.

"Yes, my father is on the bridge. He requested that you see him there, Neiluios," Nidora said with a warm smile. Neiluios bowed in acknowledgment before turning to leave. As the door closed behind him, he couldn't help but think how Nidora's beautiful smile would surely break hearts once they reached the surface. With Crelian a step behind, Neiluios made his way to the bridge—a part of the ship he never expected to see. He wished Neiaphi were with him; she would have enjoyed the view as much as he did.

"Halt. What business do you have here?" an armed guard at the bridge door demanded.

"First Agent Neiluios," he replied, steadying his voice. "Addident requested I meet him here. This is my assistant, Crelian."

"One moment, sir," the guard replied, knocking on the door. Another armed guard on the inside opened it, and the first guard announced, "First Agent Neiluios and his assistant to see Addident, sir."

"Let them in," Addident said sharply, causing the guards to start.

"Yes, sir," they replied in unison as the door swung open, allowing Neiluios and Crelian to step inside. "As well as could be expected, sir. Japster was quite vocal, but otherwise, everything went smoothly," Neiluios replied.

"Come in, gentlemen. I trust the meeting went well."

"As well as could be expected, sir. Japster was quite vocal, but everything else went smoothly for now," Neiluios responded.

"How did I get stuck with Japster? King Titern has never really liked me. I'm his third cousin and second in line for the throne if anything happens to him or his son, Itineren," Neiluios muttered.

Addident shook his head. "We'll be landing as soon as the area is dark enough. The citizens want to ensure none of the locals see the ship. They said we'll be landing some distance from Atlantis, so we'll need to travel overland to reach the city. This will give us a chance to get a lay of the land and assess the Colony's issues. I had hoped, for our families' sake, that we could land closer to the city. I'm uncertain about the dangers that might be waiting for us."

"Any last-minute instructions, sir?" Crelian asked.

"No, I'll only be here a little longer. You two may return to your families. I'll see you shortly," Addident replied.

"Thank you, sir," they said, turning and leaving the bridge.

Once in the main corridors, Crelian spoke up. "I wonder how long the trip to Atlantis will take. It should be quite an adventure."

"I was wondering the same thing," Neiluios replied. "We don't have supplies for a journey of that length. I hope the Krill citizens will have what we need."

They continued their walk in silence.

"Please return to your cabins and prepare for landing. We will be landing during a storm, so stay in your cabins and secure all your belongings," Addident's voice echoed through the ship's intercom.

Neiaphi and her parents returned to their cabin, making preparations for the events to come.

∞ 6 ∞
HOME, SWEET HOME?

THE lights on the ship flickered and then went out. It felt as though they were riding a boulder tumbling down a hill, the ship rocking and swaying violently. At one point, it seemed like they were free-falling, only to abruptly stop and climb higher into the sky before plummeting again. It was difficult to stay seated amidst the relentless motion. The storm outside must be severe to batter a ship of this size. The approach felt endless until, finally, with a tremendous crash and shudder, the motion ceased. The ship fell into silence and darkness, and it felt like an eternity before the lights flickered back on, bathing the interior in the dim red glow of the emergency lights.

"Stay in your cabins," Addident's voice ordered, echoing eerily through the still ship. No sounds came from any of the cabins. Had they landed or crashed? The ship seemed to hold its breath, the air feeling stale and thick. "High-level officials to the bridge," Addident announced finally.

Neiluios kissed his wife goodbye. "I'll return shortly. Do not leave the cabin." He walked down the dimly lit corridor to Crelian's cabin. Although Crelian might not see himself as a high-level official, his new position granted him authority. Neiluios knocked on the door, and after a moment of hesitation, Crelian opened it.

"Sorry, Neiluios. I didn't realize I was supposed to come," Crelian said.

"I thought as much. It's okay. You were just promoted yesterday. Let's go."

"Goodbye, dear. Cret, take care of your mother and sister."

"I will, Father." Crelian smiled and waved to his family before following Neiluios to the bridge.

"What happened? Did we crash?" Vanlios asked.

"Just a storm, sir. The ship is intact. We landed safely," the captain replied. He was an older man with silvery-white hair, dressed in the distinctive uniform worn by the crew. His uniform resembled a long, baggy shirt that reached down to the knees, belted at the waist, and paired with sandals laced up to the knees. While the captain and officers wore white uniforms, the other crew members were dressed in light blue.

Some of the crew wore sashes from one shoulder across their chest, attaching to their belt on the opposite hip. The guards had a similar uniform but in tan, featuring thicker belts and more sturdy-looking sandals.

"We'll be disembarking soon. Neiluios, Crelian, and I will leave the ship first to meet with the local citizens and ensure everything is in order. Please gather your families and belongings and meet in the cargo hold by midday. We hope to be back by then. Amplios, please inform Neiluios' and Crelian's families about their absence. Vanlios, notify the guards, and Haimontor, inform the rest of the officials. Gentlemen," Addident nodded to the gathered men, "if you two will follow me."

The three of them walked through the empty corridors. The ship had an eerie, unfamiliar feel. Neiluios had walked these corridors alone before, but with the dim red lighting, it felt like wandering through a dream. They entered the cargo hold, where a detachment of six guards, including Captain Heu, waited for them.

The cargo hold doors opened, and the humid night air rushed in. The storm had subsided to a drizzle, and the moon was hidden from view. Two of the guards carried torches, casting only a faint glow in the darkness. The group of newcomers descended the ramp and entered the forest. A short distance from the ship, a small group awaited them. Each member wore an oversized cloak with the hood pulled up. Several carried torches, while the figure at the front held what appeared to be a walking staff.

"Addident?" the figure with the staff asked.

"I am Addident."

"Please follow us," the local said. The group was led to a hillside where a small cave entrance was revealed.

Once inside, the torches were extinguished, and it took a few moments for their eyes to adjust to the dim light. The walls seemed to glow softly. Crelian examined them closely and reached out to touch the surface.

"The moss in this cave absorbs light and glows for a time," one of the locals explained. "Please follow me, gentlemen."

The tunnel descended deeper and deeper into the ground. As they approached the end, a light became visible around a corner. They entered a large cavern with armed guards on either side of the entrance. The guards glared at the newcomers' entourage but did not advance.

In the center of the cavern stood a large terminal. Despite its outdated technology, it appeared to be in working order. The screen displayed several cities, smaller villages, and what seemed to be a processing plant of some kind.

"Welcome, brethren. It has been some time since we last received a shipment. I have never seen one arrive myself, but my grandfather told me about the last one he witnessed as a boy." The speaker, whose appearance suggested he might be a grandfather himself, spoke from beneath his hooded cloak. "Over the next few months, we will educate you and your families about life here on Earth. After that, you will embark on the two-month journey to Atlantis."

"If I may ask," Crelian began, "what is a month, and what exactly is Earth?"

"A month is roughly equivalent to one moon cycle, and Earth is the name of this planet. The term 'Krill' is not used here. This is just a tiny part of what you'll learn over the next few months. You will stay until you've fully adapted and can pass as human. The People also refer to themselves as humans.

"It will take some time, but we have very competent teachers to assist you. We also have facilities on the surface to accommodate everything you've brought. How many of you are there?"

"Thirty officials and eighty-five guards," Crelian replied.

"Good, good. That's not too many. We can accommodate up to one hundred and fifty families. Addident, I will leave you in charge of your people's daily activities, but please defer to me and my colleagues when requested."

"Of course. We are all like children learning for the first time. Any assistance will be greatly appreciated. If there's anything we can do to help you, please don't hesitate to ask." Addident bowed his head. "May I ask your name, sir?"

"I'm sorry; you're right. I should have introduced myself first. I am Deleon. Here is a layout of the housing camp. I'll leave the housing assignment to you." Deleon handed the parchment to Crelian. "It will be light in a few hours. I'll leave you to prepare your people."

The newcomers left the cavern and returned to the ship. There was much to do and little time for sleep.

Addident left the task of housing placement to Neiluios and Captain Heu. Neiluios led the Captain and Crelian to a conference room, closing the door behind them. Although everyone had been instructed to stay in their cabins, he shut the door firmly. The ship's silence was almost eerie.

They spread the map out for everyone to see. Although crude, it was detailed enough for their needs. They would get a better sense of it in the morning. The map showed three sections in the camp, each with fifty dwellings. Captain Heu preferred the sections closest to the main gate, which perfectly suited Neiluios. The back section would offer more privacy.

It took several hours to get everything arranged, by which time the single sun began rising. Neiluios, Crelian, Captain Heu, and three additional guards left the ship to inspect their new home for the next few months.

As they descended the cargo ramp, everyone took in their surroundings. They had landed in a dense forest, where beams of light filtered through the treetops. The small group made their way through the forest to an open clearing at the base of the large mountain they had seen earlier that morning. The mountain was an impressive sight, its peak shrouded in clouds and its base extending far beyond the horizon. Dominating the clearing was a wall-enclosed village, its main gates standing open.

The camp had not been used for some time but appeared to have been recently cleaned and repaired. Each house was identical, featuring a main room with a cooking pit in the center and two side wings for sleeping. Every pair of houses shared a waste facility located between them. The camp also had four bathhouses, with separate areas for males and females. At the rear of the compound were a large gathering hall and a storage room. Just outside the main gate was an empty corral for horses and other livestock, which would need to be arranged for the upcoming journey. Everything else appeared to be in good order.

Addident would be housed furthest from everyone else, except for Haimontor, Neiluios, and Crelian, who would be placed close to each other for ease of communication. The high- and mid-level officials would be next in line, followed by the low-level officials near the center of the camp. The remaining housing units would be designated as conference rooms and schoolhouses.

After the inspection, Neiluios instructed everyone to rest before beginning the ship's unloading. They all returned to their cabins.

Altesse and Neiaphi had already packed and moved all their belongings. They left Neiluios to get some rest and headed to the cargo hold to wait for the others.

"Father looked very tired, Mother."

"Yes, dear. He's been up all night. We'll wake him before midday. I'm sure Cret, along with his mother and sister, will arrive soon so Crelian can get some rest."

They entered the cargo hold to find a small group of low-level officials already gathered, with Japster seemingly leading them. Hepluosis cast a disdainful glance at Neiaphi before turning away.

"What was that about?" Altesse asked, puzzled.

"I don't know. He's never liked me, but I'm not sure why," Neiaphi replied.

"Well, we'll stay on this side of the cargo hold," Altesse said. They moved over to some small crates and sat down. Japster appeared to be telling a story about something important he had done—or wanted everyone to think he had done. The crowd gathered around him seemed engrossed in his tale. Altesse thought to herself how often those in lower positions seemed to lead with their hearts rather than their heads, though there were exceptions. Crelian, for instance, would excel far. Moments later, Sephi and her children, Cret and Sareen, entered the cargo hold, followed by Sandorn with her three children: Xener, her eldest son; Giltorah, a very pretty little girl much younger than Neiaphi; and her toddler son, Grueosis. Sephi and Sandorn made their way over to Altesse.

"How is Grueo, Sandorn?" Altesse asked.

"He's doing well. He'll be along in a moment." Grueosis whimpered and squirmed in his mother's arms.

"There, there, little one. You can get down soon. He doesn't like being held anymore."

"My little one was the same way at that age," Altesse said wistfully.

"How have you been coping with your loss? I'm not sure I would have been able to endure it," Sandorn replied.

"At first, I didn't want to, but then I remembered I had an obligation to this one here." Altesse gestured to Neiaphi, who hugged her mother. "I had to pull through for her sake."

Sephi and Sandorn smiled but remained silent.

It was almost midday, and everyone except Neiluios, Crelian, Addident, and his family had arrived. Altesse glanced at Neiaphi, who nodded in response. Neiaphi jumped up, tugged at Cret's sleeve, and they ran from the cargo hold.

"Where are we going?" Cret asked.

"My mother wants me to wake my father, and we can get yours while we're at it."

"Oh, okay." They walked down the deserted corridors, which seemed even stranger and quieter than before. Earlier, they had heard muffled sounds coming from some of the cabins, but now the silence was complete.

They reached Cret's cabin first, but it was empty. Rushing to Neiaphi's cabin, they found it vacant as well. Exchanging worried glances, they raced back to the cargo hold. Neiluios and Crelian were just about to enter as they arrived.

"What are you two doing wandering the ship?" Neiluios asked sternly, with Crelian's expression mirroring his concern.

Neiaphi, breathing hard, replied, "Mother sent us to wake you. She was worried you might oversleep."

Neiluios wrapped his arm around his daughter's shoulders and pulled her into a hug. "I just lay there, unable to sleep. Too much on my mind. Let's go join the others. The forest is beautiful—you're going to love it." The four of them entered the cargo hold. Shortly after, the cargo hold door opened, and everyone was bathed in such bright light that the citizens at the front had to shield their eyes. It looked like a glorious day.

Addident, his wife Phebis, and their two daughters, Nidora and Surrie, were waiting at the bottom of the ramp, accompanied by Captain Heu and a detachment of guards. Neiluios, Crelian, and their families descended the ramp first. Neiluios handed a copy of the housing assignments to Addident. Addident examined the map, marked his designated housing, and then passed the map to his wife, who nodded in acknowledgment.

"High and mid-level officials, please approach first. You will receive your housing assignments first, as you will be stationed at the far end of the camp." The three high-level officials and eight mid-level officials, along with their families, descended the ramp and were handed a map layout of the camp. Next, the low-level officials and their families came down, followed by the remaining guards. Neiaphi and her mother left her father on the ship and went to explore their new home.

The camp was a fair distance from the ship; it took just under a finger of time for the first families to reach the outer gates, hauling all their belongings. In the distance, Neiaphi spotted Cret's horse, Rees, already settled in one of the corrals, contentedly munching on some local vegetation. As they walked, Neiaphi looked around, taking in her new surroundings. They were deep in the forest, where the towering trees obscured her view. The birds' chirping filled the air, though they remained hidden among the foliage. The mountain looming over the camp was immense; Neiaphi strained her neck to glimpse its peak but nearly tripped over a rock on the ground. She quickly refocused her gaze to avoid further mishaps.

As they approached the main gate, Neiaphi noticed that the walls were constructed from interwoven trees rather than stone. To her, this seemed less secure, but given that the locals lacked advanced weaponry, the walls were likely sufficient for their needs. They passed through the gate, which loomed above her, towering as high as a two-story building. A main dirt road ran down the center of the camp, flanked by smaller spur roads that branched off to the left and right, leading to the various houses.

The houses were arranged in clusters of two, each consisting of a large central square section flanked by two smaller square extensions on either end. Between each pair of houses was a space roughly the size of one of the houses. This pattern repeated continuously along either side of the main road. As they continued down the dirt path, Neiaphi noticed four large rectangular buildings, two on either side of the road. Each had a fountain in between, and they appeared to be bathhouses. They passed another set of bathhouses, then another, revealing that the camp was vast, stretching far beyond what she could initially see.

Finally, they arrived at their new home. Altesse stepped inside first, greeted by the enveloping darkness. A sliver of light filtered through the smoke hole in the center of the main room, casting faint, shifting patterns on the walls. Beneath the smoke hole, a fire pit lay cold and empty, waiting to be lit. Altesse set her bags down and opened the window by the front door, letting in a fresh breath of air before moving to the far wall. There, a shelf was crowded with cooking equipment, herbs, and spices. Neiaphi followed her mother's lead, placing her bags beside Altesse's before venturing into one of the separate rooms. Inside, she discovered a large pallet, a sturdy chest, and a small window positioned high above the pallet, casting a slender beam of light into the room. The pallet appeared large enough to accommodate three children comfortably. However, families with many children would likely find the space quite cramped, with each house being identical in size. Neiaphi moved to the next room, only to find it was the same.

"Both rooms seem to be the same," Neiaphi observed to her mother.

"Which one would you prefer?" her mother asked.

I'll take this one," Neiaphi decided, retrieving her belongings and beginning to unpack. She opened the chest and found it spacious enough to hold everything she had brought. Returning to the main room, she saw her mother grappling with a rock and flint, clearly struggling to start a fire.

"I think we'll have to wait until your father arrives to get a fire going," Altesse sighed. Just then, there was a knock at the door. Altesse opened it to find a man in a wool cloak standing outside.

"Good day, ma'am. I have a fire starter for you," he said, handing her a small wooden bowl filled with glowing embers.

"Oh, thank you. I've never started a fire with flint before," Altesse said, accepting the bowl. She glanced at the cooking pit, feeling curious and uncertain.

"You'll learn in time," the gentleman replied reassuringly. "Have a good day." With a gentle nod, he shut the door behind him, leaving Altesse to ponder her task.

"That's better," Neiaphi murmured as the room filled with a warm, comforting glow. Their new home was much smaller than their quarters in Romota, but it would suffice for now. After all, it was only temporary; they would be heading to Atlantis soon.

A sudden knock at the door broke the momentary silence. Neiaphi moved quickly to answer, her curiosity piqued. Standing in the doorway was another man cloaked in wool like the one before. His hood was drawn up, casting deep shadows over his face. Neiaphi squinted, trying to glimpse his features, but the darkness concealed them entirely.

"I've brought some provisions for you, little miss," the man said as he stepped inside, placing a large basket on the floor near the cooking pit.

"Thank you, sir," Altesse replied, already reaching into the basket, curiosity driving her movements. The man turned to leave, but Neiaphi quickly moved to hold the door for him.

"Are you a citizen or one of The People?" Neiaphi asked, her voice tinged with cautious curiosity.

"Neiaphi, that's not polite," Altesse gently scolded, glancing up from the basket.

"It's alright, ma'am," the man replied with a kind smile. "She's young, and questions like that are to be expected. I am a full citizen—one of the few that remain, I'm afraid. All who work here at the Mountain are full citizens, or nearly so. You'll learn all about us soon enough," he said before departing.

As the door closed, Altesse began sorting the items in the basket, carefully stocking the kitchen. Altesse was a skilled cook, and Neiaphi was excited to taste the local cuisine.

The rest of the day was a blur of activity as Altesse and Neiaphi worked to get the house in order. They made two grueling trips to the fountain to fetch water, each journey leaving them more exhausted than the last. Despite the hard work, Neiaphi's thoughts kept drifting to the world beyond their new home. She was eager to explore the surrounding area, but a nagging uncertainty held her back—she wasn't sure she was ready to meet one of the people just yet.

Neiluios watched his family as they made their way to their new home, a pang of longing in his chest. He wished he could join them, but his duties weren't finished yet. The day was far from over. Once everyone had disembarked, the ship's cargo was lowered to the ground remotely, its massive crates descending with mechanical precision. The local Citizens kept their distance, wary of the ship and its unfamiliar presence. Addident had offered them a tour of the craft, but his gesture was met with visible horror. They had declined with a mix of fear and astonishment. The technology used by the local citizens at the camp was rudimentary compared to contemporary Romota standards. However, to anyone living elsewhere on Earth, as they called their planet, it would appear extremely advanced and otherworldly.

A warning sound chimed from within the ship, and a door on the left side of the vessel slid open. A large crate descended to the ground, its descent marked by a low, mechanical hum. As the crate came to rest, Neiluios peered inside and saw about fifty frightened, naked citizens. Most were male, though a few females were among them, their expressions a mixture of fear and confusion. Neiluios was unaware that they were bringing in more prisoners. This must be the shipment Deleon had mentioned. From their disoriented appearance, it was clear their minds had already been tampered with. A group of guards approached the crate and opened the door. Meanwhile, some locals who had been lurking in the shadows signaled to the guards, directing them to move the prisoners toward their position.

As soon as the cargo and prisoners were clear of the ship, a warning chime sounded again. With a thunderous rush of air, the ship's engines roared to life, lifting the vessel slowly off the ground. The force of the engines created a powerful gust that slammed into the earth, pushing debris and dust around as the ship began its ascent.

Once the ship was clear of the trees, it accelerated swiftly, ascending and disappearing from view. The Officials and guards stood silently, their expressions betraying the gravity of their situation as their sole chance to return home vanished.

Neiluios felt a heavy weight settle on his shoulders. He had thought he had come to terms with the circumstances, but as he watched the ship rapidly vanish into the clouds, he realized he hadn't. A sinking heart told him he would never see his home or his parents again. The thought of whether they would ever learn the awful truth—or remain in ignorance—troubled him deeply. Shaking his head, he reminded himself that dwelling on what he could not change would only hinder him.

Once the ship was out of sight, the local citizens stepped forward to assist with the cargo. Some of it was intended for them, while the rest was for the newcomers.

Without animals to assist with moving the crates, the work was grueling. The officials, unaccustomed to such manual labor, struggled with the task. Fortunately, the guards turned the labor into a training exercise, making the process a bit more manageable. Despite their efforts, it took most of the afternoon to transport everything into the storage rooms.

"Deleon, how do we get supplies and provisions for our houses?" Addident asked as the last of the crates were being stored away.

"Firestarters and provisions have already been distributed to each house," Deleon replied. "You should find everything you need there. If anything is missing, let any of us know, and we'll check if it's available."

"Why are there no mounts or wagons?" a guard, whom Neiluios had never met, inquired.

"In the past, we learned to withhold all forms of transportation until just before departure," came the reply. "The boredom here can be unbearable for some, and removing the temptation to leave is necessary. If you leave before we deem you ready, it could jeopardize the very fabric of our civilization," Deleon warned. "We will do everything in our power to expedite your learning. For now, please return to your houses; we will reconvene tomorrow."

With a nod to Addident, Deleon turned and made his way back toward the cave.

"Addident, why did we land in that storm in the middle of the night when the ship was allowed to leave during the day?" Neiluios asked.

"I don't know," Addident replied, his concern evident. "I was thinking the same thing. I'll look into it. Something doesn't sit right with me about this."

"Did you know about the criminals on board?" Neiluios asked.

"No," Addident replied, then called out, "Captain Hue?"

"Yes, sir?" Captain Hue responded as he walked over to Addident and Neiluios.

"Were you aware that we had criminals on board?" Addident asked.

"Yes, sir," Captain Hue confirmed.

"Why didn't you inform me?" Addident demanded.

Captain Hue looked at Addident, puzzled. "Well, sir, I was told you were already aware and that I shouldn't disturb you with any issues that might arise. I was instructed to use my best judgment since you were busy."

"I see. Thank you, Captain." Addident nodded as the captain bowed and then walked back to his men.

"I don't like this one bit," Addident continued, turning to Neiluios. "I'll see you in the morning. Try to get some sleep—you look exhausted."

"Thank you, sir," Neiluios chuckled. "I will. See you in the morning."

Neiluios then made a loop around the camp, checking that everything was in order and that no major issues were arising. Finding nothing that required his immediate attention, he headed back to his house and paused briefly in front of it.

Altesse, or perhaps Neiaphi, had gathered some flowers from nearby, placed them in a bucket, and hung them in the front window. It cheered Neiluios to see his girls making themselves at home. As he walked through the door, he was greeted by two smiling faces and a delightful aroma wafting from a pot hanging over the fire.

"Hello, Father. Is everything alright?"

"Yes, it is, little one. That smells divine, Altesse. When do we eat?" Neiluios glanced around the room. His daughter had set up a crate against one wall to use as a table, and they would have to sit on the floor since the crate was low. He resolved to look into getting some proper tables for everyone.

"There's a wash basin in that corner. Wash up, and dinner will be ready in a moment," Altesse said, humming contentedly under her breath. Even Neiaphi looked happy. Just as Addident had said, something did feel off about being here. Nonetheless, Neiluios was content in this house with his family. As long as he had them, everything would be okay.

∞ 7 ∞
CAMP LIFE

NEIAPHI sat by the window in their new home, her gaze fixed outside. She was growing bored; they had been on this new planet for three days and had learned very little. Her father had told her it would take time before the schools were set up. For now, her days were filled with helping her mother with chores and staring out the window, waiting for something to change. She wasn't allowed to venture out into the compound alone, and her parents were too busy to accompany her. She hadn't seen any of the other children outside either, so they were likely following similar instructions from their parents.

A small blue bird landed on the roof of the adjacent house and began to sing a cheerful little song. Neiaphi smiled to herself, wondering what the bird might be saying.

"Neiaphi dear, why don't you go fetch the water this morning?" Altesse suggested.

"Really? I can go by myself?" Neiaphi asked excitedly, jumping up from her seat and grabbing the water basket.

"I don't see why not," Altesse replied. "We're protected here, so it should be fine. But come right back—don't delay."

"I'll come straight back. Thank you," Neiaphi said, walking briskly out of the house.

"You can walk slower if you want, dear," her mother called after her.

Neiaphi slowed her pace and looked around the camp. It was mostly deserted; the only activity appeared to be at the bathhouses and the fountains. She had visited the fountain with her mother before, but it seemed different now that she was alone.

The fountain was simple and functional, nearly as tall as a house. It featured two tiers, with water cascading down the center. The large base held a pool of water that looked inviting and refreshing.

It was shaping up to be another warm day. So far, the nights had been pleasant and the days warm. Neiaphi had asked her parents about the climate year-round. Her father had said he hadn't asked yet but promised to find out the first chance he got.

As she stood there, mesmerized by the flowing water, she was jolted back to reality when someone pushed her forward, causing her to stumble and almost fall into the fountain.

"Hey!" Neiaphi exclaimed as she caught herself.

"Hey, stranger," Cret replied with a grin.

"You could have just said hi. You didn't have to push me," she said, her voice tinged with irritation.

"Sorry, Neiaphi. I didn't mean to upset you," Cret apologized.

"I'm sorry I snapped, Cret. I'm not angry; you just scared me," she admitted. "How have you been? I've been extremely bored."

"Me too. Has your father said how long we're going to be staying here?"

"No, I keep asking him every time I see him, but he hasn't said anything."

"Same here with my father. I can't stand just sitting around and not knowing what's going on."

"I wanted to see my horse yesterday, but my parents said no—not yet. I asked them when I could go, and they just ignored me. It seems they don't know either. Do you need help with that water?" Cret offered.

"Sure," Neiaphi said, handing him her basket. He filled both baskets, then they began walking toward his house and his waiting mother.

"Good day, Neiaphi. How has your mother been?" Sephi asked.

"Very well, ma'am. She mentioned she plans to come by in a few days to visit you," Neiaphi replied.

Cret placed his basket near the cooking pit in the center of the house. Their home resembled hers quite closely.

"Well, tell your mother that I'll come by this afternoon," Sephi said.

"Yes, ma'am, I will," Neiaphi replied.

"Mother, I'm going to help Neiaphi carry her basket to her house, and then I'll return," Cret said.

"Alright, dear. See if you can lend a hand to Altesse with anything that needs a strong young man," Sephi teased. "I'm sure Neiluios is busier than your father. You've been a great help, but be sure to come straight home afterward."

"I will. Bye," Cret said.

"Bye, ma'am," Neiaphi replied, waving as she walked out of the house.

Cret and Neiaphi took their time strolling back to her house. The sunshine on her face and the sweet aroma of pine from the surrounding forest made her sigh with contentment. It felt good to be outside for a while. She was looking forward to their first chance to explore beyond the camp walls.

"Hello, Cret. It's good to see you again," Altesse said as she waited outside for Neiaphi.

"Hello, ma'am. My mother wanted me to ask if you need any help with anything."

"Not right now, but thank you for offering. I'll keep you in mind if something comes up," Altesse replied, smiling warmly at him.

"Sephi said she's coming to visit you this afternoon, Mother."

"Oh, that's good to hear. I just found out that everyone is meeting this evening, so I need to prepare the conference hall. It would be great to have some help. Why don't the two of you go around the camp and gather a couple of stems of every flower you can find? I'll use them to make a centerpiece for the head table."

"Really? We can go out by ourselves?" Neiaphi asked, her eyes widening.

"I don't see why not. Just make sure to stay out of everyone's way and don't leave the camp walls."

"My mother told me to come straight home, ma'am," Cret said sadly.

"I'll let your mother know where you are. It will be fine. Have fun," Altesse assured him.

Before Altesse had finished speaking, both adolescents dashed off toward the fountain.

On the third day of their arrival, Neiluios walked into the control room to find Addident locked in another heated argument with Deleon. Deleon had been frustratingly elusive with the information the newcomers deemed important. He was rarely around and spoke even less, with his appointed advisors and colleagues remaining silent in his absence. It was incredibly frustrating.

Addident was adamant that the schools should start immediately and saw no reason for delay. Deleon, however, insisted it was not the right time yet but refused to clarify when it would be. Today, their argument centered on the processing plant shown on the screen. Deleon remained tight-lipped about what the plant was processing. He would only say that it was a secret, that The People were unaware of its existence and must not find out, and therefore, the newcomers did not need to know either.

"Neiluios, what is the report from Captain Heu?" Addident finally asked, having given up on reasoning with Deleon.

"The guards have nothing to report, Sir. All is quiet inside and outside the camp. The guard families are all settled in. They train for these kinds of conditions and adapt quickly. The officials' families are having a bit more difficulty but seem to be coping reasonably well," Neiluios reported. He knew that Addident had only asked for the guard reports but anticipated the next question.

"Thank you, Neiluios. You're doing very well. Deleon has informed me that the schools will open in two days. Officials will be taught in two groups. High and mid-levels will have their sessions here in the control room."

"You need to select a vacant house for the Low-level officials and another for the wives. The children will all gather in the Conference Hall. There will be two teachers for the guards, and Captain Heu will assign them."

"We will remain at this camp until our teachers believe we are ready to pass as humans," Addident emphasized. Used to being a teacher rather than a student, he found it uncomfortable to take orders from someone he felt was his equal.

"Yes, Sir, I'll get right on it. Is there anything we can assign to the low-level officials? They're sitting around their houses with nothing to do, and I'm concerned that if they lounge around much longer, they'll become unproductive."

"Deleon, do you have any tasks for these officials to keep them occupied?"

"Well, it's almost planting season, but I doubt any of them have ever planted a crop," Deleon replied.

"I would assume not, Sir. Some might have done so as children, but not recently," Neiluios said. "Do you have any scribes?"

"All officials are trained as scribes before anything else, Sir."

"We have several volumes of scrolls that need to be copied. Set up some tables in the vacant houses and assign your people to the task. I will ensure they get to work."

"Thank you, Sir." Neiluios bowed deeply.

"Neiluios, you may leave. Once you have finished setting up the rooms, please have Crelian report to me. After that, you may take the rest of the day off," Addident said.

"Thank you, Sir." Neiluios left the control room to find Crelian, whom he had sent to assess the condition of the criminals. No one had spoken about the criminals, and their whereabouts remained unknown. Neiluios shielded his eyes from the blinding sun as he emerged from the cave. Once his eyes adjusted, he saw Crelian approaching with a concerned expression.

"Did you find out anything?" Neiluios asked.

"No, Sir, nothing. I couldn't even get a guard to admit that there were any criminals here. They are very well trained," Crelian replied.

"That's what I expected. All we can do is keep trying. It would be helpful to know who these current criminals are and why they were sent here. For now, we have some work to do, and then the rest of the day is ours."

"That will be nice; I haven't seen much of my family since we landed."

"Me neither. Let's go."

Cret and Neiaphi slowly made their way through the camp, zigzagging between streets and houses. They collected samples of five different types of flowers and two types of ferns, gathering four specimens of each plant type. The camp was still mostly deserted. Some houses they passed had children playing outside, though the kids stayed very close to their homes. Neiaphi and Cret spoke quietly to avoid being overheard.

"What do you think is going to happen to us?" Neiaphi asked.

"What do you mean?" Cret replied.

"Well, my father has been very quiet and upset. I don't think we're being told everything that's going on here."

Cret nodded in acknowledgment. "My father has seemed on edge, too. I don't know. It's been so long since anyone new has been sent here; maybe they feel we're intruding. Maybe they really don't need or want us here."

"That's been on my mind too. I've noticed that all the local citizens here seem to be men. I haven't seen a single woman. What do you think their status is? In school, they never taught us about the social structure in Atlantis."

"I don't know, Neiaphi. I just don't know." They fell into a comfortable silence, walking side by side and enjoying each other's company. As they made their way toward the mountainside, Cret's gaze lingered on the towering rock face. It seemed odd to him that they'd built a wall right up against such a sheer cliff, one that soared so high into the clouds that he couldn't even see the top.

There was no chance of climbing up or down the face of the mountain—it was too steep, making the wood used for the wall seem like a waste. They turned and followed the wall toward the main gate. Suddenly, Neiaphi stopped and raised her hand, causing Cret to halt in his tracks. She gestured for him to come closer.

"I hear our fathers. Can you make out what they're saying?" she whispered. Cret moved closer, pressing his ear to the wall.

"That's what I expected," Neiluios said with a sigh. "We'll just have to keep trying. It would be nice to know who these criminals are and why they were sent here. But for now, we've got a little work to do, and then the rest of the day is ours."

"That'll be a relief," Crelian replied. "I haven't seen much of my family since we landed."

"Me neither," Neiluios agreed, a hint of weariness in his voice. "Let's go."

"Did you hear what they were saying?" Neiaphi asked.

"They were talking about criminals. I didn't even know there were any on board. It seems like no one else did either."

"Criminals? But I thought Romota was peaceful. Why would anyone need to be sent to Krill?"

"That's what I thought, too. Come on; let's see if we can find out more." They continued walking along the perimeter and soon entered the guards' section of the camp, where several armed guards patrolled.

Two guards noticed them and approached. "Halt, you two," one of the guards commanded.

"Where do you think you're going?" the other guard asked.

"My mother sent me to find flowers inside the camp walls for a centerpiece she's making for tonight's gathering," Neiaphi replied, her voice firm.

"Is that so? And who might your mother be?" the other guard asked, sneering.

"My mother is Altesse, wife of Neiluios, First Agent to Addident," Neiaphi said, lifting her chin defiantly.

"You'll need to come with us to see Captain Heu. He's the only one who can authorize your wandering around the camp," one guard said. "We'll verify your identity with him."

One guard led the way while the other followed closely behind, both with their hands resting on their sword hilts.

Did they think we were going to run? Neiaphi wondered.

She and Cret walked with the guards to a house near the front gate. In the distance, she spotted Rees, Cret's horse. He seemed fine, though, from this distance, it was hard to be certain.

The two guards escorted their "prisoners" into Captain Heu's staging tent, set up next to what must have been the captain's house. Captain Heu sat at a table in the middle of the tent, glanced up with a brief smile, then returned to the pile of scrolls on his desk.

"Hello, Cret. Hello, Neiaphi. What can I do for you?" he asked. The guards straightened but remained silent. Neiaphi spoke up first.

"Hello, Captain. My mother asked Cret and me to find all the different types of flowers within the camp for a centerpiece she's making for tonight. These two stopped us," Neiaphi explained.

Captain Heu looked up from his work, his gaze so intense it could have made a weaker man falter. "Undercaptain, is this true?" he demanded sternly.

"Uh, yes, Sir… Captain, Sir. I wasn't aware anyone was allowed outside yet, Sir, and when I saw two children roaming the perimeter, I just assumed they were, uh, up to no good, Sir," the undercaptain stammered.

Captain Heu studied the undercaptain for a moment before speaking. "It's not your fault. You did the right thing by questioning their actions. However, you should familiarize yourself with the officials' children so you know who's who."

"Yes, Sir," the undercaptain replied, keeping his gaze fixed on the captain.

"Dismissed." The two guards turned on their heels and exited the tent.

"How are your mothers?" Captain Heu asked.

"They're doing well, Sir. Can we be on our way now? We're not supposed to be gone long."

"Yes, yes, of course. Here, take these." Captain Heu handed Cret two pieces of parchment. "This will ensure this doesn't happen again. Just ensure you're not up to any mischief when you use them, understood?" He looked at each of them in turn.

"Yes, Sir," they replied together.

"What is it?" Neiaphi asked once they were outside.

"It's a pass. With this, we can go just about anywhere we want," Cret explained, handing one to Neiaphi.

"Oh, look at this bright red flower. How pretty!" Neiaphi exclaimed as she knelt and picked four blooms from the low-growing bush.

They made their way back toward their houses, picking flowers along the way. It was nearing midday, and more and more citizens were out and about. As they approached the low-level officials' housing, they heard Hepluosis's voice raised in a loud command. Cret grabbed Neiaphi's sleeve and tried to stay hidden behind the houses, but it was too late—Hepluosis spotted them.

"Hey, you two! Where do you think you're going?" Hepluosis yelled.

Cret and Neiaphi stopped but did not reply. Hepluosis began walking toward them. They knew that ignoring him or running would only prompt him to chase them.

"Did you hear me?" Hepluosis asked, his tone demanding.

"Yes, we heard you. We chose to be civilized and not yell for everyone to hear," Cret replied.

"Boy, oh boy, little Cret's developing a backbone, or did Neiaphi whisper that to you?"

"Hepluosis, you're the most annoying citizen I've ever met," Neiaphi said.

"Ah, you're just saying that," Hepluosis said, interpreting her insult as a compliment. "How is it that you two are allowed to wander the camp unattended? After coming from the guards' section, you should be shackled and carried back to your mothers, crying."

"We're on a mission approved by Captain Heu, and that's all I'm allowed to disclose. Sorry, but my hands are tied," Cret said.

"We'll see about that," Hepluosis retorted before storming off.

Cret shrugged at Neiaphi, and they continued on their way.

They soon arrived at Cret's house, and he peered inside to find it empty. "They must be at your house," he said. Cret went inside to grab the empty water basket. "I should get some water before we head over to your place. It might be dark when we return." Neiaphi nodded in agreement.

When they reached the fountain, several women were gathered there, talking quietly.

"Hello, Neiaphi, dear. You're looking lovely today," Phebis said.

"Thank you, ma'am," Neiaphi replied, curtsying to Addident's wife.

"And you, Cret, are becoming quite handsome," Phebis continued. All the women smiled at him, making Cret's cheeks flush bright red. A few women giggled, causing him to redden even more.

"Uh, thank you, ma'am," Cret stammered.

"Neiaphi, come here, please," Neiluios called from a short distance away. Neiaphi and Cret excused themselves and walked over to Neiluios and Crelian.

"What are you two up to on this fine day?" Neiluios asked.

"Mother is making a centerpiece for tonight's gathering and needs flowers. Cret is helping me," Neiaphi explained.

"Altesse is so thoughtful. It should look lovely," Crelian remarked as he started heading toward his house.

"Father, I think Mother is with Altesse. There's no one home," Cret called after him. Crelian stopped and turned back.

"I was just about to fill the water basket before heading over there myself."

"I'll help you with that, son. I'm so proud of you, you know. You've been a tremendous help to your mother and me." He put his arm around Cret's shoulders, and together, they walked back to his house.

"See you soon," Cret said to Neiaphi. She waved and began walking back to her house with her father.

"Father, while Cret and I were out, we, uh, heard you and Crelian talking on the other side of the wall about criminals." Neiaphi kept her gaze on the ground as they walked. Neiluios sighed and guided her into an empty house.

"After the cargo was unloaded from the ship, another crate was lowered that contained about fifty criminals. The guards knew they were on board and assumed we did, too. They've got them held somewhere nearby, but that's all I can tell you. Do you understand?"

"Yes, Father. I didn't expect you to tell me that much." She smiled at her father, who seemed to have aged in the past few days. Dark lines under his eyes and a drawn expression marked his face.

"You little rascal, you knew I'd tell you if you looked at me with those blue eyes of yours," Neiluios said.

"Well, I thought you might, but I wasn't sure," Neiaphi teased.

"Let's get back to your mother, shall we?" Neiluios suggested.

Altesse and Sephi had prepared a feast for the evening, featuring meat for the first time. A large pork roast slowly rotated over the fire, turned by Cret's sister, Sareen. She smiled and waved when she saw Neiaphi and Neiluios arrive.

"Don't stop, Sareen," Sephi called out.

"Sorry, Mother," the little girl replied.

Neiluios approached his wife, lifted her by the waist, and twirled her around.

"Neiluios, put me down," Altesse said, playfully tapping him on the shoulder with a wooden spoon. "We have company." She was smiling broadly. Neiluios set his wife down and walked over to the cooking pit.

"Don't touch that roast," Altesse added without looking at him.

"Did she turn around?" Neiluios asked Sareen. The little girl smiled shyly and shook her head. "She has eyes in the back of her head." He tickled Sareen and then sat beside her.

Crelian and Cret arrived, carrying more wood for the cooking pit. They added the wood to the dwindling pile at the back of the main room. Crelian kissed his wife on the cheek and patted his daughter on the head. "When do we eat? I'm famished," he said.

"As soon as I get this centerpiece finished," Altesse replied. With the help of Sephi and Neiaphi, the centerpiece was completed in no time. It was a work of art, a little over a pace long and nearly half a pace wide. It would take three of them to carry it to the Conference Hall. The base of the centerpiece was a log Altesse had found behind their house. She arranged all the flowers and leaves that Neiaphi and Cret had gathered from various places on the log.

The evening meal was filled with lively conversation. Neiaphi was the only one sitting quietly, trying to follow all the discussions but struggling to keep up. She smiled to herself, appreciating how nice it was to have good friends and family close by in this strange new place.

As the single sun set behind the distant mountains, the camp grew dark, and the sky was painted in shades of blue and pink. Neiaphi and Cret sat outside her house, silently watching the sunset. Altesse stepped outside, leaning against the house as she gazed into the encroaching darkness.

"Are you two ready to go? Cret, can you help the gentlemen with the centerpiece?" Altesse asked.

"Yes, ma'am," Cret replied, standing and heading back into the house. Sephi picked up Sareen, and the women made their way to the Conference Hall, struggling with the heavy centerpiece.

"Dear, next time you make a centerpiece, please make it smaller or do it on location," Neiluios said, winded from carrying the elaborate work of art.

"Sorry. But it's going to look so good," Altesse replied with a teasing smile at her husband. Neiluios smiled back.

By the time the centerpiece was in place, Addident and Haimontor had arrived with their families. Most of the women went up to the head table to admire Altesse's creation.

The men gathered in the far corner, engaging in quiet conversation. Addident's daughters took seats on the front benches while Haimontor's son, Herctor, sat alone on the other side of the room. Cret nodded in Herctor's direction, and Neiaphi smiled as she and Cret walked over to him.

"Hello, Herctor," Cret said to the young boy. Herctor, a few solar cycles younger than Neiaphi and Cret, looked up and smiled shyly.

"Hi, Cret. Hi, Neiaphi," Herctor greeted them.

"Can we sit next to you?" Neiaphi asked.

"Sure," he replied brightly. The Conference Hall quickly filled up, leaving only standing room available. Only officials and their families were present for this meeting.

"Please quiet down, everyone," Addident called out loudly. The room's roar subsided to a whisper and then fell silent. "I'd like to introduce you all to Deleon, who is in command of this camp. He would like to speak to you for a moment about our situation."

Addident took a seat at the head table, joined by Neiluios, Haimontor, and several local citizens. This was Neiaphi's first time seeing Deleon. He was an elderly man with white hair and a white beard—a rarity, as most male citizens she had encountered were clean-shaven. Neiaphi had heard of bearded men but had never seen one before.

"Thank you all for gathering here tonight. In two days, we will begin teaching you about the planet you call Krill.

"To start with, the inhabitants of this planet refer to it as Earth, and they do not know the word Krill, nor should they learn it. The city of Atlantis is known as Atlantis, so you may use that name freely."

"The People are unaware that this planet is a penal colony, and you are not permitted to disclose this information. You will be provided with all the necessary knowledge before you are allowed to leave the encampment."

"The first thing we need to do is determine your age. Although time here on Earth is said to pass the same as it does on Romota, those you left behind will age more slowly since time on Romota moves more slowly. Your ages will also differ. People mature at a different rate here, and your instructor will assign an age that best matches your appearance."

"Let's take this girl in the front row as an example," Deleon said, pointing to Neiaphi. "Stand up, dear. What's your name?"

"Neiaphi, sir," she replied.

"Well, Neiaphi, seeing you for the first time, I would assume you're fifteen. Therefore, from this day forward, you will be considered fifteen years old. That is all."

Deleon sat back down. Addident, looking confused, stood up.

"If that is all, Deleon, we will dismiss everyone," Addident said, glancing at Deleon, who nodded in response. The local citizens stood and left the room. Addident remained, staring at the spot where they had just been, saying nothing.

"I want to apologize to everyone in this room. Dealing with that man has been frustrating. He promised to share more information than he did. In two days, the schooling will begin, and hopefully, we'll learn more at that time."

"Low-levels, please report to Neiluios two fingers after first light in this room. Deleon needs some scrolls copied. Dismissed."

Addident sat down heavily in his chair and shook his head. Everyone slowly departed the room. Neiaphi and Cret said their goodbyes, then headed back to their houses with their families.

∞ **8** ∞
FIRST DAY OF SCHOOL

NEIAPHI was up and dressed well before the single sun began to rise on the distant horizon. She sat on her pallet, gazing out the window until she heard her parents stirring. Altesse laid out fruit and bread for their morning meal and then began preparing the stew for their evening meal. Neiluios left early, followed by Altesse and Neiaphi. It was the first day of schooling, and everyone seemed excited.

Neiaphi walked into the Conference Hall alone. The benches were arranged in two groups, one on each side of the room. The head table from the night before, adorned with Altesse's centerpiece, was still in place. Cret was already seated near the front. He waved at her and gestured to the spot next to him. She smiled and started toward him, but a local citizen stepped in front of her, pointing to the other set of benches. "Girls will sit on this side, please," he said.

Neiaphi looked at him and shook her head. "I always sit next to my friend, Cret," she said firmly.

"Not today, miss. You will sit over there," he insisted, grabbing her shoulder and trying to lead her to the other side of the room.

"Now, wait a minute. Do you know who my father is?" Neiaphi asked, struggling to free her shoulder from his grip. The more she fought, the tighter his hold became. "Stop that. You're hurting me."

"I don't care if your father is Addident or Zeus himself. You will sit where you're told," he replied firmly.

Cret leaped up from his seat and confronted the citizen holding Neiaphi. "Sir, release her this instant."

"Or what will you do, young man?" the citizen snarled back.

"I will make you remove your hand, Sir," Cret replied, equally defiant.

"What is going on here?" Addident roared as he entered the room.

"Nothing I can't handle, Addident," the citizen said, keeping his eyes on Cret. "I was just explaining to these two children that we have assigned seating."

"Remove your hand from the child," Addident ordered. The citizen complied but remained still, glaring at Cret. Neiaphi rubbed her shoulder, wincing slightly.

"Are you okay, Neiaphi?" Addident asked.

"I am now, Sir," she replied.

"Will you both please take the seats you were assigned? We will discuss this later," Addident said. Neiaphi and Cret nodded and took their places. Addident turned a stern gaze on the citizen. "I will deal with you later as well." The citizen continued to stare straight ahead, avoiding Addident's gaze. Addident turned to leave but stopped just short of the door. He took a seat at the rear of the room on the girls' side. The citizen noticed but said nothing, continuing to direct the rest of the children to their seats.

Once everyone was seated, the citizen moved to the head table. His back was turned to the class for a moment, but eventually, he faced them and removed his hood. He had the same dark complexion as Deleon but sported fire-red hair. Most of the children gasped at the sight of his hair. His face was clean-shaven, and he appeared to be quite young—perhaps around twenty-five by Earth's calculations, Neiaphi thought.

"Today, I will establish your ages and teach you about the gods and goddesses you will be required to worship." The teacher went around the room, assigning each child an age in Earth terms. As he approached Addident, he scowled but remained silent. Once he returned to the front of the room, he stood with his back to the class for a moment before turning around.

"The first god you must worship is the most important for Atlantis is Poseidon, the god of the sea, horses, and earthquakes. Atlantis is his city, and all who live here must honor him. You are not to worship Athena while in Atlantis. However, you may worship any other gods or goddesses you wish and are encouraged to do so.

"Girls, your purpose is to maintain the home and bear children to continue our race. Before you and your families leave this encampment, your marriage with someone from this camp will be arranged. I suggest you learn your domestic crafts well, as it will ensure a good life for you.

"Boys, your purpose is also to further our race and civilization. You will be encouraged to use your intellect and speak up at appropriate times. Each of you will learn a trade that will benefit both yourself and others."

"That is all for today. Boys will return here tomorrow. Girls, this concludes your schooling lessons," he said, turning to leave.

"One moment, Sir," Nidora stood up. "What do you mean? Are girls on this planet allowed to learn nothing? You've only mentioned one god to worship and one not to.

"You only need to know about those two. The others will be revealed in time. Girls have more important things to focus on, and schooling on these topics will not be necessary," he stated flatly.

"Sir, this is not fair. We are smart, every bit as smart as any boy. On Romota, a woman may not have been able to hold an Official's position, but they were shop and landowners. We need knowledge so we may do the same here," Neiaphi said.

"Here, you have two choices: become a wife and mother or remain forever under the care of your parents or brother. If you are of lower status, you might serve as a noblewoman's maid, but that is the extent of your prospects. That is all. Good day."

Neiaphi glanced back at Addident, noting his displeased expression. Surrie burst into tears, fleeing to her father with her sister close behind. Neiaphi turned away, covering her face with her hands. She refused to cry—not here, not with so many watching. She composed herself and scanned the room. Aside from Addident and his daughters, no one had left. Most of the girls clung to each other, sobbing. The youngest wept only because the older ones did; they couldn't grasp what was being lost.

Cret approached as Neiaphi scanned the room, silently placing his hand over hers. Gradually, the room emptied until only the two of them remained. Neiaphi rested her head on Cret's shoulder yet still refused to cry. Could things get any worse?

Neiaphi returned home after her first and only day of school to find her mother sitting on her pallet, staring blankly at the wall.

"Mother?"

"How did school go?" Altesse asked, quickly wiping her eyes.

"I'd say about as well as yours did."

"I feared as much. Come here." Altesse opened her arms. Neiaphi sat beside her mother and embraced her. "I want you to know that I'm content with my life and that the expectations here are what I had on Romota. Still, I had hoped for something more for you."

"I'll be fine. But can I help you and Father choose my husband? I'd at least like to be able to like him."

"Of course, dear. My parents selected five suitable men for me and let me choose from among them. Most citizens of higher status do it this way. Your father and I had hoped you would have the same opportunity. With your father's new position, you now have the dowry to do just that."

"Oh, thank you, thank you!" Neiaphi hugged her mother tightly.

"Come, we need to fetch water for the evening. Let's make sure to be cheerful when your father gets home. He has so much to worry about; let's not add to it, alright?"

"Okay, Mother."

Neiluios stopped outside his house and sat on a large rock, glancing at the camp. Despite the large number of people now living there, it remained clean and well-kept. They had been here for five days, and each day seemed to bring more trouble. He dreaded what the next day might bring.

He listened intently to ensure all was well inside the house. The sound of laughter, rather than crying, was a reassuring sign. Had they not informed all the women of their duties on this planet? Neiluios looked down at his new garments.

They had been instructed to burn all their old clothing, as it did not match the current styles on Earth. His old outfit consisted of soft brown cotton pants and a tan shirt. Now, he wore an oversized shirt that reached his knees, covered only one shoulder, and was belted at the waist. He had also swapped his sturdy boots for a pair of sandals.

He shook his head, surveying the costume he would now be expected to wear every day. It resembled the uniform worn by the ship's crew. In his hand, he carried dresses for Altesse and Neiaphi, as well as sandals for both of them. He would need to get Altesse more linen and wool to make additional garments and cloaks for everyone. As dusk approached, Altesse glanced outside.

"Neiluios, what are you doing?" she asked.

"Just sitting here, thinking." He patted the rock beside him.

"And what are you wearing?" Altesse suppressed a giggle.

"This is what The People are wearing now. I also have new dresses for you and Neiaphi. We need to burn everything we brought with us."

"This day just keeps getting better, doesn't it?"

Neiluios put his arm around his wife's shoulders but didn't respond. After a few moments, they stood and headed back to the house.

∞ 9 ∞
SEPARATION

DAYS came and went at Camp Roma, as the encampment was now called. Neiluios spent little time at home and grew increasingly frustrated when he was there. Altesse seemed to handle the situation well, and Neiaphi noticed that she even appeared to be gaining a little weight.

Neiaphi, however, was bored; she wasn't accustomed to spending all her time at home. She could fetch water and visit Sephi with her mother, but she wasn't allowed to be alone with Cret. A local citizen had told her it was inappropriate for a young girl to be alone with a boy.

She was told she could visit female friends if she had any, but she didn't. Her father learned that he and Altesse could continue Neiaphi's schooling at home if they chose, so that became her only enjoyment. Cret went to school with the other boys every day but was not allowed to share what he learned with her—at least, not yet.

He told her that only after he had learned the information could he attempt to teach a girl.

Neiaphi sat in her room, holding a doll her father had brought home for her. It was made of a red clay-like substance called terra-cotta, with painted eyes and mouth and wool for hair. Though she hadn't played with a doll in years, she appreciated the gesture. Her father knew how bored and lonely she felt.

After finishing her daily chores and before she needed to help with the evening meal, Neiaphi would retreat to her room and gaze out the window. It was an exceptionally warm day, and without a breeze, the air felt thick. She longed to be out exploring the forest with her friend.

"Neiaphi."

She looked up, wondering if she had heard someone call her name.

"Neiaphi."

She moved to the window and looked out. Cret was crouched in the bushes beneath the window.

"What are you doing? You're not supposed to be here alone," she whispered.

"I need to talk to you. Can you come outside?"

"I think so." Neiaphi went into the main room and saw her mother sewing. Huddled next to the fire, she looked cold.

"Are you feeling okay, Mother?"

"Yes, dear, I'm fine. Why do you ask?"

"Oh, nothing. Can I go fetch more water? I need to get out of the house."

"I don't see why not." Her mother began to hum to herself. Neiaphi grabbed the water basket and went outside. Once outside, she veered to the side of the house where Cret was hiding.

"Cret, where are you?" she called.

"Over here." He was hiding behind the waste shed.

"What's so important that you couldn't tell me tomorrow when my mother and I visit your house?"

"Something's happening, but I don't know what. Two of the lower-level boys haven't been coming to class. The teacher says their fathers have decided to teach them at home. I asked my father about it, but he hadn't heard anything. He did mention that a new school for advanced learners is being started and hoped I would be one of the first to join it."

"Okay, so the teacher is lying. Is it worth risking getting both of us in trouble?"

"The problem is that the two missing boys weren't advanced learners. They were troublemakers who always challenged the teacher in every lesson."

"Was Hepluosis one of them?"

"No, and that's even stranger. He's been unusually silent, not saying a word."

"He's biding his time for the right moment. So, what do you think is going on?"

"I don't know. I was hoping you might have overheard something your father said to your mother."

"No, he's home very little, and when he is, they've started taking walks together. They barely speak in the house."

"If you hear anything, try to reach me and let me know, okay?"

"Okay, Cret, I will." Cret placed a hand on Neiaphi's shoulder and then left. Neiaphi started to head back to the house, only to realize she had forgotten to fetch the water. She hurried to the fountain and made her way back as quickly as she could without spilling any of the water.

"What took you so long, dear?"

"I saw a squirrel and was trying to coax it over. Sorry, Mother."

"Quite alright, dear. It's time to start dinner." Altesse stood up and nearly fell over. Neiaphi rushed to her mother's side.

"What's the matter? You've been sitting by the fire all day, saying you're cold while everyone else is sweating. And now this."

"I'm pregnant. I wasn't sure until this morning, but I am. Please don't tell your father just yet. I want to be the one to tell him."

"Pregnant? Oh, Mother, that's wonderful! I'll have a new brother or sister soon. I'll be able to help you with the baby since I'm older. This will be great. You sit back down; I'll prepare dinner."

Altesse complied, grateful for the help. It would be nice to have someone to assist with the new child and give Neiaphi something to do throughout the day. Altesse sat beside the fire, resumed her sewing, and hummed to herself while Neiaphi prepared the evening meal.

Around the time Neiluios usually returned home, a messenger knocked on the door with a letter. After the messenger left, Neiaphi handed the letter to her mother.

"Is it about Father?" Neiaphi asked.

"Yes," her mother replied. "It says he has been assigned to a remote location for additional training and assistance. He regrets not being able to inform us himself but promises to return in a few days."

"That's not fair. Couldn't they spare him a few moments to say goodbye?"

"No, it isn't," Altesse said grimly. "But there's nothing we can do. We'll just have to wait until he returns."

Two days passed, then three, then four, with no word from Neiluios. Neiaphi noticed her mother's growing anxiety but chose not to mention it. She asked Cret if his father had said anything about Neiluios, but he hadn't heard anything either. Crelian was rarely home now, handling Neiluios's responsibilities as well.

Finally, on the fifth day, a messenger arrived with a letter for Addident about Neiluios and his team. Addident decided it was best to inform the team's wives personally.

"Good day, Altesse. I have news from Neiluios. May I come in?" Addident asked at the door. It was the first time Altesse had seen him in his new garments, and he looked quite good in them. Perhaps she was just getting used to the new clothing.

"Of course, Sir. Please, can I get you anything?"

"No, my dear, I'm fine. Please, sit down." Altesse began to shake and barely managed to sit before her knees gave out.

"I received a letter from Neiluios's team this morning. They're making progress, but they'll be gone for several months."

"Months? I was told he would only be gone for a few days."

"I know. That's what I was told, too. They will send me several progress reports each week. If you'd like to send him a note, I'll ensure he gets it."

Altesse shook her head in disbelief—several months? She could be close to delivering her baby by the time he returned.

"Well, that's one way to tell him. Where is he?"

"I can't tell you, as I don't know myself. I've been informed that he's assisting at a processing plant managed by the local citizens, though they haven't specified the purpose. It's some distance away, and the local citizens have provided horses for the journey."

"Horses? Neiluios has never ridden a horse before. I suppose he made it there okay. Why wasn't he able to say goodbye?"

"There's a need for secrecy about this place. The locals don't know it exists and aren't supposed to find out about it. You mustn't tell anyone what I've shared with you."

"I will inform the other wives of those who accompanied your husband, but all they'll know is that they're assisting the local citizens with a new facility. Where's Neiaphi?"

"In her room. Why?"

"Can she hear us?"

"Most likely."

"Here I am," Neiaphi said, entering the room with her head lowered.

"The same goes for you. You cannot tell anyone what I've shared. Do you understand?"

"Yes, Sir." She looked up at him.

Addident looked into her blue eyes, trying to gauge her reaction. Finally, he nodded. "Alright then, I'll leave you to your evening. Take care of yourself, Altesse. You'll be the first to have a baby in the camp in several years. If you need anything, please let Phebis know, and she'll ensure you get it."

"How did you know? I'm not showing that much yet."

"I've been around enough pregnant women to recognize the signs. I have five older sisters, and it's quite warm in here," he said with a smile. Altesse blushed and pushed a few logs out of the fire before they lit. Addident left the two women alone in their home. Neiaphi sat beside her mother in silence as they watched the sunset. Neiaphi tidied the house, but neither felt like eating. They retired to their rooms early that evening.

The next morning, Neiaphi felt unchanged. She hadn't expected to feel better, but she had hoped for it. Today, they would visit Sephi, Cret, and Sareen, which lifted her spirits slightly. However, not being able to share what she knew with Cret was unbearable. She didn't think she could keep this secret from him.

"Are you ready, dear?" Neiaphi nodded, unable to shake the gloomy feeling inside her. She and her mother walked the short distance to Cret's house. Cret wasn't home from school yet, but he would be soon, or so she hoped. Sephi never knew when to expect him—every day was different, much like Crelian's schedule. The only certainty about Cret was that he was home every night, at least for now.

Sephi had a kettle of water boiling over the fire in the center of the room. Their house was warm, though not as stifling as Altesse kept theirs lately. Neiaphi sat next to Sareen, who was working on a lesson her father had prepared. Neiaphi was glad they had decided to start Sareen's education. Sephi poured three cups of boiling water and added a few mint leaves to each. She handed one to Altesse and then to Neiaphi, who set hers aside—it was too hot to drink just yet.

Altesse informed Sephi that Neiluios had been called away on important business and wouldn't be able to return home for several months. Sephi placed a comforting hand on Altesse's shoulder but didn't comment. She understood how difficult it was not having Crelian home every night, though at least he was still somewhere within the camp.

The afternoon passed with idle conversation. Neiaphi was glad to be out of the house, but boredom lingered. She wasn't used to having nothing to do. Back in Romota, she could have at least gone for a walk through town.

Cret finally arrived just as they were about to leave. "Mother, can I help Cret fetch the evening water?"

"Sure, dear. I'll stay within sight in case anyone stops you. Just let them know I'm watching."

"Thanks, Mother." The two friends slowly walked to the fountain. In a hushed voice, Neiaphi shared what Addident had told them the evening before, careful not to be overheard. As they neared the fountain, Cret abruptly stopped and threw the basket on the ground.

"What's the matter, Cret?"

"I can't stand it here. Not knowing anything. Being told how to act and think but never getting the whole truth. I know they're keeping things from us, just enough to keep us ignorant, but not so much that we feel completely sheltered. They're even teaching us how to speak and structure sentences. You're lucky you don't have to go to that school."

"I'd love to be told anything, anything at all. You have no idea what it's like staying in the house day after day, never being allowed to do anything without supervision. I'm not five years old."

"I'm sorry. I can imagine how hard that must be." Cret picked up the basket and walked to the fountain to start filling it.

"But what can we do?" Neiaphi asked.

"I'm working on it."

"I don't like the sound of that, Cret."

"Don't worry. I won't do anything without telling you first, okay?"

"Okay."

∞ **10** ∞
ꟼNTO THE ꟼꟼIGHT

ꟼEIAPHI and Cret returned to their mothers, exchanging heartfelt goodbyes before parting ways. Neiaphi regretted not having more time to talk with Cret, but seeing him again had eased her spirits. Altesse remained quiet throughout the evening and retired early as if burdened by unspoken thoughts. In contrast, Neiaphi lay awake on her pallet, gazing out the window at the solitary moon, unable to find rest. Tonight, the moon hung in the sky, enormous and orange. As it slowly traversed the heavens, Neiaphi listened to the distant hooting of owls and the mournful cry of a lone wolf. Soon, another wolf answered the call, followed by yet another, signaling the start of their nightly hunt. Neiaphi shivered, her mind conjuring images of what an Earth wolf might look like. If it resembled a wolver in any way, she was grateful for the camp's strong defenses.

A bird Neiaphi couldn't identify called from somewhere within the camp, its eerie cry adding to the night's unsettling atmosphere. Under the full moon, the night creatures seemed more active than ever, making it impossible for her to sleep despite her exhaustion.

Hours slipped by as she gazed out the window, contemplating her future. Her mother hadn't revealed the identities of her potential suitors, but the choices within the camp were limited. She had only seven candidates to consider unless her father encountered new people in his travels. Cret, Hepluosis, and one of the guard's sons were all her age. The four others she had seen were two to four years older than her, including two sons of guards.

The other two were Chartis and Fotis, sons of mid-level officials. Cret was the only one of similar status to hers, though he was slightly below her rank. Unlike her mother, she wouldn't have the option to marry someone of higher status. She shook her head and walked into the main room. The fire had dwindled to a faint glow, shedding no light. She added a log, and it slowly reignited. Though the flames remained low, they provided enough light for her to see. She filled a small cooking bowl with water and set it on the fire to make some tea. Perhaps she could fall asleep before the sun came up.

She sat by the fire, sipping her tea slowly. The nights and days were growing warmer, and she worried about how hot it would become before temperatures started to cool down around harvest time, as the locals had predicted.

Tap, tap, tap. The sound came from outside her window. She looked out and saw Cret crouched below."

"What are you doing?" she whispered, glancing back to ensure her mother was still in her room.

"I saw the fire start and hoped it was you. Come outside," Cret whispered back. Neiaphi returned to the main room and stirred the fire, wanting to see clearly when she returned. She went to her mother's door and cracked it open. Her mother was still asleep. Neiaphi closed the door slowly, trying to avoid making any noise. As she stepped out the front door, a shiver ran up her spine when a wolf's howl pierced the night, echoing from just beyond the walls. As long as Cret stayed within the camp walls, she didn't need to worry about the wolf.

She walked behind the house but couldn't see Cret. "Cret, where are you?" she called out. Just then, a pebble landed beside her. She glanced in the direction from which the pebble had come and spotted Cret several houses away. Quietly, she moved between the houses, trying to follow him. He didn't slow down to let her catch up. What could he be up to?

They circled the camp until they reached the spot where the guards had intercepted them and took them to see Captain Heu. It felt like an eternity ago, though it had only been a few weeks. Cret came to a large bush near the wall, stepped behind it, and vanished from sight.

Neiaphi stopped next to the bush and peered around it but saw no opening in the wall. Suddenly, a hand reached out from beneath the bush and grabbed her ankle. Her heart leaped, and she clamped a hand over her mouth to stifle a startled yelp. Mumbling about how they shouldn't leave the walls, she reluctantly followed her friend.

Once outside, Cret took her hand and guided her through the dark forest, staying hidden in the shadows as much as possible.

"Where are we going?" she whispered.

"Quiet," he replied sharply. Neiaphi's fear intensified as she realized the wolf was so close. Where there was one, there could be more.

They zigzagged and backtracked several times as if Cret believed they were being followed. Neiaphi kept glancing over her shoulder but saw no one. Eventually, Cret slowed, then stopped and crouched down. Neiaphi followed suit. In the distance, she saw a walled camp—smaller than Camp Roma but still significant. She noticed guards patrolling the perimeter with crude weapons that seemed effective enough despite their rough appearance.

"The criminals from our ship are in there. Come on," Cret urged.

"Wait, I don't want to go over there. What if we're seen?" she whispered, anxiety creeping into her voice.

"Don't worry. I've been inside before. They won't see us, I promise."

She sighed, feeling a wave of uncertainty. What was she getting herself into?

Cret inched closer to the wall, with Neiaphi so close behind that she nearly stepped on him. They reached a hole in the wall and slipped into the camp just as a guard rounded the corner. Neiaphi's heart pounded so loudly that she worried someone might hear it. Cret motioned for her to move to his left, then led her to a house near the far wall and slipped inside. The house had only one room, with a fire pit in the center. Six pallets were scattered across the floor, but only two were occupied.

"Hey, it's me," Cret said. Two boys sat up and hurried over to him.

"Cret, it's good to see you," they said in unison.

"Have you figured out why you're here yet?" Cret asked.

"Yes, and it's horrible," replied the older of the two.

"Don't say it. I can't bear to think about it," the younger boy cried as he ran back to his pallet and threw himself down, sobbing.

"It can't be that bad. Please, tell us," Cret pleaded.

The older boy glanced around nervously as if expecting someone to emerge from the shadows. He cleared his throat, wringing his hands. "They're going to erase our minds."

"What? What are you talking about? Why are you here?" Neiaphi demanded, grabbing the older boy by the shoulders and shaking him. Cret quickly grabbed her hands to steady her.

"These are the two I told you about who went to the advanced learners' school," Cret explained. "Tacitus and Colson were brought here because they refused to accept what they were being taught. They challenged the system. I warned you to keep your mouths shut. We must find a way to get you out of here before they erase your minds."

"But why would they erase their minds?" she asked, horrified.

Cret paced the small room, lost in thought for a moment. Finally, he stopped and turned to Neiaphi.

"Think about it," Cret said. "Two young boys arguing with an elder about what everyone else on this planet accepts as fact. Imagine if they're allowed to leave Camp Roma thinking the way they do—consider the damage they could do to the civilization as it stands. Does that sound familiar? Remember when Deleon said everyone would be allowed to leave Camp Roma and head to Atlantis once we understood our roles? If we don't learn it properly, they'll just erase our memories and dictate how we think."

"Why don't they just do it to everyone and stop wasting time with just a few?" Neiaphi asked.

Cret shook his head. "It makes sense if you think about it. They don't want to lose the skills they find useful. The criminals and troublemakers are kept here until their minds are 'washed' and filled with acceptable thoughts and ideas. We need to get these two out of here."

"Where will you take them? We don't know this place," Neiaphi whispered, sweat beading on her forehead as her heart rate quickened. "I've been scouting every night and found a good place to hide them temporarily."

"What about food?" she asked.

"We've been saving half of what they feed us daily," the younger boy replied.

"And I'll bring them food every night until I can move them," Cret added.

"Cret, I'm not sure. I think we should tell Addident and ask for his help.

"He won't be able to do anything. The adults don't know where this place is, and Deleon would never listen—he's focused on what he thinks is best for the planet. But it's not fair to these boys or anyone else that they get to decide who is a troublemaker."

"Okay, when do you want them to escape?"

"Tonight, right now. Are you two ready?" Cret asked.

"Yes," they replied in unison. Tacitus went to his pallet, pulled out a bundle from underneath, and slung it over his shoulder with a nod. Cret peered out the door, checking to see if anyone was watching.

"Follow me." Cret slipped out and moved behind the house, the others close behind. He led them back to the hole in the wall and out into the dark forest.

The sky was beginning to lighten as the sun peeked over the distant mountains. Cret led them deeper into the forest, where the moss-covered ground felt spongy underfoot. Neiaphi stepped carefully, her sandaled feet slipping on the rocks hidden beneath the moss. How she wished she had her boots again.

They arrived at a creek winding through the forest. The sun was still low on the horizon, casting a few rays that danced on the water's surface. Cret leaped from rock to rock to cross the creek and waited on the other side for the others to join him. Once Neiaphi had crossed, Cret smiled and began to descend a steep slope. Neiaphi ended up sliding most of the way down on her backside, screaming as she went. Cret caught her at the bottom and helped her to her feet.

"Are you all right?" he asked once she seemed steady enough to stand on her own.

"Yes, thank you," she replied. She met Cret's concerned gaze and felt her cheeks flush. Quickly looking away, Cret released her hand and led them to a small cave entrance.

The cave's interior was spacious enough for the two boys.

"You two, stay put. I'll be back tonight with more food. I've left some cooking supplies, water, and wood for a fire in the back corner. Don't go outside during the day, only at night. And don't light a fire during the day; you don't want anyone seeing the smoke. They'll be looking for you, so stay hidden. We need to head back, Neiaphi."

"Goodbye, boys. I hope you'll be all right."

Cret led Neiaphi in a different direction back to Camp Roma. "What are you going to do now, Cret?" she asked.

"I don't know yet, but I'll figure something out. I need you to act like everything is the same as before tonight. Don't tell anyone, understand?" Cret said sternly.

"Who do you think you're talking to like that? You know me," Neiaphi said, pausing to study Cret's face. "I won't tell anyone. The only person I can confide in is you, anyway. Your attitude has changed ever since you started that school. When you speak to me now, it feels like you're giving orders instead of talking to me like you used to. It scares me, Cret. Where has my friend gone?" She hugged herself, suddenly feeling very cold.

Cret stopped walking and let his arms hang at his sides. "I'm sorry, Neiaphi. You don't know what the school is like. They're teaching us how to speak to others, especially women. In this society, women have a specific role—they're considered beneath men in all respects except within the household. That's the only place they have any power, and even then, it's only over their husband and any slaves in the home."

"Slaves?"

"Yes, most wealthy citizens have slaves to handle domestic tasks. If I ever speak to you disrespectfully, please slap me. I don't want to become like they're trying to make me, but I feel myself slipping that way."

"Don't worry. I will," Neiaphi said with a straight face, but she couldn't maintain it and broke into a wide smile. "I can't imagine what you're going through. It just scared me—that's all. I thought I was losing my friend." She looked down at the ground. Cret stepped closer, and she looked up into his eyes. He gently brushed his fingertips against her cheek before taking her hand in his.

"Come on, we have to get back before everyone wakes up."

Neiaphi made it to her room and sat on her pallet just as she heard her mother enter the main room.

That was close.

∞ 11 ∞
𝕳EPLUOSIS

"𝕳EPLUOSIS woke with a start from a rustling sound outside his window. He got up from his pallet and peered out to see what it was. A shadow moved through the camp. *Is that Cret? What is he up to?* he murmured to himself. He threw his new cloak over his shoulders, the one his mother had just finished for him. He struggled to make it sit evenly, but it remained lopsided. His mother was a terrible seamstress, but what could he do?

Hepluosis crept out of the house as quietly as he could, following Cret through the camp and out into the forest via the front gate, careful not to draw the guards' attention. Cret moved with purpose, he knew exactly where he was going, it seems. After backtracking and pausing to check his surroundings several times, Cret finally stooped into a small cave. Hepluosis crouched down behind a large tree, watching.

What's in that cave? Hepluosis wondered.

When Cret emerged, the sack he had carried was gone. *He must be hiding something in there,* Hepluosis thought. Cret hurried back to the camp, with Hepluosis quietly following behind. Cret glanced over his shoulder several times but didn't notice him.

Once back in the camp, Cret moved cautiously from house to house. Hepluosis was certain they'd be spotted by the guards while reentering, but Cret seemed to know exactly when the guards would be patrolling the perimeter.

Back at his house, Hepluosis hesitated. *Is that all Cret is doing tonight? Should I keep following him?* He decided to continue trailing Cret, who walked right past his own house and stopped at Neiaphi's. "I knew it. He's up to something, and she's part of it too," Hepluosis whispered. A short time later, Neiaphi exited her house and followed after Cret.

Hepluosis lost sight of Neiaphi when she turned a corner. He quickly followed, but they were nowhere to be seen. Frustrated, he growled and pounded his fist against the nearby wall. *Where could they have gone? There must be a hole in the wall.* Hepluosis searched up and down but found nothing. Approaching a bush, he kicked it in frustration. When he stepped closer and kicked it again, he stumbled and fell into a hidden hole. "Sneaky little rats, they went down a hole," he muttered.

Hepluosis, being larger than Cret and Neiaphi, had to squeeze through the narrow opening. As he emerged, he spotted Neiaphi slipping into the forest up ahead. He broke into a run, determined to catch up before losing them again.

Hepluosis slowed down when he saw Cret and Neiaphi come to a stop. He looked past them to see what had caught their attention—another camp. *Could this be where the criminals are being kept?* The rumors circulating Camp Roma must be true, then. As Cret and Neiaphi moved toward the camp and slipped through a hole in the wall, Hepluosis stayed hidden, watching closely. *What are they up to?*

Hepluosis yawned. *They've been in there long enough,* he thought. *What are they doing? I should have followed them.* He started to rise from where he had been sitting when he saw Cret, Neiaphi, and two other boys emerge from the hole. They ran toward the forest, straight in Hepluosis's direction. He quickly jumped to his feet, finding a spot behind a large bush to conceal himself. His heart raced as the foursome passed mere feet from his position. *Who are those other boys?* he wondered, squinting into the darkness, but it was too dim to make out their faces. For now, all he could do was stay hidden and keep them in sight, as he had a good idea of where they were headed.

Cret and his group ducked inside the cave Hepluosis had seen him visit earlier that evening. When only Cret and Neiaphi reemerged, Hepluosis quietly followed them as they made their way back to Camp Roma. He stopped trailing them once they reached his house, knowing they were just headed home to avoid getting into trouble.

"Hepluosis! Where have you been?" his mother screeched.

"Nowhere, Mother," he snapped.

"Don't speak to me like that, boy. Get back inside."

"I'll do as I please, woman. Remember your place," he yelled back, glaring at her. How dare she talk to him like that? She better remember her place in public; he wouldn't want her to embarrass herself. He walked inside, retreated to his room, and lay down on his pallet. He planned to return to the camp that evening to find out what was really going on.

Hepluosis kept a close watch on Cret throughout the day. Cret made no mention of his nightly activities to anyone, nor did he visit Neiaphi. Cret seemed unusually cheerful today, humming to himself and finishing his tasks ahead of everyone else. He carried an air of smugness that went unnoticed by others, who were unaware of his activities. He had helped two criminals escape—something Hepluosis had pieced together. Cret was no better than the criminals now, and since he was the only one who knew, it was up to Hepluosis to expose the truth. But first, he needed to find out what Cret was up to and gather proof to present to Deleon. He couldn't trust Addident with this information; Cret's father was too close to him. He was certain that Deleon would take swift action once informed. The local citizens were highly concerned with preserving their traditional beliefs.

After school, Cret went home and didn't come back out. Bored with watching his house and unwilling to return to his irritable mother, Hepluosis wandered around the camp. He avoided the hole under the wall to keep from drawing attention to it but noted it was still the only unguarded section. He walked past the guard station and up to the front gate.

"Halt. You cannot leave the camp, young sir," a grizzled guard said.

"I'm not leaving. I'm just looking around. Do you know where Greish is?"

"He's near the Sentry Post over there," the guard said, nodding toward the other side of the camp.

"Thanks," Hepluosis said and headed in the direction indicated. Greish was the son of First Under Captain Seleo, second in command of the guards, and Hepluosis' only friend on this planet. He approached the Sentry Post with the air of someone with important business, a tactic Greish had advised him to use. According to Greish, if you looked purposeful and confident, no one would question you. Timid or unsure behavior, on the other hand, would attract unwanted attention. It seemed to work—no one paid him any mind.

"Hepluosis, I haven't seen you in a while," Greish said, noticing him. Dressed in full uniform, Greish was the son of a high-ranking guard and held the equivalent rank of a mid-level official himself. Though still in training, he seemed to be finished for the day. He was the same age as Hepluosis but about a hand taller and more solidly built. He wasn't overweight, just muscular for his age. His light brown hair and blue eyes gave him a commanding presence.

"You free?" Hepluosis asked.

"I will be shortly. Just wait around," Greish replied. Hepluosis made himself comfortable in the shadow of the Sentry Post. Greish was showing another boy how to use the club in his hand. Once the boy seemed to have the technique down, Greish finished up and headed toward Hepluosis.

"Let's head to my house so I can change," Greish said. When they arrived, the house was empty—his mother and three sisters must have been visiting a neighbor. It was fortunate that no women were around; Hepluosis needed to talk privately.

He explained to Greish what had happened the night before and his plans for that evening. "I want you to come with me. If we get stopped, you might be able to talk us out of it."

"I doubt that, but I'll come with you anyway," Greish said. "Just make sure we don't get caught. I'll meet you by the bush when the moon is a hand above the horizon."

With that, Hepluosis left to prepare for the night ahead.

The full moon cast a bright light over the ground, unimpeded by clouds. The increased visibility made it more challenging to move unnoticed, but Hepluosis was determined. He needed to find out what was in that camp.

Greish arrived at the meeting point just as Hepluosis did. Dressed in a black cloak, he handed one to Hepluosis. "Here, put this on. It will help us stay hidden." Hepluosis smiled and donned the cloak.

Together, they made their way to the hole in the wall, with Hepluosis going first. They moved swiftly through the forest, reaching the other camp in less than a finger of time. Greish mentioned that he had been aware of the camp's existence but hadn't known its location. It was a place for criminals and citizens deemed hazardous to society.

"That's who they are," Hepluosis said.

"Who?" Greish asked.

"The two boys Cret helped escape last night. They were removed from our school because they refused to follow the Teacher's instructions."

"So, they were sent here to have their minds erased. It's for the benefit of everyone," Greish said, his gaze dropping to his feet.

Hepluosis's eyes widened. "Not anymore. Cret helped them escape, and I know where they are.

"We need to return them before the Locals find out they've escaped," Greish said.

"They escaped last night, and no one knows yet?" Hepluosis asked, astonished.

"The guards are doing their best to keep it quiet. They should have search parties out by now. No one wants to face the consequences of allowing two boys to escape—it would reflect poorly on everyone. Come on, let's get a closer look."

"The hole in the wall is over here," Hepluosis said, leading the way.

Hepluosis and Greish approached the hole, which the guards still hadn't discovered. They slipped into the camp unnoticed. As they moved around the camp, they peered into several houses. Most had six empty pallets, though some contained pairs of criminals or more, sleeping soundly.

"Who are you?"

Hepluosis and Greish froze.

"I'm Seleo's son, Greish. Who are you?" Greish demanded, turning sharply. He had thought a guard had spotted them, but it was only a criminal in a grey tunic, barefoot.

"Seleo? Who's that?"

"No one you need to worry about, citizen. Who are you?"

"I'm... well, they haven't told me my name. I'm just called Six."

"Why are you here?" Hepluosis asked.

"There was an accident at the mine where we worked, and we lost our memories. These people are trying to help us remember."

"Come with us," Hepluosis said to Six, smiling at Greish. "I have an idea." They led Six to an empty house and stepped inside.

"My name is Hepluosis, and this is Greish. We're here to help you remember who you are."

"Oh, that would be great," Six said.

Just before dawn, Hepluosis and Greish explained everything they knew about Romota and the ship that had brought them to this planet. They told Six that he was a criminal from Romota and that his mind had been erased. Though Six struggled to grasp everything, the story made more sense than what the camp's people had told him.

"Well, it was nice talking with you, but we have to go," Greish said.

"Will I see you again? I want to learn more."

"We'll be back in a day or two. Don't tell anyone what you've learned tonight. Try to act like you're accepting what they're telling you, okay?"

"I'll try. What you've told me makes sense, but I still can't remember who I am."

"It will come back to you, I'm sure," Hepluosis reassured him.

"Thank you, both of you." Six shook their hands as they prepared to leave.

"Why did you tell him all that?" Greish asked once they were back in the forest.

"I'm not entirely sure. I thought it might help jog his memory."

"For what purpose?"

"You never know when a criminal might come in handy," Hepluosis said with a smile. He said nothing more, leaving Greish to ponder his words. They agreed to meet back at the criminal camp in two days.

∞ 12 ∞
PROCESSING PLANT

"JAPSTER? What are you doing?" Neiluios asked, his hands on his hips as he glared down at Japster.

Japster jumped, quickly stood, and brushed off his knees. "I was just—uh—just looking for something I dropped," he stammered, trying to hide his curiosity.

Neiluios raised an eyebrow. "You're supposed to deliver the report, not hunt for lost items." He held out his hand, asking for the report.

Japster shifted nervously. "The repairs won't be done by the original deadline. They've asked for an extension of two more days." Japster held the report scroll in his hand, not handing it over. "I want to send a letter to my wife and children," he blurted out.

Neiluios nodded, his expression softening slightly. "I'll ensure we get that extension approved." His hand out still waiting for the scroll. "We need to stay on top of this." Neiluios took the report and scanned it. "I'll review this and get them the necessary approvals. As for your letter, you can submit it through the proper channels, but remember, all communication is monitored and must be approved."

Japster's face fell slightly. "I understand. It's just that... it's been a while since I've heard from them."

"I know. The approval process might take some time, so be patient," Neiluios said. "In the meantime, focus on your responsibilities. If there's nothing else, you're dismissed."

Japster's eyes widened, a mix of surprise and frustration evident in his expression. "But why? Why can't we communicate with our families? They worry about us. They need to know we're all right."

Neiluios's gaze hardened. "It's a matter of security and control. If our families knew too much, it could jeopardize the operations here. We need to maintain secrecy for the safety and success of our mission. You're here to focus on your work and your duties."

Neiluios gave a curt nod. "Good. Now, return to your duties and keep your focus. If you have any further concerns, address them through the proper channels."

"How much longer do we have to wait? We've already been here for nearly two weeks. When can we finally go home?"

"You just told me the repairs will take longer than expected. Once they're finished, I'm confident we'll be allowed to go home. So, if you want to get back sooner, I suggest you do everything you can to speed up the process."

"I'm an official, not an engineer," Japster sneered.

"Watch your tone with me, Japster," Neiluios warned. "You're a low-level official, and you'll do as you're told and learn what you're taught. That will be all. Now, report back to the plant, make yourself useful, and don't delay returning."

Japster snapped to attention. "Yes, Sir," he mocked, his voice dripping with sarcasm. Neiluios turned his back, shaking his head as he walked away. Japster thought he heard a whispered "Worthless," but he couldn't be sure. He glared at Neiluios's retreating figure.

Japster headed back to the plant, though he scoffed at the term. *Plant*, he thought with disdain. The so-called plant was nothing more than a control center in a nondescript building in the middle of nowhere. It was supposed to be monitoring something, but what exactly, they were never told. Every time a team member entered the control room, the screens would conveniently shut down, obscuring whatever was being observed. The secrecy gnawed at him, fueling his frustration as he trudged back to his post.

This whole planet was full of secrets, and Japster hated secrets. He was determined to unravel this one, just as he had with others before.

Glancing around to ensure he was alone, Japster knelt again, trying to peer into the inner compound. Whatever was hidden inside was off-limits to him and everyone else, adding another layer of frustration to the already mysterious situation. But the crack in the wall revealed nothing of interest, leaving him only with his mounting curiosity.

With a sigh, Japster rose and continued on his way, but his resolve was firm. He would find out what was going on. He was patient.

He could wait.

Neiluios sat at his desk in the main tent, feeling the weight of the day's tasks ahead. His assistant, Hecto, was busy sorting through the incoming reports, stacking them in neat piles. Neiluios frowned slightly. Crelian, his preferred assistant, hadn't been allowed to accompany him on this mission, so he had to settle for Hecto, a low-level official. Hecto was nowhere near as efficient or skilled as Crelian, but Neiluios knew that even a mediocre assistant was better than none.

For a mission shrouded in secrecy, there seemed to be an overwhelming amount of paperwork. Reports, memos, and updates piled up faster than Hecto could sort them. Neiluios sighed and reached for the first report, mentally preparing himself for another long day of trying to make sense of it all.

He missed his girls terribly. He needed to figure out how to speed up the repairs—there had to be a way.

"Is there anything I should know about, Hecto?"

"Well, Sir, the supplies will be delayed a few more days. The report mentions snow in the mountains."

"What's snow?"

"I'm not sure, but I'll try to find out. I'm going for a walk and will be back soon."

"Yes, Sir." Hecto returned to his work, burying his head in the tasks at hand.

Neiluios ambled around their camp, surveying the surrounding woods. They looked similar to the ones near the camp where his family stayed, but he knew they were miles away. It had taken nearly three days to reach their destination by horseback, and this had been Neiluios's first experience riding a horse. The first day had been excruciating; his entire backside was sore and stiff, and sleeping on the ground only made it worse. The second morning was even more painful, but by midday, he had started to learn how to sit in the saddle with less discomfort. By the third day, things had improved significantly. However, he dreaded the return trip, anticipating it would be just as painful.

Birds sang in the forest canopy, and squirrels darted from tree to tree. Other wildlife rustled and snorted nearby but remained hidden from Neiluios's view. He paused and gazed at a clearing near the front of the camp, where the horses that had carried them were grazing. Neiaphi would have loved to see them; she had always wanted to ride a horse, though Neiluios had never considered it important for her to learn.

"Sir, may I assist you?" asked a man in a light blue tunic.

"No, I was just stretching my legs. Who are you?" he replied, noting that he had never seen this man before. The newcomer was of average height, with dark brown hair and brown eyes.

"I am your servant, Sir."

"My what?"

"Your servant. I've been assigned to you."

"Assigned to me? By whom?"

"Deleon, Sir. It's customary for men of higher standing to have servants. I was chosen to serve you. I'll attend to your daily needs here and assist your family as needed unless you require my help directly." He bowed at the waist.

"I don't need a servant. You can return to your previous master or whatever he's called."

"I'm sorry, Sir, but I can't do that. When you return, you'll have to speak to Deleon about reassigning me. If I disobey his orders, I'll be punished. Please, allow me to serve you."

Neiluios sighed, sensing he wasn't going to win this battle. "What do I call you?"

"I am Net, Sir."

"Net? That's an unusual name."

"As time goes on, Sir, you'll find that many things on this planet are strange to you—if you haven't already noticed."

"So, you know where I'm from?"

"Yes, Sir. I was briefed on what they considered important."

"Where are you from?"

"A village far from here, Sir. My mother is a servant at the Palace. I don't know who my father is. I was raised at the Palace and trained to serve. It's my profession."

"Being a servant doesn't sound like a profession. It sounds like slavery."

"Not at all, Sir. It's like being born into a farmer's household—if I'd been raised by farmers, I would've learned to farm. I can choose a different path if I wish, but I enjoy my life. My master sheltered, fed, and clothed me, and in return, I handled the tedious tasks. I don't mind it."

"Well, I'll allow you to help me, but only until we return to the camp and I can speak with Deleon."

"Yes, Sir. Thank you. Is there anything I can assist you with today?"

"Not at the moment. I'll let you know if something comes up."

"Very well, Sir. I'll be at your tent if you need me."

Net departed at a brisk walk. Now, he had a servant—
something he had never needed before. Life in Romota had
been easier, but here, things were different. While Net might
prove useful in assisting Altesse and Neiaphi, Neiluios still felt
he had no real need for a servant.

He continued his walk around the camp. The main
gates to the inner camp stood open, and Neiluios glanced
inside. It resembled the camp where his family stayed, but it
was much busier. Women in white tunics rested in the shade,
watching their children, dressed in white or brown tunics,
playing in the courtyards near the fountains. Men and women
in light blue tunics moved about, carrying baskets of water and
other goods—Neiluios presumed they were servants. He also
noticed men and women in light blue tunics with yellow sashes
across their shoulders engaged in more laborious tasks. He
would need to ask Net about them when he saw him that
evening. The gate slowly began to swing shut. At least he had
managed to see what lay behind the wall.

Before the last chime of the day, Neiluios returned to
the main tent. He glanced inside to find Hecto straightening his
desk.

"Do you need anything from me, Hecto?"

"No, Sir. Nothing came in while you were out."

"Then you may leave. I'll be in my tent if I'm needed."

"Yes, Sir. Goodnight. See you in the morning."

He entered his tent, greeted by the aroma of food
cooking over the fire. Although he wasn't hungry, the smell of
meat made his mouth water and stirred a pang of longing. He
missed Altesse deeply—she was the love of his life, and being
so far away from her weighed heavily on his heart.

He hadn't even had the chance to say goodbye to
Altesse or his daughter. When he entered, Net's back was

turned. Neiluios went to his pallet, retrieved the latest letter from Altesse, and began to reread it.

My Dearest,
Neiaphi and I are doing well, though we miss you terribly. I hope that all is well with you. Life here at Camp Roma (as everyone is calling this place) continues much as it did before you left. There's so much I want to tell you, but I'll save those stories for when you return. Until then, my love, know that we are always thinking of you and eagerly awaiting your return. Please hurry home to us.
Your loving wife and daughter

He hated how brief the letter was and found himself wondering what news Altesse might have that she chose not to put in writing. He refolded the letter and slipped it under the pallet.

"Sir, your evening meal is ready. I managed to get some beef for you if you'd like."

"That will be fine, Net. Thank you."

"No thanks are needed, Sir. I'm just doing my job."

Neiluios sat on a pillow that Net had provided and ate his dinner slowly. A sweet array of spices danced across his tongue, but it only made him miss Altesse's cooking even more. The meal was far superior to anything served at the Common Hall, but it still fell short of her expertise.

"Is the food not to your liking, Sir? I can prepare something else if you prefer."

"Oh no, it's delicious—better than anything I've had since leaving home. I'm just not very hungry tonight." Net bowed and moved to the corner of the tent, where he had laid out a bedroll. After Neiluios had finished most of the meal, he set the plate aside and returned to his pallet. Net then collected the plate and began cleaning the cooking area.

"What would you like in the morning, Sir?"

"Any fruit we have here will be fine."

"Very well, Sir. I'll retire now."

"Goodnight, Net."

"Goodnight, Sir."

"Please call me Neiluios in private."

"Yes, Neiluios. Thank you." Net laid down on his bedroll, facing away from Neiluios.

Neiluios struggled to fall asleep, and when he finally did, he was plagued by troubling nightmares.

∞ 13 ∞
SECRETS

"**I** don't understand why I'm not allowed to know what this plant is supposed to process. How can I tell you what's wrong if I don't know its intended function?" Neiluios asked again.

"I'll let you know when it's been fixed," said Sen, the plant leader. He was cut from the same mold as Deleon—short and taciturn.

They were informed that the plant had issues transferring the 'Product' from here to the storage holding units. They weren't allowed to examine the actual pump system or learn what the product was—whether it was liquid, gas, or solid. Neiluios had no idea. As for the storage holding units, he didn't know their locations, distances, or sizes. They were instructed to address the problem from the control center, which left him puzzled about how that would be possible.

"Let me return to the camp and discuss this with Addident. I believe we can devise a solution that will benefit us all."

"You can send a messenger with your suggestion."

"If he counters it, the resolution could take forever."

"That's the only option. You cannot leave without the rest of your party; they won't leave until the plant is operational again. We have been diverting the deliveries and must resolve this issue soon."

"What deliveries? What are they bringing?"

"You know I can't tell you. Why bother asking?"

"All right, I'll be in the main tent. Please send a messenger there later today; I'll have a letter for Addident ready by then."

Sen nodded curtly and turned away from Neiluios. Neiluios hurried out of the control center and returned to the main tent.

"How did everything go, Sir?" Hecto asked.

"Same as before—frustrating. I now understand what Addident was dealing with. Please write a letter to him. A messenger will come by later today to pick it up."

"Yes, Sir."

Three days later:

All is not well at the Processing Plant. Sen, the plant leader, refuses to disclose what the plant is processing or the exact nature of the problem. He merely states that he will inform us once it is resolved. We have examined every component of the control center but have yet to identify the issue, and the plant remains non-operational.

I have a potential solution for this problem, but it is not ideal and will require volunteers. We need to assign a team to work here permanently. Their families will have to relocate to this area, and they will be under the complete control of the locals, with no permission to leave unless granted. This is necessary to integrate our people into the plant's operations and resolve the issue. Given the current lack of trust, it appears to be the only viable solution. I await your instructions on how to proceed.

Addident folded the letter and set it on the table, his concern growing. He had feared this scenario might arise. The question remained: would anyone volunteer for such a daunting task? The messenger stood quietly in the corner of the Common Hall, where he had found Addident. At that moment,

Addident was helping Crelian organize the inventory from their most recent supply shipment.

"Crelian, I have a difficult decision to make. Can you finish on your own?"

"Yes, of course, Sir. I can handle this on my own." Addident nodded and left the Hall.

As he considered his team's final fate, a promise he had made to keep them together seemed on the brink of being broken by circumstances beyond his control. He needed to discuss this with Deleon to explore possible options. First, though, he had to find Deleon, which was no small task in itself.

He walked out through the front gate of the camp, one of the few individuals the guards would not dare stop. He entered the cave entrance, paused until his eyes adjusted, and proceeded down the long corridor to the control center. To Addident's relief, Deleon was there. Deleon glanced at Addident, gave a fleeting glare, and then broke into a large grin. It wasn't a warm, welcoming smile but rather an expression of someone eager to get things over with as quickly as possible.

"Good day, Addident. It's a pleasure to see you."

"I'm not sure I'd call it a pleasure, but a good day nonetheless. I need to discuss the Plant with you. We're encountering significant problems, and Neiluios has proposed a solution."

"I've heard about the issues. What's your suggestion?"

"We need to permanently assign you a team to handle these repairs and any future maintenance. They will be yours to keep or reassign as you see fit."

"I see. That's interesting—though not a solution I would have expected you to propose."

"There is no other solution. My people can't fix something they don't understand, especially when it's malfunctioning. They need to see the inner workings to make the repairs correctly."

"Very well. Make it so."

Addident left the control center with a heavy heart, feeling as though he were sentencing people to a grim fate.

They would likely never see their friends from home again. He wondered if anyone would volunteer for this assignment or if he would have to pick who to condemn.

Returning to the Common Hall, he found Crelian finishing up. "I see you didn't leave anything for me," Addident remarked.

"Hello, Sir. I'm sorry—I just couldn't help myself," Crelian said with a smile.

"We need to talk. Please, have a seat." Addident walked over to the head table and pulled out a chair for Crelian. "We must address the men and request volunteers for a permanent assignment to the Processing Plant. They'll be with the plant indefinitely, or at least until the locals allow them to leave."

"I'll call a meeting. How many are needed, and will any of the current team remain?"

"I'll have more information after I send a messenger. Please hold off on calling the meeting until I receive a reply. And on your way out, send the messenger back in."

"Yes, Sir." Crelian departed to carry out the instructions.

Three days later:

"Hecto, please gather all the men before the evening meal," Neiluios said after reading Addident's letter. "I have some bad news." Neiluios was worried that Addident might proceed with his suggestion, which could mean he would have to volunteer himself. He wanted Neiaphi to see Atlantis and not be confined to a camp for the rest of her life. He decided he'd better have an early meal; he might not get another chance later.

"Good day, Neiluios. I wasn't expecting you so early this evening," Net said, stirring a stew over the fire.

"I have a meeting tonight and might not return until late. Is anything ready now?"

"The stew is ready. I was planning to keep it for you, but I can serve it now if you like."

"That will be fine."

"Everyone, please be seated." Neiluios cleared his throat before continuing. "As you all know, we've been facing significant challenges. Addident and I have devised a solution, which both Deleon and Sen have agreed to. It's not an easy one, and it will be difficult to accept, but I believe it's the only solution that will work.

"I need volunteers to stay here permanently and integrate with the locals at the Plant. Your families will be moved here in one month. If no one steps forward, we'll seek volunteers from the main camp."

"What if no one there volunteers?" Japster asked.

"Then Addident and I will make the selections," Neiluios replied.

"That's not fair!" Japster yelled.

"Japster, sit down and stop yelling," Grueo said firmly.

"I will volunteer, Sir," Hecto said, standing up. Two others followed his lead. Out of the ten who were sent here, it wasn't many.

"Thank you, Hecto, Caiaphas, Georgios. Any other volunteers?"

"I'll volunteer," Japster said.

"You, Japster? I find that hard to believe," Grueo remarked.

"And why's that?" Japster challenged.

"You've never volunteered for anything in your entire life," Grueo replied.

"Well, there's a first time for everything. I want to do this. It's no secret that I don't get along with Addident—or you, Neiluios. So, here's your chance to get me out of your hair," Japster said with a smile.

Neiluios studied Japster for a moment before speaking. "What are you up to?"

"I don't know what you're talking about," Japster replied with a sheepish smile.

Neiluios didn't trust him one bit, but at least Japster would be out of their way and the locals' problem from now on. "Alright, you can stay—but you'd better behave. I doubt the locals will be as tolerant as we've been. Remember, death isn't an outlawed punishment here," Neiluios warned, motioning for Hecto to add Japster's name to the list with the others. So, they had four volunteers now, but they would need at least four more from the main camp. Addident should be pleased. "That's all for now. We'll stay and handle everything we can until the other volunteers arrive. After that, the rest of us should be allowed to return."

"Are you going to stay and help us?" Caiaphas asked.

"That will be up to Addident to decide. I'm the only one here who doesn't have the option to volunteer. Dismissed."

Everyone exited the main tent and returned to their tents for the evening. Neiluios wasn't tired and didn't want to go back to his tent. He preferred solitude, especially when his family wasn't with him.

He felt uneasy with Net around and distrusted Deleon's motives. He wouldn't put it past Deleon to use Net as a spy. Neiluios needed to be careful about what he said in Net's presence. He walked cautiously around the camp, wary of what might be lurking in the forest surrounding them.

He found a large boulder at one end of the camp, near where the horses were kept, and climbed onto it. He sat there, lost in thought until the moon was directly overhead.

"Good evening, sir," a guard patrolling the area said.

"Good evening," Neiluios replied. The guard continued on his way, and Neiluios was relieved; he wasn't in the mood for conversation. After a while, he climbed down from the boulder and headed back to his tent, hoping to finally get some sleep.

He quietly lifted the flap of the tent entrance and crawled onto his pallet. Net stirred but remained asleep. Neiluios lay there for a while, and as the sun began to rise, he finally drifted off.

∞ **14** ∞
𝒱OLUNTEERS

"**SEARCH** that cave," said Undercaptain Seleo. "We have to find those two tonight."

"I got them, Sir."

"It's about time." Undercaptain Seleo entered the cave and saw the two terrified boys huddled in a corner. They appeared to have been well supplied, but he wondered who had provided for them. "It will be alright, boys. Come with us, and we will ensure you are not harmed."

"You are going to erase our memories, aren't you?" one of them asked.

"I'm not going to erase your memories. Who told you that?" He knelt before the boys so he wouldn't tower over them.

"Just heard talk, that's all," one of them sniffled.

"I'm sure young minds can run wild. Come now, I'll let you walk if you don't try to run. If you do, you'll be carried back. Understand?" Both boys nodded. "Who helped you escape?" Both boys remained silent. "No matter. Come on, let's go." They escorted the boys back to the criminal camp.

Cret watched the entire scene from his hiding place next to the stream. He realized he would have been caught if the guards had arrived just one minute earlier. Once the guards were well out of sight, Cret hurried back to the camp. He knew he wouldn't be able to help those two again and feared he might have only made their situation worse. Yet, he couldn't have let them remain there after seeing their plight; he wouldn't have been able to live with himself otherwise.

Crelian met with Addident after receiving Neiluios's letter. Neiluios had managed to find four volunteers from his team, but the surprising choice among them was Japster. Crelian was certain Japster was up to something—he could feel it in his gut.

"Addident, I would like to volunteer," Crelian said.

"You? Why?"

"You need someone in there who you can trust to remain loyal to you while also being faithful to the Locals, and I don't know anyone else. With Japster staying, Neiluios wouldn't be a good choice—he and Japster don't get along, and I can only tolerate him myself. Additionally, Neiaphi and Hepluosis have a strong animosity toward each other. While my son Cret is learning to stand up to Hepluosis, I'm deeply concerned for Neiaphi's safety around him."

"What about your daughter?"

"Sareen has Cret to defend her. My children will be fine."

"If you are sure, I will let Neiluios know he needs to pick a new assistant."

"I will send you messages whenever possible, Sir."

"That would be very helpful. If you can, please find four other volunteers for this assignment."

"Four, Sir? I thought Neiluios mentioned they needed four additional people. With me, that will make three more."

"He included himself in that number. He figured I would send him, but I'm sure he won't be happy about you going," Addident said. "Assemble the volunteers and get them prepared to leave in one week. Their families will follow them one month later."

"Yes, Sir. I will get right on it." Crelian departed, determined to inform his family before taking further action.

"Why are you doing this to us? I was just starting to make friends," Sareen said through her tears as she hugged her mother. Sephi looked at Crelian but remained silent, willing to support whatever decision he made as long as they could stay together.

"Why a month? Why can't we go with you right away, or at least a few days behind?" Cret asked.

"They want the officials to get settled into our new jobs without worrying about our families getting settled. It will be fine, and we will be together before you know it."

Sephi finally spoke. "Will we ever get to see Atlantis?"

"I don't know. I hope so," Crelian said.

"Will I ever see Neiaphi again?" asked Cret softly.

"I don't know. I hope so," Crelian repeated, placing a hand on his son's shoulder. They had one more week at this camp together, and he was determined to make it a happy week for his family. They would not dwell on the future.

"Hi, Neiaphi. Can I help you get some water?" Cret asked from outside of Neiaphi's house.

"Mother?" Neiaphi looked at her mother. Altesse smiled and nodded. She walked outside with her daughter and sat in the shade in front of the house to keep an eye on them. Neiaphi and Cret walked slowly to the fountain.

"What's the matter?" Neiaphi asked.

"Your father will be home soon."

"We found out this morning. It's going to be great. I've missed him so much. But that's not all, is it?"

"No." Cret dipped the basket into the fountain and placed it on the ground. He turned, sat on the fountain's edge, and gestured for Neiaphi to sit beside him. She looked at him as if trying to read his mind. This was so hard. He didn't want to hurt her, but he was sure this would. They had grown closer over the past few months, relying on each other for support and comfort. Who could he turn to now? And who would she be able to turn to?

"Cret, your silence is scaring me."

"I'm sorry. I have bad news and don't know how to tell you."

"Just say it. It will be okay."

"No, it won't. My family and I are leaving. We will be living at the Plant where your father has been. I might never see you again." He looked at his friend as tears ran down her cheeks. He gently reached up and brushed them away.

"Why?"

"My father volunteered to go."

"Why?" Neiaphi stood, turning to face him.

"So, your father won't have to stay," Cret said softly. At that, Neiaphi lost control of her emotions and buried her face in her hands. Cret stood up, hesitated, and then gently touched her back. He didn't know what to say to comfort her, so he remained silent.

"I don't want to lose you," she said between sobs. "You were supposed to be here for me."

"I don't want to leave, but I have to go with my family. You understand that, don't you?"

"Yes," she replied, her voice choked with emotion, "but it's not fair."

"Nothing here has been so far. Why would this be any different? I promise I will get back to you someday."

"When? After my parents married me off to someone I never met before, or worse yet, to Hepluosis?"

"His father also volunteered to stay at the Plant."

"Oh, Cret. Don't go." She crumbled to the ground, her sobs erupting uncontrollably.

"I don't have a choice. I must." Cret knelt beside her and grabbed her hands.

Neiaphi looked at their hands intertwined and then into her friend's eyes. His face was flushed, and his lip trembled as he tried to contain his emotions. She closed her eyes and slowly composed herself. Finally, she leaned toward him, hugged him, kissed him on the cheek, and then ran back to her house with the basket of water. Cret stared after her but did not follow. He would try to talk with her tomorrow after he was released from school.

Neiaphi ran to her mother, dropping the water basket on the way. She flung herself into her mother's arms. Cret watched helplessly, recalling what she had said about being married to someone she had never met before. *What did she mean by that?* he thought.

"Why, Mother? Why?"

"I know, dear. Sometimes, things just don't go our way; there is nothing we can do."

"You knew?"

"Addident told me when he told me about your father coming home. I'm sorry I didn't tell you, but I thought you should hear it from Cret, not me."

"Oh, it is not fair, it's not fair."

"I'm sure your father will do everything he can to get him back here as soon as possible."

"I don't want to talk about it anymore." Neiaphi went to her room and lay on her pallet. She soon cried herself to sleep.

Immediately after school the following day, Cret headed to Neiaphi's house.

"Good day, Cret. I don't think Neiaphi wants to see anyone right now." Altesse was getting wood to start their fire for the evening.

"I don't blame her. Can you give her this note for me?" He handed her a carefully folded piece of parchment with 'Neiaphi' written neatly on the front. "And please keep this copy in case she burns the first one. She is upset with me right now."

"She is not upset with you, Cret; she is upset with the situation, that's all. She will be fine in a few days. You're not leaving for over a month. You two will have plenty of time to talk about it."

"No, I asked my father if I could start my training early, and he received permission from Addident for me to leave with him in a few days."

"I understand. I will make sure she reads this letter. May I read it in case she burns the second one, too? I will tell no one else."

Cret looked into Altesse's eyes; Neiaphi had her mother's eyes, so beautiful. "That would be fine. She must know how I feel about her. I will be back for her. I will."

Altesse hugged Cret and wished him farewell. She decided to wait until Cret and his father had left before giving Neiaphi the letter. She was afraid that she might burn the letter without reading it. Cret would have been a good match for Neiaphi; he might still be someday if he was allowed to return. Altesse didn't think it was likely that they would ever see them again, however.

∞ **15** ∞
GOODBYES

OVER the next few days, Neiaphi moped around her house methodically, doing what was required of her and nothing more. When she went outside to bring water to the house, she scanned the area for Cret. If he was around, she stayed inside. She knew she would have to talk to him before he left, but she had some time before that happened—she would be able to see him before the month was up. Her mother kept bringing him up, but Neiaphi would not let her talk about him. Her mother looked sad but said no more.

On the morning that Crelian was leaving, Neiaphi convinced herself to speak to Cret. She needed to be there if he wanted to talk about anything. He was going through a lot, just like her. She realized it was selfish to be mad at him; besides, it was not his fault.

"Morning, Cret," she said as she stood behind him. He jumped and spun around.

"So, you're talking to me again?" he said. She could tell he was hurt and angry with her.

"I'm sorry. I have been acting childish. I wanted to say goodbye to your father, and we need to talk."

"Didn't you read my letter?" His tone softened.

"What letter?"

"I gave your mother a letter to give to you. Oh well, I'm sure she had reasons for not giving it to you yet. I am leaving with my father today."

"What? Oh no, Cret. I'm so sorry, I didn't know. I thought we still had a month together. What did you say in the letter?"

"You will have to read it to find out."

"You can't leave me. Please don't." She threw her arms around him, and he hugged her back.

"I will be back. I promise."

"Don't make promises you don't know if you can keep. You promised me a ride on Rees, which has not happened." She kept hugging him, unable to bear looking at him.

"That's not my fault. I wanted to and still do; you can't blame me." Neiaphi leaned back.

"And not coming back to me won't be your fault either. Don't promise. It's not fair to me." She kissed him gently on the cheek and ran back to her house.

Crelian kept a reasonable distance from his son while he said his goodbyes to Neiaphi. They would have been good for each other. He had been in the process of arranging a marriage between them, but that would be on hold until they knew what was going to happen. He would have to tell Neiluios not to mention it to her and, if another young man entered her life, to let it take its course. Neiaphi kissed Cret and then ran away. Getting her out of his head would be more challenging, Crelian feared.

"You ready, Cret?" he asked after a moment.

"Yes, Sir," Cret replied, following him to the waiting horses. Cret would be taking his horse, Rees, with them, and in this new place, he would be given more free time to do as he liked. He would be training to take Crelian's place someday, and the locals would need to trust him.

"How long is the trip, Father?"

"Three days, I have been told. Rees hasn't been ridden in quite a while; do you think he can manage?"

"I hope so; he is all I have left to remind me where we come from." Cret patted Rees's slick black neck and mounted. Rees snorted and shook his head. His long mane whipped back and forth. "Easy, boy. It is going to be alright." Rees calmed down under Cret's light touch and the soothing way he spoke. It was going to be a long ride.

It rained on the second day of the trip to the Processing Plant, forcing them to postpone their travel. They had set up tents the night before and were now confined to them. Sheets of rain poured down, thunder rumbling overhead, and lightning cracking closer than anyone liked. The sky was dark despite it being mid-morning. None of them had ever seen a storm like this before. Crelian was thankful his wife and daughter were still back at the camp under a more stable roof. Cret arranged some parchment into a makeshift tablet or journal and began to write. Crelian wanted to ask him how he was handling the situation, but he knew Cret wouldn't want to talk about it, just as he wouldn't have. Crelian left him to his thoughts as his own drifted to how long it would be before he saw his wife again.

On the fourth day, they arrived at the Processing Plant Camp. The main gates were closed, and several tents were set up outside the camp walls. Neiluios saw them and waved, greeting Crelian with a warm smile.

"How was the journey?" he asked.

"Wet, but we arrived safely."

"Cret, good to see you again, but I must say I'm surprised to see you here already," he said, shaking Cret's hand.

"Hello, Sir. I requested to start my training early."

"I see. Very well, then. We have been housed here, but I've been told you will be allowed to live within the main village. Come, come. The servants will see to the horses. My tent is this way." Neiluios led them to his tent. Net had prepared a midday meal for the two of them but, seeing Cret, began preparing more.

"This is Net, my servant."

"Your servant. When did that happen?" Crelian asked.

"A while ago, Deleon, it appears, thought I needed a servant."

"I see." Then, in a hushed voice, he asked, "Can we talk around him?" Neiluios shook his head.

Net served the three of them and then left the tent. Neiluios went to the flap and looked out. Net was walking toward the main camp.

"Okay, we can talk now."

"Good. As you know, I am going to be taking your position here. I'll work to gain the Locals' trust and remain faithful to them, but my loyalty is still with Addident and you. I'll send messages whenever possible."

"I hoped as much. I thought I'd have to stay, and that would have been tough. They already don't trust me, and I doubt they ever will," Neiluios said, shaking his head.

"You are probably right. What have you been able to find out since your last message?"

"Absolutely nothing. These people are very tight-lipped."

"Hopefully, they'll open up to me, or all this will be a waste of time." Neiluios nodded his agreement. They finished their midday meal in silence.

Net returned a few fingers later with another man in servant's clothing.

"I have been assigned to you, Sir. I am Camtis, your servant," Camtis said to Crelian.

"Thank you, but I do not need a servant."

"Don't fight it. It won't work. You'll just have to get used to having him around. I don't know how I'm going to break it to Altesse. She has never liked the idea of servants," Neiluios said.

"Okay, fine," Crelian stated. "Hello, Camtis. I am Crelian, and this is my son Cret. My wife Sephi and daughter Sareen will be here in a few weeks."

Camtis bowed at the waist. "I have been briefed on your entire family, Sir. Please follow me; I have your house ready."

"Well, this looks like goodbye. I hope to see you again, Neiluios. Take care of your family." They shook hands.

"Sir, can you give Neiaphi this letter for me? Um, please don't read it. It's not bad, just private. I gave Altesse a letter before I left and said she could read it, so I suppose she could read this one as well, but please not you." Cret kept his gaze on Neiluios as he spoke.

"I will give this letter to Altesse, and if she says it's okay, then Neiaphi will receive it. Take care of yourself, Cret, and look out for your sister."

"I will, Sir. Thank you." Cret shook Neiluios' hand and followed his father and Camtis to their new home.

The walls and main gate of the camp looked the same, but the houses were laid out a little differently. The houses were larger, and each had its courtyard. Some even had their fountain and bathhouses attached to the courtyard. Most, however, used the ones in the common area in the center of the village.

Camtis led them to a house near the rear of the village. The house was one story, like all the others. Their courtyard was connected to a bathhouse and fountain shared by three other houses. Camtis had already brought their belongings in from the horses. The house's main room was about fifty percent larger than their last house near the mountain camp. Three rooms branched off the main room. At the rear of the main room was the cooking area, where a small fire was burning in the cooking pit.

"Where do you sleep, Camtis?" Crelian asked.

"Here in the main room, Sir. My bedroll." He pointed to the opposite corner from the cooking area to a neatly rolled bedroll and several folded tunics.

"Cret, do you mind sharing a room with your sister?"

"No, Sir. It has been fine so far. I don't know how well she likes it, though."

"For now, Camtis, you sleep in the empty room. We will decide your permanent sleeping area after my wife arrives."

"Thank you, Sir." He bowed and retrieved his bedroll and belongings.

"How are you holding up, son? Ready to get to work?"

"Ready as I will ever be. What are you going to be doing?"

"I have no idea."

Crelian and Cret spent the rest of the evening in their courtyard. Neither had much to say, so they sat silently, listening to the bustling village on the other side of their private little wall. After the sun had set, they retired to their rooms.

"Morning Sir. A message came for you this morning." Camtis handed him the message.

Crelian,
Welcome to Minopolis. From this day forward, Minopolis will be your home. Future reassignments may be possible, but not for some time. Please have your servant show you the location of the Control Center. I will see you shortly.
Sen

"Not very friendly, is he?"

"Sir?" Camtis asked

"Nothing. I need you to show me to the Control Center."

"Yes, Sir."

"Come on, Cret. Time to get working."

"Coming, Father," Cret called from his room.

The walk through the village to the control center was short. Set off by itself, the building was nondescript—completely square, made of white stone with a flat wooden roof, no windows, and only one door. Camtis left them at the entrance. Crelian and Cret exchanged a glance before entering the small building.

The control center buzzed with activity. Crelian and Cret were the first to arrive from the new team. Today, they would all learn what this plant did and what was wrong with it. Crelian was eager to get to work so he could report back to the others.

Net had packed Neiluios' belongings and was waiting by the horses shortly after the morning meal. Neiluios had hoped Net would stay behind, but it seemed he was joining him.

The journey back was just as boring and painful as the journey to the plant. The letter to Neiaphi from Cret rested in the pouch around his waist, feeling as though it added extra weight. He knew it was only his imagination, driven by the temptation to read it. He had promised Cret he wouldn't, and he never went back on his word. Still, he hoped Neiaphi would share it with him.

Altesse, Neiaphi, and the rest of the wives and children of his returning team were at the main gate waiting for them when they arrived. They broke the line of guards holding them back and ran to the men. Altesse and Neiaphi about knocked Neiluios from his feet, but he didn't mind. He was home at last. He looked at Neiaphi. She had grown in the few short months he had gone. He then looked Altesse up and down; it seemed she had grown to it.

"How long?" He placed a hand on her stomach.

"About five months now." Neiluios picked her up and carried her back to their house. His wife would not be doing anything laborious during this pregnancy. Neiaphi and her dear departed brother were born healthy, but it had been hard on

Altesse. He had thought he was going to lose her with his son. He was now delighted that Net had come with him and would be put to good use.

Net followed them closely back to the house. Neiaphi eyed him cautiously. Neiluios gestured with his head for Net to stay outside for a moment. He entered his home with his girls and placed Altesse carefully on her feet.

"The man who followed us is Net. He is our servant. Deleon thought he could come in handy. I now see that he was right." He pointed to Altesse's belly.

"Oh Neiluios, I'm fine. This one is going to be just fine, don't worry. We don't need a servant; you know how I feel about them."

"I know how you feel, but you must be off your feet. I will not lose you."

"What are you two talking about?" Neiaphi asked.

"Your mother almost died when she had your brother, and you were not easy on her either."

"Mother, why didn't you tell me that? I should have been helping out more."

"Because I feel fine. I felt weak with you and with your brother, I could hardly stand. I'm fine. Really!"

"I don't care; you are to relax. I will instruct Net not to let you do anything that looks like work. You can sew, that's all."

"Really, Neiluios, that is not necessary." He gave her one of his looks that said there was nothing left to talk about, and she dropped it.

"One thing about Net," Neiluios said in a hushed voice. "Deleon sent him to us. I do not trust him at all. We are not to talk around him except about unimportant matters, understand?" Both women nodded.

Net looked around the camp. It was clean and well-kept but lacked signs of life. That would change once more servants arrived to help get things in order. These people needed to look like they were born on this planet. That would be a challenge.

The first thing to do was to give the camp a lived-in look. Children needed to play in the open, laugh, and run about, while women needed to relax and enjoy themselves in their courtyards. He looked at the houses; there were no courtyards. Well, they could sit out front in the shade under the watchful eye of their servants. He would also seek to get a woman for his household. With two women, one of whom was pregnant, they would feel more comfortable having another woman around.

"You may come in, Net," Neiluios called. This was all new to these people, but they would adjust soon enough.

∞ 16 ∞
SIX

HEPLUOSIS and Greish visited Six almost every night for a couple of hours. Six was keenly interested in learning more about his origins and had a multitude of questions. Hepluosis and Greish answered his questions as best as possible, but they couldn't address the one he found most important: Who is he?

That night, he wouldn't need to ask them that question. Since meeting the two boys, he had been plagued by dreams of his past life every night, which troubled him deeply. He didn't remember being the malevolent figure from his dreams, but he was certain it was him. The boys were late for their meeting that evening, and he had drifted off to sleep momentarily. He woke in a cold sweat, fully aware of his name and identity. Things would never be the same. He realized he was indeed the malevolent figure from his dreams—the horrible, despicable person he had feared. Could he change? Was this his chance to start over?

He had never met his parents, who had died when he was an infant. His father's brother reluctantly took him in as a servant. With three children already to support, his uncle couldn't afford to feed another mouth without expecting something in return. As soon as he could walk, he found himself doing chores for the family.

He often thought it would have been easier not to know they were his family. It might have been simpler to accept the cruelty of those who had merely purchased him. Six's three cousins relentlessly beat him whenever he made a mistake, and even when he stopped making errors, they continued to beat him for sport.

His uncle was no better. He would punish Six for the mistakes his children made, turning a blind eye to the beatings they inflicted. The only one who showed him any kindness was his aunt, but she died suddenly when Six was twelve. No one knew why she climbed onto the roof and jumped, but Six was sure she hadn't done it willingly. He tried to tell her parents, but his uncle, who owned their home, refused to listen. After her death, his life deteriorated even further.

When he was sixteen, while gathering household supplies at the market, he was struck from behind by a rock thrown by his eldest cousin, Imp, who was twenty at the time.

Six was consumed by rage. Until then, the abuse had been confined to the house; they had never attacked him in public. Dropping the basket he was carrying, Six chased after Imp. Imp darted into an alley and tried to hide behind a crate, but Six found him and attacked.

He ended up killing Imp. He couldn't explain how he managed it; Imp was much larger, and Six was a scrawny child from malnutrition. Yet, somehow, he had done it. He felt numb—his anger had dissipated, and he experienced no remorse, pain, or even a sense of relief. He was simply empty.

He looked around; no one had witnessed what he had done. He fled the alley and returned to the market square, approaching the shopkeeper who had seen him chase after his attacker.

"Did you see which way he went? I lost track of him. Do you know who he was?"

The shopkeeper replied, "The young man was a stranger to me. I saw him run into an alley, but he came out a short time later." Six thanked the shopkeeper. He wasn't sure if the man was lying for him or genuinely believed he had seen Imp emerge from the alley, but it didn't matter. When Imp was found, people would assume he had been mugged. Six grabbed his money pouch and fled the scene. A few months later, Six's cousin Thedoro was discovered floating in the river near their home. The general belief was that he had fallen in while fishing despite everyone knowing he couldn't swim. There were no more tragedies for the family until Six turned eighteen. For the past few years, Six's uncle had been preoccupied with work and paid little attention to him. As for Fayia, the youngest cousin and just a year older than Six, she avoided him whenever no one else was around. Since her brothers had disappeared, she had grown timid and dependent, lacking their support.

Fayia always dressed scantily around the house, which confused Six. In his youth, he had thought of her—and all women—as pure. He had always adored Fayia and never blamed her for the abuse he endured; he held her brothers responsible for forcing her to partake in it.

Over the past few months, Fayia had entertained many suitors at the house while her father was away. Lacking a maternal role model, she seemed to be running wild. Some of the suitors were her age, but most were much older—men whom Six knew to have wives and children of their own. But who could resist a young woman as beautiful as Fayia?

One summer day, Fayia dressed in a manner very different from her usual attire. She wore a sheer, flowing dress that left little to the imagination. Six, concerned for her safety, decided to follow her discreetly, curious about where she was headed and whom she might meet.

Fayia approached a grand house in the center of the city belonging to an Upper Official. She knocked on the door, and a servant, eyeing her carefully, answered without comment. The servant gestured toward a side entrance that led to the back courtyard, indicating where Fayia should go. Fayia nodded and stepped through the gate, followed closely by Six, who ducked behind a nearby bush. In the courtyard, four 'gentlemen' awaited her arrival.

Fayia hesitated, clearly surprised by the number of people waiting for her. She forced a wide smile and approached them. The 'gentlemen' quickly surrounded her, gagged her, and carried her into the house. Six lingered in the courtyard for several hours, torn between the urge to return and his concern for Fayia's fate.

As dusk fell over the city, the house door creaked open, and Fayia was roughly dragged out. The men hauled her through the courtyard and unceremoniously tossed her into the alley. When they went back inside, Six ventured into the alley and found Fayia's battered body lying in the shadows. She was dead, having succumbed to the brutal treatment she had endured. Six left her where she lay and hurried home, overwhelmed by the uncertainty of how to face his uncle. He feared being blamed for her death, though he knew he was innocent in this instance.

"Where have you been?" his uncle demanded, his voice booming.

"I was following Fayia," Six said, his voice trembling. "She went to someone's house and was murdered."

"What? You killed her, didn't you? Just like you killed my sons."

"I didn't kill her. I loved her," Six protested.

"You liar!" His uncle's rage erupted as he struck Six repeatedly, leaving him battered and unconscious.

When Six regained consciousness, he found his uncle sprawled in the courtyard, a jug of wine lying beside him. Fury coursing through him, Six stood over his uncle, seized the jug, and struck him with all his strength. That night, Six stayed in the house, but with the first light of dawn, he fled the city, never to return.

Afterward, fear of being hunted drove him to constant motion. He moved from place to place, always staying hidden. To survive, he did what was necessary: killing when he had to and stealing what he needed. He drifted from town to town, lurking in the shadows to avoid detection.

He had spent five years living on the streets before being captured and sent to the ship that brought him to this planet. Now, he had a chance to begin anew and build a better life for himself. He hoped for a fresh start. Killing had come easily to him, and he found himself strangely untroubled by it. Even now, reflecting on his past, he was haunted by the question of why it didn't disturb him. Decent people should grapple with moral dilemmas about taking a life. Was he not a decent person? Despite everything, he still felt that he was.

"Six, are you there?" Greish called out.

"Come in, boys," Six replied.

"Did you remember anything new tonight?" Hepluosis asked.

"I remember everything," Six said, his voice heavy with sadness.

"You do? Great. Tell us everything about yourself. Start with your name," Hepluosis instructed.

"My name is Six. I was a criminal sent to this planet as punishment. I was given a chance to start over with a clean slate, but thanks to you two, that chance is now ruined. I have to build a new life with the burden of my past, and that will be a challenge."

"What do you mean? You were so eager to uncover your past. Tell us what you did to end up here."

"I've done a great deal, and much of it hasn't brought me here. What I've done is none of your concern. I'm focused on starting over and building a new life. We were informed today that we'll be assigned to officials who need servants. Our job will be to assist them and their families in exchange for food, clothing, and shelter. Over time, we'll have the opportunity to move on and seek new work. I'm committed to performing my duties well for my master."

"I'll have my mother choose you to serve our household," Hepluosis said.

Six sighed in response. "That's fine."

"I can't keep coming here, but I need to know more about your past, so I'll keep pestering you until you tell me."

"Pester away, young sir, but I will never tell," Six replied.

The three talked for a while longer before the boys returned to their camp. Six was left with much to ponder. What kind of life did he want, and how would he achieve it?

∞ **17** ∞
𝕿HE 𝕷ETTERS

HEPLUOSIS sat in class, staring at the teacher but not listening. They were supposed to be choosing their servants soon, but he hadn't heard any updates yet.

"Hepluosis? Are you with us?" the teacher asked.

"Sorry, Sir. Please continue with the lesson," Hepluosis replied, straightening in his chair and nodding respectfully.

"As I was saying, your families will be assigned servants tomorrow. These servants are aware of who you are and where you come from. They will also serve as your teachers. Remember, servants are not slaves. They work for their families in exchange for food, clothing, and shelter; it's their profession. They must be treated with respect and kindness at all times. If your parents choose to, they may acquire additional servants or purchase slaves in the future. Meanwhile, your assigned servants will teach you how to be proper citizens and integrate into society.

"Many young men come to rely on their servants as close friends or even father figures when their own are absent. Your mothers and sisters will receive this information tonight; you and your fathers are the first to be informed within your families, as it should be."

Hepluosis drifted back into thought. At last, he could have his mother select Six as their servant. But if all the criminals were informed about their future employers and their origins, wouldn't they start recalling who they were? Oh well, the locals aren't that perceptive. He could hardly wait.

As soon as the teacher dismissed the class, Hepluosis dashed out of the classroom. He needed to inform his mother before she heard it from the locals. He sprinted past the fountain and headed straight for the front door. Upon arriving, he saw a local leaving. He scowled at the man, who gave him a curious glance in return. They had beaten him to it. How dare they? He vowed that one day, he would rise to a position of power and make everyone around him tremble at his presence.

He stormed into the house and sat down by the fire. "What did he want?" he demanded of his mother.

"We'll be assigned a servant tomorrow, that's all," his mother replied, avoiding his gaze. He had finally managed to assert his dominance over her and was determined to keep her in line. She needed to be properly trained before they joined his father at the plant. His father would be grateful for his efforts.

"What do you mean, assigned? Aren't we allowed to pick our own?"

"He said they would be assigned, son. That's all I know. If you'll excuse me?" She bowed her head and walked toward her room.

She couldn't stand being in his presence and feared him, as she should, Hepluosis thought. He sat alone in the main room, staring at the fire for a while.

As dusk approached, Hepluosis left the house and wandered around the camp. He spotted Neiaphi fetching water from the fountain and slipped into the shadows to observe her. She glanced around nervously. Since Cret had left with his father, Hepluosis had seen little of her. They had been each other's strength; apart, they were vulnerable targets. As the single sun of this strange planet continued to set, his shadow shifted, and Neiaphi caught sight of him.

She quickly gathered her water basket and hurried back to her mother. He found it odd that she was fetching water when they already had a servant. People were often strange and different from him, he reminded himself. One day, everyone would recognize his greatness.

Neiaphi glanced around the camp. Women, children, and a few men moved between the houses and the bathhouses, but no one paid her any mind. The camp felt emptier since Cret and his father had left. While she was grateful her father was back, she couldn't shake the unfairness of losing her best friend. She glanced to her right and saw Hepluosis lurking in the shadows. Startled, she wondered how long he had been standing there, watching her. His intense gaze was unsettling. There was something distinctly different about him, unlike anyone else in the camp. Neiaphi quickly gathered her water basket and hurried back to her house.

"Neiaphi, you shouldn't be fetching water. Let me handle it. It's not becoming of you to be doing that kind of work," Net said.

"I know, Net. I just like to be alone sometimes. I'm sorry."

"Your mother asked me to find you. She wants you in her room."

"Thank you, Net." Net bowed at the waist and took the water basket from her.

"Mother, you wanted to see me?" Neiaphi asked as she entered her mother's room.

"Yes, dear. Come in," her mother replied, patting the pallet next to her, inviting Neiaphi to sit. "Cret left a letter for you, and he also gave me a letter for your father to pass along to you."

"He allowed me to read both letters and decide if and when you should read them. I believe you're finally calm enough to do so," her mother said. "If you need to reply, your father said he would make sure Cret receives your letter. Take your time reading them and try to keep your emotions in check until you're finished."

Altesse handed Neiaphi two meticulously folded parchments, each labeled with her name on the front.

"The top one was given first," Altesse said, patting Neiaphi's shoulder before leaving the room.

Neiaphi held the letters in her hands, slowly tracing the lettering with her finger. Cret had mentioned a letter on the day he left almost two weeks ago, but she hadn't pressed her mother about it. She trusted that her mother would give her the letter in due time. She hadn't expected there to be a second letter, though.

Neiaphi stood up, walked to her room on the other side of the house, and sat on her pallet. She carefully opened the first letter, then closed her eyes before slowly reopening them. She didn't read the words just yet; instead, she examined the script. Cret had clearly invested a lot of time in writing this letter; his letters and spacing were impeccable. She placed the first letter face down on the pallet and opened the second one. The handwriting was the same but appeared more hurried. The second letter had dirt and water stains on the parchment, suggesting Cret must have written it while traveling. Neiaphi refolded the second letter and picked up the first one once more.

Dear Neiaphi,

I wish I didn't have to leave Camp Roma, and I'm sorry for the hurt my departure caused you. I believe it's best for me to go with my father rather than wait a month and travel with my mother and sister. I am and will always be your friend. I only wish I could be closer to you and offer you more. If you ever need anything, please find a way to let me know, and I will do everything I can to help. I've cherished our brief time together as close friends in this new world. You have the chance to make your life great, no matter what the locals say. I will miss you and will try to write to you often.

Your friend,
Cret

Neiaphi carefully refolded the letter and set it aside. She wiped her eyes before picking up the second letter.

My Friend, Neiaphi,

I'm sorry you didn't get to read the first letter before I left. I think it might have been easier that way, but I'm sure your mother had her reasons. I can't predict how our lives will unfold on Earth, but we must remain strong and strive to make our lives extraordinary.

You are so bright and full of potential. If I can't return to you soon, I hope your parents choose a suitable husband for you. You deserve to use your mind and spirit freely, without being constrained by an overpowering man. Despite any doubts you may have had about their decision to move you here, your parents have always had your best interests at heart. I'm confident they will make the right choice.

Please remember that we are only good friends, and try not to dwell on my absence if I cannot return. I hope we'll meet again someday. I'll think of you often and write when I can, but I fear we may lose touch once the rest of the team moves to Atlantis. Have a wonderful life, my friend, and be happy always.

Cret

Neiaphi reread both letters. It was clear that Cret was subtly encouraging her to move on without saying it outright. He didn't expect to see her again, nor did she expect to see him again. How could everything in her life change so suddenly? It felt like only yesterday when her parents first told her they were moving to Krill for a few cycles, and now this. She was stranded on a strange planet, surrounded by people she was only beginning to love and trust, and now they were being torn apart. Who would the locals take next, and how many would be taken?

"Neiaphi, we're heading to the Meeting. Would you like to join us?" Neiluios asked.

"Yes, Father. I'll be right out." Neiaphi went to her trunk and carefully placed the letters near the bottom, under her garments. She closed the lid of the trunk and gazed out the window. The sun had fully set below the distant horizon, and the full moon cast a dim light over the camp. Neiaphi wiped her eyes and went to join her parents.

"Are you alright, Little One?" Net asked.

"Yes, Net. I'm fine," Neiaphi replied.

Altesse put her arm around Neiaphi's shoulders and led her out of the house. Together, they walked to the meeting at the Conference Hall. They were among the last to arrive. Neiluios guided his family to the rear of the Hall. Although he wanted to be present for the meeting, he decided to stay out of the way, given that he already had a servant.

Deleon sat at the head table, flanked by a group of men and women wearing identical light blue tunics similar to the one Net was wearing. Most of them appeared to be in their mid-to-late twenties, based on Neiluios's judgment. Addident was seated next to Deleon, a scowl fixed on his face. Since their arrival, Addident's expression had seemed perpetually set in a frown. Their situation seemed to weigh more heavily on him than on others. Responsible for all the citizens at Camp Roma, he felt a deep sense of helplessness. He had no control over their lives or insight into what the future held for his team.

Having their families with them was both a blessing and a burden. Neiluios glanced at his loved ones, a soft smile tugging at his lips. He was grateful for his wife's unwavering support, but a deep sadness and fear gnawed at him for Neiaphi and the uncertain future of their unborn child. Back in Romota, he would have already selected a few suitors for Neiaphi, and she might have already embarked on her chosen career path. He couldn't imagine Neiaphi being content staying at home like her mother. But then, when he first met Altesse, she had grand ambitions of her own—ambitions she eventually chose to set aside. He had encouraged Altesse to pursue her dreams, but she insisted on caring for their home instead. Perhaps Neiaphi would follow in her mother's footsteps after all.

"Everyone, please take your seats," Deleon said, standing at the front of the room. "Each family has been assigned a servant to help ease your transition into life here." We chose to let you fend for yourselves for a while so you could understand just how tough life is on this planet. However, given your status in our society, you won't have to endure much of that hardship again.

"Each family will begin with two servants, one man and one woman. In Atlantis, most households have at least one servant, and some may even have a few slaves. Servants have more freedom; some live within the households they serve, while others live independently. They will work for you in exchange for basic food and clothing. If they choose to live on their own, you are not responsible for their household. Many guards' wives work as servants to provide for their children and themselves while their husbands are away. Servants will work for you until you decide otherwise. If a servant wishes to leave, they must find a replacement unless you instruct them otherwise. In contrast, slaves are owned by you in the same way as livestock. They can be purchased from slave traders or other households.

"You must treat them kindly and provide shelter, food, and clothing, but they can never leave you unless under extreme circumstances. While you have the option to release them, doing so is costly, and most remain with their masters for life. Keep this in mind before making a purchase. Each servant has been assigned to a household and will depart for their designated home now. They will greet you when you return this evening. Do you have any questions?"

"I have a question, sir," Hepluosis said, standing up.

"Yes, young man?"

"When do we get to choose our own servants?"

"Eager, aren't you? You can select additional servants before those assigned to the plant depart."

"And how do we acquire slaves?" Hepluosis asked.

Slaves are generally not permitted at the plant, but others may purchase slaves after leaving this camp on their way to Atlantis. Any other questions?" The room fell silent. "Very well. You may retire to your homes." Deleon exited the hall, and the rest of the assembly followed.

"Two servants? We don't need two," Altesse remarked as they headed home. "No offense, Net, but we don't really need you."

"No offense taken, ma'am, but it's customary for Upper officials to have both house servants and personal servants to assist with business matters. Since you're expecting a child soon, and I have no experience with that, you'll need someone who does. I've selected a very experienced woman named Cleop to assist you."

Altesse sighed, about to speak.

"Don't fight it. It won't help," Neiluios said. Altesse smiled and nodded in agreement.

When they arrived home, Cleop was already waiting in the main room. She was a short, slender woman in her mid-twenties with blonde hair and striking blue eyes. Her expression, however, was cold. She stood with her hands clasped behind her back. Net introduced Cleop to the family, and she acknowledged them with a curt nod, saying nothing more. Neiaphi's parents exchanged puzzled glances but remained silent.

"Cleop, where are you from?" Neiaphi asked.

Cleop paused, looking at Neiaphi for a moment before replying. "I come from a small village on a distant island. My family was poor and arranged for me to come here. May I retire for the evening, ma'am, sir?"

"Yes, of course. Where are you sleeping?" Neiluios asked.

"All servants have been given quarters next to yours. Cleop and I will be just next door if you need us." Net bowed, and the two of them left the house.

"That was strange. She doesn't seem as happy about being a servant as Net," Neiaphi said.

"I think she's just not very friendly, that's all," Altesse replied.

"Now, you two, that's enough," Neiluios interjected. "We don't know her, and she doesn't know us. Let's give her some time."

"You're right. We just need to give her some time," Altesse said.

After a while, they all gathered around the small fire in the main room before retiring to their pallets for the rest of the evening.

"What's the matter with you? You were quite rude to your new family," Net said.

"I'm here to do a job, not to make friends. I'll assist Altesse with the baby and help you around the house, but that doesn't mean I have to act cheerful."

"You seemed like a different person when I picked you up this morning. What happened?"

"I don't know what you're talking about. I'm the same as I've always been. Now, if you'll excuse me, I have a long day ahead and need some sleep."

Cleop left Net standing in the main room of their new home. There was something strange about her. That morning, she had been full of smiles and pleasantries, but now she was as cold as stone. He would have to ask around to see if she had a love interest she hoped to be stationed with. Something was clearly wrong with her. His family was already dealing with enough without having to tiptoe around an unhappy servant. He would consider relocating her if necessary, but that was a matter for another day.

Net knelt by the cold cook pit and stoked a small fire. He placed a bowl of water over the flames and sat down. He enjoyed his work; he had been trained to be a servant for as long as he could remember. When he was ten, he faced a choice: stay in the household with his mother or take up an apprenticeship at the palace. He spent a week talking with the carpenter, the bricklayer, and the farrier at the stables. In the end, he decided he would rather work in a household, caring for people.

It was a good, clean job with plenty of free time. He was a skilled basketmaker, and over the years, he had sold enough to buy his own horse. He enjoyed taking a break now and then to go riding. He would have to see if Neiaphi knew how to ride. All girls liked horses, even if they were too polite to admit it. He didn't think Neiaphi would be too proud or shy to express her interest in something she enjoyed. Net picked up the basket he had been working on but set it aside, lost in thought.

Neiaphi sat on her pallet, staring at her trunk and the letters it contained. She knew what the letters said but felt the need to reread them. She approached the trunk, slowly lifted the lid, and retrieved the letters. Once back on her pallet, she gazed at the letters in her hands. They were her only reminders of Cret. She traced the elegant script on the front of the top letter with her finger. Cret's handwriting was perfect— something she could never quite replicate. Neiaphi opened each letter, reading them slowly, then reread them with the same careful attention. Finally, she lay down with the letters resting on her chest and cried herself to sleep.

Neiaphi, Neiaphi," a distant, unfamiliar voice called to her. Neiaphi looked around but couldn't recognize anything, though it felt oddly familiar. She found herself near a large body of water.

She started down a rocky path leading to the water. A large tree stood by a bend in the path. As she approached the tree, a handsome man walked toward her. He had the darker complexion of The People, with very dark brown hair and striking grey eyes. Neiaphi felt she had seen him before but couldn't quite place where. He smiled as he walked past her, but she stopped and looked back. He was now standing in the path, gazing at her. "Hello, Neiaphi," he said.

"Hello. Who are you?"

"Who I am isn't important. How are you adjusting?"

"Adjusting to what?"

"Sorry, I must go. Until we meet again, Neiaphi. Keep walking down the path; you might find what you're searching for," the man said with a warm smile and a wave goodbye.

He turned and continued up the path. Neiaphi watched him until he disappeared from view.

Following the man's advice, Neiaphi continued down the path, rounding the bend. As she curved around the tree, she was awestruck by the sight of the ocean. She had never seen such a vast expanse of water before.

She wasn't sure if it was an ocean or a sea, but it was stunning. The blue waves gently lapped against the rocky cliff below the path. It was a long way down to the water, and the path was narrow.

Neiaphi considered the path. She wasn't sure what she was looking for or if venturing onto the narrow ledge was worth the risk.

Maybe she should go back and try to find the man again. But no, she followed his advice and continued as he had suggested.

She straightened her back and carefully descended the switchback path to the water's edge. Small trees grew from the ledge where the wind had carried their seeds. Some seemed barely clinging to the rocks, as though a slight breeze could tear them from their precarious perch. The air was calm and hot, with the bright yellow sun beating down on Neiaphi relentlessly. She tried to shield her eyes, but it felt as though the sun was growing even brighter. Determined, she continued down the path to the first switchback. Next to the path was a small, furry animal. Neiaphi bent down, keeping a safe distance from it. "Rosk, is that you?" she asked the little animal. The squirrel chirped in response and scampered up a small evergreen tree.

Neiaphi shook her head and continued on her way. Her pet Rosk was with a friend back in Romota, a place far, far away that she might never see again. Tears began to streak down her face, blurring her vision. She struggled to see the path ahead and stopped, sitting down in the middle of the path. Was she lost? Was this just a dream? Where was she?

"Neiaphi, Neiaphi," the voice called again.

She tried to stop crying. "Get a hold of yourself. Crying won't get you anywhere," she said to herself. Taking a deep breath, she stood up and wiped her face.

"Neiaphi, Neiaphi."

"Who is that? Where are you?" she called out to the distant voice, but there was no response. Neiaphi resumed walking. The water below remained stubbornly distant as she walked on and on. After what felt like an eternity, she finally reached the ledge above the surf. Each time a wave crashed against the rocks, spray misted onto the path. The water appeared rougher up close—perhaps a storm was moving in. The path ended at a beach that hadn't been visible from above. The sun's reflection off the white sand was blinding. Neiaphi squinted, trying to see her way across the beach. On the other side of the beach was a dense forest, and a man stood before it, gazing at the sea. He didn't seem to notice her as she made her way across the soft sand. When she was within easy sight, she tried to get his attention, careful not to startle him or provoke any hostility.

"Hello? Excuse me? Hello?"

He didn't respond. Neiaphi continued to approach him slowly, stopping a safe distance away. "Hello, sir. Excuse me." When he remained unmoving, she cautiously walked around to face him. He was tall and muscular, with short, sandy brown hair.

He wore the same clothing as the man on the path. As Neiaphi walked in a slow circle around him, she noticed a sword belted at his hip. Taking a few steps back, she moved before him, trying to catch his attention.

"Who are you?" he demanded. "Where did you come from?"

"I'm Neiaphi, sir. I came down this path and have been trying to get your attention. I apologize if I startled you."

"I knew you were there," he said. "I was hoping you would walk away. What do you want?"

Neiaphi looked into his green eyes. They seemed strangely familiar.

"Who are you?"

"A person who is too busy to be talking to a child. State your business here or leave."

"I don't know where 'here' is. I just followed a path that led me to this place. I don't know anything else."

"Then why did you follow the path here?"

"A man up there told me to follow the path to find what I was looking for. The path led me to you. Who are you?"

"What man?"

"I don't know who he was. He said his identity wasn't important. He had dark brown hair and grey eyes, and he wore clothing similar to yours, but with a green shirt instead of maroon."

The man paused, thinking. "I don't know him. What do you want?"

"I want to know what you're looking at," Neiaphi replied. She was curious about his identity but suspected he wouldn't answer that question.

"I am looking at an island I've dreamed about—an island where I plan to build my own home with my beloved by my side."

Neiaphi looked out at the sea but saw no island. "Why are you just looking? Why don't you go there with her?"

"Because I don't yet know where the island is, and my beloved doesn't even know I'm alive, nor does she know how deeply I still desire her."

"Who are you?"

The man drew his sword and pointed it at Neiaphi, who jumped back several feet. "I told you to leave me alone, child."

"I'm sorry. I'll leave. Please don't hurt me." Neiaphi ran back across the beach and up the path.

"Neiaphi, Neiaphi."

She heard the voice again, now much closer. Looking back, she saw that the man was gone. Had he been calling her name? As she turned toward the path, she found a large wolver standing just five feet away, growling menacingly. She fell backward, screaming...

Neiaphi woke up in a sweat. It had all been a dream, but such a vivid one. Who were those two men who seemed to know her yet refused to reveal their names? And what was that wolver doing in her dream? It was nearly dawn before she could drift back to sleep, her questions still unanswered.

∞ 18 ∞
GIFTS AND SURPRISES

"**GOOD** morning, young one," Net said as Neiaphi entered the room the following day. "We have some fresh fruit and nuts for breakfast."

"That sounds lovely, Net. Good morning, Cleop. How was your first night?"

"Fine, Miss." Cleop continued chopping vegetables for the evening meal without looking up. Neiaphi glanced at Net, who shrugged in response. Altesse and Neiluios then walked into the main room from outside.

"Where have you two been?" Neiaphi asked.

"We went for a walk this morning. Good morning, Net, Cleop," Neiluios replied.

"Good morning, sir," Net said. Cleop merely nodded in acknowledgment. "Sir, I have a horse, and I was wondering if Neiaphi would like to go for a ride today if that's alright with you."

"That's fine with me. Neiaphi?"

"I would love that. When do we leave?"

"Shortly. I have a few things to finish up first." Net replied with a smile.

Neiaphi sat on the ground near the cooking fire and hummed to herself as she ate.

"I'll have a surprise for you this evening when you return," Neiluios said with a smile.

Neiaphi looked up at her father, her eyes bright. "Oh, tell me now! What is it?"

"You'll have to wait and see." He smiled warmly at her, and Neiaphi's face lit up with excitement.

Net's horse was a large bay stallion with four white legs and a star on his forehead. When the horse saw Net approaching, he nickered in recognition. Net responded by offering him a piece of carrot.

"I've acquired a horse for you to ride today. I'll be right back," Net said. Neiaphi approached the bay stallion and gently petted his nose. Net soon returned, leading a dapple-gray mare with one hand and carrying his saddle with the other. He handed the reins to Neiaphi and proceeded to saddle his horse.

"What's your horse's name?" Neiaphi asked.

"I'm terrible at picking names, so I just call him Bay. The mare is an extra mount, and I don't think she has a name. I'm sure no one would mind if you named her."

Neiaphi patted the mare's neck, considering a name for her. Net helped Neiaphi into the saddle before mounting Bay himself. They rode away from the camp at a slow walk, and no guards attempted to stop them. Neiaphi looked around, taking in her surroundings. This was the first time she had been away from the camp since Cret, and her previous excursion had been to the prisoner camp. She realized she had never asked Cret about the two boys they had helped escape.

A bluebird flew through the trees overhead. Although she had seen these birds inside the camp before, seeing one flying freely without any walls was a new experience. Her gaze followed the bird as it moved behind her, and she twisted her body to get a better look, nearly unseating herself.

"Careful, young one," Net said as he reached over to steady her.

"Thanks, sorry. I haven't been outside the walls since we first arrived here."

"That's why I thought you'd enjoy a ride. Now that you're properly supervised, you can venture outside more often. I know your father has been giving you lessons, but I'd like to teach you as well. I can tell you about this planet and The People, though I'll leave the mathematics to your father."

"That would be wonderful. I've been asking my father questions he doesn't have the answers to yet." As they rode at a careful walk, Net described the trees, plants, and animals they encountered. There was so much information that Neiaphi's head was spinning by the time they reached the camp's main gate again. Net unsaddled the horses and walked Neiaphi back to their house.

"How was the ride, dear?" Altesse said. She was sitting in the shade with Cleop, sewing.

"It's so much fun, and Net is teaching me about this planet. I now know the name of this flower hanging in the window I planted here. It is a Lavender." Altesse smiled. Cleop looked up but did not say anything.

"Your father will be here shortly; he saw you coming and went to get your surprise. Why don't you go inside and clean up?"

"Yes, Mother, of course. Please excuse me."

"Thank you, Net, for doing that for her. She hasn't been herself since her best friend left."

"I was curious but didn't want to pry. It was my pleasure. Riding with someone is always more enjoyable, and I love sharing what I know. If you'll excuse me, I'll check on dinner. Cleop, please join me." With that, Net and Cleop went inside.

Neiluios arrived at Captain Heu's command tent. A guard announced his arrival, "Sir, the First Agent is here to see you."

"Neiluios, good to see you. Come in, come in," Captain Heu said, gesturing for Neiluios to enter. Neiluios stepped inside the tent, where the light was dim, illuminated only by a small candle on the table. It took a moment for his eyes to adjust to the low light. Captain Heu smiled warmly and clasped Neiluios's wrists in welcome. "What can I do for you this fine day?"

"I've come to inquire about the present for my daughter. I spoke with you about it a few days ago."

"Ah, yes. I have it right here. I'm sure she'll be very excited—it's the best of the lot. You won't be disappointed. When she's ready, have her bring it back, and I'll help her train it." Captain Heu moved to the rear of the tent and retrieved the present. Neiluios thanked him and then left the tent.

Everyone he passed on his way back home stared and pointed. Neiaphi was sure to become much more popular.

Altesse was sitting outside alone when he returned. She smiled up at him and glanced at the wriggling present in his arms. "She's inside cleaning up," she said. He helped her to her feet with his free hand, and she followed him inside. Neiaphi wasn't in the main room. Neiluios quickly ducked into his room and called for her. Neiaphi emerged to find Altesse and Net with large, beaming smiles on their faces while Cleop looked down as usual.

"Father, where are you?" Neiaphi called out.

"Kneel and pat your legs," her father replied from the other room. Neiaphi glanced at Altesse and Net, but neither offered any explanation. Neiaphi followed the instructions, and a small, fluffy tan and black puppy trotted out from the room. She squealed with excitement as the puppy waddled over and licked her hand. Neiluios stepped into the main room. "You've been so lonely without Rosk and with Cret gone. Your mother and I thought you could use a new friend."

"Where did you get him?" Neiaphi asked, still in awe.

"Captain Heu is raising guard dogs for the outposts, and he allowed me to take one. When the puppy is older, he said to bring him back, and he'll teach you how to train him as your personal guard."

"Thank you so much. Today has been the best day," Neiaphi said, hugging her parents. She then carried her new puppy into her room.

Neiaphi closed her door to keep the puppy in her room and then sat down on the floor. The little tan and black puppy crawled into her lap and nestled in, closing its eyes.

"What should I call you?" she asked softly. The puppy whimpered but remained still. She gently stroked his head, pondering the perfect name.

"You'll be my protector and friend, so you need a name that won't be laughed at. Zeus? No, that might not be right. I need something easy to say in a hurry or if I'm in danger. How about Cypress? Yes, that sounds good. Little puppy Cypress." Cypress lifted his head and barked at Neiaphi.

"Cypress it is, then," she said with a smile. "Let's see about making you a collar and leash so you don't wander off." She gently moved Cypress to her pallet and rummaged through her trunk, searching for materials that would work.

She found an old belt from Romota among her clothes that she had kept. Measuring it around his neck with extra room for growth, she cut it to fit and tied the ends together securely. Next, she removed a rope belt from one of her tunics and attached it to the collar. It wasn't pretty, but it would do for now. As Cypress fell asleep on her pallet, she gently petted him.

After a while, Cypress woke up and began sniffing around the room. Neiaphi quickly jumped off her pallet, grabbed the makeshift leash, and headed towards the door. "I'll be just outside, Mother."

"Don't go too far," came the reply.

"I won't," Neiaphi assured her as she walked Cypress to the back of the house, where the waste shed was located. In the distance, she spotted her father and Net walking together, but they were too far away for her to overhear their conversation. She tried to approach them, but her father noticed her and moved further away. Knowing she had a habit of eavesdropping, he was determined to keep their conversation private this time. *Oh, well,* she thought. With a new puppy to keep her occupied, she let it go and began considering asking Net for another ride, maybe a chance to learn more about the planet. Humming contentedly, she walked Cypress around the house before settling down in the shade with him.

Out of the corner of his eye, Neiluios noticed Neiaphi approaching slowly with her puppy. He signaled Net to continue moving away from the house.

"How was your ride this morning?" Neiluios asked.

"Lovely, Sir," Net replied. "Your daughter rides quite well, especially considering she's never ridden before."

"She is quite graceful. Altesse mentioned that you've even begun teaching her about the planet."

"Yes, Sir. I hope I didn't overstep my bounds. It's customary for servants to help tutor children, but only with permission."

"You have my permission. I don't know much about this planet either, so any help you can provide to Altesse and me would be greatly appreciated."

"Of course, Sir. May I say something?"

"Yes, of course."

"You don't trust me," Net said. Neiluios remained silent, not meeting Net's gaze. "You don't have to answer that. It's not always the master's place to trust their servants. I apologize for even bringing it up."

"No, you're fine. I appreciate honesty and asking hard questions, no matter how difficult they are. I admit I find it hard to trust you. You were assigned to me by Deleon, who seems to dislike me and anyone on our team. He has many secrets, and I've noticed some of his people spying on us."

"I understand. I wouldn't trust me either if I were in your position. I respect your caution. You're a careful man, protecting your family. I'll always be honest with you. Deleon handpicked me because I'm easygoing and not shy about getting necessary answers. He did require me to report your movements to him, but I haven't done so yet. I wanted to get to know you and your family first."

"Deleon painted a rather bleak picture of you, and I've told him so since we returned. He's not pleased with me at the moment. As long as you and your family do not intentionally harm our society, I will report nothing and assist you however possible. I chose Camtis for Crelian because I trust him implicitly. I can send letters to him for Crelian that no one else will see."

"That could be useful," Neiluios said. "For now, I don't need to send anything, but I appreciate the offer." He paused briefly before changing the subject. "Now, about Neiaphi. Are you willing to continue her riding and planet lessons?" He gestured broadly, trying to encompass the entire planet.

"It would be a great privilege, sir," Net said, bowing at the waist.

"Good. Let's head to the stable and find her a horse."

"You're a generous father," Net remarked with a smile. "First a puppy, and now a horse. She's a lucky young lady."

"She's had a tough time lately," Neiluios replied, his voice softening. "Her brother was killed by a wolver a few months before we left for here. She had to leave her pet behind, and she and Cret were the first to discover that we'd be stranded. And now, Cret is gone."

"What is a wolver, and how could two young children uncover such important information before an adult?" Net asked curiosity piqued.

"It's a long story, and I promised not to share the details. You'll have to ask her yourself. A wolver is a large creature resembling a wolf but about twice its size. No one I know understands where they come from or what they truly are. Somehow, one got into the city, leaped into our courtyard, and killed my son. He was only three years old."

"I'm so sorry, Sir. I didn't know."

"Altesse prefers not to talk about it, so please avoid bringing it up. Also, let Cleop know that Altesse had complications during labor. Our son's birth nearly cost her life, but she insists she feels great."

"I will, Sir. You have nothing to worry about."

At the stable, Net showed Neiluios the horse Neiaphi had been riding. Neiluios negotiated with the Horse Master to secure the little gray for Neiaphi, a sorrel gelding for himself, and a two-horse bay team with a carriage for Altesse and Cleop. He wanted to ensure all the horses were ready when it was time to move to Atlantis.

"Since you are closer to the locals than we are— actually, you are one," he corrected himself with a shake of his head, "have you heard when we will be leaving for Atlantis? I hope Altesse can make it before she delivers."

"I haven't heard anything yet, sir, but I'll keep a close ear out for any information."

∞ 19 ∞
MARKETPLACE

NEIAPHI woke up in a sweat, disturbed by the recurring dream. This time, though, something was different. She was older, and Cypress was with her, now fully grown, his once-black fur streaked with gray. The gray mare she had ridden the day before was there too. The man with the gray eyes didn't appear, nor was anyone calling her name. She left the horse at the top of the switchback path and hurried down to the beach, but the other man wasn't there either. As she turned to head back up the path, the wolver appeared, blocking her way, growling. Cypress leapt in front of her, his growl matching the wolver's. The two animals circled each other, hackles raised, ready for a fight.

Suddenly, the dream shifted, and Neiaphi jolted awake. She was still fifteen, still in her room at Camp Roma. What did the dream mean? Was it a glimpse of her future? Had getting Cypress somehow altered that path? The first time she dreamt it, she had been fifteen, but now it seemed to show her at around twenty-two. Unable to fall back asleep, she heard movement in the main room and decided to get up. Cypress woke as well, wagging his tail and letting out a soft whimper.

"Let's go see who's awake," Neiaphi whispered to Cypress. She peeked out of her room and saw Cleop sitting by the fire, her eyes puffy as if she'd been crying not long ago. Though her tears had stopped, the sadness lingered. Neiaphi cleared her throat and, a bit louder, said, "Come on, boy, let's go outside."

"Good morning, Neiaphi," Cleop said, smoothing out her tunic.

"Good morning, Cleop. You're up early this morning."

"So are you."

"I had a bad dream and couldn't get back to sleep. How about you?"

"Similar."

"If you don't mind me saying, you don't seem very happy," Neiaphi noted.

Cleop sighed but didn't respond.

"Well, I don't want to pry. I'll be out front with Cypress," Neiaphi said, ducking outside, leaving Cleop standing in the middle of the room. After a moment, Cleop sighed softly and followed her. Neiaphi and Cypress had stopped a short distance from the house, standing beneath a large tree.

"Neiaphi, can I confide in you?"

"Sure, but wouldn't my mother be a better person to talk to?"

"I don't think I should be discussing this with you. But I need to talk to someone, and I don't feel comfortable speaking with Net about it."

"But I'm just a child."

"You're fifteen—almost a woman. If your parents follow tradition, you'll be married soon. Have they chosen a husband for you yet?"

"Not that I'm aware of."

"I was once married," Cleop said, pausing. Neiaphi waited, sensing more to come. "My parents arranged the marriage when I was a young child. I met him for the first time when I was ten. He was much older and already a successful merchant. We were married when I turned fifteen." Cleop paused again, her voice quieter now. "I'm unable to have children, it seems, so he sold me back to my parents three years later. That's when they decided I would be better suited to serve others."

"They arranged my first job. He was a kind old man, but he passed away shortly after I started working for him. My next master... he wasn't kind. I spent several years with him until he decided I had 'served my purpose.' Then, I was given to a young couple. They had five children while I was with them. That's where I gained my experience with children. The woman had three younger sisters, and I helped with the births of their children as well." Cleop's voice wavered for a moment before she continued. "Later, the man was reassigned to a camp near where Deleon's team was stationed. The couple decided it would be best if I 'served society'—so they transferred me to you.

"I'm sorry for being rude to you and your parents," Cleop began, her voice trembling. "But I'm afraid that once your mother has her baby, you'll no longer need me, and I'll be discarded like everyone else has done to me. I am a person with feelings, not just a servant, though that's how I've been treated. If you hear your parents considering releasing me from service, could you please speak to them about keeping me around?"

Neiaphi considered Cleop's words as she looked into her eyes, noticing tears falling once again. "You haven't given us much reason to keep you around, you know? You need to be happier—or at least, not so unkind if happiness is too much to ask. My parents are good people. They may not be used to having servants, and they certainly won't keep slaves, but they want to fit into society here. They'll want to maintain the appearance their status requires. If you work hard and try to be happy, they won't let you go. But if you stay miserable, they might think you don't like them or want to leave."

"I'll try to be happy and work hard," Cleop replied, wiping her tears. "That's why I'm up early—I wanted to have breakfast ready before your parents woke. Thank you for talking with me. I've never shared my story with anyone before, and it feels good to finally do so. If you ever need to talk, please trust me. I was your age once, and I know how hard it can be. At least you have kind parents who have your best interests at heart."

"I'm sorry you've had such a hard life. It's not fair to go through so much so quickly. I understand, and I'm sure I'll have questions only you can answer." Cleop hugged Neiaphi tightly before running back to the house.

"Cypress, you're such a good boy, just sitting there so quietly. Would you like some breakfast?" Cypress jumped up and barked excitedly. "Shhhh, you'll wake everyone up. Come on."

"Are you ready for your lesson, Neiaphi?"

"Yes, Net. Can Cypress come with us?" she asked, holding Cypress, who was wriggling to get free.

"Not yet, I'm afraid. He's a bit too young and undisciplined to be around the horses."

"I'll watch him for you, Miss," Cleop offered. Net looked at her in surprise, as Cleop had spoken without being asked. She even smiled at the puppy as she took him from Neiaphi.

"Very well. We'll return later." Net and Neiaphi then left the house to get the horses.

Neiaphi noticed a new horse in the pen as they approached Bay's corral. "Did you get another horse?" she asked.

"No, that's your father's sorrel gelding. And over there is the gray mare you rode last time—she's yours now. The other two are for your mother's and Cleop's carriage."

"Are we leaving for Atlantis soon?"

"Not that I'm aware of," Net replied. "Your father just wants everything in place for the move. He mentioned something about not being prepared last time, but I'm not sure what he meant."

"When we left to come here, we didn't know it would be a permanent move. We left behind a lot of things." Her voice grew quiet, and she looked down sadly.

"How cruel."

"Yes, it was." They saddled the horses in silence and rode out of the camp, entering the shadowy forest.

"Net, is it true that most girls marry around fifteen?"

"Yes, it is. Who told you that?"

"Cleop and I talked a bit this morning, and she mentioned she was married at fifteen. How old are boys typically when they marry?"

"What did you and Cleop talk about?"

"I can't share the details. She just needed to talk to someone about some fears she had. She says she's going to be a hard worker from now on. Everything has been worked out with her."

"Did she mention if she has a love interest?"

"She didn't mention anyone since her arranged marriage husband. But, as I said, I can't discuss it unless she permits me. How old are boys?" she asked again.

"Usually around eighteen," Net said thoughtfully. "Sometimes as young as sixteen, but that's less common. Most boys wait until they have a stable income, their own house, and maybe a servant or two. So, sometimes the woman they marry ends up waiting a few years longer than her parents might have planned. Why the sudden interest?"

"Well, I'm fifteen now, and my parents haven't chosen anyone for me, as far as I know. They said they'd choose a couple of candidates and let me make the final choice, but things could change. I'm not sure."

"Your father hasn't mentioned anything about that to me. I'll let you know if I hear anything."

"Thanks, Net." Neiaphi looked into the sky as a large bird with a long neck and legs flew overhead. "What kind of bird is that?" Neiaphi asked.

"That's a crane," Net explained. They rode for a while, making a slow loop back to camp. Net quizzed her on the things he had taught her previously and introduced a few new ones. Neiaphi was quick to learn, catching on effortlessly.

By the time they returned to camp, Neiaphi had chosen a name for her horse: Nexus, after the current Queen in her homeland. Net had never heard the name before and advised her to tell anyone who asked that she had just made it up.

"Get your cloak, Neiaphi," Altesse said as Neiaphi and Net returned from their lesson. "We're going to the village marketplace."

"Really? That should be fun. What's the village called?"

"Uralpolis," Cleop replied.

"I'll gather a few baskets for you, ma'am, and come with you."

"Thank you, Net. Cleop has a few baskets here, but we might need more. I'm not sure what they'll have there. How long is the walk, Cleop?"

"Not too far, ma'am. You can't see it from here because of the forest." The four of them gathered their cloaks and baskets and began walking toward the village, with Cypress trotting along behind. The guards at the front gate questioned them but soon allowed them to pass. As they neared the village, Altesse stopped when the criminal camp came into view.

"Who is in that camp?" she asked.

"I don't know, ma'am," Net replied abruptly, continuing to walk. Altesse watched him closely, sensing he was withholding something. She didn't believe his answer—he knew who was there but either couldn't or wasn't allowed to say.

Cleop was right; Uralpolis wasn't far, and they soon arrived. The marketplace reminded Neiaphi of the one in Romota she used to visit daily. Merchants loudly hawked their wares and stands, and carts overflowed with everything imaginable—from strange-looking fruits and seafood to jewels Neiaphi had never seen. Cleop helped Altesse select some fruit while Net showed Neiaphi a collection of hair beads adorned with pearls and crystals. Neiaphi showed the beads to her mother, who nodded in approval. She paid the merchant and asked Cleop to help put them in her hair, feeling the absence of her jewelry from Romota.

They soon came upon a large shop with bolts of cloth in every color displayed in front. Net excused himself to visit a shop across the way.

Altesse, Neiaphi, and Cleop selected several beautiful fabrics, with Altesse planning to make finer tunics and cloaks. The wool would be perfect for travel and cold days, while cotton was ideal for everyday wear. Having elegant clothing for special occasions was essential. Cleop assured Altesse that she was an excellent seamstress and could create the garments beautifully. After purchasing the fabric, they left the shop and saw Net approaching with three goats in tow. The buck was pulling a small cart, ready to carry their baskets back.

"Goats! Oh, how wonderful, Net!" Cleop clapped her hands in excitement. Net smiled, relieved to see that Cleop seemed to have found peace and was genuinely happy. "We'll have fresh milk tomorrow and cheese before winter. This is fantastic."

"Thank you, Net. That was very thoughtful. I wouldn't have considered raising our own goats," Altesse said.

"Most families keep at least one female," Net explained. "But with your family growing, two females are better. And since no one else in your village has a male, you'll be the first. You can rent him out once more female goats arrive."

"Have you ever had a goat before, Mother?" Neiaphi asked.

"No, but my grandmother did. I remember them being a handful. We can keep the goats but no chickens. We'll trade milk and cheese for eggs." She glanced at Net, who nodded.

"As you say, ma'am," Net replied, though he seemed unconvinced.

The group of four, now accompanied by the three goats, continued down the bustling street, browsing the shops and carts along the way. Most houses were single-story, with the occasional two-story building standing in the distance. The marketplace was alive with color, as vibrant awnings shaded customers from the unrelenting sun while the buzz of lively conversations and merchant calls filled the air. By midday, the weary group began their walk back to camp, their baskets full and arms tired. Neiluios would be home soon, and since he hadn't known about their outing, they decided to return before he arrived.

Neiaphi skipped merrily ahead of the adults, her heart light despite the fatigue. The marketplace reminded her so much of Romota that a wave of homesickness had briefly washed over her when she first saw it. But with her mother beside her and her father close by, she was beginning to accept their new home. This planet held countless wonders, and she would get to explore them, not just read about them from a tablet.

Cypress barked suddenly, stopping in his tracks. Neiaphi laughed as she scooped him up. "What's the matter, Cypress? Are your legs tired?" The little puppy licked her face and squirmed playfully until she found a way to carry him that kept him content. They passed the unfamiliar camp in silence. The camp itself was eerily quiet, with no signs of life, and once again, Neiaphi's thoughts drifted to the two boys she and Cret had helped escape. She hoped they were okay. Cret had told her about three other boys who had been sent to 'The Special School' and never returned. He had thought it too risky to try helping them. Since Cret and his father had left, Neiaphi hadn't heard about more boys being taken, but she knew that didn't mean it wasn't still happening.

As they walked back into their camp, curious eyes followed them, and a few people approached to see the goats and the goods they had brought from the village. The women buzzed with excitement, chatting animatedly. Neiaphi felt like she was hearing four conversations at once as Altesse and Cleop expertly fielded a barrage of questions. Neiaphi doubted she would ever master that skill.

After the crowd dispersed, they continued toward their home. Net excused himself to take the goats to one of the storage houses when their house came into view. Neiaphi, meanwhile, led Cypress to the nearby fountain. She cupped water in her hands for him, and the puppy drank eagerly, his small tongue lapping at the cool liquid. Altesse and Cleop, engrossed in their own conversation, hadn't noticed that Neiaphi had paused. She sat at the fountain's edge, gazing up at the clouds as they drifted lazily across the sky, lost in thought.

"Hepluosis sneered from behind her. 'Where did you get that mangy-looking beast?' Neiaphi jumped at the sound of his voice and spun around, causing Cypress to leap and squeal in surprise. "What a wimpy little mutt," Hepluosis added with contempt.

"He's not a wimpy dog. My father got him from Captain Hue. Cypress is the pick of the litter if you must know."

"The pick to be killed, you mean. Just look at him—so small and scared. What a wimp."

"He's just a baby. You'll see. And then, I dare you to come around and bother me."

"Well, I'll be leaving in a few days to join my father, so you'll have to show off your so-called dog to the other boys. Have you ever wondered why no one else talks to you, Neiaphi? You're the dullest-looking girl here. I only talk to you to humor you so you don't feel entirely left out." He chuckled to himself.

"Oh, so you're doing me a favor, then?"

"Yes, I am," he replied proudly.

"Well, you don't need to. I don't require your pity; I'll be just fine without it."

"Really? Then who has your father chosen for your husband?"

"He hasn't chosen anyone yet. Why do you care?"

"My wife has already been promised to me, and it's the same for the other boys. I think you and two or three other girls are all that's left. You might have to settle for a local or someone far beneath you. That would be a shame. The locals want us to remain pure and will surely look down on anyone who even mingles with one of their own." He laughed, clearly thinking himself clever. Neiaphi took a deep breath, determined not to let him get the better of her.

"Well, whatever my future holds is none of your concern, Hepluosis. I hope you enjoy your life on this planet. We probably won't see each other again... so, farewell." She waved and turned to walk away, but Hepluosis grabbed her shoulder, spinning her back toward him.

"You don't walk away when a man is speaking to you. You wait until you're properly dismissed."

"That's funny," Neiaphi retorted, "I don't see any men around—just a spoiled boy."

Fury flared in Hepluosis's eyes. Without warning, he pulled his arm back and punched Neiaphi with all his strength. She collapsed, nearly falling on top of Cypress.

He bent over, grabbed her by the hair, and slammed her head into the ground repeatedly. Cypress whined and licked her face when Hepluosis finally stopped. When she didn't respond, the puppy growled and snapped at Hepluosis.

Enraged, Hepluosis swung his foot, aiming to kick the troublesome puppy, but Cypress was too quick. The puppy leaped, biting onto Hepluosis's tunic and tugging fiercely. With a roar of frustration, Hepluosis kicked out again, this time connecting. Cypress was sent sprawling, landing on top of Neiaphi.

Hepluosis stood over her, laughing triumphantly. Neiaphi groaned, beginning to stir, her head throbbing as if it were being pounded deeper into the ground. Hepluosis delivered a brutal kick to her stomach, followed by a vicious blow to her ribs. She curled in a ball, grunting as the air was knocked from her lungs. Hepluosis prepared for another strike, positioning himself to kick again.

"Hold it right there!" Net shouted, sprinting toward the fountain. Seeing him, Hepluosis bolted in the opposite direction, with Cypress barking furiously at his heels.

"Neiaphi, are you all right?" Net asked, gently lifting her. She groaned at the jostling movement.

"I d... don't know. Cypress!" Neiaphi called weakly.

"Cypress, come on, boy," Net urged. The puppy hesitated, barking one last time at Hepluosis before racing back to Neiaphi. He whimpered up at her, his eyes full of concern.

"It's okay, Cypress. Come on," Net said gently. He carried Neiaphi back to the house, noticing the bruise already forming on her cheek. He hoped nothing was broken.

"Neiaphi! What's wrong with her?" Altesse cried out upon seeing Net carrying her.

"A brute attacked her—punched her in the face and kicked her," Net explained. "I think she'll be okay, but I can't be sure just yet."

"Who did this to you?" Altesse demanded.

"It was Hepluosis," Neiaphi gasped between wheezes. Net gently laid her on her pallet and adjusted the blanket over her. As he began to examine her face, she moaned, "Oh, don't."

"Lie still. I need to make sure nothing is broken," Net instructed gently. Altesse took her daughter's hand, touching her forehead and noticing the feverish heat. Meanwhile, Cleop stoked the fire, preparing boiling water in case Net needed it. As Net worked his way down Neiaphi's chest and ribs, she winced but didn't cry out. "You've got a few bruised ribs, but nothing seems broken. That's a relief. Now, what happened? Why were you out there by yourself?"

"I'm sorry, Net, Mother. I've been to the fountain alone before, and nothing like this has ever happened." Neiaphi's hand flew to her cheek, and she moved her jaw slowly. "I've even spoken with Hepluosis alone, and he never acted this way. I don't know what got into him."

"Think back to your conversation with him. What were you two discussing?"

She closed her eyes, her voice slowing as she recalled the events. "He was mocking Cypress, as I expected. When I turned to leave, he spun me around and said I wasn't dismissed yet, and only a man could dismiss me. I told him I didn't see a man, just a spoiled boy. That's when he hit me." A sob escaped her lips, and her body tensed as a wave of pain shot through her.

Altesse laid a hand on Neiaphi's shoulder to comfort her.

"Cypress tried to help you, and Hepluosis kicked him too, but don't worry—he's not injured," Net reassured her before leaving her side and heading into the main room.

"What is it between you two?" Altesse asked.

"I don't know, Mother. He's never liked me. He claimed he was just humoring me by talking to me and that no one else would because I'm the dullest girl here. He also said that all the boys already had their brides chosen and that only two other girls and I were left to be promised. Not that I'm in a hurry or anything, but… have you and Father thought about my future yet?"

"We have, but we're not in any rush. No one in this camp seems suitable to us, so we'll wait until after we leave here. How concerned are you about maintaining pure blood?"

"Not at all, I suppose. Before we left, I was horrified at the idea of intermingling with the locals on this planet. But after meeting Net and Cleop and getting to know them, I realized they're no different from us on the inside. And that's what really matters, right?"

"Right." Altesse smiled softly. "Now, try to get some rest. I'll be back in a little while to check on you." She leaned over and kissed Neiaphi on the forehead, relieved to feel her cool down a bit.

Neiaphi was asleep when Neiluios returned home for the evening. Altesse and Net quickly informed him what had happened, and he immediately hurried out of the house. Cleop brought Neiaphi some broth for her evening meal, then quietly left her to rest.

Neiaphi remained in a deep sleep throughout most of the night, and her usual nightmare was absent. Instead, her dreams were haunted by visions of Hepluosis attacking her. Cypress stayed by her side, barely moving, his small body a constant presence of comfort.

Neiluios returned home late. His face shadowed with frustration. He told Altesse that speaking with Hepluosis's mother had been useless—she had become submissive, unwilling to intervene. Afterward, he informed Addident and Deleon about the potential problems with the boy. Addident, clearly concerned, immediately wrote letters to Japster and Crelian. Deleon, however, remained indifferent, remarking that soon it wouldn't be his concern. Still, he agreed to pass the information about Hepluosis to Sen at the plant.

Altesse and Neiluios slept fitfully that evening, troubled by their concerns for their daughter. They needed to find a way to keep her away from Hepluosis over the next few days without confining her to the house.

∞ **20** ∞
ᛒRUTE

ᕼEPLUOSIS sat in his room, glaring at the door. Neiaphi's father had come earlier, confronting him and his mother about his behavior toward Neiaphi. While his mother had listened silently, she said very little.

Hepluosis seethed, glaring after Neiluios. How dare he question how he treated women? According to what the Teacher had told him, he was in the right, and Neiaphi was in the wrong. If anything, her parents should reprimand her for how she had disrespected him. Women were supposed to be submissive and respectful—those were the rules on this planet, rules that Neiluios seemed willing to ignore.

When Neiluios didn't flinch under his heated stare, Hepluosis stormed off to his room. A short while later, he heard Neiluios leave, and his mother retreated to her quarters, softly closing the door behind her. He didn't expect his mother to say anything—she was well-trained, after all. Neiluios, on the other hand, would struggle in this world, letting his women act as they pleased. It was weak, foolish.

From the main room, Hepluosis heard movement—it had to be Phartar, their male servant, preparing the evening meal. The female servant was rarely around when he was home. She'd barged into his room without knocking on her second day of employment. Hepluosis had struck her for her insolence, and she hadn't seen much of her since. What was her name again? He couldn't recall—it wasn't important. She served his mother, and that was all that mattered.

As their departure to the Processing Plant approached, Hepluosis grew more anxious. They still hadn't selected the additional servants who would accompany them. Hepluosis had every intention of keeping Six with him. A criminal in his employ could prove useful—someone he could manipulate and control. He grinned at the thought, rubbing his hands together in excitement.

"Evening meal is ready, sir," Phartar said meekly from the doorway. Though Hepluosis had never punished him, Phartar remained cautious, especially after witnessing what had happened to the female servant. Hepluosis reveled in that power, eager for the day when everyone would fear him in the same way.

"Coming," Hepluosis replied. He entered the main room, where his mother and sister sat on the floor, their bowls placed in front of them. They waited for him to sit. Handing his bowl to Phartar, Hepluosis watched closely as the servant tasted the stew with his own spoon and handed the bowl back. Hepluosis inspected him for any signs of deceit or poison. Satisfied, he took a small bite. It tasted acceptable, so he nodded to his mother and sister, signaling them to begin eating. Phartar was a better cook than his mother, and the female servant had made him some decent tunics and cloaks. He was pleased with the results.

"Son, I hear we'll be allowed to select additional servants tomorrow. Are there any you would prefer?" his mother asked.

"Finally. Yes, I'll be selecting a personal servant for myself. You may keep these two if you wish, Mother. I won't have any use for them soon."

Thank you, my son. You are very good to me." His mother spoke without looking up from her stew. Hepluosis nodded, satisfied with her praise. They finished their meal in silence. Afterward, his mother and sister retired to their room on the other side of the house.

Lilen sat on the floor, quietly playing with her doll, while Jankin sat on her pallet, watching her daughter with a faint smile. Life on this planet was not what she had anticipated. Back on Romota, her family had been content, and Hepluosis had once shown her respect. Now, that felt like a distant memory. What had happened to him? Jankin lived in constant fear of displeasing her son, dreading the day he might turn on her again, as he had done after starting school. She wasn't sure what they were teaching him, but from what she heard from the other mothers in the camp, her son was the only one behaving this way. The thought of him growing older, stronger, filled her with dread. He was already spending much of his time with Undercaptain Seleo's son, Greish, training with the primitive weapons of this planet.

How she missed Japster. He would never have allowed Hepluosis to behave this way. Though he could be harsh and always sought an advantage in business and politics, he was kind to her. Everything he did aimed to improve her life and their children's lives. He had been gone for so long, and soon, she would have to traverse this strange world to be with him. She had been told it would be a three-day journey. She disliked sleeping in tents; even this hut she now called home felt too primitive for her. Back in Romota, her family had been wealthy. She had four sisters and two brothers, and being the youngest meant her dowry was modest. As a result, she had been forced to marry below her status. She resented her parents for having so many children and for not being able to provide for them at an appropriate level until Hepluosis was born. Despite this, she was thrilled to have a child, finding new meaning and purpose in her life.

When Lilen was born, she told Japster she would have no more children, and he agreed that two was enough. At that moment, Japster promised her that he would ensure Lilen had a good dowry and would marry above her status, and so far, he was keeping his word. He was determined to make the Locals recognize his value and planned to rise through their ranks. Addident and Neiluios seemed intent on holding him back, driven by jealousy over her husband's drive to succeed.

The front door slammed shut as Hepluosis left the house. Jankin sighed; he would be gone for a while. She went to the main room, where Phartar cleaned up after the evening meal. Melain, having seen Hepluosis leave, felt safe enough to enter the house and help Phartar with the cleanup. Melain was a lovely woman of average height with fire-red hair and green eyes. She was exceptionally skilled at sewing, which was a blessing since Jankin was dreadful at it and had to rely on Melain to fix or remake all her attempts. Melain also mentioned a nearby village where they were allowed to shop, offering Jankin a new opportunity to find what they needed. She planned to make a trip to the village before they left. Jankin looked out the window at the strange single sun sitting low on the horizon. With Hepluosis often staying out late, it would be some time before he returned. She settled down near the cook pit fire to enjoy a cup of tea.

Hepluosis stormed out of the house, slamming the door behind him. He needed to blow off some steam and hoped Greish would be available for a sparring session. He longed to escape the weakness of his home planet and looked forward to proving his greatness to everyone someday.

The following day, Hepluosis woke late after a long night. When he first arrived at the training ground, Greish was busy, so Hepluosis waited, restless with anticipation. Once they began sparring, Hepluosis pushed himself until his arms trembled and he could no longer lift the heavy sword. Afterward, they sat down and talked about their future plans. Greish mentioned that he and his father would be staying at

Camp Roma for the time being. The Locals didn't need any more guards at the Processing Plant, a disappointment for Hepluosis, who had hoped his only friend on this planet would be leaving with him. Never mind, he thought. He would make new, stronger friends. He bid Greish farewell and returned home just as the sun peaked over the eastern horizon.

Neiaphi drowsily opened her eyes. The sun was up, though still low in the sky. She hated waking up late; it always felt like she was wasting the day. Her ribs ached, her head throbbed, and her vision blurred slightly. She attempted to open her mouth, but the sharp pain made her eyes water, and she cried out softly. Altesse, sitting just outside her room, heard her and rushed in.

"What's the matter, dear? Are you all right?" Altesse asked gently. Neiaphi shook her head, wincing as she held her bandaged cheek. Altesse sat beside her and carefully began undoing the bandage. She reached for a small wooden bowl beside the pallet, scooping out a slimy green paste, which she spread across the fresh bandage before reapplying it to Neiaphi's face. The coolness of the paste soothed her feverish skin, and its calming scent helped ease the throbbing pain. Neiaphi closed her eyes, leaning back in gratitude for the relief.

"Try to drink this," Altesse said gently.

Neiaphi opened her eyes again, accepting the cup her mother offered. She slowly parted her lips, wincing but managing to sip the cool, refreshing liquid. After finishing, she handed the cup back and closed her eyes once more. Sleep came quickly.

"How is she doing?" Neiluios asked from the doorway.

"She's in a lot of pain. Net said her jaw isn't broken, but she can barely open her mouth, and the swelling is still pretty bad," Altesse replied.

"She'll feel better tomorrow. That boy is a brute," Neiluios muttered, shaking his head. "Come on, let's give her some quiet so she can heal." He extended his hand to help his wife off the pallet. They quietly left the room, closing the door behind them.

At the foot of Neiaphi's pallet, Cypress looked up as they departed. He rested his head on his front paws, his watchful eyes never leaving Neiaphi as she slept.

∞ 21 ∞
ℋEALING

NEIAPHI scanned the room, her mind still foggy. How long had she slept? Outside, darkness pressed against the window, though the moon's pale light seeped through, casting a faint glow. Cypress stirred, leaping up and padding over to her, his warm, concerned eyes fixed on her. She reached down, her hand brushing through his soft fur, gently patting his head. Slowly, Neiaphi pushed herself upright, her feet swinging over the edge of the pallet. The room swayed, and a wave of dizziness washed over her. She squeezed her eyes shut, focusing on her breath—slow inhales, slow exhales—until the sensation passed. When she opened her eyes again, the room had stilled. Tentatively, she stood and made her way to the window. The moon hung high, its silver light serene, but the eastern sky was beginning to brighten with a faint, promising light. Dawn was approaching. Neiaphi moved cautiously to the door and stepped into the main room. Cleop was tending the fire, its flames casting a warm glow, while Net had gone outside to fetch water.

"You shouldn't be up," Cleop said, rushing to her side.

"I had to move. How long was I asleep?" Neiaphi asked, her voice groggy.

Cleop guided her toward the fire, but Neiaphi shook her head, refusing to sit.

"Two days, off and on, thanks to Net's special broth. You're looking better. How do you feel?" Cleop asked, watching her closely.

"A bit stiff and sore, but mostly hungry," Neiaphi replied.

"You've only had that broth since the attack. Let me get you something more substantial." Cleop knelt down to reheat the stew from the night before.

"Good morning, Neiaphi. You're looking better today," Net said with a smile.

"I'm feeling better. Thank you for taking care of me."

"No trouble at all, Little Miss. It's my job." He gave a small bow at the waist.

After Neiaphi settled beside the fire, Cleop handed her a bowl of stew. The warmth and rich flavors comforted her. She ate slowly, carefully chewing the tender lamb, her gaze fixed on the flames. Cleop and Net left her in peace, quietly returning to their tasks.

Neiluios was already gone for the day, leaving earlier and earlier each week.

Altesse emerged from her room once the sun was above the horizon. "Good morning, everyone." She sat beside Neiaphi, gently touching her cheek and forehead. Nodding with a warm smile, she said nothing.

"Ma'am, Deleon is allowing everyone to choose additional servants today if you'd like. I just thought you should know."

"Thank you, Net, but you and Cleop are more than enough for us." Net nodded in acknowledgment.

"Can we go to the selection and watch?" Neiaphi asked.

Altesse looked at her, surprised. "Why would you want to do that?"

"I think it would be good to know who works for whom, and we might hear more about when we leave for Atlantis."

"I don't see the harm in that, as long as you stay close to Net. Hepluosis will likely be there, and I don't want to give him any opportunity to get you alone."

"Agreed." Neiaphi smiled, then winced as pain shot through her cheek. Altesse gently patted her shoulder in comfort.

Hepluosis hurried out of the house after Phartar informed him that additional servants would be selected just after midday. He approached the first local he saw, asking where the selection would take place. The Conference Hall seemed like the most logical choice, but he wanted to be sure. After confirming the location, he headed to the guards' section, looking for someone in need of a sparring partner. He didn't want to appear too eager by arriving at the hall early, so he made a point of lingering in the practice area. As usual, it wasn't hard to find someone willing to spar. With his extensive training, Hepluosis was more skilled than most of the guards-in-training when it came to swordsmanship.

Soon, the midday bell rang across the camp. Hepluosis returned home briefly to freshen up before heading to the Conference Hall. He arrived early, securing a spot near the front of the room.

As most of the camp gathered, Deleon made his entrance. He sat in the front of the room beside Addident and Neiluios, whispering something to Addident that caused him to frown.

"May I have your attention, please?" Deleon asked. "Those of you leaving tomorrow will have the first pick of servants. We have mostly males available, but there are a few females as well."

"First, a few rules. Your current servants have reported that you're learning quickly and rarely mention your origins. That's good. These new servants don't know who you are and shouldn't learn. Treat them as you would anyone else from this planet. If you handle this well, it will be time for the rest to depart for Atlantis."

"The servants are located at a nearby camp. Those of you who have traveled to the village may have seen it. We'll walk there now for those of you who need or want additional servants."

Deleon, Addident, and Neiluios departed first. Hepluosis jumped to his feet to follow them, hoping to overhear their conversation and find a way to help his father.

Altesse started to walk toward Neiluios but noticed Hepluosis trailing closely behind. She hesitated, deciding to give him some space. The last thing she wanted was to provoke any unnecessary tension.

The walk to the other camp was brief, and no one was in a hurry. Most people chatted as they walked, while a few approached Altesse and Neiaphi to inquire about what had happened. Altesse explained that Neiaphi had tripped and reassured them that everything was fine. Most people seemed skeptical, but no one pressed the issue. While Altesse had shared the truth with a few, she saw no need to create a scene in this setting.

At the camp, the servants stood in two neat rows. Hepluosis and Neiaphi recognized them as criminals from their home planet, though no one else was aware. Neiaphi was eager to observe who selected each servant and to keep an eye on them. Hepluosis scanned the crowd for Six but couldn't spot him initially. Eventually, he saw Six in the second row, trying to hide. Hepluosis knew he needed Six, and Six needed him. As Jankin approached, Hepluosis felt her presence and shot her a sharp glare when she stood beside him. Her confidence faltered, and with a quick bow of her head, she stepped back without a word.

"Jankin, since you're upfront, why don't you pick first?" Addident suggested.

"Thank you, Addident, but I'll let my son choose for us." Hepluosis walked along the line, scrutinizing each servant as he passed.

"How many can we pick?" Hepluosis asked.

"One to start," Deleon replied. "You may choose more at the end, but remember, you must be able to afford them.

When Hepluosis reached Six, he glanced at him briefly before continuing down the line. "Make your choice, Hepluosis," Addident urged impatiently.

Hepluosis sighed. "Very well, I pick that one," he said, pointing at Six. Six bowed and stepped forward.

"All right, who's next?" Deleon asked. The rest made their selections much more quickly. Soon, only a few servants remained, most of them female. Males were more valuable, as they could do more work and were preferred by the officials who were learning to farm and would need laborers.

Hepluosis scanned the remaining criminals one by one, but none stood out to him. With a nod to his mother and sister, he signaled for them to follow. They fell in line behind Six, who led the way.

Altesse and Neiaphi joined Neiluios after most of the camp had chosen their servants. "Let's get home. I have some news to share," Neiluios said, his tone grim.

"What news, Father?" Neiaphi asked, her voice urgent, even before they were all inside the house.

"We'll be leaving here very soon, but we won't go straight to Atlantis."

"Where are we going?" Altesse asked.

"We'll be making a long trip to a couple of outposts first to resupply them, and then we'll head to Atlantis. It will take us several months, and we might have to winter at one of the outposts before reaching Atlantis. However, we should arrive by spring."

"Oh, I had hoped to have this child either here or in Atlantis," Altesse said.

"I'd hoped so, too. I'm not looking forward to this, but don't worry—I've already arranged for a carriage for you and Cleop. You should be comfortable on the journey."

"You're such a thoughtful husband, Sir. I wish all men were like you," Cleop said, her gaze dropping to her hands.

"Thank you, Cleop," Neiluios replied, uncertain of what else to say.

"I don't know where Atlantis is, Sir, but I do know it's nowhere near here." "Some travelers I've spoken with have never seen it but have heard of it in their journeys. I'm afraid the trip might be much longer than you think," Net said.

"Deleon hasn't always been forthright with information, but it's been reliable so far when he does share. He volunteered this; let's hope we can trust it."

The next day, the entire camp gathered at the main gates to bid farewell to those leaving for the Processing Plant. Neiluios discreetly handed two letters to a man departing in secret—one for Crelian and the other for Cret from Neiaphi. The Locals were not to learn of either letter.

Hepluosis sat tall on a striking black-and-white stallion, chin held high, with a sword belted at his hip. His arrogance was palpable as he gazed down at everyone as though they were beneath him. Beside him, his new servant rode a sturdy honey-blonde gelding. Neiaphi shook her head in quiet disapproval. Hepluosis had spared no expense on his horses and personal servants, yet his family and their remaining servants sat crowded in a simple wagon pulled by two tired-looking donkeys. He clearly prioritized his comfort over theirs. After many tearful embraces and hushed farewells, the small group departed from Camp Roma.

Neiaphi stood among the onlookers, tears silently streaming down her cheeks. She didn't have any close friends in this group, but the weight of their departure felt final. It struck her that she would never see them again—just as she would never see Cret again. In her letter to him, she had written of their upcoming journey to the outposts, her hope for his well-being, and her relief that his mother and sister would soon join him. Yet deep down, she longed to see him one last time. When the departing group disappeared into the trees, everyone returned to their homes in silence.

The next few weeks settled into a predictable routine. The boys continued their schooling, and Net took Neiaphi on morning rides for her lessons. The camp seemed to be finding its rhythm again, though it was clear that things had changed irreversibly. The mention of Romota had faded from the conversation, which left Neiaphi with a sense of loss. She worried that she might soon forget what Romota looked like. She was growing accustomed to the white and gray clouds and the single sun. When she tried to picture the sky of her home planet, it now seemed distant and unfamiliar. Her favorite time of day was sunset when the clouds sometimes took on a pinkish hue.

Altesse appeared strong and healthy, often humming contentedly throughout the day. Cleop and Net managed the daily chores, gently shooing her away from any task she attempted. Most of her days were spent outside in the shade, where she sewed clothes for the baby. Neiaphi assisted with some chores and worked through the lessons her father had left her. Once her tasks were complete, she would take Cypress outside. Despite being just a puppy, Cypress was remarkably intelligent; she had already taught him to sit, stay, and come.

Neiluios was rarely home, frequently citing the extensive preparations needed for their departure. Occasionally, he allowed Neiaphi to accompany him on errands, but such opportunities were infrequent.

That evening, Neiluios informed his family that they would leave in one month. Net and Cleop immediately began packing their belongings and gathering supplies for the journey. Altesse repeatedly told Net that he was packing too much. They would reach Atlantis in a few months, but he insisted on bringing extra items and continued to pack them.

A couple of days before their departure, Neiaphi assisted Net in delivering some of his baskets to the Uralpolis Marketplace in exchange for two donkeys and a wagon. Neiaphi was surprised by how little the merchant required in exchange for the team. She recalled Hepluosis's mother, sister, and their two servants traveling in a similar wagon, realizing that he hadn't had to trade much for his family's transportation.

Two days later:

"Neiaphi, what a beautiful horse you have," Chartis said. Chartis was Amplios's only child, a few years older than Neiaphi. He had light blonde, almost white hair, light pinkish-blue eyes, and very pale skin, even by Romota standards. Cypress sprang up from his spot in the shade, barking and growling at Chartis. Startled, Chartis jumped back.

"Cypress, no. He's a friend. Come here!" Cypress looked at her and then back at Chartis. "Come, Cypress," she repeated. Cypress obeyed and sat at her feet. "Hello, Chartis. I'm sorry about that."

"That's okay. This is a hostile place; having someone watching your back is best. What's your horse's name?"

"This is Nexus."

"Nexus? Do you think that's wise?"

"Net, our male servant, said that if anyone asks about the name, I should say I made it up."

"Well, they might believe you. Still…" He shook his head and smiled. "How are you holding up?"

"Fine, I guess. I haven't seen much of you around camp or even on the ship."

"I've been working with my father. He's been keeping me busy. I haven't seen you around camp much since Cret left."

"I'm not allowed to go off by myself. You know, being a helpless girl and all."

"I've been meaning to talk to you. You know there aren't many boys your age or older here, and I was wondering if I could speak with your father." She stopped brushing Nexus and looked at Chartis. He looked down to the ground and shuffled his feet. She wouldn't describe him as attractive, nor would she call him ugly.

"Why don't we try being friends first? We hardly know each other." Chartis looked down, kicking at a pebble.

"I'd like that. Can I ask what happened to you?" He gestured to her face, indicating the healing bruises.

"Hepluosis didn't like the tone I took with him, so he tried to show off how strong he was."

"I'm so sorry. Too bad your puppy wasn't with you. He seems pretty protective."

"He tried to protect me, but he's too small, and Hepluosis kicked him out of the way. That's why he reacted the way he did."

"Well, that shouldn't happen again," Chartis said. Neiaphi nodded and resumed brushing Nexus. Chartis sat on the ground and called Cypress to him. Cypress looked at Neiaphi and whined.

"It's okay, boy. He's a friend," Neiaphi reassured him. Cypress wagged his tail and trotted over to Chartis.

Neiaphi moved from horse to horse, brushing them carefully to prepare for the journey ahead. Her father's horse, a large and sturdy animal, stood patiently as she led him over to a boulder to reach his back. He seemed calm, as usual. After returning him to the pen, she pulled a small piece of carrot from her pocket—a treat she'd managed to sneak from the house. The horse nickered softly as he accepted the carrot from her hand. She patted his neck affectionately, then glanced around. Chartis was still playing with Cypress while Net was finishing packing the wagon. He glanced in her direction and smiled. He'd probably been watching her the whole time or at least keeping an eye on Chartis. She didn't mind. Chartis was harmless, but she felt comforted knowing Net was nearby, just in case.

"I'm sure I'll see you soon. Take care. Come, Cypress," Neiaphi said, her voice warm as she called her companion.

"Bye. It was nice talking with you," Chartis replied, waving as Neiaphi turned to leave.

Neiaphi then walked over to Net, her thoughts lingering on the conversation she just had.

"Who was that?" Net asked, his curiosity piqued.

"Chartis, Amplios's son," she replied softly, her gaze dropping to the ground. "He wanted my permission to speak to Father about me."

Net paused, glancing at her from the corner of his eye as he carefully placed the last item in the wagon. His expression remained neutral, but there was a hint of something unreadable in his eyes.

"And what did you tell him?" Net asked, his tone steady but probing.

"I said we should start as friends, and he agreed," she said, her voice contemplative. "He's nice, and his status is almost as high as mine, but... I don't know." She sighed, uncertainty clouding her expression as she trailed off.

"But he's not Cret, is he?" Net asked, a hint of teasing in his voice.

"Cret? I—I never said anything about Cret. That's not what I meant," she stammered, flustered. "Anyway, I just don't like him that way."

Net smiled knowingly, sensing her discomfort, but mercifully let the subject drop. Neiaphi quickly turned away, her cheeks flushing with embarrassment, hoping he wouldn't press further. *Why did Cret's name have to come up?* She wondered, trying to shake off the heat rising in her face.

A grand celebration was planned three nights before they departed from Camp Roma. The men and boys gathered in the Conference Hall while the women and girls made their way to the center of the camp, waiting until the sun had fully disappeared beneath the western horizon. As darkness settled, several female servants assembled a massive fire near one of the fountains in the heart of the open square. Others constructed an altar from stones gathered and brought into the camp. Once the fire roared to life and the altar stood complete, two servants emerged from a nearby house carrying a large basket filled with oil, incense, and bread.

All the women and girls gathered close to the altar. On this planet, religion and rituals were deeply woven into the fabric of society, and they needed to learn these customs to convincingly blend in and appear as if they truly belonged here. Back in Romota, rituals had faded into obscurity long ago, dismissed as barbaric relics of the past. But here, they would have to adapt. The servants had selected a few gods for them to worship and would guide them through the necessary rituals. Tonight, they would begin by learning about the goddess Artemis.

The basket was placed beside the altar. One of the older servants stood beside it, resting a hand on the stone surface and bowing her head in reverence. All the other servants bowed their heads in unison. The women and girls of the camp glanced around, some bowing their heads while most kept their eyes wide open, eager to see what would unfold.

After a moment of silence, the servant at the altar turned toward the crowd of women and raised her hands. "Tonight, we honor Artemis, goddess of the hunt, wild animals, wilderness, chastity, and childbirth. Hera, the Queen of the Gods, almost denied her life. To give birth, Leto, her mother, had to seek refuge from the Queen."

"Artemis was born first and helped her mother with the birth of her twin brother, Apollo. When Artemis was three years old, she sat on her father's knee, Zeus, King of the Gods, and made several requests of him."

"She asked for perpetual virginity, lop-eared hounds to pull her chariot, and nymphs to serve as her hunting companions. Zeus granted her requests. As a result, all those who serve in her temples are bound to remain virgins or face her wrath."

"Tonight, we will begin with prayer, accompanied by the burning of oil and incense. Please repeat after me as I teach you the prayers to honor her."

The old woman repeatedly recited a series of prayers. Neiaphi and her mother joined in with the others, their voices blending. Servants distributed small bowls of scented oils, incense, and bread as they chanted. One by one, they approached the growing fire and cast their offerings into the flames. As the fire consumed the gifts, they recited one final prayer and observed a moment of silence.

"Now, we will hunt," the old woman announced. Everyone picked up the sticks placed by the fire and followed her outside the camp's walls. The female servants began chanting and dancing, ceremoniously stabbing the air, the ground, and the trees.

Nothing was hunted, but the ritual was performed with intent. After a few moments, some of the Romotian women joined in. Altesse handed one of the sticks to Neiaphi and gestured for her to join as well. They danced until the eastern horizon began to glow with the first light of dawn. The ceremonial hunting spears were then taken to the dying fire and thrown in, causing the flames to leap back to life.

"Now, one of us must stay with the fire until Artemis is satisfied and lets it burn out. We need a young, unmarried woman to volunteer. In villages that worship Artemis, this ritual is a sacred tradition. The High Priestess would normally fulfill this duty, but since we have no temple here, any willing woman will suffice." One of the servants stepped forward.

"I will watch the fire, wise one," she said.

"Come forward, child," the old woman responded. "Do you swear by the wrath of Artemis and the might of Zeus that you are pure?"

"I am pure, or may the Lady of the Hunt strike me down on this very spot." The old woman stepped back as if expecting Artemis to do just that. "I have the courage to protect the fire, or may the Hand of the King fall upon me now."

Nothing happened. "May Artemis be with you." The old woman bowed at the waist and walked away. As the others departed, the newcomers to this planet hesitated, unsure if the ritual had ended. Cleop approached Altesse and Neiaphi, guiding them away in silence. She finally spoke only when they were some distance from the dwindling fire.

"The one who protects the fire must remain until every member has gone cold. Sometimes, rain comes quickly, and the duty ends soon after. But other times, it takes much, much longer. I've even heard that some priestesses have died while waiting. They are allowed no food or water while performing their duty. It is said that if Artemis does not find the fire's protector worthy, she will not let the fire die until the protector herself perishes."

"How barbaric," Altesse said.

"How can people allow this to happen?" Neiaphi asked.

"It's what's believed. Don't question it if you wish to live in a village that worships her. This goddess is not widely revered where you are going.

"We have been told that this is why she was chosen. You may choose to worship others in time. During our journey, you will be taught all the ceremonies for Poseidon—there are many. We must finalize our preparations for departure; we'll be leaving very soon." With that, the three women returned to the empty house, the stillness hanging heavy in the air. The men had not yet returned.

When Neiluios and Net finally arrived, the sun was high in the sky. Neither was in the mood to eat, and both retired early for the night, wearied from the day's tasks.

The old woman was the first to leave the Protector of the Fire, but instead of returning to her household, she slipped around a corner and made her way to the main gate. Pausing for a moment, she glanced around. The area was deserted; no one had noticed her. With a furtive glance over her shoulder, she hurried into the forest. "Hello? Deleon, are you there?"

"We are done, Sir."

"Very good, Leness. Are they ready?"

"As ready as they can be, given their time here, Sir."

"Do they question you anymore?"

"No, it seems they've given up and accepted their situation."

"Good. You and the others have done well." Leness bowed her head in gratitude.

"Sir, may I ask why we hide so much from them? They're smart—smarter than most of the people here on Earth. I'd think they could keep the secret better than anyone."

Deleon sighed, pacing as if the weight of the question pressed on him. "Atlantis sent a message to Romota, requesting additional officials, guards, and new machinery. They weren't supposed to send anyone else here—ever again. Especially not more criminals. But we've grown stronger while they've grown weaker. We intercepted their signal and altered it. Originally, we planned to eliminate them as soon as they landed. But then, the plant started having problems.

"I want these people to disappear. But I can't just eliminate them myself—they've been seen in Uralpolis. So, I've made arrangements for their disappearance. Don't worry. You'll be allowed to return once it's done."

"Why are you allowing some of them to stay at the plant?"

"We decided long ago that the plant needed to be shut down. It no longer benefits us, and they're always behind on payments. Technology is neither needed nor wanted anymore; its time has passed. But we're under pressure from our clients to repair some of the aging components. They also want us to upgrade the system to handle larger shipments, and, unfortunately, they hold more power than we do." He spread his hands helplessly.

"Okay, that explains why some are staying, but why have we spent so much time teaching the others to adapt to our way of life?"

"We had hoped that some would come around to our way of thinking, but it hasn't happened. It could with more time, but they're growing restless sitting idle here. They need to be dealt with before they become a threat."

"I understand, Sir. We'll find a way to deal with them. We won't allow them to reach Atlantis. You need not worry."

"That is why I have hand-selected all of you."

"Some may have strayed, but most remain loyal. I will personally deal with those who have deviated." She bowed once more and departed.

∞ 22 ∞
LOYALIST

WHETHER the sun was rising over the eastern horizon was unclear to Neiaphi. Dark storm clouds shrouded the sky, and a drizzle fell as they finished loading the wagon. Altesse and Cleop were busy preparing the carriage. They had arranged plenty of horses and donkey carts for the journey. Everyone stood in the rain, looking miserable as they waited to depart. Neiluios helped Altesse into the carriage before mounting his horse. Cleop took his place in the driver's seat at the front, ready to lead the team of horses. Net tied Neiaphi's horse to the back of the carriage and then helped her inside. After securing his horse to the wagon, he placed Cypress inside and climbed aboard to drive the donkeys. Neiluios guided his family to the front of the group, where Addident and his family waited.

"Everyone looks ready, Sir," Neiluios said.

"Good. Let's get going."

"Can't we wait until the rain stops, Sir?" Amplios asked.

"No, Deleon has requested we leave immediately. I'm not sure why, but I'm eager to get moving and explore more of this planet. Let's go." He raised his hand, standing in the saddle. "Everyone, mount up and move out. We'll take it easy today and set up camp early tonight." Addident spun his horse around, falling in behind their guide—Cham, appointed by Deleon, who rode a small, wild-looking black mare. Cham glanced over his shoulder to ensure everyone was following. Neiaphi peered out of the carriage at him. His wild black hair and thick beard covered most of his face, leaving only a small gap for his large, bulbous nose and two squinty eyes. He was round and shorter than most of the men Neiaphi had known back home. Shaking her head, she leaned back inside the carriage.

"What's the matter, dear?" her mother asked.

"I was wondering if more of the men on this planet will look like our guide or the male servants."

"The servants and locals we've met so far don't look too different from us. Some are tanner, but Cham—he's unlike anyone I've seen before."

"I was wondering the same thing. I think the locals are still close to their pure ancestry, while the servants were handpicked. Deleon chose ones we would find more acceptable. I'm afraid that most people we encounter away from here will look more like Cham."

"I was afraid of that," Neiaphi said, saying no more. She closed her eyes and listened to the rain, which drummed steadily on the leather top of the carriage. The rhythmic sound was mesmerizing. She took a deep breath. It rained on Romota, but this felt different somehow.

Neiluios glanced back at the camp they had called home for the past several months. It felt like they had disembarked from the ship that brought them to this planet only yesterday, yet it also seemed like a lifetime had passed. He recalled their first night—landing in the storm and watching the ship depart once the skies had cleared. It was a memory he often revisited. Why had they been forced to land in such a storm, anyway?

His thoughts drifted to the plant. He hoped the letter he had sent to Crelian had reached him and that a reply might soon follow.

He needed to start piecing together this puzzle. The locals had contacted Romota, requesting additional guards and officials. Yet, they were told their presence was no longer required upon their arrival. Then, they were sent to the Processing Plant, where it became clear they were needed, but many details remained shrouded in secrecy. None of it made sense—unless Deleon and his followers had overthrown those who originally requested help. The journey had taken five solar cycles, roughly twenty-five years. A lot could happen in that time. Once they were en route, there would have been no way to recall them, leaving the locals stuck with their arrival. Deleon's concern that they wouldn't fit in now seemed suspicious. Perhaps he had hoped they'd never reach Atlantis and uncover the truth.

Neiluios looked ahead as they traveled downhill, away from the Processing Plant. They approached a large cliff, where a narrow trail wound down to the valley below. Heavy gray clouds obscured the ground, but the guide assured them the trail wasn't long. The descent was slow and unnerving— there wasn't much room for carriages and wagons on the narrow path. Fortunately, the horses and donkeys remained calm, unable to see the sheer drop through the fog.

Once they reached the bottom, they set up camp. Though they had only traveled for a short time, the rain made it feel much longer. Neiluios helped Net and Cleop set up their two tents before heading off to find Addident. When he finally located him, Addident was deep in conversation with Cham.

"How far is the first outpost?" Addident asked.

"About four days, considering the pace I expect everyone will be able to manage," Cham replied.

"Can you tell me anything about it?" Addident asked.

"This is one of the first outposts established in this area and one of the smallest we'll visit on our way to Atlantis. It's called Kranapolis. Can we step inside the tent? I have some grave news to share." Addident nodded and gestured for Neiluios to join them. "I need to update you on some history before we continue. Shortly after Poseidie settled on this planet and established Atlantis—"

"You know about us?" Neiluios interrupted. "We were told you didn't."

"Deleon and his followers don't know everything about me," Cham replied. "I'm part of a group of Loyalists dedicated to preserving our old ways. They're part of a suppressive society trying to crush us."

"After Poseidie found the perfect location for his main base and established Atlantis, he began creating mini-colonies across the planet. He built mines, processing plants of all kinds, and various industries, aiming to live comfortably while amassing great wealth to take back home. Most of the workers came from Romota, but Poseidie also handpicked many from the criminal population, undoing their mind erasure to build a large labor force.

"The Gods were pleased with Poseidie and invited him to Mount Olympus. They tested and challenged him and then granted him the powers of the gods. He became Poseidon. Since he created the island where Atlantis sat, he gave him rein over the oceans.

"When the first replacements arrived, they were appalled by what Poseidie—now called Poseidon—was doing. They believed he was exploiting both the planet and its inhabitants. Most of the replacements stayed to try to stop him, but Poseidon was too powerful, especially with his ten sons helping govern the planet. They seemed to be everywhere at once.

"Deleon and his followers are descendants of those replacements, while I am descended from the originals. The Society, as they call themselves, went underground for many years. But during my great-grandfather's time, they resurfaced. Outside of Atlantis, they control most of the planet. That's why we reached out to you. Unfortunately, our signal was intercepted. They've been waiting and preparing for you for a long time."

Neiluios and Addident shared a look but kept their opinions of the story to themselves. "Why do they use technology if they want to suppress the old ways?" Neiluios asked instead.

"They use only what they absolutely must," Cham replied. "If it were up to them, all technology from Romota would have been destroyed long ago. As long as we possess technology, they must use some of it to keep up with us."

"The Processing Plant near Camp Roma—do you know what it's processing?" Neiluios asked.

"No, and not in my lifetime," Cham replied. "The Society's influence doesn't extend much beyond this region, with only small pockets of power here and there. They hold no real sway where we're heading. We came as quickly as we could after learning you had landed. I was sent to be your guide and protector. We have much work ahead of us."

"First, we must get as far from here as possible—and quickly. We're likely being followed. I was instructed to lead you into the wilderness and abandon you without supplies. Rest assured, I won't do that. But we're in danger as long as we remain here. We leave before first light tomorrow."

"Second, we must identify which of your servants are truly loyal and which are working for Deleon. In a few days, we'll reach a cave equipped for this. Third, we'll use another device in that cave to reverse the mind erasure on the rest of your servants."

"Mind erasures? What are you talking about?" Addident asked, alarmed.

"Your new servants—the ones they allowed you to choose—are criminals from your planet," Cham explained.

"Criminals? That makes sense," Neiluios muttered, shaking his head. "I've been wondering what had happened to them."

Addident's expression darkened, but he remained silent for a moment before finally speaking. "Neiluios, keep this information to yourself until we reach the cave. I don't want anyone loyal to Deleon catching wind of this."

With that, Neiluios and Cham left Addident to contemplate the situation alone. That evening, Neiluios got his family to bed early, but sleep eluded him.

∞ 23 ∞
SPIES AMONG US

THE sky was brightening, though still overcast with storm clouds, but the rain had stopped. Neiaphi's father had remained silent since his meeting with Addident, and his troubled thoughts were evident. Neiaphi's mind raced, wondering what could be weighing on him. Meanwhile, Cypress ran happily around the wagon and carriage, his tail wagging. Neiaphi called him over, hugging his still-damp neck. He had grown so much since her father first gave him to her. Cypress licked her cheek before wriggling free from her embrace. She reached for him again, clipped the leash to his collar, and secured the other end to the wagon. Cypress whined and pulled on the leash for a moment before settling down. Neiaphi smiled and patted him on the head.

Altesse was already seated in the carriage while Cleop and Net nearly finished packing the tents. Neiluios paced restlessly in front of the wagon. Addident called for everyone to mount up, and those who weren't yet fully packed scrambled to finish. No one wanted to be left behind and must catch up later.

Cham sat on his unruly black mare, his grim gaze sweeping over everyone. Neiaphi felt uneasy around him, unsure of his intentions and plans for them.

"Neiaphi, why don't you ride beside me today?" Neiluios asked.

"Okay, Father." Neiaphi went to Nexus, untied her from the back of the carriage, and mounted. Nexus tossed her head and nickered. Neiaphi patted her neck to calm her and guided her over to her father. "What's going to happen to us?" she asked.

Neiluios smiled at his daughter and patted her arm. "We'll be fine in a couple of days. We just must make it until then. You need to stay strong no matter what happens, okay?"

"Of course, Father."

The group slowly moved out, with Cham setting a brisk but manageable pace for the donkeys, burdened by their heavy loads. The valley they traversed was mostly flat, with distant hills lining the horizon. Small clusters of trees dotted the landscape, and meandering streams wove through the valley. Occasionally, the sun peeked through the clouds, but short rain showers quickly followed these brief moments of light. They pressed on until midday, stopping by a large pool of water for a brief rest. The horses and donkeys were unhitched from the wagons and carriages and allowed to drink and graze. Servants unpacked food for their families and then tended to the animals. Small groups formed as people gathered to chat and rest, with Neiluios setting up camp next to Addident's.

The conversations were trivial, and Neiaphi quickly grew bored. Nidora whispered with her mother and Altesse while Surrie played with a doll near their wagon. Neiaphi sighed and returned to their wagon to sit with Cypress.

Most of the girls in the camp were either much younger or older than Neiaphi. Nidora was seventeen, and Surrie was only nine. There were also very few boys her age.

She hugged Cypress, her only companion, and quietly began to cry. She had promised her father she would be strong, but it was harder than she imagined. She still felt like a child, forced to grow up too quickly. Back on Romota, she would have been living a carefree life with few worries. But in the past few months, she had faced loss after loss. How did the people on this planet survive in such a harsh, primitive world?

"Are you okay?" Chartis asked. He set down the tablet he had been working on and sat beside her. Neiaphi quickly wiped her eyes and looked up.

"I'm fine, just feeling sorry for myself. How about you?" Neiaphi made a half-hearted attempt at a smile.

"I'm okay, I suppose. Have you heard anything about where we're going?" Chartis asked.

"No, why would I?" she replied.

"Well, I thought you might have overheard something, given your father's position as the First Agent," he said with a shrug.

"Oh, I see," she teased. "Normally, I would have heard something, but my father has been unusually quiet lately. I'll let you know if I find out anything. I should get back to my parents now. I'll see you later." She waved and walked back to her family.

"Yeah, see you later," he said, though he had hoped for a longer conversation. He didn't want to push her, figuring she would open up in time. He could wait. He picked up his tablet and headed back to his parents.

"Everyone, please prepare to move out," Cham called out, his voice carrying across the camp. It was the first time Neiaphi had heard him speak. She had expected a deep, gruff voice, but his tone was soft and almost sing-song.

The group resumed their journey at the same steady pace. The afternoon brought a welcome change in weather as the grey clouds finally parted, allowing the sun to warm the cool air. However, the relief was short-lived. As the humidity increased and insects emerged, everyone grew increasingly uncomfortable. True relief came only when the sun finally slipped below the horizon. Cham kept them moving well into the night, but when his horse stumbled over an unseen object, he finally called for camp. The sky was clear, and most of the group opted to sleep either in their wagons or beneath the stars, knowing they only had a few hours of rest. The distant howls of wolves punctuated the stillness of the night, but aside from that, it remained peaceful.

Neiaphi yawned and stretched as dawn arrived far too quickly. Cham was already mounted, prepared to move out before the sun had fully risen. The camp slowly came to life, hushed voices drifting through the early morning air as parents roused their children.

"Please, everyone, we need to keep moving. I promise we'll be able to rest more tonight," Cham called out, his voice reassuring yet firm.

Addident nodded in agreement. "We will stop early tonight and rest most of the day tomorrow."

"Cham wants us out of this valley before the rains start again," Addident urged, prompting everyone to pick up the pace.

They skipped their usual midday break and set up camp well before dark. The horses and donkeys were unsaddled and unharnessed while the tents were quickly erected.

Cham wandered around the camp, sizing up the servants as he went. His gaze lingered on each one, trying to gauge their thoughts. An elderly woman, hands firmly planted on her hips, stormed up to him. This was the person he'd been searching for. "We need to talk," she declared.

"Yes, we do. But I need to address everyone first," Cham replied, his voice calm but authoritative. "I've received last-minute instructions from Deleon. Once everyone is settled, we'll meet in the clearing to the east. Every one of you must attend. Do you understand?"

"Yes, sir. We'll be there. What about the other servants?"

"We'll handle them in the morning, along with the rest."

"About time," she said, nodding before walking away.

Cham exhaled slowly, relieved. He had managed to convince her he was speaking for Deleon. He'd been concerned she wouldn't believe he had new orders.

He scanned the camp and noticed a young woman with brown hair and deep blue eyes watching him. At her side was a large black and tan puppy. That must be Neiluios's daughter, he thought to himself. Everything will be okay, young lady.

After the evening meals were finished and the camp had settled down, Deleon's appointed servants parted from their families and vanished into the forest. Neiluios and Addident walked through the camp, reassuring everyone that all was well, before following the path taken by the servants, accompanied by several guards.

Leness stood before her followers, who waited anxiously for Cham to arrive with their new orders. When Cham finally entered the clearing, his cloak obscuring his tunic, she didn't hesitate. "What are Deleon's new orders?" she demanded before he had a chance to speak.

Cham waited until he was directly in front of her before speaking. "I have no new orders from Deleon. You are under arrest. Please do not resist."

"Under arrest? By whose authority?" Leness demanded, clearly surprised.

"By the authority passed down to me through my blood from Poseidon and Atlas," Cham replied. "I will use force if necessary. Please come with me peacefully, and you will not be harmed." As he spoke, he threw back his cloak to reveal a purple tunic, the color of Poseidon's followers.

"You're one of them," she sneered. "I don't recognize your authority and won't submit to you." As she spoke, the guards emerged into the clearing, surrounding the servants with weapons drawn. Some of the women screamed while the men stood stiff and silent. Neiluios and Addident approached Cham and Leness, their expressions tense.

"If you resist, you will be killed. If you come with us, you will live. The choice is yours. Please make the wise decision," Addident said calmly.

"You'll have to take us by force!" she screamed. Two guards stepped forward and seized her arms. She struggled wildly at first but soon ceased her resistance, collapsing into their hold.

"Please, sir, some of us don't share the same views as Leness and Deleon. We were all chosen to help Cham with his plans against you, but some of us have changed our perspective. You're not the monsters we were led to believe. Your good people," Net said slowly and carefully. "Please believe me: I never intended to let Cham harm you or your families, and I'm deeply relieved he's on your side now. I wish to continue serving you, Neiluios." He dropped to his knees, holding out his hands, palms up, to show he was hiding nothing.

"I want to believe you, Net, but it's difficult. I hope you understand that," Neiluios said gravely.

"There is a way," Cham interjected. "Net, will you volunteer to be the first to take the Test of Truth?"

Without hesitation, Net replied, "Yes, please. I'm deeply ashamed of the deception I was part of. I'll do whatever is necessary to prove my loyalty."

"Everyone, follow me," Cham instructed, walking toward the forest with Net trailing behind. The other servants exchanged uncertain glances, looking toward the guards for guidance. After a few followed, the rest hesitantly joined in. The two guards holding Leness had to carry her as she refused to walk. Neiluios and Addident brought up the rear as Cham led them to a small, secluded pond nestled among towering trees, with a graceful waterfall cascading over a rocky ledge. Cham stepped behind the waterfall and disappeared from view.

Neiluios made a mental note of the location—he wanted to bring Neiaphi here before they left. The sight was breathtaking. Behind the waterfall was a cave entrance, wide enough to accommodate the entire group. Inside, several ancient-looking machines were scattered throughout the spacious chamber.

"Net, please sit here," Cham said, gesturing toward one of the machines. It was a formidable metallic chair, complete with straps to secure the occupant, and a console in front connected by a tangle of wires. Net eyed the contraption warily.

"It will hurt if you lie, and it may kill you if you resist," Cham warned. "Relax and answer the questions truthfully. Do you understand?"

Net nodded and took a seat in the chair. Cham moved to the console and activated the machine. It emitted a low whine and a steady hum as the buttons on the console began to glow softly in the cave's dim light.

"Where is the power source for these machines?" Addident asked.

"I'm told they're powered by the sun, with hidden wires bringing the energy down here," Cham replied. "Now, Net, is your name really Net?"

"Yes," Net replied.

"Where are you from?"

"I'm from a city just south of here."

"Were you born a servant?"

"Yes."

"Who did you work for?"

"King Umphis."

"And after that?"

"Deleon and The Society. King Umphis is part of The Society, and when they called for servants, he sent me."

"Who do you work for now?" Cham asked, locking eyes with Net, watching closely for any sign of pain from the machine if he lied. Cham knew from experience that no one could deceive the Truth Machine.

"Neiluios and his family. I have severed all ties to the Society in my mind," Net answered. His response appeared to be truthful.

"If someone were to try to harm Neiluios or his family, what would you do?" Cham asked.

"I would protect Neiluios, Altesse, Neiaphi, and the unborn child with my life if necessary," Net replied.

Cham nodded, then unstrapped Net from the chair. Net walked over to Neiluios and knelt before him, his gaze fixed on the ground.

"Please forgive me, sir, for the harm I may have caused you and your family. I am at your service and will do whatever you wish. I want to continue serving you, but I will leave if you instruct me to." Net briefly met Neiluios's gaze before looking down again.

"I will let Altesse make that decision," Neiluios said.

Net folded his hands before him, backing away on his knees while repeatedly mumbling, "Thank you, thank you."

"Who wants to go next?" Cham asked.

"I will," Cleop said, stepping forward. Cham strapped her into the machine and proceeded with the same line of questions. After her questioning, she didn't plead her case to Neiluios. Instead, she walked over and stood next to Net.

"Keep up the good work, Cham. We're going to retire for the night. We won't be traveling tomorrow—this seems like a good place to stay for a day or two while you sort through these people," Addident said.

"I'll report back when I'm finished. After that, we'll deal with the other servants. Please have fresh guards posted before dawn," Cham replied.

Neiluios nodded and followed Addident out of the cave.

When Neiluios returned to the camp, he conveyed the grim but unsurprising news to Altesse and Neiaphi.

"I wish I could have been there for the questioning," Altesse said. "Seeing their reactions would have made my decision easier."

"He seems sincere now," Neiluios replied. "But he never tried to mislead us before. I don't know what caused him to change his mind or when it happened, but he's been loyal to us. Cleop has also been doing well. I'm not sure how many of the servants are truly loyal, but I suspect only a few will be."

"We'll need every one of them to get through our first winter here," Altesse noted.

"Then it's settled. They can stay, but they'll have to earn our trust," Altesse said.

"Agreed," Neiluios affirmed.

"Good morning, Addident. I've sorted through all the servants and compiled a list of those who are loyal," Cham reported.

"Already? I thought it would take much longer," Addident replied, surprised.

"After Cleop, a man named Rem came forward and lied. He fought the machine with every ounce of strength he had and died for it. The rest were easier to get through. Some, like Leness, refused the test, insisting their loyalty to Deleon was enough without the machine. In the end, you will retain eighty-two of the two hundred twelve servants appointed by Deleon."

"It could be worse, I suppose. Thank you for your help, Cham," Addident said.

Cham bowed his head. "When would you like to begin with the others?"

"After midday," Cham said, "I need to rest before proceeding. There are two machines I must use. The first will place the criminals into a trance so we can uncover what they were convicted of before performing the memory erasure. If they are true criminals, we'll leave them as they are. In the past, when shipments were frequent, we could often erase most of their memories due to the nature of their crimes. Simple theft for food or street fights aren't significant offenses here. However, murderers are a different matter."

"What will we do with the one hundred and thirty servants who remain loyal to The Society?"

"I will erase their memories of their time with us and send them on their way. The criminals whose minds we leave erased will need to be sent with them as well. Memory erasures can be reversed if their memories are triggered."

"We'll leave this to your discretion. Please join my family for the evening meal tonight."

"Thank you, sir," Cham replied, bowing before walking back to his tent.

Net and Cleop were allowed to return to Neiluios and Altesse shortly after Cham left the cave. A meeting would be held before the remaining eighty servants were released. Net glanced back at the cave, shaking his head. He had hoped that more of the servants would have changed their minds after meeting their new leaders. Cleop was silent, her tears seemingly dried. She had spent most of the night crying in a corner of the cave. Net had tried to comfort her and asked why she was crying, but she only replied that he wouldn't understand.

Altesse was sitting outside the tent when Net and Cleop arrived. Both knelt before her and bowed their heads to the ground.

"Please forgive us, ma'am. I was led to believe that Cham would leave you stranded without supplies. I've been leaving small bundles of provisions along our path so we could retrieve them after he departed. I wasn't going to let anything happen to you. I wish I had told you sooner, but I was afraid

Deleon would replace me if he knew I no longer followed him. We were told you were monsters coming to destroy our way of life and enslave us all. I feel like a fool for believing them."

"Net, please be silent and let me speak. You and Cleop may stay with us, but you are not yet forgiven. You must prove that you truly regret what you conspired to do. While the Truth Machine may have revealed your feelings, we need to see actions that match your words."

"Thank you, ma'am. You won't regret it," Cleop blurted out, and Net nodded in agreement.

"We'll be here for the rest of the day and probably all of the next," Altesse said. "I want to review your supplies to see what you packed."

Net and Cleop immediately jumped up and hurried to the wagon to fulfill her request.

Addident met with each family individually, sending their servants—those who had once been criminals—over to Neiluios for questioning in the cave. After informing everyone of the situation, he returned the remaining eighty servants to their families. Only one family refused: Nestor and his wife, Adelpha, declined to take back their female servant, Dela. Adelpha had never felt safe with Dela at Camp Roma and didn't want to see her now. Addident assured them he would employ Dela and keep an eye on her. Thankfully, they were the only ones to refuse their servant's return. Most others accepted Neiluios's and Altesse's methods of punishment for the deception.

That night, the camp was eerily quiet as most retired to their tents early. The only sounds were the distant cries of owls and the occasional howl of a lone wolf.

∞ 24 ∞
KRANAPOLIS

CRET stood on a white sand beach, a dense forest behind him. He gazed over the choppy ocean, where white-capped waves slapped against the shore. To his right, a young woman with long brown hair walked away, accompanied by a large dog. She made her way toward a path that wound up a nearby cliff, never turning back. Who is she? Cret wondered.

As the woman and the dog neared the path, a massive wolver—the largest Cret had ever seen—leaped in front of her. The dog lunged at the wolver, and the two began to circle each other, snarling. Cret drew the sword belted to his hip and ran to assist the unknown woman. She grabbed a large piece of driftwood and swung it at the wolver, but the driftwood split in two without making an impact.

Cret pushed her aside just as the wolver's back was turned. He swung at its hind legs, but the creature jumped and spun in the air, barely evading the blow. The wolver pounced at him, but Cret blocked the attack with his sword. At the same moment, the dog leaped onto the wolver, sinking its teeth into its ruff.

He hesitated to act, fearing he might accidentally hit the dog. The two animals tumbled on the ground for a moment before separating. The wolver, tail between its legs, fled into the forest. The dog spun to pursue it but abruptly stopped and trotted over to the woman instead.

"Are you alright? I'm sorry I pushed you down," Cret said.

"I'm fine, thank you for helping me," she replied. "But what were you doing on the beach? I tried to talk to you, but you ignored me."

"I don't know. I'm unsure how I got here or even where 'here' is. Who are you?" Cret asked.

The wolver let out a long howl, answered by what sounded like hundreds of others in the distance.

"Let's move before it brings in reinforcements," Cret said, extending a hand to help the woman up from the sand. She stood and brushed herself off.

"I have a horse up top. We'll be able to get away much faster on her. Come on," the woman said.

Cret, the unknown woman, and her dog stepped onto the path and began the climb.

Cret woke with a start, unsettled by the strange dream. Why did the woman seem so familiar? He wondered how old he had been in the dream—probably in his early twenties.

It was still dark outside, and sleep eluded him. He stepped outside and gazed up at the stars. *Is Neiaphi looking at these same stars?* He wondered.

Neiaphi lay in her bedroll under the stars, staring up at them. Sleep eluded her once again. She had that dream again—the one where the young man on the beach didn't respond to her. As in the last few times, the wolver was present, always a fixture in the dream now. What could a wolver be doing on this planet? she wondered.

Cypress lay with his back pressed against her side as she gently petted him. He had spent the entire day chasing rabbits and was now sleeping soundly. He finally caught one before the evening meal, which Cleop had added to her delicious stew. Neiaphi was grateful that Net and Cleop were allowed to stay with them. She had grown accustomed to their presence and enjoyed their conversations.

Earlier in the day, they learned they would be staying at the campsite for another day. Cham had informed them it was another two difficult days' journey to Kranapolis, but they would have a few days to rest there. Neiaphi lay in her bedroll, gazing at the sky until she finally drifted back to sleep.

The camp stirred to life with the sunrise. Cham announced that most of the criminals would have their memories restored by the end of the day. Of the thirty individuals, only ten were deemed too dangerous—their minds would remain erased, and they would be released alongside the Society members.

The remaining twenty would be informed that their new role was to serve as servants, though they could negotiate with their masters for a different position. If they refused the role, their memories would be erased again, leaving them to spend the rest of their lives unaware of their past.

The rest of the day was spent resting and socializing. Neiluios made several rounds through the camp, ensuring everyone was doing well. On his final round of the day, he invited Neiaphi to join him. Together, they strolled through the camp, engaging in conversations with the others. They then walked toward the clearing, where the criminals received their memory restorations. Arriving at the small pond with the waterfall, Neiaphi stood in awe, her mouth agape. She had never seen a waterfall like this before.

Back in Romota, she had never ventured outside the city and had only seen fountains. Even when she helped Cret rescue the two boys from the criminal camp, they had only crossed a small cascade, barely a few feet high. This waterfall, however, soared several times her father's height. Neiluios guided her to a large rock and gestured for her to sit beside him.

"Chartis spoke with me today," Neiluios said, breaking the awkward silence.

"He did? What did he say?" Neiaphi asked, her gaze fixed on the ground. She already knew what had been said and why they were out here alone.

"He's mapping our journey and doing a marvelous job. It would be easier with a ship, but he has a real knack for detail and direction."

"I noticed he's been using a tablet since we left Camp Roma. I was curious about what he was doing," Neiaphi said.

"Do you know what else he discussed with me?" Neiluios asked.

"I have an idea," Neiaphi replied.

"Why didn't you come to me about it sooner?"

"I told him we needed to get to know each other better before I'd discuss it with you. I hardly know him myself," Neiaphi explained.

"I see. Well, he has asked for your hand in marriage," Neiluios said.

"What did you say?" she asked slowly, without looking at her father. She felt too young for marriage but trusted that her father would only do what he believed was best for her. Cret was firmly against his parents choosing his bride for him, but Neiaphi felt powerless. On a planet where women were often treated as little more than property and had few rights, what could she do?

"I told him I would discuss it with you before making any decisions. He wasn't too pleased about that. I suspect he thought I would agree to his request without consulting you."

"From what Cret told me, their school taught them how to control women and keep them in their place. Women here have no rights and are considered property." A tear slowly slid down her cheek. Neiluios reached over and gently brushed it away.

"My women have all the rights of men and are no one's property. Do you understand? I will make sure you marry someone who shares that belief."

"Cham has told me that in Atlantis, women have the right to vote, hold office, and own businesses and land. You will have more rights there than you would in Romota. There's even a city where women are trained to be warriors."

"Really?" Neiaphi asked, her curiosity piqued.

"I wouldn't lie to you, but if Cham is, you can't hold that against me," Neiluios replied, leaning over to tickle her side. She giggled and hugged him tightly.

"Thank you, Father. I love you and Mother so much."

"How would you like to learn how to swim?"

"Really? Oh, that would be wonderful!"

"I meant to teach you when you were younger but never found the time. We'll frequently travel by water on this journey, so I think it's wise for you to learn how." They spent the rest of the evening swimming. When they returned to camp, Cleop had their evening meal ready. Neiaphi didn't dream that night and enjoyed a much-needed, restful sleep.

"What are we going to do, Leness?"

"Be quiet, Europ. They'll hear you. We'll return to Deleon and turn in this traitor, Cham, as soon as they release us. Then, we'll come back and destroy them ourselves."

"Leness, come with me," a huge, rough-looking guard said. He grabbed her by the arm and yanked her to her feet before she could stand up on her own.

"Where are you taking me?" she demanded.

"Cham needs to speak with you," the guard replied. "I must blindfold you. Hold still." Another guard stepped forward, tying a strip of cloth around her head, covering her eyes.

"Is this necessary?" she asked.

"Cham says it is. Come on." The guard pushed her forward, still holding her arm. He led her back into the cave and forced her into the mind-erase machine. After strapping her in, he removed the blindfold.

Her eyes slowly adjusted to the cave's darkness. When they finally did, she gasped in horror. They were going to erase her memory. The thought was unthinkable. The idea of having this technology used on her was revolting. She would rather die than endure this.

Her desperate pleas went ignored as Cham activated the machine. Her screams gradually faded, swallowed by the hum of the device as it worked. Cham had assured Neiluios and Addident that only her memories of their time together would be erased. But he couldn't risk allowing a member of The Society to return.

Instead, all of Leness's memories—of her childhood, her adulthood—were wiped away, replaced with a fabricated history. In this new life, she had grown up in Atlantis as a dutiful servant of the Royal Household. Once the process was complete, she and the others would be sent to a nearby village that had been expecting them. There, they would be cared for, and they would no longer pose a threat to anyone.

The sun had yet to rise, but they had already been on the move for some time. Cham had roused everyone early, insisting they reach their next destination swiftly. The group departed the picturesque valley and plunged into the dark, humid forest surrounding it. Relentless insects made the journey equally miserable for both animals and humans.

As dusk approached, they finally emerged from the dense foliage of the forest. Confused whispers drifted from the group's rear as those in the front stopped moving.

"Wow, you have Hovers?" Amplios asked, clearly astonished.

"Yes," Cham replied with a hint of pride. "We may not have a lot of technology, but we guard what we do have fiercely. All animals and wagons will go in the last two; everyone else will ride in the others. We'll make excellent time but need to travel under the cover of darkness. This area is relatively uninhabited, but we must be cautious—we're in the Society's territory, and they'll destroy these if they find them."

Neiaphi stared in awe at the large, flat metallic discs. Made specifically for transport, they had little amenities on board. Each Hover consisted of a flat metallic surface with a short railing circling it. A single seat with a small control panel sat at what she assumed was the front of the craft.

As she drew near them, parts of the silvery metallic vessel almost disappeared from sight. *Camouflaged paint,* she assumed with delight.

Once everyone and everything was securely stowed, the Hovers lifted off, each guided by a Loyalist pilot. The terrain blurred beneath them as the Hovers followed their pre-set route. Neiaphi clung tightly to a shivering Cypress, who was clearly overwhelmed by the experience. She wondered how the horses and donkeys were faring, hoping someone had given them a sedative or something to ease their distress. As the sun began to peek over the horizon, the Hovers dove into the cover of the trees. Everyone disembarked, knowing they'd have to finish the rest of the journey on foot. They had covered a significant portion of the distance already, though it would still be a grueling two days of travel. But it could have been much worse.

The next two days passed long and uneventful. Chartis hadn't attempted to speak with Neiluios or Neiaphi again, which suited her just fine. Still, she felt apprehensive, knowing she would soon have to confront him. Her mother had advised her to set things straight with him—leaving him in the dark wasn't fair. Neiaphi knew she was right, but she dreaded the task. She should have addressed it the first day he approached her.

Occasionally, she could feel Chartis's gaze on her, and whenever she turned, he quickly looked away. Neiaphi hoped he would lose interest and find someone else. Most of the children in their group were male, so the females were being chosen quickly. He might have to settle for someone much younger—or even a Local—and she knew he'd want to avoid that.

As the second day drew to a close, Kranapolis became visible in the distance. Not long after, a small group of heavily armed men from the town approached them. Cham, Addident, and Captain Heu rode out to meet them, and the rest of the group halted, following Neiluios' lead, giving the men from Kranapolis space to speak and feel at ease. Their group had doubled the town's population, with twenty-one officials, eighty-five guards, and their families and servants. After a brief conversation, Addident signaled for everyone to move forward.

They camped outside the town's wooden walls due to a lack of space inside. Once the camp was set up, small groups entered the town to explore. Neiluios went with his daughter and wife, while Cleop and Net stayed behind to watch over the animals and belongings. Net believed this was the wisest course of action, as he didn't trust the townspeople and was wary of potential theft.

Kranapolis resembled Uralpolis but on a smaller scale, with a large central meeting hall dominating the landscape. After dark, all the men were expected to gather there for a town meeting to decide how many officials and guards needed to remain behind. Cham assured them that Kranapolis's governing body was loyal to Atlantis.

"We're so pleased to see you all. Did everyone make it out safely?" the Governor of Kranapolis asked.

"We're down by nine, Sir," Neiluios explained. "Deleon is dealing with issues at a processing plant, and some of us stayed behind to assist. This was before we fully understood what Deleon was, of course."

"We'll see what we can do to get them out, but I fear they might be lost," the Governor said.

"We've been thinking the same," Neiluios replied. "We've already lost some fine people and good friends." Most of the gathered men lowered their heads in respect for a moment.

"Is there anything we can assist with here?" Addident asked.

"We could use a guard or two, but we don't need any more officials. Our government is running smoothly, but with The Society so close, we could use extra hands to bolster our defenses."

"You'll have as many volunteers as you need by the end of the day tomorrow," Neiluios assured.

"Very good. Two or three would be sufficient. You're all welcome to stay as long as you like. You've traveled far and endured much to get here."

"Thank you for your kindness, Governor," Addident said, offering a brief bow at the waist. The Governor mirrored the gesture.

"Thank you all for coming. You're dismissed." Though dismissed, many of the men lingered, exchanging words for several minutes.

Neiluios quietly slipped out of the meeting hall, eager for a solitary walk through the town. The quaint charm of Kranapolis was pleasant enough, and he found himself hoping they might settle here, even if Atlantis remained out of reach. The road ahead would be long and arduous. If Altesse could endure the journey, they would reach their destination. If not, Neiluios was certain they'd find another place to call home.

He wandered around the camp before finally making his way back to his family. As he approached the flickering remains of their fire, he noticed that Net was still awake.

"Good evening, Sir. Did everything go well?" he asked.

"It appears so. They need some of the guards to stay but no officials."

"I'm sorry to see more of you leave, but I'm relieved we're moving on from here," Net said.

"I'm certain that more of us will be lost at one outpost or another. It's the reason we were sent here in the first place. It saddens me that groups like the Society seek to destroy us, keeping everyone on this planet in the shadows of their past. We should be advancing our technology to trade with Romota and others. A simple life has its merits, but clinging to primitive, backward thinking is, in my opinion, a waste of potential. We must work to change this mindset. Have you learned anything from the people living here in Kranapolis?"

"Not much," Net said. "The locals are wary of newcomers, especially those of us from this planet. They seem more accepting of you than of us—they suspect we might be spies for the Society."

"Well, that thought has crossed our minds, too," Neiluios said with a half-grin.

"And rightly so. I asked around about the Processing Plant to the north, but no one's been there. They mentioned strange objects falling from the sky several times a week, only to disappear shortly after. No one knows what they are, but they suspect it's connected to the Plant."

"Who was in charge of the plant before Deleon's people took over twenty-five years ago?"

"Likely people from Uralpolis. When the Society takes over an area, they control the government and schools, imposing their ideology. Those who disagree are forced to flee—or face death. Their way becomes the only way once they're in command. Those who managed to escape, if any were allowed to, would have gone much further south than Kranapolis. Anyone from Uralpolis would be recognized instantly if they came to trade here."

"Objects fall from the sky and then vanish." Neiluios looked up into the dark sky, where millions of stars twinkled back. "They must be ships, but from where? And what are they delivering or collecting? I'm afraid we may never know—unless there are more plants like this," Neiluios said, shaking his head.

"Quite likely. From what I've learned about Poseidon, he established various types of Plants all over the planet. If any are still operational, we might stumble upon one controlled by a Loyal."

"Loyal? What's a Loyal?"

"That's what Cham says his people call themselves. They're Loyal to Poseidon, Atlas, and Romota, so they are the Loyals."

"Do they have a name for us?"

"Yes, they call you the Olympians."

"Olympians? Isn't that what the Gods are called?"

"Yes, Sir. To these people, you're considered Gods."

"I'll need to address that with him. We're just people like you, only from the home planet. We're no more special than you."

"I beg your pardon, Sir, but you are different. You and the other Olympians are taller than most of us, both men and women, and you're notably fit, attractive, and intelligent."

"Deleon was taller than me, though not as tall as Addident or Captain Heu—few men are. I've seen some beautiful women here in Kranapolis. As for intelligence, we benefited from better schooling. If you had attended the same school I did, you'd be just as smart."

"I doubt it, Sir, but thank you all the same."

"Well, there's no use arguing about it. I'll speak with Cham, but until then, please don't call us Olympians, okay?"

"Yes, Sir. Goodnight." Net left the fire and Neiluios alone with his thoughts.

Neiaphi walked down a long corridor in a grand palace. White columns lined either side, with windows set between them. Through these windows, she gazed out over a sprawling city encircled by water. The buildings, rising three or four stories high, were crowned with spires and towers. They were adorned with gold, silver, bronze, and other gleaming metals Neiaphi did not recognize. Colorful awnings provided shade for the front doors of most houses and shops.

She continued down the curving corridor until she reached a vast circular chamber. In the center stood the largest statue she had ever seen: a magnificent figure of Poseidon, crafted entirely from gold, riding in a chariot drawn by six majestic Pegasi.

She was in Atlantis—how marvelous! She approached a mirror set into one of the far walls and examined her reflection. She appeared only slightly older than in the recurring dream she always had. Her attire was strikingly different: she wore fine silk adorned with numerous jewels on her wrists and fingers. Her hair was also decorated with beads and gems. *I must be wealthy,* she thought.

A deafening explosion shook the palace. Neiaphi rushed to a window and saw smoke and flames erupting from several points around the city. *What's happening?* she thought.

"Ma'am, we need to leave immediately," a guard shouted as he approached her.

"Leave? Where to?"

"We're under attack. We must get you to safety."

"Lead the way, please." The guard shot her a puzzled glance but kept running down the corridor she had just come from. He halted at a tapestry on the wall, pulling it aside to reveal a hidden passage. He stepped into the passage after opening the door and grabbing a torch from the wall. Neiaphi shrugged and followed.

They reached a long flight of stairs spiraling downward. Faint voices drifted up from below. At the bottom, the stairs opened into a vast cavern deep underground. A crowd of people stood around, their anxiety mirroring Neiaphi's own.

"Oh, thank the Gods, there you are," an older woman with an infant in her arms said as she approached Neiaphi. "I've been so worried. Please, don't wander off alone like that." She gently handed the child to Neiaphi. "Here is your son."

"My son? Are you certain?" Neiaphi took the boy hesitantly from the woman.

"Where did you find her? Did she get hurt?" the woman asked the guard.

"She was in Poseidon's chamber again. She seemed fine to me," he replied.

The woman touched Neiaphi's forehead to check for a fever. "Are you feeling all right, Neiaphi?"

"Yes, I'm fine. My son—what a handsome little man you are. What's his name?"

"His name? You want to know his name? You gave him his name."

"Just tell me his name," she snapped, frustration evident in her voice. She shook her head in disbelief. Who was she?

"Yes, ma'am. You named him Creluios, after your father and your husband."

"Husband? Cret?"

"Yes, ma'am. Please, come over here and sit down." Neiaphi complied, still shocked that she had a son and was married to Cret. When had he come back to her? Oh, this must be a dream. I'm torturing myself. She handed the child back to the nurse and rose to her feet. "Where is Cret?"

"He is not here, remember? He is off battling The Society."

"Then who is attacking us?"

"The Society must have broken through our defenses, ma'am." The walls shook again, and more people came rushing into the chamber.

"The city is collapsing! It's crumbling to ruins!" one person wailed.

"No, this can't be real. I have to wake up—wake up, Neiaphi! Snap out of it!"

The scene shifted abruptly. Neiaphi now found herself on a beach, but it wasn't the one from her previous dream. Before her stood a heavily pregnant version of herself, with the same man from her earlier vision beside her, it was as if she were watching a play with an actress who resembled her playing the role.

"This is the island I've dreamed about ever since we were separated in childhood," he said enthusiastically. "I'm going to build a magnificent city here, where we'll be safe and

secure. I've already started building a powerful navy. It's going to be wonderful, Neiaphi. You'll see."

"But Cret, why can't we live in Atlantis? It's already a magnificent city, and I have considerable influence there. You could be King, and I'd be Queen. Our child would grow up in the most splendid place on this planet."

"But I'll be King here, and you'll be my Queen. We'll raise our family in safety. Atlantis has become a symbol that the Society is hell-bent on destroying. They won't stop until it's gone. Here, though, we can live freely and out of their reach. It will be years before they even discover our existence. You'll see."

"I can't bear the thought of leaving Atlantis; it's become my home. We fought so hard to reach it, and now you want to leave it all behind. With your navy, we could protect Atlantis."

"Atlantis is too vast to defend," Cret countered. "This island is a much safer option. Please, Neiaphi, trust me on this." The pregnant Neiaphi gazed into Cret's eyes, then leaned in to kiss his cheek.

"I'll do as you ask, Cret."

"Thank you, Neiaphi," he said, his gaze softening as he sighed.

"We'll stay in Atlantis. Let's go back now." With that, Neiaphi wrapped her arms around him, holding him tightly.

Neiaphi shook her head as she watched the two lovers board a small boat. Cret and three other men rowed the small vessel into the calm waters toward a large warship. Neiaphi sighed, trying to grapple with her thoughts. Had her decision, convincing Cret not to build his city here, led to the destruction of Atlantis? She recalled the other dream, where the man had mentioned searching for an island to take his beloved. She vowed to ensure this island city would be built if this dream was destined to come true.

Neiaphi awoke to Cypress's warm, wet tongue on her face. "Stop that, you silly puppy," she said, gently pushing him away. Sitting up, she wondered if her dreams were mere fantasies or glimpses of a possible future. Would she truly marry Cret and have a child with him? She hoped with all her heart that it was real. With that thought, she settled back into her bed, sleep finally came, and without dreams.

∞ 25 ∞
FIRST VOYAGE

THE weary travelers from Camp Roma spent several peaceful days in Kranapolis, socializing with the locals and trading goods. Meanwhile, Neiaphi was preoccupied with thoughts of her dreams, though she kept them to herself. *They were just dreams,* she told herself, trying to dismiss their significance. The next leg of their journey would be by boat. They had secured several large ships to transport themselves and their belongings. Weather permitting, the trip would take five days along the shoreline of an inland sea. Most of the group had never sailed before and were anxious about embarking on the wooden vessels.

"May I have your attention, please?" Neiluios addressed the gathered group. "Cham and I have decided on a more fitting name for us. As many of you know, Cham has been referring to us as Olympians, a term associated with the Gods. I believe this name is unsuitable, as our goal is to integrate into society rather than impose ourselves upon it.

"Some of you have suggested calling ourselves Romans. However, I believe this is also unsuitable, as we need to move past Romota and accept that we will not return there. Instead, we will be known as Laosans, which means 'People.' If anyone inquires, we will say that we come from a distant land to the east called Laos.

"Cham has arranged boats for us, and the generous people of Kranapolis have already loaded our belongings and animals. Please proceed to one of the two remaining ships so we can set sail. The journey will take approximately five days to reach the Outpost of Turber. There, we'll find only a small guard post—no town or village—serving to protect this inland sea. We won't be staying there long," Neiluios said. "Please gather your belongings so we can set sail." He assisted Altesse onto the first boat, noting her impending due date with concern. He hoped she would manage to wait until they were safely on shore again.

Neiaphi ran to one of the railings and looked out at the sea with Cypress at her side. The sea was choppy with white foam-capped waves. The boat gently rocked from side to side from where it was tied to a pier. She had to sit down; she was getting lightheaded.

"Are you all right, young one?" Net asked with concern.

"I'm feeling a bit ill," Neiaphi replied. "I'm not sure why."

"It's the motion of the water. Some people get seasick," Net explained. "You'll feel better by morning. Rest here for a while, and I'll bring you some water." Neiaphi nodded, resting her head on her knees. Her head felt like it was spinning, and nausea was setting in. Net soon returned with a wooden bowl of water. "Here, drink this slowly," he said, handing it to her.

"Will this feeling get worse once we set sail?" Neiaphi asked, concern evident in her voice.

"Let's hope not," Net replied. "Come to the center of the boat. It should be more stable there than at the edges." He guided her toward the main mast. Neiaphi sat on the deck, leaning against the mast with closed eyes. Altesse soon joined her, sitting down beside her.

Once Neiaphi felt steady enough to stand, she followed her mother below to the mid-deck and located their cabin. The cabin was very small, featuring four hammocks arranged two on each side, with one hammock stacked above the other. There was barely a pace of space between the hammocks, and a small round window was set opposite the door. Their belongings were already stowed in one of the hammocks.

Neiaphi settled into the hammock beneath their things and sat down.

"Stay here for a while, dear. I'll check on you soon," her mother said.

"Thank you, Mother," Neiaphi replied.

Altesse closed the door gently behind her. The cabin was dim, with only a faint light seeping through the small window. Neiaphi lay down and closed her eyes, relieved that the ship's motion had eased considerably.

"Little Miss, are you awake?" Net's voice called from outside the cabin.

Neiaphi jolted awake, surprised to find she had fallen asleep. "Yes, Net, I'm up," she responded, opening the door.

"You should come up. It's a beautiful night, and Cleop has saved you some food," Net suggested.

"It's already dark? Why didn't anyone wake me sooner?" Neiaphi asked, surprised. She followed Net back up to the upper deck.

Net was right: sleeping it off was the best remedy when feeling ill on a boat. The night was indeed wonderful, and Neiaphi was feeling much better. The sky was clear, with a full moon shining brightly overhead and stars twinkling across the dark canvas. A gentle breeze rustled the sails. Cleop approached her and handed her a bowl of warm fish and root vegetables. Despite its strong fishy flavor, the meal was comforting, and the last remnants of her nausea soon faded. As she looked around, she noticed several others on the boat appeared to be experiencing the same discomfort she had earlier.

Neiaphi scanned the deck for Cypress but couldn't see him. She heard a cheerful bark and walked to the rear of the boat, where she found Herctor tossing a stick for him to fetch. When Cypress spotted her, he barked joyfully and dashed over.

"Hello, boy. Are you having fun?" Neiaphi asked, smiling at the playful puppy.

"Hello, Neiaphi. I hope you don't mind me playing with him. He seemed a bit lonely," Herctor replied.

"Not at all. I'm glad he's found a friend. You might want to ask Captain Heu if he has any more puppies," she suggested.

"My father already asked about more puppies," Herctor said. "He said they're in training and unsafe for children right now, but I can choose from the next litter."

"Well, if you ever want to play with Cypress, just come over," Neiaphi offered.

Herctor's face lit up with a smile. "Thanks!"

Neiaphi picked up the stick and threw it for Cypress. After watching them play for a moment, she waved goodbye to Herctor and Cypress and headed back to her parents.

On the third day, a storm rolled in, and everyone was forced to stay in their cabins or on the mess deck, which was one deck further down. People huddled in corners of the deck, passing the time with card and dice games. Chartis, who had somehow ended up on the same ship as Neiaphi, sat at a table by himself, working on his map. Neiaphi steadied herself, took a deep breath, and walked over to him. She cleared her throat. "Can I sit down?" she asked.

Chartis looked up in surprise, quickly pushing his tablet aside. "Of course, please have a seat," he said with a warm smile.

Neiaphi took a seat and said, "We need to talk. My father mentioned that you spoke with him about me, and I wanted to let you know that I don't think we're a good match."

Chartis's expression faltered. "I had hoped you'd changed your mind. I don't understand why he's letting you decide," he said, his brow furrowing.

"My father doesn't share the Society's beliefs. In Romota, women had some rights, remember? Cham told me that in Atlantis, women could vote and even hold office. My father supports this idea of equality, which is why he's given me the choice." Chartis's face tightened. "He won't allow me to marry someone who would suppress those rights, even if I wanted to. Do you understand? You were influenced by the Society back in Camp Roma. Addident is going to find someone else to travel with us and teach at your school—someone who isn't affiliated with the Society."

"My father has been trying to undo some of the teachings I received. It's difficult because they were skilled teachers and had months to instill their beliefs. Their way is easier to accept; they taught that men are superior to women and that women are here to serve us, like servants."

"How are you supposed to treat a female servant?"

"You really don't want to know. Slaves are treated even worse." Chartis looked down at the table.

"I have an idea. Cleop, our female servant, has shared stories about her past masters. You don't have to follow that path. If you change and I'm older, I might reconsider. Everything is happening so quickly and is so new right now; I need time to adjust. What I need is a friend, nothing more. Can we just be friends?"

Chartis gazed into Neiaphi's blue eyes, a mix of determination and resignation in his expression. He sighed, nodding slightly. "I'll try, but I can't promise I won't keep trying to change your mind."

Neiaphi's lips curved into a teasing grin. "If you do, I'll just walk away and pretend I didn't hear you."

"Fair enough." He chuckled, the tension easing between them. "Would you like to see the map I've been working on?"

"I was hoping you'd offer," she replied, her voice softening. "My father says you're doing a remarkable job."

"That means a lot coming from him." Chartis smiled broadly. Chartis and Neiaphi spent the rest of the afternoon in conversation, slowly unraveling the layers of each other's lives.

Neiluios observed them from a distance, a small smile forming on his lips. Perhaps she was finally opening up. If so, he would ensure that Chartis cherished her as she deserved.

On the morning of the fifth day, they busied themselves with gathering their belongings, readying to disembark from the boats. Outpost Turber loomed on the coastline, its detachment of guards already in position, awaiting their arrival. Captain Heu was the first to step ashore, moving briskly to meet the guards. From her vantage point at the front of the boat, Neiaphi strained to catch snippets of their conversation, but it was clear—they wasted no time in getting straight to business.

"We need ten guards to remain here. Their families will be stationed a day's ride to the north. You all have one day to rest before moving on. These waters aren't safe for women and children," the leader stated, his tone leaving no room for argument.

"A day's ride north?" Captain Heu questioned, a hint of concern in his voice. "How often will they see their families at that distance?"

"We're rotated every ten days—ten days here and then ten days back in the village."

"And what's the village called?"

"Turber."

"I thought that was the name of the outpost."

"Turber Village and the Outpost at Turber are how they're distinguished," the leader explained with an air of impatience. "Please keep all your belongings on the boats and prepare to leave at first light. You may disembark, but only for short periods. Have the ten guards report to me at dusk." With that, the Turber guards turned on their heels and marched back toward the outpost.

Captain Heu went back to the boat to update Addident. Everyone had hoped for a day on solid ground before moving on, but that wasn't to be. Cham informed them that their next stop would be a large city where they could finally rest. It would be another day and a half journey to Bacapolis.

While some chose to remain on the boats, most eagerly disembarked to feel solid ground beneath their feet once more. As soon as he was off the ship, Cypress began chasing after rabbits, squirrels, and anything else that moved.

"Good day, Neiaphi," Captain Heu greeted. "Your pup is growing up nicely and seems ready for training. I'll send Greish over to assist you."

"Why Greish?" Neiaphi asked; instant fear gripped her throat, making speaking hard. "I thought you would help me train him," she asked quietly.

"Greish is now in charge of all the dogs," Captain Heu explained. "He'll have more time to work with you and your pup. What did you name him?"

"Cypress," Neiaphi replied.

"Good, strong name." Captain Heu nodded approvingly before walking away, his hands folded behind his back.

Neiaphi watched the captain walk away. *Greish? Why did it have to be Greish? Hepluosis's best friend, this is a nightmare,* she thought with a shudder.

A few hours before dusk, the Captain rang the ship's bell to gather everyone's attention.

"Hurry up! We need to leave immediately."

"What's going on?" Addident asked as he boarded the ship.

"Look over there," the boat captain said, pointing to the eastern horizon where several ships were approaching. "Get those staying off the boats immediately, or they'll end up coming with us."

"Captain Heu, are your men and their families unloaded?"

"Yes, Sir. Just a moment ago."

"Good. Please help everyone aboard. We need to leave before those ships get too close."

"Those are warships," the boat captain replied. "They're smaller and will move much faster than we can. Let's hope they're heading for the Outpost and not us." He harrumphed and strode back to his platform. "Prepare the ship to sail and man the oars!" he shouted to his crew. Women gathered their children and hurried back on board while the youngest cried out in confusion. The chaotic scene left everyone uncertain about what was happening.

"Make way, row with all your might!" the boat captain bellowed. "Row as if Zeus himself is after you!" The boats slowly pulled away from the shore and into what appeared to be a wide river. "Keep us in the middle, Medline," he directed. "Let's put as much distance between us and those predators as possible."

"Yes, Sir," Medline responded.

The warships didn't appear to be in a hurry or overly concerned about catching up with them.

Neiaphi huddled with her mother in their cabin as the boat swayed and creaked, struggling to pick up speed. Neiluios and most of the men remained on the main deck, keeping watch. The warships were heading toward the Outpost, and Neiluios could see guards prepared with flaming arrows notched and ready. As the warships drew closer, flaming arrows arched through the sky from both the Outpost and the ships. The arrows crossed paths midair, striking their targets with precision. Neiluios whispered a silent prayer for the men and families left behind. With the warships focused on the Outpost, their small group was granted a reprieve and allowed to escape without immediate pursuit—for now, at least.

The boat captain refused to let his men rest until the Outpost was far out of sight. Addident and Neiluios peered through a spyglass at the horizon behind them. The captain marveled at the glass's impressive range. "Zeus, save us," he whispered. "Medline, increase the pace. We're being followed."

"Followed?" Neiluios asked, taking the spyglass and focusing on the horizon. After a moment, he spotted a distant mast bobbing in the surf.

"They think they're far enough behind us not to be detected," the captain explained, "but thanks to your spyglass, we can keep track of them and stay ahead." The boat gradually increased its speed. Maintaining that pace would be difficult, but reaching the next Outpost and getting off the ship was their only option.

Before the sun had fully set in the western sky, Addident spotted the distant city. They would reach it before dawn if they could maintain their current pace.

∞ 26 ∞
THE TEST

"QUICKLY, quickly! We need to get off these ships as fast as we can. The warships will be here soon, and this vessel has no defenses. Move swiftly, everyone," Addident urged, his voice calm but carrying an unmistakable urgency.

How can he remain so calm in a situation like this? Neiaphi wondered, her eyes fixed on the approaching ships and the storm clouds gathering ominously behind them.

Everyone scrambled off the boats in a frantic rush. Blindfolded animals were hurriedly shoved down the ramps, and carts were quickly rolled into place. The teams were hitched as fast as possible. Just as the Laosans got underway, the three warships arrived. The incoming warships opened fire on the defenseless boats. Two of the four boats were quickly engulfed in flames, and men leaped overboard in desperation. The remaining two boats managed to escape, but the warships were in hot pursuit and gradually gaining on them.

Cham shook his head. "Those are our last boats. It will be a shame to lose them."

"Can't you build more?" Amplios asked.

"Poseidon built those boats; we no longer have the technology or knowledge to replicate them. Look at the size and shape differences between our boats and the warships. The warships weren't designed that way solely for speed. That's the only way the Society knows how to build them. That technology will be lost forever once they catch those last two boats." He sighed heavily, turning his gaze away from the inevitable. "Poseidon's vessels were designed for durability. They were large, sturdy ships capable of transporting many people and resources across the planet. They've withstood the test of time and weather."

The group made their way grimly toward Bacapolis. Although it was not a port town and was some distance from the sea, a well-maintained road led into the city. The surrounding countryside was dotted with small farms and orchards.

The city was the largest Neiaphi had seen on this planet, nearly as vast as Romota but lacking an outer wall for protection. Instead, guard towers were positioned on every road leading into the city, and others were scattered seemingly at random. Well-armed, grim-faced men manned the towers. Captain Heu signaled for everyone to halt and approached the nearest guard tower alone. A runner and one of Captain Heu's messengers were dispatched to the city.

"We'll wait here until someone from the government can meet with us," Captain Heu said. "We're too large a group to enter the city at the moment. We can set up camp here. It might be a day or two before someone arrives to speak with us."

"I haven't been identified as part of your group yet. I'll go in and see what I can find out," Cham said. He maneuvered behind their camp, swapping his horse for one of the donkeys loaded with a large pack of blankets. Pulling his cloak tightly around him, he began to limp toward the guard tower. The guards eyed him but didn't stop him; he appeared to be a peasant come to trade.

The Laosans quickly set up camp and settled in, hoping their stay would be brief.

.

Greish grumbled under his breath. He had hoped to avoid interacting with Neiaphi, especially after his friend Hepluosis had warned him about her arrogance. However, an order was an order. Captain Heu wanted her dog trained to protect her, and Greish couldn't fathom why the well-being of an official's daughter mattered so much to him. He watched from a distance as Neiaphi played fetch with her dog, her family some ways off.

Let's see how good this dog really is, he thought. He grabbed a boy of similar age but of much lower rank. Greish had risen through the ranks swiftly—faster than anyone he had ever heard of. He might even out-rank his father soon. Captain Heu had taken him under his wing and was training him personally.

"I need you to help me test that dog over there," Greish instructed. "Sneak up on Neiaphi from behind and grab her. Don't hurt her—just scare her a bit. But be cautious of the dog; I'm unsure how he'll react."

"Yes, sir." The young guard snapped to attention and then moved stealthily from rock to rock, then from tree to tree, approaching Neiaphi with careful speed. She remained unaware of his presence, focused on a bird that had landed nearby. Greish watched anxiously, noting that the boy was nearly within reach, and Neiaphi still hadn't noticed him. *Where is the dog?*

"Oh, help, help!" the young guard yelled. The dog had snuck up behind him and jumped onto his back. Missing his neck, the dog was tearing at the boy's shirt. Greish sprang into action, rushing to the boy's aid.

"Down, boy. Come," Neiaphi commanded sternly. The dog complied immediately. The young guard ran toward Greish and didn't stop until he reached the main camp. Greish slowed to a walk. "Sorry about that, Neiaphi. I needed to test the dog's reactions. It looks like you've done a lot of good work with him. What's his name?"

"This is Cypress. What was the boy supposed to do?" Neiaphi asked, her face marked with a scowl.

"He was just supposed to grab you from behind. I told him not to hurt you, so don't worry." Cypress began to growl softly. "Can you control him?" Greish eyed the young dog.

"I can," Neiaphi replied, kneeling beside Cypress and wrapping an arm around his neck.

"Can you get him to stop growling at me?"

"I'm not sure yet. Are you friends with Hepluosis?"

"Yes, or at least I was. Why does that matter?"

"Hepluosis and I have never gotten along. I assumed you knew that. He didn't mention what he did to me?"

"I know you have a history with him, but he never told me anything. What happened?"

"Did you hear about my accident?"

"Yes, you fell and hit your face on a rock. Isn't that what happened?"

"No," she said, looking away. "Hepluosis and I argued. He insisted that, as a man, I should bow to him, more or less. I told him he was nothing but a boy, and he responded by beating me up. That's why Cypress is so protective—he tried to defend me, and Hepluosis kicked him."

"Look, I had no idea; what he did was inexcusable. I didn't attend the same school he did and thought his ideas were just a bit misguided, but I had no idea he was becoming abusive. I'm truly sorry. I wish I had known. I was teaching him how to use weapons, and now I deeply regret that." Greish scowled and shook his head. Neiaphi met his gaze. "Will you let me help you finish training your dog? He has a solid foundation but needs some fine-tuning. With the surprise attack he just performed, Herha should be dead or at least wounded."

"You seem sincere, but please understand if I find it hard to believe you," Neiaphi said. "However, since Captain Heu wants this, I'll allow it. But only because of that."

"Fair enough." Greish extended his hand, and Neiaphi took it, shaking firmly.

"Oh, help, help!" a boy yelled as Cypress leaped onto his back. Fortunately, the dog missed his neck and only shredded his shirt. Neiluios and Net rushed over to assist, noticing another boy in a lieutenant's uniform hurrying toward the scene. Neiaphi called Cypress off, and the boy ran past the lieutenant, heading in another direction. Neiaphi stood and spoke with the lieutenant. Their conversation had concluded by the time Neiluios and Net arrived within earshot.

"What's going on here?" Neiluios demanded of the lieutenant.

"Sorry for the confusion, Sir," Lieutenant Greish replied. "I'm Greish. Captain Heu asked me to help with your daughter's puppy training, and I needed to test the dog. Neiaphi was never in any real danger."

"Are you okay?" he asked.

"Yes, Father. Cypress protected me."

"You are to have Net with you at all times when we're not at home—wherever we may be staying. Do you understand?"

"Yes, sir." She dropped her gaze to the ground.

"Net, please?" Neiluios asked.

"I will guard her with my life, sir."

"Thank you, Net." Neiluios hugged his daughter before heading back to the camp. Net walked over to a large rock and sat down.

"You have many people who care about you, don't you?" Greish asked.

"It seems I do," Neiaphi replied, watching her father return to the others. "How do we start training Cypress?" she asked, returning her attention to Greish.

Greish smiled. "You're direct and to the point. I like that." Neiaphi returned his smile.

Chartis glanced over at Neiaphi when he heard the shouting. Cypress was attacking someone. He set his tablet aside and rushed over to help. As he approached, he saw Neiluios, their male servant, and Greish heading in her direction. Chartis slowed to a walk as he arrived, finding that Neiluios and the servant had already reached the scene. Neiluios left, and the servant took a seat on a nearby rock. Neiaphi continued her conversation with Greish and then smiled. It seemed he would now have competition for her attention. Well, he was sure Neiaphi would value brains over brawn.

He returned to his tablet, eager to finish the section he had started before darkness fell. Working by candlelight wasn't the same; he made too many mistakes if the light wasn't bright enough.

Later that night...

"Welcome back, Cham. Would you like to join us for the evening meal?" Neiluios asked.

"Very kind of you, Sir, but I must decline," Cham replied.

"What did you find out?"

"I'm afraid it's not good," Cham said. "The Society is everywhere. They're not in power yet, but it's only a matter of time. I hope their influence doesn't extend to the Altaian Sea, which we'll cross next. It never reached this far before. Addident is not with his family, so I thought I should let you know. Can we take a walk?"

"This way," Neiluios said, leading Cham away from the firelight. Neiaphi waited until they were out of sight before slipping away from the fire to follow them.

"We must be cautious," Neiluios said. "As soon as we reach the next Outpost, we should start traveling in smaller groups and avoid the large towns. I'll enter them to see if the governments need additional officials or guards, and then I'll report back to you or Addident. We're drawing too much attention to ourselves with so many members of The Society around."

"Agreed. Can our groups stay within range of each other for support, or do we need to keep a greater distance?"

"I think we'll need to keep a greater distance," Neiluios said. "We can send runners back and forth, but only when we get close to large towns and cities. In the open, we can camp together." They walked into a stand of trees toward a man hiding in the shadows.

"This is Agathon; he's a spy for us and works as a servant in a Society member's household," Neiluios introduced.

"What can you tell me about the Society here?"

"Let me start with a bit of history. I'm not sure how much you already know about them. They are the descendants who came to replace Poseidon and his group. They disapproved of how Poseidon was managing things, believing he was exploiting the planet. Their goal was to overthrow him. However, Poseidon and his sons had a strong hold on the local populace and were eventually overpowered.

"They retreated to the east, far from Atlantis. Over the past fifty years, they've been making a comeback, promoting their ideology of superiority and suppression. This has gained acceptance in some areas. Atlantis mostly keeps to itself and only intervenes if the Society gets too close to the island. Meanwhile, the outlying towns are left to fend for themselves and are being gradually taken over."

"Doesn't Atlantis realize that by protecting the outlying towns, they would be safeguarding themselves? If the Society takes over everywhere else, Atlantis will be vulnerable," Neiluios said.

"They feel secure on their island. They believed you would land near them and bring enough new technology to help them secure their position and overthrow the Society once and for all," Agathon replied.

"You're very well informed. Who do you work for?" Neiluios asked.

"I worked for Deleon before he left for Uralpolis to await your arrival. He left me with his brother, who is the leader here, during his absence."

"Given that Atlantis expects us to bring new technology close to them, how is it that we landed so far away?"

"The Society intercepted the signal that Atlantis sent. A few weeks later, the society sent a follow-up message stating their needs had changed. They wanted to cancel your mission but feared Romota might send you anyway. So, they requested that all technology be left behind, citing concerns that it might fall into the wrong hands. They also altered the landing instructions. The Society believed they could either use you or, if not, dispose of you."

"They attempted the latter. Thankfully, Cham was sent to assist us. Do you know what the processing plant is working on?"

"No, sir, I'm sorry, but I don't know what the processing plant is working on, and it doesn't matter right now. We need to get you to Atlantis as quickly as possible. We'll assign a few Loyals to assist you on your journey. Cham can't be with all the groups simultaneously; each will need guides. I wish I could join you. I would love to see Atlantis one last time."

"You've been to Atlantis? We haven't met anyone who has," Neiluios asked.

"Oh yes," Agathon replied. "I was born in that marvelous city. When I was about twelve, my mother took me on a trip to visit her parents on the mainland. She fell ill during the journey, and we never reached our destination. A Loyal household adopted me as a servant, and I was later trusted enough to become a spy for the Loyals."

"You're being modest, Agathon. You're very skilled. He has convinced the Society of his loyalty, and they've assigned him to spy on us. He feeds them information that we deem safe, and he's been doing this for five years now with great success," Cham said.

"Thank you, Cham. I must go now before I'm missed. I have some freedom, but not much. Take care and make it safely to Atlantis. May the Gods smile on you." He shook hands with Cham and vanished into the night.

"Can we truly trust him?" Neiluios asked.

"Oh yes, sir. I would trust him with my life, and I have in the past. If you see Addident before I do, please inform him of what you've learned this evening.

"The Government Official will arrive in the morning. He'll inform you that we are not welcome in the town but may stay on the outskirts for as long as we need. If everyone agrees, we'll leave the following morning. We'll have to wait at the coast for a few days for the next boats, and then it's a short two-and-a-half-day journey to the other side. I'll see you in the morning. Goodnight."

"Goodnight, Cham."

Cham disappeared into the darkness, heading in the same direction as Agathon. Neiluios sat on a rock, contemplating the information he had just received. This journey was bound to grow increasingly perilous as they continued.

"Father," Neiaphi called quietly.

"Come here, young lady," Neiluios replied with a sigh. How did he know she would follow him? "Why are you here?"

"You know me, Father. I just must know what's going on," she said with a sly smile.

"So, what do you think?"

"I think we need to reach Atlantis quickly without losing anyone else. We should bypass all the Outposts to prevent them from taking anyone," Neiaphi said.

"I considered that," Neiluios replied. "But those Outposts need help as well. We may have to leave people behind, knowing that Atlantis won't be able to assist them. That might be their only hope."

"Father?"

"Yes?"

"Never mind. We should get back before Mother starts to worry." She decided not to mention her dreams, dismissing them as just dreams after all.

Neiluios took his daughter's hand and walked her back to their camp, wondering what might be troubling her.

Altesse paced anxiously but relaxed when she saw them return together.

"Sorry, Mother," Neiaphi said.

"Please stop running off by yourself, dear," Altesse replied, kissing her on the cheek.

"Yes, Mother. Goodnight."

Once Neiaphi was settled, Altesse turned to Neiluios. "What are we going to do about her? She's too wild for this planet. I shudder to think what else she might do."

"I'm only worried about what I already know she will do," Neiluios said, shaking his head and remaining silent after that.

After the brief meeting with the government official, the Laosans packed up camp and headed for the western shore. They had voted unanimously; no one wanted to remain near a place that did not welcome them. The recent attack by the warships was still fresh in their minds, and they were determined to distance themselves from the Society as much as possible.

After a long day's journey, they finally reached the coast of the Altaian Sea, a vast expanse stretching beyond the horizon in every direction. With the boats for their crossing still several days away, they set up a more comfortable camp to await their arrival.

∞ 27 ∞
THE LOYALS

"**WELCOME**, brethren. We're so glad you could join us," Cham said warmly as he greeted a group of people they had been observing for some time as they traveled up the coast.

"Cham, it's been a long time. We're glad to be called upon to help. I hope you don't mind, but we've brought our families with us," said a slender man with greying black hair and a mustache.

"Of course, I don't mind. It was expected and welcomed. You're all most welcome. Please, come with me, Aner. I'd like to introduce you to Addident and Neiluios."

Neiaphi squeezed through the crowd, eager to see the Loyals who had arrived to assist them. Several boys and girls around her age were among the group.

"I am Aner," the slender man said with a bow. "These are Mace, Paragon, and Baccus. We've come to help Cham guide you to Atlantis. It's a pleasure to meet Olympians from Romota. We were eager to bring our families along; it would have been a great disappointment if they missed the chance to meet you."

"It is a pleasure to meet you all, but we have one request. We are not gods and do not come from Mount Olympus. Please call us Laosans from Laos, far to the east," Neiluios said.

Aner nodded respectfully. "Understood. I'll make sure to use the term Laosans from now on. We're here to support you and ensure your safe passage."

"Please, make yourselves comfortable. Don't hesitate to ask if there's anything you need or any questions you have." Addident said.

"I'm glad we can make this work. Let me introduce you to my family. My wife, Iris, and our two daughters, Kayo and Nemie. Over here, we have Mace's wife, Miry, and their son, Andonis. Paragon's family includes his wife, Anthie, their daughter, Alexa, and their son, Alexen. And these are Baccus's twin sons, Bacceon and Aristas."

"It's a great honor to meet you all," Neiluios said. "Please follow me, and I'll introduce you to everyone. This is my wife, Altesse," Neiluios continued, "and my daughter should be around here somewhere. Ah, there she is!" Neiaphi came running over. "This is Neiaphi."

"It's a pleasure to meet you, Altesse and Neiaphi," Aner said with a deep bow. The group continued following Neiluios and Addident around the camp, meeting everyone.

"Oh, this is wonderful, Neiaphi. There are some girls your age here. Perhaps you'll be able to make some friends," Altesse said.

"That would be nice," Neiaphi replied, her attention focused elsewhere. She was watching the newcomers with curiosity. They didn't seem very different from themselves; in fact, most of the people they had encountered so far looked quite similar. While many were a bit shorter on average, and some were rather round, she had noticed several men taller than Addident.

Many of the men had facial hair, a feature Neiaphi had never seen back in Romota. Most people in Romota had light brown or blonde hair, with a few having white hair, which she hadn't seen on this planet yet. Some, like her mother, had red hair. It wasn't until she arrived here that she saw hair so dark it almost looked black, like Cham's.

She studied the newcomers, trying to memorize their names. They were all dressed similarly to everyone else on this planet. Neiaphi still found it strange that she wasn't allowed to wear pants occasionally. While the tunics were usually comfortable, they were less practical when she was riding her horse. As the group walked around the camp, they eventually disappeared from Neiaphi's view.

She reached down to scratch Cypress behind the ear, glanced around the camp, and saw Greish approaching. Noticing the sky, she realized it was time for Cypress's lesson. "Good day, Greish. Are the Gods smiling on you today?" Neiaphi asked as Greish drew near.

"What?" Greish asked, looking puzzled.

"That's something I overheard two servants saying to each other," Neiaphi explained. "I think it means, 'Are you having a good day?'"

"Oh, I see," Greish replied, shaking his head with a smile. "Well, yes, I suppose I am. You seem to be in a good mood yourself today."

"I am," Neiaphi replied. "I'm not sure why, but today I feel really good. What are we working on today?"

"Today, your pup will learn to stop regardless of what he's doing."

"He already knows how to do that," Neiaphi said.

"Then it should be a quick lesson, won't it?" Greish said with a playful grin, placing his hands on his hips. "I want to start with the basics and then move on from there. Is that alright?"

She shrugged and smiled back. "Okay. You're the teacher."

Neiaphi was right; the lesson was quick. No matter what Greish tried, he couldn't distract Cypress. Usually, Greish stayed around to chat for a while, but today, he excused himself immediately after the lesson. Neiaphi and Cypress spent the rest of the day chasing rabbits and sticks. Thanks to Cypress, she managed to catch three large rabbits to bring home.

As the sun set over the water, the sky blazed with fiery hues, and the water shimmered like molten lava. The camp settled into the evening routine, with campfires being lit all around. Neiaphi helped Cleop clean up after their meal while Altesse sat quietly beside the fire, humming to herself. After a while, Altesse struggled to her feet and asked, "Neiaphi, are you ready to go?" Being almost eight months pregnant, bending down had become increasingly difficult for her.

"Go where Mother?" Neiaphi asked.

"We're heading to Addident's tent," Altesse explained. "All the women and girls are gathering to get to know each other. It should be fun. Come on."

"Alright, Mother. Let me grab our cloaks." Neiaphi quickly fetched their cloaks, and she and Altesse silently walked the distance to Addident's tent. Nidora stood at the entrance, welcoming the women as they arrived.

"Nice to see you, Altesse. You look lovely tonight," Nidora said with a warm smile.

"Thank you, Nidora. Any prospects for a husband yet?" Altesse inquired.

"Not yet, I'm afraid. Unless I marry one of the guards, I'm older than the rest of the boys here," Nidora replied with a rueful smile. "I'm sure I'll find someone eventually. But thank you for asking. Do you have anyone in mind for Neiaphi?" Nidora added with a smile, glancing at Neiaphi.

Neiaphi smiled back. Though she and Nidora didn't usually interact, Neiaphi thought they might get along well if they did, but Nidora often kept to herself.

"No, we're still searching. See you inside," Altesse replied, and they continued into the tent.

Altesse and Neiaphi ducked inside the tent. Most of the women had already arrived and were gathered around the fire in the center of the tent. The girls over five were huddled near the back, chatting amongst themselves.

"Neiaphi, over here. Sit next to me," Rhoda, Kamkrates's daughter, called out. "This is Neiaphi, daughter of First Agent Neiluios," she added proudly.

"It's a pleasure to meet you, Neiaphi. What a beautiful name you have," Kayo said warmly. "I'm Kayo. This is my sister, Nemie, and this is Alexa. It's so wonderful to meet someone from our home planet. Could you tell us more about it?"

Neiaphi studied Kayo, wondering if she was trying to trap them into saying something inappropriate. "Home planet? I'm not sure what you mean. We are Laosans from a place far to the east called Laos. It's a beautiful place. If you're ever in the area, you should visit."

"Oh, very good," Kayo said, clapping her hands. "We were just testing you, and you passed wonderfully. It's clear you've been well taught. We can safely talk about Romota with you now, but we understand if you choose not to. We know you're trying to fit in and focus on your new surroundings."

"How old are you?" Surrie asked, abruptly changing the subject.

"That's not very polite, Surrie. I'm sorry, Kayo," Neiaphi said.

"That's quite all right," Kayo responded with a smile. "She's young, and we can overlook her forwardness. I'm sixteen, my sister is twelve, and Alexa is fifteen."

"We're the same age, Alexa!" Neiaphi exclaimed.

"Really?" Alexa responded with a wide grin.

"So, are any of you promised yet?" Kayo asked.

"Some of us are, and some are not," Rhoda replied. "I am, as are Surrie, Chara, and Dela. Hestia, Kore, Leda, and Dione are still too young."

"What about you, Neiaphi?" Alexa asked.

"Not yet," Neiaphi replied, shaking her head.

"That's surprising," Kayo said. "Other than Nidora, you're the oldest here, so I would have thought you'd be promised by now. I saw several boys your age and a few older."

"My parents haven't found a suitable match for me yet. Chartis has asked, but since he's of lower status…" She shrugged. "And my parents won't consider a guard," Neiaphi explained.

"That makes sense," Kayo said. "I'm promised to Bacceon, but Nemie and Alexa aren't promised yet. Plenty of boys are here, so I'm sure they'll find matches before we reach the next Outpost."

"I hope not," Nemie protested. "I'm still too young."

"I was your age when I was promised. You'll learn to accept it," Kayo said.

"When are you marrying Bacceon?" Neiaphi asked.

"I'll marry him when I turn seventeen," Kayo replied. "My parents want Bacceon to mature a bit more before we wed. He's only a year older than me. If I had chosen an older boy, I'd probably be married already. That's why I picked someone close to my age." She winked.

"Your parents let you pick?" Surrie asked.

"They did," Kayo explained. "They suggested several matches and then let me make the final decision. I advise choosing a boy close to your age, if possible. However, some parents don't give their daughters a choice in their husbands."

"Mine didn't," Chara said, and the other girls nodded in agreement.

"I'm sorry to hear that," Kayo said, placing a comforting hand on Chara's shoulder.

"That's all right," Chara replied. "I like Xener, and he seems to like me. He's two years older than I am."

"Have your parents set a marriage age for you?" Nemie asked.

"I'll wait until I'm sixteen," Chara said. "So, I still have six more years to enjoy being a little girl."

"That's not too bad, then," Nemie responded.

The rest of the evening was spent exchanging questions and stories. Neiaphi soon grew bored and began to look around the tent. Addident's tent was much like theirs, sparsely furnished with only a few belongings. The women chatted animatedly, their voices blending in a cacophony that Neiaphi couldn't distinguish. She noticed Alexa watching her and saw her gesture toward the back flap of the tent. Neiaphi nodded in understanding. She stood up, walked to the back, and stepped outside. A few moments later, Alexa joined her outside.

"I thought maybe we could talk out here," Neiaphi suggested. "I know some of those girls are only a year younger than us, but it still makes a difference…"

Kayo emerged from the tent, looking relieved. "I'm so glad you two came outside. I was so bored. Little girls talk about the most mundane things."

"I was just thinking the same thing," Alexa giggled.

Neiaphi joined in the laughter, enjoying the moment. It had been a while since she laughed so freely for no particular reason.

"Do you have any brothers or sisters?" Kayo asked Neiaphi.

"I had a brother back home, but he was killed…" Neiaphi replied, her voice tinged with sadness.

"Oh, I'm so sorry. How old was he?" Kayo asked gently.

"He was almost three," Neiaphi said. "But my mother is pregnant again and due any time."

"That's wonderful news. Babies are so much fun," Kayo said with a smile.

Neiaphi returned the smile, hoping that would be the case. "Would you like to meet my dog?"

"Sure, where is he?" Alexa asked, looking around.

Neiaphi whistled, and a dog barked in the distance. Cypress came running at the call, quickly making his way to Neiaphi and sitting in front of her.

"This is Cypress. He's my friend and protector," Neiaphi said with a smile.

"He's so pretty. May I pet him?" Alexa asked.

"Of course. He's very friendly with nice people," Neiaphi replied.

"So, you said Chartis has asked for you?" Alexa asked.

"Yes, he has," Neiaphi said. "But I don't feel the same way about him. I told him I just wanted to be friends, but he said he wouldn't stop persuading me otherwise. He's nice enough, but I'm not sure."

Neiaphi shook her head and looked down, her thoughts weighing on her.

"He's not bad-looking. He seems interesting. I've never seen white hair and pink eyes before. Do you mind if I go talk to him?"

"Not at all," Neiaphi replied.

"How about Fotis? He's Dione's brother, isn't he? Do you know if he's promised yet?"

"I don't think so," Neiaphi replied. "He's quite a bit older than the other girls here. You might want to ask Dione; she would know for sure."

"I'll just observe for now. I don't like being too forward," Alexa said, her cheeks flaring bright red.

"What's your status?" Neiaphi asked the two girls.

"Based on what we've learned about statuses on Romota, I'd guess we're Mid-Level," Kayo replied.

"We don't have those classifications here," Kayo explained. "We have Royalty, Officials, Guards, Townsfolk, and Peasants. We fall into the Official class since our fathers serve in the government."

"Where is your home?" Neiaphi asked.

"We're from about two days south of here, from a town called Topolis," Kayo explained. "It's smaller than Bacapolis, but not by much."

"Most of the towns we're visiting have 'polis' in their names. What does that mean?" Neiaphi asked.

"It's another word for 'city,'" Kayo explained. "It's strange how we speak the same language, but there are still so many words and differences we don't know."

"People here must have invented words to suit themselves or adopted them from the original inhabitants of this planet," Neiaphi suggested.

"That must be it," Kayo agreed, though she didn't look entirely convinced.

"Have you ever traveled by sea before?" Alexa asked.

"Just recently," Neiaphi replied. "It wasn't too bad. I was sick on the first day, but I've been fine since then. Have either of you?" Neiaphi asked.

"No," Kayo replied. "Our town is next to a small river, but I've never even considered getting into a boat."

"I tried once," Alexa said, "but my cousin started rocking it, so I got out and never tried again."

"I can't wait to get to Atlantis. I hope the boats arrive soon," Neiaphi said.

"We're excited, too," Kayo agreed. "We've heard so many stories about Atlantis, which sounds wonderful. I hope it lives up to everything the storytellers say."

"Neiaphi, are you out here?" Altesse called.

"Yes, Mother," Neiaphi replied.

"Oh, it's nice to see you again, girls," Altesse said, addressing Kayo and Alexa. "You're Kayo and Alexa, correct?"

"Yes, ma'am," they answered in unison.

"It's time to go now, dear," Altesse said gently. "You can continue your conversation tomorrow. Goodnight, girls."

"Goodnight, ma'am. See you tomorrow, Neiaphi," Kayo and Alexa said.

"Bye, see you tomorrow," Neiaphi replied, waving to her new friends as she followed her mother back to their tent. She looked back one last time, feeling hopeful about having friends again.

"Are either of them promised?" Altesse asked as they walked.

"Kayo is promised to Bacceon, but Alexa isn't," Neiaphi said. "She's interested in Chartis and Fotis."

"Well, that could solve your problem with Chartis if he likes her," Altesse noted.

"That would be nice," Neiaphi agreed.

Altesse glanced at her daughter and sighed.

When they returned to their tent, they each settled onto their pallets. Net and Cleop were already asleep. Neiluios didn't return until nearly dawn.

Neiaphi was jolted awake by her mother's moans just as the sun crested the horizon. Cleop rushed into the tent and then hurried out again, calling for Net to get the fire made and water boiling. Neiluios sat beside Altesse, trying to offer comfort.

Neiaphi moved to the other side of her mother. "It's all right, dear. I'm just having the baby now. Go outside and see if Cleop needs any help," Altesse said between gasps.

"Yes, Mother," Neiaphi said, rushing outside and accidentally bumping into Cleop. "Sorry, do you need any help?"

"Go get Dela. She's with Addident. Tell her to hurry," Cleop instructed, ducking back into the tent, Neiaphi at her heels. "Neiluios, sir, you must leave. This is no place for a man. Do not argue. I need Altesse to focus on me. Please, just go."

"It's all right. Please go," Altesse wheezed.

"Neiaphi! Dela, please hurry!" Cleop shooed her out of the tent.

Neiaphi jumped and ran to Addident's tent.

"Dela, Dela," Neiaphi whispered urgently as she found her.

"Yes, who is it?" Dela asked, peeking out of her tent.

"I'm Neiaphi. Cleop says she needs your help with the delivery. Please hurry."

"Oh, Altesse is having her baby already? So soon," Dela said, surprised. "I'm coming. Don't worry, child."

Dela emerged from the servants' tent and hurried back with Neiaphi. "Stay out here," Dela instructed as they reached the tent.

Neiaphi sat on the ground by the fire, joining Net, and watched her father pace anxiously in front of the tent.

"Would you like some tea, sir?" Net asked.

"No," Neiluios snapped.

"Father! Please, come sit. You're not helping anyone, including yourself," Neiaphi said.

"I'm sorry, Net," Neiluios apologized. "It's just that Altesse has a hard time with deliveries. We weren't supposed to have any more children. She nearly died with Neiaphi's brother. I want to be by her side. I can't stand this."

"It could anger the Gods if you're inside, so Cleop and Dela won't let you in. Please try to calm down. From what I hear, she's in good hands. Dela has saved many children and mothers when others thought there was no hope. Here... at least drink this while you pace. It will help calm you down," Net said, offering the tea.

Neiluios took the wooden bowl and sipped the tea. Net then handed a bowl to Neiaphi before pouring himself a small serving. The tea was sweetened with mint, but Neiaphi could also taste a hint of a bitter root.

Time seemed to drag on as Altesse continued to moan and cry in pain. With every sound, Neiluios grew more agitated. Most of the camp was now awake. Kayo and Alexa joined Neiaphi, sitting beside her in silence. Several other female servants had gone into the tent to help but were sent out with the reassurance that everything was going well.

Suddenly, Altesse cried out loudly, followed by the distinct sound of a baby's wail. Cleop poked her head out of the tent. "Altesse wants to see you," she said to Neiluios.

Neiluios rubbed his hands together nervously and then entered the tent.

A moment later, Neiluios emerged from the tent, holding a naked newborn above his head.

"A son!" he announced.

The camp erupted in applause. Neiluios carried the baby over to Neiaphi so she could see her new baby brother. Just then, another baby's cry pierced the air from within the tent. Neiluios and Neiaphi exchanged surprised glances and hurried back inside. They ducked into the tent to find Altesse holding a second baby.

"You have twin sons, sir," Dela said.

"Twins? How are you feeling? Are you all right?" Neiluios asked, concern evident in his voice. Cleop stepped forward to take the baby from Neiluios, wrapping it in a cloth.

"I'm fine. Take our sons and show them to everyone," Altesse said, smiling up at her husband.

Neiluios gently took his second son from Altesse and headed outside with Cleop, who carried the first baby.

"Twin sons," Neiluios announced, holding the second baby up. The crowd erupted in applause once more. Several men approached Neiluios to offer their congratulations.

"Are you sure you're all right, Mother?" Neiaphi asked, staying close to her mother's side.

"I feel fine. Just fine. I'll be on my feet in no time," Altesse assured Neiaphi.

"Twins! Did you have any idea?" Neiaphi asked, still concerned.

"No, I had no idea," Altesse replied with a smile. "They're quite small and came earlier than expected. I thought I just had one very active baby inside me."

Cleop and Neiluios reentered the tent. Cleop handed the firstborn back to Altesse and took the other from Neiluios, wrapping him carefully in a cloth.

"Would you like to hold your brother?" Cleop asked.

Neiaphi extended her arms in the manner she had seen Cleop do and took the baby, one of her new brothers. She had never held a baby before and was both excited and nervous.

"Do you have any names picked out yet?" Neiaphi asked her mother.

"Not yet. I'll decide on something in a day or two," Altesse replied. "Hand me my other son so he can nurse."

Neiaphi carefully carried her brother over to her mother and handed him to her.

"Okay, everyone out. Mother and the babies need to rest," Cleop said, shooing everyone out of the tent.

Neiluios and Neiaphi sat beside the fire, grinning from ear to ear.

"Two brothers, wow!" Neiaphi exclaimed. Neiluios nodded in agreement.

"How are they?" Kayo asked, approaching them.

"My mother says she's fine, and Dela and Cleop both say the babies are healthy," Neiaphi replied.

"That's good to hear," Kayo said. "Are you going to hold the Naming Ceremony, sir?" she asked Neiluios.

"A Naming Ceremony? I've never heard of that before," Neiluios said, puzzled.

"I'll have my father explain it to you, sir. It's not appropriate for me to go into detail," Kayo said, her cheeks flushing. She stood up quickly and ran to find her father.

"So many ceremonies here," Neiluios said, shaking his head. "These people are so concerned with pleasing the Gods."

"It's their way, Father, and now it's our way too. We must adapt," Neiaphi replied.

Neiluios smiled at his daughter. "It's good that so many people are willing to help us."

"Neiluios, my daughter mentioned that you need instruction on the Naming Ceremony," Aner said as he approached, grabbing Neiluios by the forearm in greeting.

"Yes, I've never heard of it before," Neiluios admitted.

"The ceremony must take place before the sun rises tomorrow. Come, let us walk, and I'll explain how to perform it," Aner said, leading Neiluios away from the camp.

Neiluios spent most of the day preparing for the Naming Ceremony, so Neiaphi helped Cleop with the twins while Altesse rested.

"Has your mother chosen their names yet?" Cleop asked.

"I don't think so. What is the Naming Ceremony?" Neiaphi asked.

"It's when the father announces the new child's name to everyone nearby. It's crucial to let the Gods know the names of all new citizens as soon as possible. If something were to happen to the child before the ceremony, the Gods wouldn't know how to find the infant and guide it into the afterlife," Cleop explained.

"None of us had a Naming Ceremony when we were born. What about us?" Neiaphi asked.

"Well, two things," Cleop replied. "First, you can talk to the Gods can ask you your name directly if needed. Second, you don't believe in the Gods anyway."

"That's true," Neiaphi said with a smile, gently humming to the infant she was rocking in her arms. "I just thought I'd ask."

"I have to be naked? Are you sure?" Neiluios asked, clearly startled.

"That's how it's done," Aner confirmed. "You must present yourself to the Gods in the same way you entered this world, just as you present your children."

"Why?" Neiluios asked.

"Well… I don't know. It's just the way it's always been done," Aner replied.

"Well, I won't do it," Neiluios said firmly. "We're from Laos, where the ceremony is different. I'll wear minimal clothing, but I won't parade around naked in front of my daughter and everyone else in the camp. Besides, I came into this world fully clothed."

Aner chuckled. "Do as you see fit. I hope the Gods accept the ceremony."

Neiluios studied Aner, trying to gauge if he was joking. He wasn't. "What happens if the Gods don't accept the naming?"

"It is said that Zeus will send a lightning bolt from the heavens to show his displeasure."

"Have you ever witnessed this?" Neiluios asked, his skepticism evident.

"I haven't, but I met a traveling storyteller who claimed to have seen it once."

"I will risk it," Neiluios said with a scowl. "I must return and announce to the camp that the ceremony will occur tonight. Thank you for your help."

"I will inform everyone. You focus on your wife."

"Thank you again, Aner." They gripped forearms in farewell before parting ways.

"Neiluios, there you are. Come and hold your sons." Altesse settled beside the fire, cradling one infant while Cleop held the other. Neiluios joined his wife and gently took his son from Cleop.

"Have you decided on their names yet?"

"I have a few options, but I'd like your help choosing their final names."

"If you'll excuse me, I need to prepare the evening meal," Cleop said, rising to leave the tent. "Neiaphi, could you help me fetch some water?"

"Yes, Cleop."

As the sun began to set, the sky transformed into shades of purple and orange. Fires and torches were lit, casting a warm, flickering glow over the ground and tents. Aner and Mace kindled a large bonfire in the center of the camp for the Naming Ceremony. As the flames grew bright, the camp's inhabitants gradually approached the bonfire.

"Come, Neiaphi, stay close to me," Net said.

"I was planning to help Cleop with the twins," Neiaphi protested.

"She can manage on her own," Net replied. "Besides, you're too young and unwed to be involved in the ceremony. We don't want to risk offending the Gods."

"Okay, you're right. Can we sit close?"

Net nodded with a smile, feeling proud that she wanted to learn their ways. He had heard from other servants that some families, especially the older ones, were reluctant to embrace new traditions. Net shook his head in bemusement.

"What's the matter, Net?" Neiaphi asked.

"Oh, it's nothing," Net replied. "Just remembering something I forgot to do. I can take care of it later. Let's find our spot."

Cleop helped Altesse settle into a chair positioned in front of the crowd. Altesse appeared quite uncomfortable; she had always disliked being the center of attention. Neiaphi scanned the gathering but couldn't spot her father or the twins. Aner approached the bonfire and tossed a handful of powder into the flames, causing them to leap and crackle. The people closest to the fire recoiled, and an expectant silence fell over the crowd. Altesse, sitting right beside the blaze, shifted away from the intense heat.

Aner raised his hands skyward toward the heavens and the unseen Gods. "Let all the Gods take notice this night and remember the names of the children born on this day," he declared. "I am Aner, fulfilling the wishes of the Gods. Smile upon us always and guide us safely to your holy city, Atlantis."

He bowed deeply and then turned back to face the fire. For a moment, he stood silently as the flames crackled loudly, and another log split open from the intense heat. "Thank you, Gods, for gracing us with your presence this evening." He bowed once more. "Now, let the Naming Ceremony begin."

Neiluios emerged from behind the fire, carrying one naked son in each arm. He wore only a loincloth himself. Altesse gazed at her husband and their two newborn sons, her face lighting up with a smile.

"Thanks to the Gods and to everyone who has gathered here today," Neiluios said, doing his best to bow without dropping either of his sons. He approached the front of the assembly, turned toward the fire, and bowed again. After the fire crackled anew, Neiluios faced his family and friends. "From this day forward, let everyone assembled here and the Gods above hear the names of my sons. I am Neiluios, and these are my sons. My firstborn will be named Annas, and my secondborn will be named Praxis. I proclaim this for all to hear. Please welcome my sons."

"Greetings, Annas. Greetings, Praxis," the crowd intoned in unison.

Neiluios paused, glancing at the sky for any signs of storm or lightning. "Mighty Gods, know my sons, Annas and Praxis. They will not join you soon, but be aware of them for when the time comes." He lifted his sons as high as he could into the air, offering them to the Gods. Still, there was no sign of lightning. Zeus must not be displeased, Neiluios thought, and a smile crossed his face. Aner added more powder to the fire, causing the flames to flare up once again.

Neiluios walked through the crowd, carrying his sons and making a full circuit before stopping in front of Altesse. "Here are my sons," he said. "Take them and care for them. This is your purpose in life; fulfill it well." He gently handed each son to Altesse, one at a time.

"I will take care of your sons," Altesse said. "I will make them strong, while you will impart wisdom to them. Annas and Praxis, you are now known." With these final words, the crowd dispersed silently, leaving only the new family by the fire. Altesse and Neiluios were required to stay by the fire until it burned down, as it was believed that since the Gods had been invited to the ceremony, they would extinguish the fire upon their departure. Leaving before the fire had died would be seen as disrespectful. Cleop brought several cloaks and blankets to keep them warm.

"Let's return to the tents now," Net told Neiaphi.

"Can't I stay here?" Neiaphi asked.

"No," Net replied firmly. "Only the new child and its parents should remain. Your presence might confuse the Gods. Come with me." He extended his hand to her. Neiaphi hesitated for a moment, then took his hand and followed him back to the tents.

∞ 28 ∞
MAKING NEW FRIENDS

"**HOW** long do we have to stay here?" Altesse asked, pulling the blankets tighter around herself and her sons.

"Until the fire is nothing but embers, I'm afraid," Neiluios replied. "It would reflect poorly on us to leave before then." For now, he was grateful for the warmth from the fire, but he eagerly anticipated its dying down so they could return to their tent. "I'm sorry for what I had to say earlier. I didn't mean it, you know."

"Oh, my sweet husband, I understand," Altesse said softly. "I know you don't see my only purpose as bearing your children. Everything here is so different from where we came from. We must adapt." Neiluios carefully held his wife close, sharing their warmth against the biting wind from the water, which seemed to cut straight to their bones.

The fire finally burned down enough for them to return to their tent, as the sun was just a sliver on the horizon. Altesse had managed to fall asleep, and to their relief, the twins also slept through the night. However, Neiluios had stayed awake throughout the night. The sky was bright with stars, and the full moon hung low over the water, sometimes seeming to dance upon its surface. Neiluios and Altesse slipped quietly into their tent to avoid waking Neiaphi. Neiluios went to his daughter's side and gently kissed her forehead. She stirred but remained asleep. Cypress, their faithful dog, whined softly and wagged his tail. Neiluios bent down and patted the dog's head.

"Neiluios, come to bed," Altesse whispered. He turned toward her and nodded. The soft blankets on their pallet were a welcome relief from the cold ground they had been lying on by the fire. Sleep came quickly to them both.

"Is Mother or Father awake yet?" Neiaphi asked Cleop as she emerged from the tent, carrying Annas and Praxis.

"Your mother is awake," Cleop replied. "She'll be out shortly."

"What a beautiful day!" Altesse exclaimed, stretching her arms out to either side. "Neiaphi, how about we go for a walk this morning? Cleop, could you please watch the boys? We won't be gone long."

"Yes, ma'am," Cleop replied.

They walked toward the choppy, angry-looking water, where white foam-capped waves crashed onto the beach. Cypress raced along the shoreline, barking at the waves.

"Have you had a chance to make any friends yet?" Altesse asked.

"I've spoken a bit with Kayo and Alexa. They seem nice," Neiaphi replied.

"I'm glad to hear that. Have you discussed the boys with them at all?"

"Not really," Neiaphi said, stopping and facing her mother. "Alexa asked about a few people in our group, and they told me a little about the ones in theirs, but not much. Why?"

Altesse sighed. "You're reaching the age where we need to consider your future."

"I thought you and Father said I had plenty of time and didn't need to think about that yet."

"Well, yes and no," Altesse explained. "We don't need to choose someone for you right away, but we do need to give the impression that we're considering it. I've heard that in some of the larger cities, powerful men might take women as brides if they're considered too old to be unengaged. I don't want that to happen to you."

"I don't want that either. It would be terrible. I might as well be a slave in that situation," Neiaphi said, shuddering.

"That's pretty much how it would be," Altesse agreed. "Are there any boys around your age?"

"Aristas and Andonis are a couple of years older than me, and Alexen is a couple of years younger. I haven't actually met any of them yet; the past two days have been so busy."

"That is very true." Altesse tripped over a piece of driftwood but managed to catch herself.

"Are you okay, Mother? Do we need to go back?" Neiaphi asked, grabbing her mother's elbow to steady her.

"I must still be a bit weak," Altesse said. "We'll start back, but slowly."

They walked silently for a while, gazing out over the water they would soon be traveling on. Neiaphi reflected on their first boat journey and the fiery sight of their sinking vessels. Cham had mentioned that those had been the largest boats they had left. Neiaphi didn't want to think about the size of the vessels they were expected to sail on now; this was a much larger body of water.

"I want you to try to befriend the two boys who are older than you," Altesse said. "It never hurts to have many friends. Get to know them and keep an open heart and mind about the possibility of becoming promised to one of them."

"If I have to, I'll try," Neiaphi replied, looking down at the sand and kicking a large shell. "But I can't promise that anything will come of it."

"Do you still think about Cret?" Altesse asked.

Neiaphi hesitated before answering. "Sometimes I dream about him."

"What other dreams do you have?" Altesse inquired gently. She had often woken to hold Neiaphi's hand during her nightmares, and Neiaphi sometimes mumbled in her sleep.

"I dream about what our future here might bring, that's all," Neiaphi said, lying.

"Do you ever have a recurring dream about someone other than Cret?" Altesse asked gently.

"There is one man I dream about sometimes," Neiaphi admitted. "I don't know who he is. But it's just a dream. It's not real. It doesn't matter."

"You know you can tell me anything," Altesse said softly. "I won't share it with anyone."

"I know," Neiaphi replied, still staring at the sand as they walked. Altesse let the subject drop for now and would try again later.

Neiluios was sitting by the cookfire, holding one of the twins, when Altesse and Neiaphi returned. "A beautiful day for a walk, wouldn't you say?"

"Oh, yes. It was splendid," Altesse agreed. "Any news on when we'll depart?"

"Not yet. I suspect we'll hear something in a day or two. Neiaphi, a girl named Alexa, came looking for you. I told her I'd send you over to her when you got back."

"Do I need to complete any lessons today?" Neiaphi asked.

"No, you can have the day off," Neiluios replied.

"Thank you, Father," she said, kissing him on the cheek. "I'll be back before the evening meal." Neiaphi whistled for Cypress to join her and began walking through the camp toward Alexa's tent.

The camp was bustling with activity. Servants and women were busy organizing and repacking their belongings while children ran about, playing. Neiaphi walked through the camp, smiling and waving whenever she caught someone's gaze. She noticed Chartis looking her way. He smiled briefly before quickly looking away. Ever since the newcomers had joined them, he seemed to be around less often. She had grown accustomed to his gaze, and it felt strange now that it was absent.

The newcomers were camped on the opposite side of the camp, clustered together and keeping to themselves, creating the impression of two separate camps. Alexa was sitting outside her tent near their fire, sewing. When she saw Neiaphi approaching, she looked up and smiled. "Greetings, Neiaphi. I pray the Gods are smiling on you today," she said.

"Yes, they are, thank you. Are you well?" Neiaphi responded, still unsure of how to handle that type of greeting.

Alexa giggled. "I am well. Please, sit. The usual response would be, 'Yes, and you as well,' but what you said wasn't bad either."

"Thanks. You came by this morning?" Neiaphi asked.

"I was hoping we could get to know each other better and…" Alexa hesitated, clearing her throat.

"What is it?" Neiaphi prompted.

"Well, I've been asked to introduce you to Aristas and Andonis," Alexa admitted, looking down and wringing her hands. "But I'm not sure how to do that without making it obvious what I'm trying to do. I don't feel comfortable trying to arrange a promising."

"You weren't supposed to tell me that, were you?"

"No, I wasn't. But once I began, it would've been obvious, and I don't believe in deception. I want to be honest with you... I want us to be friends."

"I'd like that. This morning, my mother suggested I get to know Andonis and Aristas. Maybe you could introduce us, and in return, I'll introduce you to Chartis and Fotis."

"That sounds perfect! I've been trying to figure out how to meet them. My parents are already nudging me to choose a husband."

"I could also introduce you to Greish if you don't mind a guard. He's nice, and he's handsome in a rugged kind of way. Plus, he's been helping me train Cypress for protection."

"Sure, why not? You never know what might happen."

"What are you working on?"

"Oh, this?" She lifted the cloth she was sewing. "Just fixing a tear in my brother's cloak. He's so careless! I keep telling my mother that if she made him do his own repairs, he might finally learn, but…" She gave a slight shrug. "How are your brothers?"

"They're doing well, according to Cleop. Want to take a walk?"

"I'll just let my mother know, then we can go." She ducked inside the tent and returned a moment later. "All set."

As they walked, their conversation flowed naturally. Neiaphi shared stories about their journey from Camp Roma, describing the landscape and events leading up to when Alexa's group joined them. In return, Alexa spoke fondly of her home, painting a vivid picture of where she came from.

"Alexa!" someone called out. She turned to see cret approaching—a tall, lean figure with brown hair and matching eyes that gleamed with curiosity. The two girls paused, allowing him to catch up. "Hi, Alexa. Who's your friend?"

"Neiaphi, daughter of Neiluios," Neiaphi replied with a gentle smile.

"Oh, right! My apologies." Andonis gave a polite bow. "We met so many people the other day that I've forgotten most of their names. I'm Andonis, son of Mace. Where are you two headed?"

"We're just out for a walk," Alexa said. "Would you like to join us?"

"If I'm not intruding," Andonis said with a friendly smile directed at Neiaphi.

"Not at all," Neiaphi replied, matching his smile.

As they walked, Andonis led the way toward the water. They eventually reached a large pile of driftwood and settled down. Andonis busied himself gathering some of the wood and soon had a small fire crackling. "So, Neiaphi," he said thoughtfully, "how are you finding things so far from home?"

"I think I'm adjusting well, but it's such a big change."

"How so? Is it the land or more the people?"

"Oh, everything," she replied, gesturing with her hands as if trying to capture it all. "The land feels both familiar and foreign at the same time, but it's the people, the culture, and especially the religion that are so different. That's been the hardest part to adapt to."

"What do you want out of life here?" Andonis asked, his voice steady as he fixed his gaze on her.

His eyes bore into hers with an intensity that made her pulse quicken. Neiaphi felt an almost magnetic pull to look away, but his gaze seemed to hold her captive. She swallowed hard, fighting to regain her composure and willing herself not to break under the pressure.

"Well, back home, my path was clear: finish schooling, get married, and manage a household. When we first arrived here, I assumed my life would follow the same course. But since formal schooling isn't offered to girls here, I suppose I'll keep learning from my father and our servant Net until I marry. It doesn't seem like women have many choices here, does it?"

"There are a few, but not many, you're right. My mother's sister owns a pottery shop, but she's one of the rare exceptions. Most women don't get that far. I've heard that in Atlantis, though, it's different—many women-run businesses, and some even hold political power." "Please don't think I'm being too forward. I just want to get to know you better. As you probably know, there aren't many pairing options for your people right now. I've been encouraged to connect with any girls around my age. I imagine you've been told something similar." Neiaphi nodded. "I'm sure you'll meet plenty of boys on our way to Atlantis, but that doesn't mean we can't be friends."

"I agree. It's important to have friends. I'm really glad to know you both, Andonis, and you too, Alexa."

"Let's go. I'll introduce you to Aristas." Andonis stood, offering a hand to each of them as they got to their feet. He smothered the fire with sand, ensuring it was fully extinguished before leading the way.

They found Aristas and his twin brother, Bacceon, sparring with swords. They were nearly identical, with blonde hair and piercing blue eyes, making it difficult to distinguish between them at a glance. The only noticeable difference was that Bacceon sported a thin line of facial hair above his upper lip, while Aristas remained clean-shaven. After a tense exchange, Bacceon managed to catch Aristas off guard. With a swift spin, he moved behind his brother and delivered a controlled thrust, pressing the flat side of his sword against Aristas's back to assert his dominance. Aristas grunted from the impact, stumbling forward before collapsing to the ground. But he quickly rolled onto his back, just in time to parry Bacceon's follow-up strike.

Bacceon laughed loudly and then thrust out his hand to assist his brother.

"Take a breather," Andonis suggested, nodding toward the girls. "Go sit with Alexa and Neiaphi. I'll avenge you."

"Thanks, I need a break." Aristas pulled off his shirt, wiping the sweat from his forehead with it. He nodded in agreement, grateful for the reprieve.

He walked over to the box of swords and carefully placed his inside. After blotting his forehead and neck again, he approached the two girls. He had been told both were available as potential matches. Alexa, he knew well—they had grown up together. She was a beautiful girl, with soft brown hair and warm eyes, but she was a bit too short for his liking.

Neiaphi, on the other hand, had rich brown hair and striking blue eyes that seemed to sparkle in the sunlight. Her pale skin, almost like polished ivory, contrasted sharply with her dark hair. She was taller than Alexa, and her slender frame gave her an elegant, almost statuesque presence.

"Good day, Alexa. Good day, Neiaphi," Aristas greeted with a nod.

"Good day," the girls responded in unison.

Aristas sat beside Alexa, his gaze drifting back to the sparring match. Andonis was holding his own against Bacceon, pushing him hard. Aristas knew Andonis was smart—he never challenged either of the twins when they were fresh, knowing they trained more rigorously. Still, it was impressive to see him keep pace with Bacceon despite practicing less often.

"It's a glorious day. Have either of you heard when we'll be departing?" Aristas asked, glancing between the two girls.

"No, not yet," Neiaphi replied. "My father said we should know more in a day or two."

"Your father is Neiluios, correct?" Aristas confirmed.

"Yes," she nodded.

"And he's... second in command?" Aristas asked, hesitating as he tried to recall the title.

"Yes," Neiaphi clarified, "he's the First Agent."

Aristas nodded thoughtfully. "Alexa, could you fetch us some water?" he asked.

"Of course. I'll be back in a moment," Alexa replied, rising to her feet.

Neiaphi began to stand as well, ready to assist, but Alexa gently waved her off. "Why don't you stay here? I won't be long," she said with a reassuring smile.

"Okay." Neiaphi settled back down, absentmindedly fiddling with the fabric of her dress.

"Have you or your parents made any plans for your future yet?" Aristas asked, his tone direct.

Neiaphi glanced at him, eyebrows slightly raised. "You're straightforward."

Aristas shrugged, a hint of a smile on his lips. "Time is short, and I prefer to get to the point."

"I can see that," she said with a chuckle. "Andonis was the same way. No plans have been made yet. For now, I'm just getting to know any boys close to my age."

"That's sensible," he replied. "Have you heard about the Taking practice in some cities?"

"Is that when men take a bride if she's too old to be promised?" she asked.

"Yes, it is," he said. "In my opinion, it's a barbaric excuse to take a young bride, but it's still widely practiced in some areas. Some men even take more than one bride if no suitable men can be found. They believe it offends the Gods to let a woman of age remain unwed."

"How horrible," Neiaphi said, her voice filled with distaste.

"I agree," he said. "I know everyone is worried about this and wants their daughters promised before we reach the next town. They understand it might not be possible to arrange all the promises in such a short time. So, I have a proposal for you and your parents. Since we've just met and don't know each other well yet... But if you're still unpromised by the time this situation arises, would you allow me to say that I've spoken for you?" He raised his hands to stop her from responding. "This doesn't mean we're formally promised, but it indicates that I'm negotiating with your parents. It would allow you to explore your options without risking being Taken."

"I'll need to discuss it with my parents first, but it sounds reasonable," she said. "But why would you do that? Wouldn't it hinder your chances of finding someone?"

"Not necessarily," he replied. "I can still look. I knew a man who spoke for three girls at once and chose the first one who agreed. It's not that I don't want to get to know you better—I do. But I'd hate to see you, or anyone else, be Taken like that." He looked away, and Neiaphi studied him, trying to gauge his feelings. At first, he seemed so confident, but now he appeared almost embarrassed. Leaning over, she gently placed a hand on his knee. He met her gaze, caught in the depth of her blue eyes.

"That's very sweet of you. Thank you," Neiaphi said softly. She withdrew her hand as she noticed Alexa returning.

"Did I miss anything?" Alexa asked as she sat down and handed a waterskin to Aristas.

"Nothing much, just Andonis losing badly," Aristas replied, taking a long drink from the waterskin.

"It was a pleasure meeting you, Aristas," Neiaphi said with a smile. "But I promised Alexa I'd introduce her to some people. Will you excuse us?"

He stood and helped both girls to their feet. "Of course. Please feel free to come by anytime so we can continue our conversation. May the Gods shine on you both." He gave a deep, respectful bow.

Alexa took Neiaphi's hand and pulled her into a brisk walk.

"Goodbye, Andonis. It was nice meeting you," Neiaphi called over her shoulder.

Andonis, momentarily distracted from his sparring, glanced their way. Bacceon seized the opportunity to tap him on the shoulder with his sword. Andonis grunted and jumped back.

"Sorry!" Neiaphi shouted back with a smile.

"So, what did you and Aristas talk about?" Alexa asked.

"He asked similar questions to those Andonis did," Neiaphi replied. "Then he proposed that if I'm not promised by the time we reach the next city, he'll say he's spoken for me to prevent me from being Taken."

"Really? He talked to my parents about the same thing last evening. They agreed. I think he just wants to have all the options available," Alexa said, giggling as she doubled over.

"Do you really think so?" Neiaphi asked, frowning and coming to a halt. She had thought Aristas' offer was a sign that he liked her and wanted to get to know her better.

"Oh, not at all," Alexa said, noticing the concern on Neiaphi's face. "Don't worry. Aristas is just incredibly kind and considerate. He looks out for everyone he knows and doesn't want anything bad to happen to them. My father says he'll make a great leader someday. Besides, I've known him my whole life—he's like a brother to me."

They made small talk as they walked back to the main camp and toward the guard section.

One of the guards on patrol approached them. "Greetings, Neiaphi. Have you heard the news?"

"Hi, Greish. What news?" she asked.

"Camp Roma was attacked."

Neiaphi's hands flew to her mouth. "H—how do you know?"

"Cham received a report, and I overheard Addident and Captain Heu discussing it. Apparently, there was a control room inside the large mountain behind the camp, and it was destroyed."

"Was anyone hurt?" Alexa asked.

"Some," Greish replied. "But they were all members of the Society."

"Was the Processing Plant attacked?" Neiaphi asked urgently.

"Not that I've heard. Why do you ask?" Greish looked at her with concern.

"We left a lot of friends behind," Neiaphi said. "I just want to know if they're safe."

Greish shook his head. "You're still thinking about Cret?" he asked gently.

"Sometimes," Neiaphi answered softly.

"You must try to forget him," Greish said gently, placing a hand on her shoulder. "Holding on is only hurting yourself. You're growing into a very beautiful woman; you'll find someone else."

"He was just a friend," Neiaphi replied, brushing his hand away. "I'm only concerned about his safety." Greish shook his head but didn't press the matter further.

"Greish, I'd like you to meet Alexa," Neiaphi said, shifting the topic.

"Nice to meet you, Greish," Alexa said, her cheeks flushing slightly as a small, shy smile appeared on her lips.

Greish bowed deeply. "It's a pleasure to meet you, Alexa. I saw you from a distance and had hoped to introduce myself. I hope this isn't too forward, but... well, are you promised yet?"

Alexa's blush deepened as she looked down and whispered, "Not yet."

"I'm introducing her to you, Chartis, and Fotis for that reason," Neiaphi said with a broad smile.

"Well, I'd love to get to know you better if you'll allow me," Greish said warmly.

"I'd like that," Alexa replied.

"We should keep moving. I see Fotis over there," Neiaphi said, taking Alexa's hand and gently pulling her away. "I'll see you tomorrow, Greish, for Cypress's lessons."

"See you tomorrow. It was nice meeting you, Alexa," Greish called after them.

Once they were out of earshot, Alexa glanced back at Greish, who was still watching them. "You were right. He does seem very nice."

"He does... lately," Neiaphi grumbled.

"What do you mean?" Alexa asked, stopping and looking intently at her friend.

"Well, back in Camp Roma, Greish was friends with a boy named Hepluosis. I'm unsure what we ever did to him, but he hated me and Cret. He would follow us around, always trying to get us into trouble. After our group split up and we started traveling, Captain Heu ordered Greish to help me train Cypress. He didn't want to help at first," Neiaphi continued. "He said that Hepluosis had told him I was a horrible person. But "He said that Hepluosis had told him I was a horrible person. But later, he admitted that he realized I wasn't. I never knew he thought I was becoming beautiful, though." Neiaphi glanced back in Greish's direction.

"I wouldn't pursue him if you don't want me to," Alexa offered.

"Oh no, you can if you like," Neiaphi replied. "My father would never agree to a marriage with a guard. He's still stuck on the idea of marrying within your status or above. And besides, Greish has never mentioned anything like that before. I think he was just being nice."

"If you don't mind, I might talk to him tomorrow," Alexa said.

"You can join me for Cypress's lesson," Neiaphi suggested. "Oh, look, there's Fotis."

They spotted Fotis sitting alone in the sun, his eyes closed. They approached him quietly until Neiaphi cleared her throat. "Fotis, do you have a moment?"

Fotis turned his head, noticing Neiaphi and Alexa approaching. "I have a moment, but not much more," he replied.

"Fotis, this is Alexa," Neiaphi said. "I'm introducing her to all the boys in our group."

"How old are you?" Fotis asked as he stood up, looking Alexa up and down.

"I'm fifteen," Alexa replied cheerfully, her cheeks flushing as she spoke. Fotis was very tall, with blonde hair and striking green eyes. Alexa couldn't help but beam at him, finding him incredibly attractive.

"You seem nice enough," Fotis said, "but a three-year age difference is too much for me. Have a good day, both of you. Goodbye." He gave a slight bow and then walked away.

"He's not very friendly, is he?" Alexa remarked.

"I never thought so," Neiaphi replied. "I think he's aiming for Nidora, but I doubt Addident will approve." She shook her head with a sigh. "Oh well, Chartis is nice."

"He's the one who's asked for you, right?" Alexa asked.

"Yes, but he's been ignoring me ever since your group arrived," Neiaphi replied. "He's probably at his tent, working on his map."

They continued to speak quietly to each other as they made their way to Chartis's tent.

"Good day, Dia. Is Chartis around?" Neiaphi asked.

"Good day, Neiaphi," Dia replied. "He was here a moment ago. Oh, there he is. Chartis, you have some visitors."

Chartis was sitting a short distance away under a large tree. Hearing his mother's call, he looked up and waved.

"Thank you, Dia."

"My pleasure, dear," Chartis's mother replied before ducking inside their tent.

"What do I owe the honor of this visit?" Chartis asked, glancing up.

"This is Alexa," Neiaphi said, introducing her. "I'm introducing her to all the boys in our group."

"Oh, I see. Nice to meet you, Alexa," Chartis said, though a flash of hurt briefly crossed his face.

"Nice to meet you too, Chartis," Alexa replied with a warm smile. "Neiaphi has told me so many nice things about you. I'd love to get to know you better if you don't mind."

"Um, I don't think so. Can you excuse us for a moment?" Chartis asked, gesturing to Neiaphi.

"Oh, sure," Alexa replied. "Come on, Cypress. Let's go see if we can find that squirrel." She gave Neiaphi a nod and then hurried off after Cypress.

"Why are you introducing her to me?" Chartis asked, turning back to Neiaphi. "I've already asked for you. Unless this is your answer." He reached for Neiaphi's hand but hesitated when she flinched.

"No, that's not it," Neiaphi said, shaking her head. "I don't know how to explain it. You're so sweet, and I consider you a great friend, but I don't have those kinds of feelings for you. I thought you might like to meet Alexa because I'm learning that a man can speak for several girls and choose later. I'm not sure if that's how it works here, but I wanted you to meet someone. Kayo is closer to your age, but she's already promised."

Neiaphi paused and looked up at him. "I don't want to hurt you. I just thought you might appreciate getting to know one of the new arrivals."

"I'm sorry," Neiaphi said, looking down. "I guess I wasn't thinking. I'll let her know you're not interested." She turned to leave, but Chartis placed a hand on her shoulder to stop her.

"Thank you for your honesty," Chartis said. "I'll get to know Alexa for your sake, but I can't promise anything will come of it. I'm still asking for you."

"At least get to know her before making a decision," Neiaphi said with a smile.

"I can do that," Chartis replied. "Who else have you spoken with today?"

"We spoke with Greish first. He's interested in getting to know her better," Neiaphi explained. "Then we saw Fotis, who said she's too young. So, it's between you and Greish. But there's also Aristas, one of the boys in her group. He has an agreement with her parents that if she isn't promised before we reach the next town, he'll claim he's spoken for her and negotiate with her parents to prevent her from being Taken. He's proposed the same arrangement for me if I want it."

"Taken? What does that mean?" Chartis asked, frowning.

Neiaphi hesitated, her discomfort evident. "In some areas, when a woman reaches a certain age and is unmarried with no prospects, any man can take her as his wife, even if he's already married. They believe it offends the Gods for a woman to remain unwed."

Chartis's eyes widened in surprise. "I've heard of some strange things on this planet, but that has to be the craziest yet. Well, you can tell Aristas that I've already done that—for real. I'll get to know Alexa for your sake, but I'm not withdrawing my offer to you."

"That's fine," Neiaphi replied.

"So, do you like Aristas?" Chartis asked, glancing at her out of the corner of his eye.

Neiaphi shrugged. "I don't know. I just met him. He was very blunt and to the point. Andonis was a little more subtle."

"So, are those my only two competitors?" he asked, half-jokingly.

"I suppose," Neiaphi replied, though her thoughts drifted to the man with the grey eyes from her dream. She shook her head, reminding herself it was just a dream—he wasn't real.

"Well, at least I know who to keep an eye on," Chartis said with a grin. "I thought Greish might be competition too. You two spend a lot of time together."

"Only because of Captain Hue's orders," Neiaphi replied. "Greish is helping me train Cypress. He's never mentioned liking me before. Though today, he did say I was becoming beautiful. He's never said anything like that before." She frowned slightly.

"Well, he's right. The man who wins you over will be very fortunate. I hope that man is me."

"We'll see," Neiaphi replied, attempting to smile, though it felt strained. Her comfort level dropped noticeably. "Thank you for being willing to get to know Alexa. She has few choices, just like me."

∞ 29 ∞
CHOICES

"**NEIAPHI,** you must choose. You must choose now. Which of us do you want?" Chartis's voice trembled with urgency. Neiaphi's gaze swept down the line of young men— Aristas, Andonis, Cret, the man with the grey eyes, and finally, Chartis—each one staring at her, waiting, their expressions a mixture of hope, fear, and expectation.

"I do not need to be promised yet," Neiaphi protested.

"Choosing will put your mind at ease," Chartis insisted. "You don't know where your family will go, and you'll need someone beside you—to protect you."

"But I want to explore this new world without being tied down. How can I do that if I'm promised to someone?" Neiaphi's voice wavered with uncertainty.

"By letting one of us join you on your adventures," Chartis replied, his tone growing more urgent. "Choose now!"

Neiaphi stepped toward Chartis. "You are a good friend, Chartis, and I will always cherish that." Her voice was soft but resolute. She shook her head gently, then walked past him.

"Aristas, Andonis," she continued, "I have just met you both, but I still do not truly know you." They smiled but remained silent, their expressions a mixture of understanding and uncertainty.

Finally, she turned to Cret. She tenderly placed a hand on his cheek and whispered, "Cret, you were my first true friend. I don't know if I'll ever see you again. I've had dreams about our child," Neiaphi said softly, searching Cret's eyes. "Does that mean we'll meet again, or are you lost to me forever?"

"Time will tell," Cret replied, his voice tinged with a bittersweet calm.

Neiaphi shook her head, unable to linger on the uncertainty. She turned to the last man, the one with the grey eyes. "And you," she began, her voice laced with curiosity and frustration, "I've dreamed about you so often, but nothing ever happens in those dreams. Who are you?"

"It is true that you do not know me," the man said, his gaze unwavering. "But you will, soon. I can say no more. You'll know me when you see me. I await you."

"How can I be expected to choose between you all when there are so many unanswered questions?" Neiaphi demanded, frustration edging her voice. "You will have to wait. Leave me so I may rest."

With a sharp flick of her hands, they vanished in a blinding flash of light. Neiaphi shielded her face, squeezing her eyes shut against the overwhelming brilliance. When Neiaphi opened her eyes, she was alone, standing in an endless abyss of white nothingness. She closed her eyes again, concentrating on the beach she had visited so often in her dreams. In an instant, she was there.

She spun in a circle, taking in the familiar surroundings, searching for Cypress. Then she heard it—his joyful barking in the distance. Her heart lifted as she spotted him. Cypress saw her, too, and sprinted toward her, his tail wagging with excitement.

"There's my good puppy. My, how you've grown." Neiaphi smiled as Cypress sat at her feet, his bushy tail wagging happily. Slowly, she lowered herself onto the sand beside him, her hand gently stroking his fur.

"What am I going to do, Cypress?" she murmured, her voice tinged with uncertainty. "Why do I have to choose my

husband now? There's still so much I want to explore, and we haven't even made it to Atlantis yet."

"That's not why you can't choose," a female voice said.

Neiaphi jumped to her feet, scanning the empty room with growing anxiety. "Who are you? Where are you?"

"It's not important who I am," the voice replied. "What matters is who you are. You are Neiaphi, destined for great things."

"What's stopping me from choosing?" Neiaphi asked.

"The reason is clear," the voice responded. "You love Cret, yet you don't know if he's alive. You have three promising suitors before you and dream of a possible fourth—who may or may not be real. You're giving yourself an escape, fearing that choosing now might make you miss out on someone in the future. Rest assured; the choices you must make will soon be right before you. For now, focus only on those who are present."

"That might be part of the reason, but there's still so much to discover in this new world."

"You can explore with a companion; that won't hinder you. No, the real reason is, as I've said. You need to come see me in person so we can talk."

"Who are you, and where are you?" Neiaphi pressed.

"You'll find out soon enough. You possess a great gift, young one."

"How will I recognize you if I can't see you now?"

"You will be traveling to my home soon," the voice assured. "Don't be afraid to make your decision before you arrive. You won't be married before we meet. I must leave you now."

"Please don't go. How am I supposed to choose? Please help me." Silence was the only answer. Neiaphi found herself alone with Cypress once more. "What am I to do, Cypress?" She hugged his neck tightly and began to cry.

Neiaphi woke with a start, finding herself back in the tent with Cypress curled at her side. *That was a strange dream,* she thought, glancing around. Her parents and brothers were still asleep, their breathing steady and calm.

Quietly, she slipped out of the tent, wrapping herself in her cloak. The fire's embers glowed faintly, casting long shadows across the camp, while the full moon hung high in the sky, bathing the world in an eerie light. Everything seemed to move forward in a rush, and she felt like she was struggling to keep up.

She wandered toward the edge of the camp, her gaze fixed on the sea. The water shimmered like glass under the moonlight, and in the distance, she could make out the silhouettes of four masts—ships approaching. They would be departing soon, but where were they headed?

The voice from her dream echoed in her mind, saying she would see it soon and have chosen her husband by then, though she would not be married yet. Maybe if she chose someone now, she could change her mind later. But no, that wouldn't be fair to whoever she chose, she thought.

Slowly, she walked back to the fire and sat beside it. As if sensing her distress, Cypress emerged from the tent and settled beside her. She rested her head on his soft side and soon drifted back to sleep.

"Neiaphi, what are you doing out here?" Neiluios asked, emerging from the tent.

Neiaphi sat up, rubbing her eyes. "I couldn't sleep last night, so I came out here and must have fallen asleep. Have the ships arrived yet?"

"What ships?" Neiluios asked, emerging from the tent.

"The four large ships I saw on the horizon last night. Oh, there they are." She pointed to the distant vessels. "They're still quite far off."

"Tell your mother I'll be back soon. I need to speak with Addident about our departure.

Addident was watching the approaching ships when Neiluios joined him. "They're smaller than the last vessels we were on but not as small as I had feared," Addident remarked.

"Yes, I thought the same," Neiluios agreed. "When do you think we'll be leaving?"

"Cham mentioned the ships should arrive tomorrow. We can begin loading them the day after," Addident replied. "We'll need to ask the captain about the duration of the trip to our next destination."

"Do we know how much farther it is to Atlantis?"

"No one knows. None of us have ever been there before." Addident shrugged and turned back to the camp.

"I'll alert the camp to start preparing for the journey."

Addident nodded. "That's good. I wonder how many will abandon us before we arrive."

Neiluios sighed. "I hope it's not too many, but I fear only a few of us will reach Atlantis."

"You and I will," Addident assured him. "I'll make sure of it. How are your wife and children?"

"They're well, Sir. The boys don't sleep much at night, but they seem healthy. I hope the sea voyage doesn't upset them too much."

"I'm sure they'll be fine. I'll see you later."

"Yes, Sir. I have a lot to do today. Good day." Neiluios turned and headed back toward the camp. Most of the camp was already up, watching the ships slowly approach. A few men spotted him and met him halfway. He instructed them to start packing, as they would leave in two days.

Neiluios stood, gazing at the ships, lost in thought. He reflected on their plans and the future they had envisioned here, only to have those hopes altered by their current situation. Now, his only concern was the safety of his family and friends.

"Alexa, come look! Can you see the ships over there?" Alexen called excitedly as he climbed onto a boulder for a better view. "Can you see them? Do you see them?" The young boy bounced up and down with excitement.

"Alexen, be careful," she warned her brother. "Yes, I see them! Has Father said when we'll leave?"

"He's talking with the Laosians right now. What do you think Atlantis will be like?" Alexen asked, beaming down at her.

"I don't know. It should be similar to home, just larger. Tell Mother and Father I'll be back soon." She left her brother and headed toward the Laosian camp.

"Are the gods smiling on you today, Cleop?" Alexa asked as she approached.

"Ah, good day, Alexa. The gods are indeed pleased with me today. Neiaphi is out with Cypress," Cleop replied, gesturing toward the water as she spoke.

"Thank you, Cleop." Alexa spotted Neiaphi a short distance away and waved as she approached.

"Hello, Alexa."

"Good day, Neiaphi. Do you know when we're leaving?"

"In a couple of days. They say the ships will arrive tomorrow morning, and we'll depart as soon as we're loaded," Neiaphi replied, sighing and kicking at a shell.

"You seem troubled today."

"It's nothing. I've been having strange dreams since we arrived here, and the one I had last night is still on my mind."

"Do you want to talk about them?"

"Not yet. I need some time to work them out for myself. Have you had a chance to speak with any of the boys yet?"

"I talked with Greish last evening. He seems nice and caring, which isn't common, as you might have heard. How about you? Andonis seems to like you; I can tell."

"He seemed nice, but I'm not sure. Do you remember hearing Greish mention a boy named Cret?"

"Yes." Alexa reached down to scratch Cypress behind the ear.

"He was a friend back home who came with us and became my best friend. His father was sent to the Processing Plant to help repair it. The Plant is under the control of The Society."

"I'm so sorry. You cared about him a lot, didn't you?" Alexa took Neiaphi's hand and gave it a comforting squeeze.

Neiaphi nodded. "I dream about him often. I've been told I need to choose a husband, but I can't make that decision until I know what happened to him."

"You have to accept that you may never see him again. The plant was near Camp Roma, wasn't it?" Neiaphi nodded. "That's a long way from here. I don't see how you could ever find him again."

"It's good that the choice is yours and not your parents'. I agree with them, though; we both need to decide. It won't be so bad, you'll see. We can choose now but ask our parents to set the union date for when we're seventeen or eighteen after we reach Atlantis. That way, we won't have to think about it again until the date approaches. We have plenty of time."

"You're right. But... is it acceptable to break a promise if the future doesn't turn out as expected?"

"I've never heard of anyone breaking a promise like that, but I haven't heard that it's not allowed either. I guess it depends on the situation. Why do you ask?"

"You never know what the future will bring, so you must prepare as best as possible. We've all learned that the hard way." She gestured toward the camp.

"You have a point." They stood silently for a moment, watching the incoming ships and contemplating their futures. "Have you seen Chartis? I told him I'd meet him today."

"I haven't seen him, but his tent isn't far from here. I'll walk you over."

"Thank you, Neiaphi. I'll find you before I head back to my tent and let you know how it went."

Neiaphi walked Alexa to Chartis's tent and then started back toward her own.

"There you are, dear," Altesse said, approaching from behind. "I need your help packing. The ships are due to arrive this evening, and your father wants our belongings onboard first."

"Yes, Mother." Neiaphi fell into step beside her. "Mother, when did you know that Father was the right person for you?"

"I didn't know right away. Your father is several years older than me, so I didn't meet him until he was already promised. I was fourteen; he was eighteen and scheduled to marry the following year. I thought he was handsome immediately, of course, but I didn't think anything would come of it. We spoke occasionally, socially, but soon lost touch. The year passed, and things changed."

"One day, I ran into your father the following year at the market near our old quarters. He offered to carry my purchases back to my home. I assumed he was already married, so I didn't ask. Later, I discovered the girl he had been promised to have left the city with her family. With my modest dowry, I was still unpromised."

"I sought him out, even though I thought I had little chance. He was my only hope. A few days later, I managed to arrange another encounter. We got to know each other better, and soon, he asked for my hand in marriage, telling my parents to keep my dowry. He said they needed it more than we would. We were married a few months later, and you were born the following year."

"That's such a lovely story, Mother. I hope to have a story like that."

"Your story will be special in its own way, I'm sure. Have you gotten to know any of the other boys?"

"I've met Andonis and Aristas. They're both nice and handsome. Oh, Mother, why did Cret have to be sent to the Processing Plant? Why?" She broke down into tears.

"Come here, dear," Altesse said, opening her arms. Neiaphi crumbled into them. "Oh, my sweet child. What heartache you've endured." Altesse gently patted her on the back. "I know you long for Cret to be by your side. I wish I could say something to make you forget him, but I'm afraid that isn't possible." "It was either him or your father. If we had known more about our fate at the hands of the Society, I'm sure we would all still be together, but that wasn't meant to be. I've learned that since Chartis has asked for you, you're not at risk of being Taken, so you don't need to choose right now. You have some time. Try not to worry about it at the moment."

"Are you sure?"

"Yes, dear. I'm certain the right person will present himself to you when the time is right."

"Thank you, Mother. I feel better now. I couldn't sleep last night, thinking about having to make a hasty decision."

"Do you want to talk about your dream?"

Neiaphi hesitated, then sighed. "I dreamed that Andonis, Aristas, Chartis, Cret, and another man were all telling me to choose. I told them I couldn't decide yet and asked them to leave me alone." She chose not to mention the woman's voice who said she would meet Neiaphi soon. She wasn't ready to explain that part.

"Do you know who the other man was?"

"No, I've never seen him before."

"I think I might understand," her mother said gently. "He could represent the unknown. As you'll be meeting many new people, your dreams might just be giving you a face for what's to come. Try not to dwell on the unknown or Cret for now. Focus on the three before you. If the unknown becomes clearer, we can address it then. Thank you for opening up to me. Remember, I'm always here to help you; I'm your mother."

"Thank you, Mother. My dreams never seem to make much sense while I'm having them, and even less when I try to explain them to you."

"I understand. Thank you for sharing with me."

Crying reached their ears from the direction of their tent. Altesse quickened her steps and ducked inside. Neiaphi patted Cypress' head, feeling a weight lift from her shoulders. She was grateful for his comforting presence. The pressure to choose a husband immediately had eased; she could take her time. Perhaps the woman from her dream was real and could offer her guidance. Neiaphi continued to pack the items they wouldn't need in the morning, moving slowly and thoughtfully.

Later that afternoon, Alexa returned from her visit with Chartis. "How did it go?" Neiaphi asked as Alexa plopped down beside her.

"He seems nice enough, but it's clear he's not interested," Alexa said with a sigh. "I'm sorry, Neiaphi. I tried. After a while, I could sense he was bored and wanted me to leave. I pressed on, showing genuine interest in his maps—they're quite fascinating and well-done—but in the end, I had to give up." Alexa said with a deep sigh.

"Thanks for trying. What about Aristas and Andonis? Do you like either of them?"

"I grew up around them. They're both like big brothers to me. It would feel strange," Alexa said. "I'd better get back to my mother. I'll see you tomorrow." She stood up and waved goodbye.

"Bye, Alexa. See you tomorrow," Neiaphi replied, offering a small smile. She wandered over to a large rock and sat, her gaze fixed on the rhythmic waves of the sea. The soothing sound calmed her as the sun dipped lower in the sky, casting long shadows across the shore. She remained there until Cleop called her in for the evening meal.

That evening, the camp was bathed in the warm orange glow of countless campfires flickering in the light breeze. The air hummed with the bustle of activity as everyone prepared for the upcoming journey. The sounds of conversation, laughter, and the occasional clatter of supplies being packed echoed through the night, blending with the crackling of the fires. Even as the stars began to dot the sky, the camp remained alive with energy, the anticipation of departure hanging in the air.

"We'll load all the wagons and your belongings onto the ships first. Animals and people will be brought on board before dusk. I want us to set sail as soon as the sun disappears," shouted a plump man standing on the bow of the nearest ship to the crowd gathered around the four ships.

The tide was high, allowing the ships to get reasonably close to shore. They had three small boats and a flat ferry for the animals, all tied to large trees near the water's edge. Everything needed to be loaded onto these boats first, then transferred to the larger ships. It would take all day to get everything onboard.

Addident informed everyone that the journey would take four to six days. They would be at sea for two days before hugging the shoreline until they reached their departure point. The captain would get them as close to the next Outpost as possible, but they would still need to travel about a day overland to reach it.

"Let's get moving, people!" the captain yelled. "I'll make sure you're loading this ship in the dark if necessary. I've heard about the problems with the last ships you traveled on. That won't happen with my vessels. We'll sail by midday tomorrow at the latest, whether everyone is on board or not."

"You heard the captain, everyone. Let's get packing. Once your belongings are on the boats, I want you and your families to stay onboard," Addident commanded in a gruff, authoritative tone.

The camp was quickly dismantled as the small boats and ferry were loaded. One load at a time was transported to the waiting ships.

Neiaphi approached Nexus, gently patting the mare's muzzle. Nexus responded with a soft nicker. "Sorry I haven't spent much time with you, girl, but we'll be traveling more now." A crew member stepped forward, taking Nexus's lead and guiding her onto the ferry.

Neiaphi watched the horses board before returning to help Cleop load the last of their belongings onto the boat. She caught sight of her father, deep in conversation with several Loyals nearby, though they were too far off for her to hear.

Most of the camp was loaded before the sun slid below the western horizon.

Neiaphi sat on the beach, watching as the sun disappeared and the sky darkened. The full moon provided little light, obscured by shifting clouds. Stars appeared one by one, only to be swallowed by the velvety, cloudy black sky. Neiaphi watched as one of the last families was ferried out to sea in the transfer boat.

"It's time for us to board one of the boats, dear. Come on," Altesse urged, determined to be the last family onboard to ensure everyone received the help they needed.

"Yes, Mother," Neiaphi replied. She glanced back at the bare ground where their camp had been, now seemingly erased. She sighed and climbed into one of the small boats. "Do you know which boat Alexa and her family will be on?"

"No, dear. I'm sorry, I don't," Altesse said, placing a comforting hand on her daughter's shoulder. The small boat lurched into the water as four strong men rowed them toward the lead ship.

As the sun set, the water grew choppy, and the four men struggled to keep the boat steady alongside the ship. A large basket was lowered for Altesse and the twins while everyone else had to climb a long rope ladder. Cleop muttered a prayer under her breath as she ascended.

Neiluios and his family were the last to board the boats. He glanced back toward the shoreline, but the night was so dark that he couldn't distinguish where the water ended and the land began. Once the crew hoisted the small boats up along the sides of the ships, the oarsmen began their work, slowly maneuvering them out to sea.

"I'm impressed by how quickly you and your group managed to get on board. I've never seen such a large group move that fast," the captain remarked.

Neiluios jumped slightly, surprised by the captain's sudden presence. The captain was a stout man with a face covered in blonde hair. Despite his size, he moved with surprising lightness.

"We've had a lot of practice lately. How long did you say until we touch land again?" Neiluios asked.

"Four to six days, depending on the weather. It took us six to get here, but we sailed through a severe storm. All indications point to milder weather now. It'd be best if you headed below for the night. Not much going on up here," the captain replied.

"I think I will. Good evening, Captain."

"May the Gods grant you a peaceful sleep." The captain nodded, and Neiluios bowed his head slightly before heading below deck. His family was already asleep when he entered their cabin. He quietly slid in beside Altesse and fell asleep quickly.

∞ **30** ∞
IN PURSUIT

THE small vessels rocked with each wave, water spraying onto the deck and creating a slick, almost oily surface. Most of the Laosians gathered on the upper deck, gazing at the turbulent sea, while only a few Loyals were visible. Many of them had never been at sea before and were likely staying out of sight.

Neiluios and Addident had arranged for all families with children around Neiaphi's age to be placed on the same boat. They believed that building friendships would be easier in such close quarters.

On the second day of the voyage, a group of young men, a mix of Laosians and Loyals, gathered near the ship's stern. Their laughter and shouts carried over the sound of the waves. Curious about the commotion, Neiluios made his way toward them. He soon saw that one of the Loyals was sparring with Greish, who was giving him a vigorous workout.

"Who's Greish sparring with?" Neiluios asked Chartis.

Chartis glanced up from his map, brushing his hair out of his eyes. "A Loyal named Bacceon, Sir. He claims to be the best with a sword and challenges anyone who thinks they can beat him. His twin brother, Aristas, says no one has ever bested him."

"I see. I hope this doesn't create a rift between them," Neiluios replied.

"No, Sir," a young man said, approaching Neiluios and Chartis. "My brother is smart enough to know when he's been bested. He'll handle it well. The real problem will be for me," he added with a snort.

"How so, Aristas?"

"He'll just insist that we practice more, that's all," Aristas replied. "Oh, look out, brother!"

Aristas's warning came too late. Greish had already swept Bacceon's feet out from under him, sending him crashing onto his back with a grunt. Greish raised his sword high and thrust it into the deck beside Bacceon's head. Bacceon shut his eyes and let go of his practice sword. With a nod of satisfaction, Greish withdrew his blade and extended a hand to help Bacceon up.

"We're very well matched. I'm glad we're on the same side. That could have gone either way," Greish said, grinning from ear to ear.

"No, you're better than me, but thank you. That's the best workout I've had in a long time. I'd be honored to spar with you again."

"I'd like that," Greish replied. "Not many among the guards can even come close to the skills of Andonis, let alone you."

"Hey, now. No need to insult me," Andonis called out with a grin. Greish shrugged, raising his arms in a playful apology.

"I will avenge you, brother," Aristas laughed, bowing theatrically to Greish before flourishing his practice sword.

"Let me grab some water, and then we'll see about that," Greish replied.

Satisfied that the mood remained light, Neiluios made his way to the bow of the ship. A smile crept onto his face when he spotted Neiaphi and Alexa sitting a short distance from the boys, quietly watching the sparring match.

The two girls huddled close, speaking in hushed tones.

"Wow, I've watched Bacceon spar for years and never seen him defeated. Greish must practice even more—and that's saying a lot. Bacceon trains nearly every waking hour," Alexa murmured, her voice filled with awe.

"I don't think he practices that much. Before coming here, he'd never even touched a sword. They're not used back home. He said it just came naturally to him."

"He's something," Alexa said, her voice full of admiration.

"Have you talked with him much?"

"A little. I'm hoping to speak with him again soon. If he agrees, I think he might be the one I present to my parents."

"Really? You picked quickly."

"Not many options," Alexa shrugged. "I thought I'd like Chartis more, but he's distracted and doesn't talk much. He's trying, but his heart just isn't in it."

Neiaphi sighed. "Yeah, I didn't think it would work out anyway. I want you to choose the one who makes you happiest."

"I think that might be Greish," Alexa said, a hint of excitement in her voice. "He's strong, smart, and handsome. I believe he'll go far wherever we're headed. I hope he makes it to Atlantis. I've always wanted to see the Great City."

Neiaphi tilted her head slightly. "I've never heard you call Atlantis the Great City. Is that common?"

"Oh, yes." Alexa nodded, "Atlantis is our founding city, the largest one I know of. Everything starts there, and according to what's written, everything will end there too."

"What do you mean everything will end there?" Neiaphi asked, a bit puzzled.

"It was written long ago that the Great City would fall someday, and with it, our society," Alexa explained, her tone softening. "But I don't believe it. The City has stood for so many years, and no one is strong enough to destroy it—not even the Society. They keep their distance from the areas the City can easily reach. They're cowards."

Neiaphi considered this. "It's strange to think of something so grand being vulnerable."

Alexa shrugged. "Maybe, but I think it's just a story. Atlantis has always been a beacon of strength. I can't imagine it ever falling."

"Where I come from, prophecies are mostly dismissed. But from what we've observed, the Society has a strong foothold here. If no one intervenes, they could pose a serious threat to Atlantis—unless it's far better fortified than any town I've encountered."

"Oh, Atlantis is filled with wonders and marvels beyond imagination. They're extremely selective about who they allow near the city, and their defenses are formidable."

"What do you mean, selective about whom they let near the city? How do they keep people away?"

"The city is located far from shore and is invisible from the mainland. Only authorized ships are permitted to approach the island. There's an outpost at The Gateway, and you must pass through it and undergo a test before you're granted access to the city. I've heard of people who tried to bypass the testing—they're never heard from again. Their ships are destroyed before they even catch a glimpse of the island. I hope we're worthy to gain entrance." Neiaphi noticed the awe in Alexa's eyes and silently hoped she was right.

"I never knew that. I always thought anyone could visit the city to help it thrive."

"That's all I've heard. I've never met anyone who's been there." Alexa shrugged.

Aristas and Andonis were now sparring, appearing evenly matched, though Aristas was already winded from his earlier bout with Greish. Neiaphi glanced around and noticed Chartis sitting with his back against the ship's outer railing, focused on his map. He occasionally looked up to watch the match. Greish and Bacceon were deep in conversation about Greish's sword, while Fotis stood nearby, looking completely bored and distant. He turned away from the sparring pair and stared out at the sea. The waters were calming, but the ship still rocked gently back and forth.

In the evening, everyone gathered in the main hold, socializing and eating their meals. Most retired early, as there was little to do aboard the ship.

Neiaphi lay wide awake in her hammock, the moans of several seasick passengers echoing through the ship. She groaned and buried her head under the blankets, but it did little to muffle the sounds. Eventually, exhaustion won out, and she drifted off to sleep.

Neiaphi watched in horror as their ships came under attack. She tried to scream for her father, but no sound escaped her lips. It felt as though she were an audience member, watching a play unfold—powerless to intervene.

Three smaller ships fired strange weapons at their vessels. Onboard the Laosian ships, men frantically handed out weapons to anyone willing to fight. She saw herself grab a bow, taking position beside her father, with Andonis on her other side. Captain Heu and Addident barked orders as the guards rushed to their posts.

The attacking ships withdrew, and the weapons were stowed away. The ship's captain appeared delighted, while the rest of the crew looked visibly relieved. The rest of the night passed uneventfully. Neiaphi noticed her father and Andonis talking quietly as they kept watch throughout the night.

As Neiaphi wandered the ship, she pondered what she was meant to see or learn from this dream.

Just as the sun rose over the still waters, attackers boarded the ships and took them by surprise. With their weapons stowed away, the Laosians and Loyals were defenseless. Those on the top deck were quickly herded into a tight group near the ship's center.

The men surrounding them closed in. Neiaphi heard screams from below deck, their haunting cries seeming both distant and uncomfortably close. Neiluios shoved Neiaphi behind him. The man nearest to him grinned cruelly and drove his sword into Neiluios's stomach. Neiluios grunted, his eyes widening in shock. His knees buckled, and he collapsed to the ground. Neiaphi's scream pierced the air, mingling with Neiluios's final, agonized cry.

Neiaphi woke up screaming.

"Neiaphi, wake up. It was just a dream. You're safe; you're here with us," her mother's soothing voice reassured her. Neiaphi reached out, clinging to her mother as her body trembled, tears streaming down her face. "It was just a dream," her mother repeated, her tone soft and gentle.

"No... No, it wasn't," Neiaphi choked out between sobs.

"What do you mean?" her mother asked, concern in her voice.

"I don't know. I have these dreams... I know I'm dreaming, but they don't feel like dreams. They feel real."

"What kind of dreams?" Neiluios asked, his brow furrowing.

"About the future—my future, our future. Oh, Father, you *died*," Neiaphi sobbed, reaching out to cling to him, her tears streaming down her face.

"I'm fine. I'm not dead; it was just a bad dream," Neiluios said, shaking her head. She struggled to find the words to explain how real the dreams felt.

She sighed deeply, sensing that her parents might not understand. "You're right. I was just so scared. It was only a dream. I feel better now." Neiluios gently patted her on the head and helped her settle back down.

"Try to get some more sleep. It'll be light soon," he said, leaning over to kiss her forehead.

"We'll talk tomorrow, okay?" Altesse said gently.

"Okay, Mother," Neiaphi replied. She lay awake the rest of the night, too afraid to fall back asleep.

"All hands on deck! All able-bodied men on deck! Hurry, hurry!" The shout echoed across the ship. Neiaphi leaped out of bed, quickly throwing on her cloak as she rushed from the cabin, beating her father to the deck. The ship shook and rocked violently. Neiluios followed close behind, sprinting to the upper deck.

Chaos erupted on deck. People darted around in confusion, and the air was filled with the terrified cries of women and children. At the stern, Addident stood surveying the scene. Neiaphi froze in horror as she spotted three boats closing in on them.

"Neiaphi, what's wrong?" Neiluios asked, his voice filled with concern. Neiaphi's face had turned ashen, and she was trembling uncontrollably. "Neiaphi?" He shook her gently. She turned her terrified gaze toward him.

"You're going to die," she whispered, her voice breaking as she sank to her knees.

"What are you talking about?" Neiluios knelt beside her, bewildered and alarmed.

"This is my dream. The ships chasing us—they're from the Society. We'll draw our weapons and wait for them to catch up. Then they'll back off, and we'll put the weapons away."

"That doesn't sound so bad. What else?" Neiluios asked. Greish approached, silently handing him a sword. Neiluios stared at the weapon, then glanced around the deck. Net was busy distributing weapons to anyone willing to take one.

"Those ships will back away, and we'll stow our weapons. But by morning, they'll catch up and board us. I... I saw them kill you," Neiaphi whispered, her breath quickening as she began to hyperventilate.

"Okay, calm down," Neiluios said, trying to soothe her. "This might just be a coincidence. Just because the ships are here doesn't mean the rest will happen."

"Please, Father, you have to believe me." Her voice was desperate. He nodded, helping her to her feet.

"Come on," he said quietly. They walked over to Addident in silence.

"The Society seems to have found us again," Addident said grimly. "The captain says we can't outrun them. We need to prepare to be boarded." He turned to Neiluios, his tone firm and commanding. "Do everything you can to keep them off the ship. I want several men stationed by the hatch to the lower decks. None of them are to get below. Understood?" Addident's tone was firm and commanding.

Greish quickly assembled a group of men and led them to the hatch while Andonis moved closer to Neiaphi and Neiluios, ready to protect them.

"Can I be of assistance, Sir?" Andonis asked.

"You can stay by my daughter's side and make sure she isn't hurt," Neiluios replied firmly.

"Please, we have to stop this before they board us," Neiaphi pleaded.

"Stay next to her and keep her safe," Neiluios instructed Andonis, dismissing Neiaphi's plea.

"Yes, Sir. You can rely on me," Andonis responded with determination.

Neiluios nodded and refocused on the approaching ships. Andonis stepped closer to Neiaphi, offering her a bow and quiver. She accepted them, glancing up at him. He appeared proud to be entrusted with her protection, but she shook her head, aware he had no idea of the danger to come—though she did. Relieved when he didn't follow, she took a small step away from him.

"I want all bows at the stern. Do not fire until I give the order," Addident commanded, his voice carrying across the deck.

The ships loomed ever closer, their dark silhouettes growing larger by the second. Neiaphi stood at the railing, her father on one side and Andonis on the other, her heart pounding in her chest. The wait was agonizing, each second stretching into eternity. She knew what was coming, tears streaming down her cheeks as she looked up at her father.

Then, unexpectedly, the pursuing ships slowed, no longer gaining on them. The captain of their ship stepped forward, his face twisted in a scowl. He raised his fist high and shook it at the enemy vessels.

Suddenly, the captain burst into a deep, throaty laugh. "They're backing off! They must see us as too great a threat. Good work, everyone." Indeed, the pursuing ships were retreating, gradually turning away as they distanced themselves.

Once the ships were far enough behind and withdrawing, the captain grunted, "Come on, let's stow those weapons and celebrate." Addident glanced at the other ships and saw their crews also putting away their weapons.

"Stow the weapons. The threat seems to have passed," Addident ordered.

Andonis placed a reassuring hand on Neiaphi's shoulder. She looked up at him, tears in her eyes. "The threat is over; you're safe now. It's time to be happy, not sad," he said gently.

"The threat is not over," she replied, turning to her father. "Father, please, you must believe me. Everything I've told you is true. Don't let them stow the weapons. We'll need them."

Neiluios met her gaze, his expression softening. He gently cupped her chin and wiped a tear from her cheek with his thumb.

"Addident, we need to talk in private. Hold off on stowing the weapons for now," Neiluios said firmly.

Net and Greish paused, glancing at Addident. He nodded, signaling them to wait, and led Neiluios aside for a private discussion.

"What's going on?" Andonis asked Neiaphi, his voice low and concerned.

She shook her head, unable to explain.

Neiluios and Addident huddled together, whispering urgently. Addident occasionally glanced at Neiaphi, his expression a mix of curiosity and skepticism. Neiaphi looked away, her face flushed with anxiety. She hoped he would believe her.

"Keep your weapons close tonight," Neiluios instructed. "Greish, signal the other ships to do the same."

"The ships are gone," the captain protested, frowning. "Your weapons aren't needed anymore."

"We've been tricked by the Society before," Neiluios said firmly. "We won't let it happen again. It doesn't bother you if we keep our weapons ready, just in case they decide to launch a night attack, does it?"

The captain harrumphed in frustration. "Of course not. Do as you like." He turned sharply and stormed away.

Addident gave Neiaphi a reassuring wink before refocusing on the last known position of the Society's ships.

"Thank you, Father, for believing me," Neiaphi said, her voice breaking as she burst into tears once more. Neiluios enveloped her in a tight embrace.

"It's going to be all right," he reassured her. "We'll stay vigilant tonight for any potential attacks. Keep dreaming, little one. Your dreams have helped us today."

"My dreams scare me," she admitted softly.

"What other dreams have you had? Have any of them come true?" Neiluios asked gently.

"I mostly dream about my future. They started on the ship coming here, but so far, only this one has come true," she replied.

"Then how did you know this one would?" Neiluios asked, his curiosity piqued.

"I don't really know. I have ordinary dreams—silly things—but these feel different, more real. It's hard to explain. In most of them, I'm much older. Sometimes, I'm in the dream, and other times, I'm just watching. Does that make any sense?" she asked, glancing around to ensure no one was overhearing their conversation. Andonis stood a short distance away, his back turned to them.

"Not really, but I'm here to listen to any dreams you want to share and help you make sense of them," Neiluios said gently. "I'm going to check on your mother. Why don't you see what Andonis needs?" He gave her a reassuring smile before walking away.

Neiaphi wiped her eyes and cheeks, taking a deep breath to steady herself. Once composed, she walked over to the railing where Andonis stood.

"Thanks," she said softly.

"For what?" he asked, turning to face her.

"For wanting to protect me."

"You don't have to thank me for that. It was nothing," he replied with a modest smile.

"No, it was more than that." She turned to him, genuinely looking at him for the first time. He was tall and handsome, and his eyes showed genuine warmth. "No one's really shown they cared about me since my friend Cret left. It means a lot to me."

"He went to the Processing Plant with his family, right?" Andonis asked.

"Yes," Neiaphi nodded, her voice tinged with sadness. "I miss him so much."

"You liked him more than just as a friend, didn't you?"

"I don't know... I think so," she admitted, her thoughts swirling. "Everything's happened so fast. I don't know what to think anymore."

"How did you know about the attack?" Andonis asked gently.

Neiaphi sank to the deck, sitting against the railing with her back to the sea. Slowly, Andonis lowered himself beside her, waiting for her to answer.

"I don't know about that either," Neiaphi confessed, her voice trembling. "I have dreams that feel so real, and this one actually was. I'm terrified; I don't know what will happen to us." Tears began to slip down her cheeks. "I'm sorry. I used to be able to keep my feelings in check. I had better control before we came here."

"It's okay to be scared," Andonis said softly, his voice full of understanding. "Our lives are in turmoil right now. All we can do is keep our families and friends close and pray to the Gods for protection."

"Gods? Do you really believe in them?" Neiaphi asked, her curiosity piqued.

"Well… I guess so," Andonis replied, shifting to face her. "I was raised to believe in them. It gives me peace of mind, knowing there's something greater than myself to seek guidance from. Haven't you ever prayed to something, anything, to find comfort?"

"I was taught to look within myself for answers," Neiaphi said thoughtfully. "I never considered praying to something I couldn't see. My people used to believe in gods, but those beliefs faded over time. I'll have to think about Poseidon's reasons for starting a religion here."

"This is nice," Andonis said with a slight grin, his tone softening as he looked at her.

"What is?" Neiaphi asked.

"Just sitting here, talking with you, without Alexa around," Andonis replied with a smile. "We should do this more often. I really want to get to know you better. You're intriguing. From the moment I saw you, I knew you would be."

"Thanks," she said, smiling shyly. "I've enjoyed this too."

"I see I have some competition, though," Andonis teased gently.

"Who? Do you mean Chartis? Sure, he likes me and has asked for me, and he's nice, but I don't see him that way."

"That's not who I meant," Andonis said, his tone more serious. "I mean Cret."

"Cret? He's not competition," Neiaphi said, her voice tinged with sadness. "I don't even know if he's alive. The camp we stayed at after we first arrived was attacked not long after we left, and no one knows if the Processing Plant was hit too."

"In your dreams, is he alive?" Andonis asked gently.

"Well, yes, but that doesn't mean he is," Neiaphi replied, uncertainty clouding her voice.

"After today, I'd guess he is," Andonis said, a hint of confidence in his tone. "But that doesn't deter me. I think you're worth fighting for."

"I don't know what you mean," Neiaphi said, looking at him with a puzzled expression. His goofy grin made her smile despite herself.

"That's okay," Andonis said warmly. "We'll be on this ship for a few more days, and I'd like to spend as much time with you as possible."

"I think I'd like that," she admitted. Andonis placed a hand on top of Neiaphi's and gave it a gentle squeeze.

Neiaphi sat on the deck, letting the gentle rocking of the ship lull her into a rare state of calm. The day was bright, the sky clear, with only a soft breeze stirring the sails. Since their first night aboard, the weather had been unusually pleasant—a blessing, she thought. Yet, despite the fair conditions, there was an undercurrent of unease among the crew. They muttered about the 'cursed voyage,' casting wary glances toward the horizon.

Weapons remained at the ready, day and night, as the Society's vessels continued to tail them, lingering just out of reach. It felt as if the enemy ships were waiting for a signal to attack, though it never came. The ship's captain scowled whenever he caught sight of one of his passengers armed and on high alert, clearly displeased with the constant tension.

The day after the encounter, Neiaphi spent her time playing with Cypress and chatting with Alexa and Andonis. Chartis tried to approach her several times, but Andonis's steady presence seemed to keep him at a distance. With little to do aboard the ship, Greish, Bacceon, Aristas, and Andonis took to sparring several times a day, their matches providing a welcome distraction from the looming threat that followed them across the sea.

On the fifth day at sea, the distant shoreline finally appeared. The spirits of everyone on board lifted at the sight of land, though an undercurrent of nervousness was palpable. Tomorrow, they would land—but they would also flee for their lives. The Society's ships were closing in once more. Addident and Neiluios worked tirelessly, coordinating the three vessels, determined to expedite the unloading process. They knew that, this time, they would have even less time to get everything off the ships.

"Father, how do they keep finding us so quickly?" Neiaphi asked, watching as their belongings were hurriedly packed and brought to the top deck. Cleop was helping Altesse soothe the boys, while Net wrestled a bag from Cypress, who had stubbornly claimed it as his own.

"I've been trying to figure that out," Neiluios replied, his brow furrowed in thought. "They must be using some of our own technology against us."

"But the Society despises technology. Why would they use it to catch us?" Neiaphi asked, puzzled.

"I think they believe that using a bit of technology to catch us is better than letting us reach Atlantis. They seem truly fearful of what we represent," Neiluios replied.

"But we didn't bring any new technology with us. We're no threat to them."

"Ideas and thoughts can be powerful weapons," Neiluios said, his voice tinged with seriousness. "We've taken many who were loyal to the Society, and without even trying, we've swayed their way of thinking. They've seen beyond the twisted teachings of the Society and, for the first time, are thinking for themselves."

"Why do people so willingly accept the teachings of the Society, like Hepluosis?" Neiaphi asked, her curiosity piqued.

"I think I can shed some light on that, Sir," Net interjected. "The Society offers easy answers to those who prefer not to think for themselves. When they take over a town, they seize control of everything—government, regulations, trade, you name it. They promise order and security in exchange for unquestioning obedience. For many, it's simpler to follow than to resist.

"Everything is divided equally among the townspeople; it seems fair as long as you adhere to their rules," Net continued. "But if you question or defy them, they expel you from the town. Most people find it easier to accept their teachings. It's a safe environment where everyone has food and shelter—at least at first. But only the leaders get rich, and they intend to keep it that way. Weak-minded and power-hungry individuals often fall in line easily."

"Well, that explains Hepluosis," Neiaphi said, "but you were among them, Net. You're neither weak-minded nor power-hungry. Why did you follow them?"

"I grew up with their teachings," Net replied. "It wasn't until I met you and your family that I truly began to think for myself, to consider what I wanted out of life. I reflected on what I had seen and looked beyond the surface. I owe you all my life. Thank you," he added, with Cleop nodding in agreement.

"No thanks needed, Net. It's been a pleasure knowing you, and we're honored to have helped you," Altesse said warmly.

"Thank you, ma'am. I hope we can get you all away from the Society and safely to Atlantis," Net replied earnestly. "That's what we're all hoping for," Neiluios added with a nod.

∞ 31 ∞
WOLVES

ADDIDENT ordered the ships to be beached on the approaching shoreline. The surrounding terrain was cloaked in darkness, the absence of the moon making their task even more challenging. Unloading the ships was difficult, with only a few hidden torches to avoid detection by the looming Society vessels. With a bit of luck, the Society wouldn't find the ships until they had already departed.

Sensing the tension, the animals stomped the ground nervously as the servants hastily hitched them to the wagons. Addident watched proudly as everyone worked with remarkable speed, unloading the ships with quiet efficiency. Without a word, the group began moving inland, away from the Altaian Sea, slipping into the night as they put more distance between themselves and their pursuers.

Nervous eyes scanned the darkness, shadows dancing with every movement. The only visible threat was the Society ships in the distance, their decks glowing with the light of many torches. The group moved cautiously, sticking to the shadows. Silence was their ally as they increased the gap between themselves and the shoreline. The faint sounds of the Society's search grew dimmer. Urgency and fear drove them forward into the unknown terrain ahead.

They traveled through the night and well into the next day. Progress slowed as exhaustion set in. Near midday, Addident finally called for a rest.

"We'll stay here through the evening and continue in the morning," he announced. "We'll split into three smaller groups, staying within a couple of hours' ride of each other to avoid being noticed. The next outpost is Chrysafi. Aner mentioned they have a large gold-mining operation near the city of Neospolis, not far from the outpost. We won't stay long. We need to reach Atlantis before winter arrives."

"How long do we have before winter comes?" Addident asked. "A couple of months," Cham replied. "The planting season has passed. We're now in the third of the four growing months. After that, the harvest months will be upon us. The weather will turn colder, and the winter months will arrive. We'll need to stay in or near a city through the winter, then continue as soon as the planting months return. I want us to travel as much as possible before winter. We'll be stalled for several months and can rest plenty then. The sooner we reach Atlantis, the safer you'll all be. Rest today and be ready to move out at first light."

Neiaphi stared into the flickering flames, her thoughts as restless as the wolves howling in the distance. Their chilling cries seemed to echo from all directions, unsettling her. She pulled her cloak tighter, trying to stave off both the cold and the rising fear gnawing at her. The sliver of moonlight offered little comfort, leaving the woods around them cloaked in darkness. The soft nickers from the horses and donkeys provided a small sense of security, reminding her she wasn't entirely alone in the night. Yet sleep remained elusive, her mind tangled in thoughts as the sounds of the night pressed in around her.

Cypress, her loyal companion, lifted his head and let out a soft woof in response to the distant howls. Neiaphi reached down, gently patting his head until he settled back into a light sleep. She returned her gaze to the fire, willing herself to find some measure of peace, but just as her eyelids began to grow heavy, a new sound from the surrounding forest jolted her awake. Footfalls—faint but unmistakable—rustled through the underbrush. Neiaphi sprang to her feet, and Cypress leapt beside her, her ears pricked and her muscles tense.

"Hush, be quiet," she whispered to him, her voice barely rising above the crackling fire. Shielding her eyes from the fire's glow, she peered into the dense shadows beyond. Seconds ticked by, each one heavier than the last until she finally spotted them—several pairs of golden eyes glimmering from the darkness. A low, haunting howl followed, this time much closer. Eerily close.

"Neiaphi, are you out here?" Neiluios asked softly as he emerged from their tent.

"Quiet," she whispered urgently. "There's something out there."

Neiluios froze, his voice dropping to a whisper. "What's out there?"

"I heard footfalls," she replied, her eyes scanning the darkened forest. "Then I saw several pairs of golden eyes staring at me. But when you stepped out, they vanished."

A howl pierced the night, closer than before, quickly followed by another. Within moments, the once-quiet evening erupted into a cacophony of howling wolves. The deafening sound came from all directions, surrounding the camp. Men rushed out of their tents, weapons in hand, their eyes wide with fear as they scanned the darkness. The eerie, relentless howling drowned out any cries of fear or distress.

Addident and Cham hurried over to Neiluios.

"How long has this been going on?" Addident asked.

"Only a few moments," Neiluios replied. "Neiaphi was by the fire when she saw several pairs of eyes watching her and heard footfalls. They scattered when I came out. Any idea how many there are?"

"I'd estimate hundreds by the sound," Cham said loudly. "I've never heard such a noise. I didn't know they gathered in such numbers. Let's bank all the fires to keep them away. No one leaves the camp without an armed escort."

"Agreed," Neiluios and Addident said in unison.

Within moments, the camp was bathed in the light of the fires. Everyone was awake now. The howling continued for about an hour before stopping abruptly. Neiaphi sat beside her father, her eyes wide and alert. As the sun began to rise, the howling resumed briefly but was short-lived and came from a greater distance.

The camp was quickly dismantled after the morning meal. Addident and Cham led the first group, setting off early. Amplios, Aner, and Baccus took charge of the second group, departing mid-morning. Neiluios, Mace, and Paragon led the third group, moving out in the early afternoon.

The Laosian officials and guards were evenly divided among the three groups, with scouts assigned to travel between them throughout the day to ensure they stayed on course and remained safe. They planned to travel until dusk each day and set up camp. The journey to Outpost Chrysafi was estimated to take two days.

"That's interesting," Neiaphi said, adjusting her saddle. "So, Chrysafi means 'gold' and Neospolis means 'New City.' It's good to know these details. They might be useful as we move forward."

Alexa nodded, still smiling. "Yes, understanding the local language and culture is always helpful. It might give us an edge in navigating new places. I once met a traveler who claimed to speak six different languages."

"Back home, we have a few dialects, but the main language is quite consistent. It's common to know a second dialect, especially if you travel a lot or are involved in trade. But hearing multiple languages from a peddler? That's intriguing. Did he say which languages he spoke?" Neiaphi asked.

"He said things in all six, but I don't know if he was saying real words or not."

Both girls burst into laughter as they mounted their horses.

"So, only one language on the entire planet of Romota?" Alexa asked.

"Well, centaurs and giants have their own languages," Neiaphi said.

Alexa turned in her saddle to stare at Neiaphi. "What's a centaur?" she asked slowly. "I can imagine what a giant might be, but I've never heard of a centaur before."

"You haven't? Oh, I didn't realize. I assumed you knew all about us and our world. My mistake. A centaur is a remarkable creature. It has a horse's body, but from the torso up, it looks like a human."

"That's quite strange," she said.

"A giant is indeed large—very large—and they resemble humans, though their teeth are different, and some have only one eye. They're not actually human, though. Some can be quite friendly, but others have a temper. We were told that Poseidon brought centaurs, giants, griffins, and pegasi with him. I'm not sure if there were any other creatures he brought."

"I've learned about pegasi from Poseidon's history lessons but never heard of a griffin."

"Oh, those are beautiful creatures too. Griffins have the body of a lion but the front legs, head, and neck of an eagle. They also have powerful eagle wings; you can train them to fly with you. Cret's family had one named Bol, and I had the chance to ride him a few times. It was an exhilarating experience."

"Have you ever ridden a pegasus? I've always dreamed of riding one," she asked.

"No, they went extinct long before I was born. It's been a dream of mine as well. I hope there's still one in Atlantis that I can at least see."

"That would be wonderful."

"Are you girls all ready?" Paragon asked.

"Yes, Father," Alexa replied.

"Yes, sir. Could Alexa ride with my family, sir?" Neiaphi inquired.

"I don't see why not. Just make sure you don't wander off."

"We won't," they said in unison.

By mid-afternoon, the third group was on their way. They traveled steadily and comfortably until the sun began to set. Since they had left late in the day, they didn't cover much distance. When they stopped, the first scout arrived to check on them. He reported that everything was going smoothly with the other groups and departed as swiftly as he had come.

As soon as the sun had fully set and darkness began to envelop the camp, the distant howls of wolves echoed through the night. Fires were quickly lit, encircling the camp to keep the wolves at bay.

Alexa and Neiaphi huddled together around their family's shared cooking fire.

"Well, at least there aren't as many as last night," Alexa remarked.

"Not yet, anyway," Neiaphi replied.

"Oh, don't say that. I've never been so scared. The howling was deafening."

"They were so close. I heard their footsteps and saw their eyes staring at me. Thankfully, my father exited the tent, and they ran off."

"How terrifying. I hope they don't get that close tonight," Alexa said, hugging herself tightly.

"Me too," Neiaphi agreed.

"Come on, girls, you need to try to get some sleep," Net said, peering from the tent. "I've made some tea that should help."

"Yes, Net," they replied in unison.

The howling continued throughout the evening, but it sounded like typical hunting calls—single howls occasionally answered by one or two others. It was nothing like the previous night, much to everyone's relief. Clouds gathered during the night, and a brief shower fell on the sleeping travelers.

At first light, the camp was packed up, and they set out once more. The sky was overcast, and the ground was soft from the rain. Neiaphi and Alexa rode together in silence for a while. Alexa then pointed to the ground between their horses, where large wolf prints were clearly visible in the fresh mud. The tracks led toward the camp and then away again.

"Have you ever seen paw prints that big before?" Neiaphi asked.

"No, I haven't," Alexa replied. "My grandfather once took me on a hunting trip and taught me how to distinguish different paw prints. We came across several wolf prints, and he mentioned one was the largest he had ever seen. These are easily twice that size."

"Wolves on this side of the Altaian Sea must be bigger. I hope they keep their distance," Neiaphi said.

The wolf tracks seemed to be following the other two groups. Faint prints were visible beneath the second group's tracks, with more recent prints on top of theirs. Several well-armed guards stayed a short distance behind, scanning the surrounding forest for any wolves. If there were any, they remained hidden. Scouts came and went in pairs throughout the day, reporting that the other groups feared wolves were stalking them, but none were ever seen.

The travelers made camp one last time before reaching Chrysafi. Although the wolves were out again, their howls seemed more distant.

"Everyone halt and stay here. The first group is near Chrysafi, and Cham has ridden ahead to check if it's safe for us to proceed," a scout announced. They had been traveling since sunrise, and now the sun was directly overhead. Neiaphi and Alexa took the chance to dismount and stretch their legs.

The sound of steel clanging against steel echoed through the still afternoon as Andonis and Greish sparred a short distance from the others.

"Those two never stop. What is it with men on this planet and swords?" Neiaphi asked.

"Swords are a means of defending oneself and one's family. All able-bodied men know how to use a sword—it's just a part of life," Alexa explained.

"I keep forgetting that things are more primitive and barbaric here. Sorry," Neiaphi said.

"Don't worry about it; you haven't been here that long. Come on, let's go watch," Alexa replied.

Neiaphi nodded, and Cypress happily bounded after them, chasing butterflies along the way. Andonis seemed to be improving; Greish only barely managed to best him.

"Good match," Greish said, helping Andonis up. "You'll be able to beat Bacceon the next time we see him."

"I don't know about that. You barely beat him. I'm not sure how I could," Andonis said.

"I'll teach you. I studied his techniques when he sparred with you and Aristas and noticed a weakness. He needs someone to expose that weakness, or it could cost him his life," Greish replied.

"Hello, Neiaphi, Alexa. How long have you been sitting there?" Andonis asked, noticing them.

"Not too long," Neiaphi replied, feeling her cheeks flush.

"Long enough to see you get planted," Alexa teased with a grin.

"Very funny. I'd like to see you try," Andonis retorted as he sat on the ground. Cypress immediately ran over and jumped into his lap. "Nice to see you too, Cypress. Get down, you silly puppy."

Greish placed his sword next to his pack and sat down beside Alexa. "I can't wait until we reach Atlantis," he said.

"I can't wait either," Alexa said excitedly. "Ever since my parents mentioned that we had the chance to see The Great City, it's all I've been able to think about."

"What do you two hope to do once we reach the City?" Neiaphi asked the boys.

"I'll probably be assigned to the guard posts," Greish replied. "I hope to be stationed as close to the Palace as possible."

"My father was a senator back home, so I'd assume he'll seek a similar position in Atlantis, and I'll continue my training for the same role. Our family also owned a large vineyard that our servants managed. My father brought several small vine stems with us and plans to acquire land to start a new vineyard. I was responsible for managing the servants who handled the cultivation and harvesting of the grapes," Andonis continued. "Now that my schooling is nearly complete, I plan to venture into the city and find work if necessary. Atlantis is a large city, so there should be plenty of opportunities. How about you two? Any plans?"

"I will marry, and my husband will provide for me and our children," Alexa replied, keeping her eyes downcast.

"I don't know. I haven't given much thought to the future yet," Neiaphi admitted.

"Who do you plan on marrying, Alexa?" Andonis asked with a wink.

Alexa's cheeks flushed bright red. "I have someone in mind, but I won't tell you, Andonis." She glanced at Greish from the corner of her eye to gauge his reaction. He looked unconcerned but was smiling. When their eyes met, she quickly looked away. Neiaphi smiled, knowing Alexa had feelings for Greish and suspecting he might feel the same, though he hadn't spoken of it yet.

"Neiaphi, we haven't trained with Cypress in a while. How about a quick lesson?" Greish suggested.

"Sure. I'll be back in a bit, Alexa," Neiaphi said.

"Andonis and I will stay here and watch. Right?" Alexa asked.

"Why not? I don't have anything else to do," Andonis replied.

Neiaphi and Greish walked a short distance away, out of earshot of Alexa and Andonis.

"So, what do you think about Alexa?" Neiaphi asked.

"She's nice and very pretty. Why do you ask?" Greish replied, giving Cypress a few hand signals. The dog obeyed promptly.

"She likes you but isn't sure if you like her. Do you?" Neiaphi asked.

"She likes me? How do you know?" Greish asked, surprised.

"She's told me. Do you like her?" Neiaphi inquired.

"Of course I do. But she doesn't know that?" Greish replied.

"Well, she thinks you like her, but she's unsure how you feel," Neiaphi said.

"Am I the person she has in mind?" Greish asked slowly.

"Would you like that?" Neiaphi asked.

"Yes, very much," Greish replied.

"Then yes, you are the one she has in mind. But don't tell her I told you. She wanted you to make the first move. You should talk to her about becoming promised if you're serious."

"I'll think about it. I haven't given much thought to my future here either. Everything has happened so fast."

"Can I ask you something?" Neiaphi asked.

"Go right ahead," Greish replied.

"Something has been bothering me since we first started training Cypress."

"What is it?" Greish asked, calling Cypress to sit beside him.

"Why were you friends with Hepluosis? You two are nothing alike."

"I've been thinking about that a lot," Greish said. "Hepluosis was different back then. The things I've learned about him from others since then really disturb me. I saw glimpses of the Hepluosis you knew when we followed you and Cret to the Criminal Camp. He befriended one of the criminals and helped him regain his memory."

"You followed us? You never mentioned it," Neiaphi said, surprised.

Greish shrugged.

"Why did Hepluosis help a criminal regain his memory? That could be very dangerous. Do you know who chose the criminal as a servant?"

"Hepluosis did," Greish replied. "He said you never know when a criminal might come in handy. Six never told us what he did to end up there."

"Six? That's an unusual name," Neiaphi remarked.

"That was the number he was assigned when he arrived at the camp. He never revealed his real name, even after he supposedly regained his memory," Greish explained.

"Maybe he doesn't truly remember. Perhaps he just said he did to stop you from trying to make him recall," Neiaphi suggested.

Greish thought for a moment. "That's possible, I suppose. I'm just concerned about what Hepluosis might want to use him for. At the time, I thought he was just messing around, but I've since seen a different side of him. I hope the Society can keep him in check."

"I think they'll most likely use him," Neiaphi said. "Consider this: they have the perfect asset. The Society believes their way is the only right way and sees themselves as superior to us. Hepluosis thinks he's better than anyone. He'll rise quickly in their ranks. I suspect they'll use him to help undermine us. He knows all about us because he was once one of us, and he despises us. He's the perfect candidate. My father shouldn't have allowed his father to volunteer at the plant, but we didn't know about the Society back then."

"You make a good point. He'll make a formidable soldier for them. I've trained him well with a sword—he was a fast learner. I just hope we never cross paths again," Greish said.

"What will you do if that happens and he's with the Society?" Neiaphi asked.

"I'll kill him," Greish replied sternly. Neiaphi met his gaze, looking into his hazel eyes. He returned her stare, his eyes intense and unyielding. Neiaphi eventually looked away, breaking the stare.

As dusk approached, campfires sprang to life around the camp. "Well, I'd better head back," Neiaphi said, glancing over at Net, sitting a short distance away. He was rarely far from her these days.

Greish walked Alexa back to her family while Andonis accompanied Neiaphi to hers. "That was quite a long conversation you and Greish had," Andonis remarked.

"Are you worried?" Neiaphi asked.

"No, of course not. Why would I be?" Andonis replied, a bit flustered.

Neiaphi giggled at his reaction. "I was asking him if he liked Alexa."

"Does he?"

"He says he does and is considering asking her about becoming promised. I think she'll be pleased."

"Have you thought any more about us?" Andonis asked.

"A little, but I still think it's too soon. One of my dreams told me to wait until we reach a certain place, so I want to see if that comes true before making any decisions," Neiaphi explained.

"A dream told you to wait until you reach this place? Where is it, and how will you know when you get there?" Andonis asked, puzzled.

Neiaphi sighed. "The woman in my dream told me I would just know when we were close. She said I would recognize the moment. I understand how that might sound, but I've come to trust my dreams. I need to see if this one comes true. I hope you understand." She looked up at Andonis, trying to gauge his reaction. He met her gaze with a serious expression.

"I can wait. I'd like to see if your dream comes true as well," Andonis said. "What did this woman say to you?"

"She said she could help me choose. And she mentioned we had other things to discuss. She said..." Neiaphi hesitated.

"What did she say?" Andonis asked.

"Oh, I feel silly repeating it," Neiaphi replied.

"Don't be. I want to know," he insisted.

"She said I was destined for great things," Neiaphi admitted.

"I think she might be right. You're very intelligent for your age and quite pretty," Andonis said.

Neiaphi turned her head, her cheeks flushing red. Andonis smiled and gently patted her shoulder.

Net was sitting by the fire when Andonis and Neiaphi arrived. After exchanging goodnights, Andonis left. Neiaphi walked over to the fire and sat down next to Net.

"He seems like a nice young man," Net commented.

"Yes, he is," Neiaphi replied.

"He seems to like you," Net observed.

"He does," Neiaphi confirmed.

Net smiled. "Do you like him?"

Neiaphi sighed. "I don't know, Net. He's nice and handsome, but I'm not sure if he's right for me. It feels strange even considering the possibility of marrying someone from this planet."

"Why is that?" Net asked.

"Don't take this the wrong way, but before we came here, my teacher asked if we were excited about meeting one of The People. That's what you're called back on, Romota. I shuddered at the very thought of meeting—please excuse the term—'apemen.'"

"Apemen?" Net asked, puzzled.

"Oh, it's not important," Neiaphi said quickly. "While we were still on the ship, I had a dream about meeting one of The People. I thought he was handsome in the dream, but then I started to scream. I had very wrong notions about what to expect when we arrived. I realize now how mistaken I was. Most of the people we've met here, like you, Andonis, and Alexa, have been very kind. We're fortunate to have made such good friends."

"I'm glad we're not the 'apemen' you feared," Net said with a smile. "I admit, I was nervous about meeting you too. I'd heard stories about the evil ones from the sky for most of my life. When I was selected as the first servant, I was terrified. I didn't know what to expect from you. I didn't even know if you would look human. When I met your father, he seemed decent enough, though a bit wary of me. But seeing you, your mother, and how warmly you all greeted each other—and all the other friendly faces of your fellow travelers—made me realize that what I'd been taught was flawed. That's when I decided to prove myself to you and your family."

"It has been such a pleasure having you with us, Net," Neiaphi said warmly.

"Thank you, little miss," Net replied with a smile.

At that moment, Neiluios and Altesse arrived, having been out walking around the camp with the twins. Cleop emerged from the tent and ushered the twins inside.

Just as Neiluios and Altesse settled next to the fire, the quiet of the night was shattered by the eerie howls of hundreds of wolves. Neiaphi and Altesse jumped, clutching at Neiluios. Net dashed into the tent, grabbed their swords, and handed one to Neiluios. Neiaphi shielded her eyes from the firelight, her gaze drawn to the golden eyes glaring back from the edges of the surrounding forest.

"Can you see them? They're everywhere," Neiaphi whispered, her voice trembling.

"I see them," Neiluios said firmly. "Altesse, you and Neiaphi get inside the tent."

"But Father, we can help," Neiaphi protested.

"Now, child, don't argue with me. Altesse, please get inside the tent," Neiluios said firmly.

Altesse grabbed Neiaphi's arm and pulled her into the tent. Inside, Cleop was cradling the twins, trying to comfort them. Altesse took one of the twins from her and settled onto her bedroll. Neiaphi sat beside her, both trying to find reassurance in each other's presence.

"What do they want, Mother?" Neiaphi asked, her voice quivering.

"I wish I knew, dear. I wish I knew," Altesse replied softly.

"I've heard stories about wolves stealing infants and raising them as their own. They say that's the only time wolves will get close to humans—when they're taking children," Cleop said quietly, hugging the infant in her arms a little tighter.

"That's just talk, I'm sure. My husband and Net will protect us. Don't worry," Altesse said, wrapping her arm around Neiaphi and pulling her close.

The wolves continued their haunting howls throughout the evening. Neiluios and Net remained by the fire until the sun began to crest the horizon. Some wolves ventured close to the tents, lingering just out of the firelight, but none crossed into the circle of flames. Net observed their size as they passed by. They were the largest wolves he had ever seen or heard of, and there were so many. Such a large gathering was unprecedented, but this was his first experience on this side of the Altaian Sea. It might be normal here; he resolved to ask the first person he saw about it.

As the sun rose, the wolves dispersed, and the men retreated to their tents for some much-needed rest. By midday, scouts from Addident's group arrived, greeted by a small delegation of Chrysafi citizens who reported that it was safe for small groups to enter the town to gather supplies.

"Did anyone see the wolves last night?" Neiluios asked the lead scout.

"We heard them howling all night, Sir, but none were spotted. Did you encounter any problems?"

"The wolves got close to our camp, but it seems none entered. Please deliver this report to Addident." Neiluios handed the scout a carefully folded letter. The scout accepted it, placing it securely in his pack. He snapped to attention and signaled the other scouts to mount up.

"Addident asked that you stop by his tent when you pass by on your way to Chrysafi."

"Tell him I'll see him soon," Neiluios replied.

The scouts departed at a quick trot, leaving a cloud of dust in their wake. Neiluios turned to the small group that had gathered around him. "All right," he began, "we need to organize who will go into Chrysafi and what supplies are most urgent."

The group huddled closer, the morning light casting long shadows as they discussed their needs.

∞ 32 ∞
REPAIRS

SEPHI and Sareen returned home from the local market, accompanied by their male servant, Camtis. The village near the Processing Plant was small yet self-sustaining, where outsiders were met with suspicion. Adapting to this new life had been a slow and difficult process for them, with the locals offering little in the way of tolerance or assistance. Despite Sephi's efforts to blend in and avoid trouble, Crelian had already been informed of her "misconduct" on multiple occasions.

Crelian had more than enough to worry about. He and Cret left by dawn and often did not return until well after sunset. Weeks ago, Sephi had stopped asking Crelian about his daily activities. Each time she inquired, he would simply shake his head, kiss her on the cheek, and quietly leave the room.

The village buzzed with activity as preparations for an evening ceremony honoring a God whose name Sephi had forgotten were underway. The sheer number of Gods, each with their own cycle of celebrations, made it difficult to keep track. Villagers hurried about, intent on their tasks, with much to do and little time to finish it all.

Sephi hoped they would soon be finished with their work here so they could begin the journey to Atlantis. Even if they had stayed with the main group, she knew there was always a chance they might have been left behind in a village if they were needed. But at least then, they would have seen more of this planet. So far, all they had encountered were endless trees stretching as far as the eye could see.

"Do you think Father and Cret will join us tonight, or will they be working late again?" Sareen asked.

"Your father wasn't sure. He'd forgotten about the ceremony tonight. Are men and women allowed to be together for this event?"

"Yes, Hebe, the goddess of youth, is a minor deity and isn't very strict about such things."

"I'm so relieved you remember all that we're taught. I can hardly keep track," Sephi said, smiling at her daughter.

"You'll catch on soon enough. Just give it time," Sareen reassured her.

Crelian sat at his desk in a cramped room adjacent to the Processing Plant's control room, thumbing through the daily reports. He had finally pieced together that the plant received shipments from an undisclosed source. This facility mixed various liquids and pumped them into underground caverns. The nature of these liquids remained a mystery to him, but the small insights he had gained were proving valuable in addressing the issues the locals had been unable to resolve.

The plant featured several holding tanks for different liquids, each equipped with pumps that transported the substances to the mixing room. Once mixed, the liquid was sent via additional pumps to underground caverns located miles away. From the maps Crelian had managed to glimpse, the most distant cavern was several hundred miles to the north and buried even deeper underground. The plant grappled with a problem involving a series of bulge pumps designed to transfer the remaining sludge out of the mixing tanks. Crelian and his team were working on adjusting the composition of the final liquid to ensure that the sludge could be moved through the main pump more effectively. Unfortunately, this adjustment was proving to be more challenging than simply repairing the bulge pumps.

A knock echoed through the small room, and Crelian looked up from his reports. Cret stepped inside with a wide grin.

"Father, we seem to be making some progress," Cret said, beaming.

"Finally. How much longer do you think it will take?"

"I'd estimate about a week or two at most. Most of the liquid is now flowing through the main pump, and we've removed around 85% of the sludge."

"That's excellent news," Crelian replied, visibly relieved.

"I've been trying to figure out how to get the remaining sludge out of the tanks, but I don't think it's possible without the bulge pumps."

"Have you come up with any solutions?"

"Just one. We need to mix the remaining sludge with another liquid to thin it out enough for the bulge pumps to handle."

"That should work, but we'll need to repair the bulge pumps first."

"We can start on that first thing tomorrow. I think it'll be easier and faster this way. I doubt we can alter the mix any further."

"Good. Inform the crew. Let's start on the bulge pumps tonight, though. And if you see Japster, send him my way—I have an errand for him."

"Yes, Sir." Cret departed, leaving Crelian staring after his son for a moment. Cret was learning quickly, starting to take charge of the other men. He had the qualities of a natural-born leader—most of the crew followed him without question, except for Japster and Hepluosis.

Japster and his son Hepluosis were troublemakers, always scheming to curry favor with the Locals. Crelian had long suspected that Japster was deliberately sabotaging their progress, ensuring they'd be stuck here longer, but he lacked the evidence to prove it. He eagerly anticipated the day they could leave this village, the plant, and, with any luck, Japster and his family behind.

A light, careless knock sounded on the door. "Come in, Japster," Crelian called out.

Japster entered, looking amazed. "How did you know it was me?"

"Lucky guess. Sit down, please," Crelian replied.

Japster stood for a moment, then took a seat in the only other chair in the cramped room. He glanced around, noting the small desk piled high with reports, two chairs, and a short bookcase overflowing with more papers. The air felt thick in the confined space. Shifting in his seat, Japster caused the chair to groan under his weight. "I need you to ride back to Camp Roma and deliver a message to Deleon."

"Deliver a message? I'm not a messenger. Send one of them," Japster protested.

Crelian, who had been focused on the reports in front of him, slowly lifted his gaze, his eyes locking onto Japster with a deliberate intensity. "This isn't a task for just anyone. I don't trust the messengers with something this important. I need one of our own—someone I can rely on. Can I trust you?"

Japster glanced down at his hands, then quickly met Crelian's unwavering gaze. "Of course, you can trust me. That's a stupid question. What does the message say?"

"It's not for your eyes," Crelian replied, his voice firm. "That's why I need someone I can trust. You are to deliver it directly to Deleon and place it in his hands, no matter how long it takes to find him. Do you understand?"

"Sure, I understand. When do I leave?" Japster asked, his tone steady.

"In a moment. You'll need to pack quickly and leave immediately," Crelian replied, not missing a beat as he pulled out a clean piece of parchment. "You can take your son or your servant with you if you wish." He scribbled a quick message, then rolled up the parchment with practiced efficiency. Reaching into the desk drawer, Crelian retrieved a stick of wax. Holding it above a lit candle, he let the wax drip onto the rolled parchment. Once the wax had melted, he pressed a stamp into it, sealing the document with an official mark.

"Here's the message," Crelian said, handing the parchment to Japster. Japster examined the sealed document with a scowl.

"You wrote that pretty fast for something so important," he remarked.

"Important messages don't need to be long or flowery. Deleon prefers them short and to the point. You will deliver this to him and wait for a reply," Crelian said, settling back into his chair and returning to his reports, signaling the end of their conversation.

Japster stared at him, muttered something under his breath, and then left the room. Crelian watched him go, a smile tugging at the corners of his mouth. This should keep Japster occupied for at least a week, if he took his son with him, all the better. It would allow Crelian's team to complete the repairs without interference.

Crelian sighed, glancing down at the stack of reports cluttering his desk. The locals inundated him with seemingly meaningless paperwork, all unrelated to the repairs. His primary task was to distill these reports into a single summary for Sen.

Standing up to stretch his legs and back, he decided the reports could wait a little longer. He left the room to find Cret and assess their repair progress.

The pumps were screeching and squeaking, struggling to remove the remaining liquid from the holding tanks. Crelian walked onto the catwalk above and looked down. Cret had been right—the majority of the sludge was gone. Suddenly, the pumps abruptly stopped, and a loud bell chimed as fresh liquid began rushing into the tanks.

The mixing augers began to churn slowly. It was remarkable what the locals could achieve with minimal technology and machinery. The augers were powered by burros turning a large wheel, while the pump engine was operated by solar power. As the liquid flow ceased, another bell chimed, signaling that the pumps had come online again. Crelian looked down and saw Cret waving at him. He smiled and made his way to the lower level.

"Everything seems to be working well. Good job, everyone," Crelian praised.

"So far, everything is running smoothly. We're about to activate the bulge pumps," Cret explained. "Last time, the pressure buildup caused a jet of sludge to shoot up and cover the catwalks. I figured you wouldn't want to be up there if that happened again."

"Thanks for the heads-up. That would have been quite a mess." Crelian patted Cret on the back.

"Here we go. Let's hope this works this time." Cret flipped a switch and held his breath. The bulge pumps roared to life with a loud grind and clank. The sludge jetted upward but stayed clear of the catwalks this time. The liquid-sludge mix started to swirl, and the pumps began to draw the sludge out of the tanks. But just as they picked up speed, the pumps ground to a halt. Cret threw his hands in the air in frustration. "What now? Will these infernal pumps ever work consistently?"

"I'm confident you'll have them working by the end of the week. Cret, I need to speak with you privately," Crelian said.

"Yes, Sir." Cret turned to Georgios. "We need to disassemble the pump and check the tubes from each tank. They might be clogged again."

"Yes, Sir," Georgios replied with a nod.

Crelian and Cret walked a short distance away, out of earshot. "I've sent Japster to Camp Roma with a message for Deleon. He should be gone for about a week. I told him he could take Hepluosis with him if he wanted. Hopefully, he did."

"When is Japster leaving?"

"I instructed him to leave immediately."

"In that case, he won't be taking Hepluosis with him. He's currently feeding the burros."

"Feeding the burros! How did you manage that?"

"Hecto is supervising him now. He seems to listen to Hecto, albeit reluctantly, with only minimal complaints. Hecto promised him a day off tomorrow if he completes everything today. Surprisingly, Hepluosis has been quite helpful and quiet."

"I hope that's harmless. Keep me updated on any developments. Clean out the tubes and inspect the pumps tonight, but hold off on running them again until tomorrow. Make sure everyone is here bright and early. If all goes well, we'll have the women start packing. I'd like us to be well on our way before winter arrives."

"How are we going to get to Atlantis? We don't know the way."

"I haven't figured that out yet. I'm hoping we'll encounter people who can guide us along the way."

"How far do you think the others have gotten?" Cret asked quietly.

"I'm not sure. I hope they're making good progress. Atlantis should be just a few months' hard journey from here. I'm hoping they're nearly there by now. I have a report to finish, and then I'll join you at home."

"See you there, Father," Cret said, and Crelian patted him on the shoulder before heading back to his office.

When Crelian arrived at his office, a few more reports awaited him on his desk. With a weary sigh, he settled into his chair and picked up the last report he had been reviewing. It detailed that the grain bins were prepared for the upcoming harvest, but most of last year's crop had been depleted, leading to a projected shortage before the new harvest could begin. Crelian jotted a note about this on a separate piece of parchment to include in his summary report, then turned his attention to the next document.

By the time Crelian finished his report for Sen, the sun had fully set. He carefully stacked the individual reports on his bookcase, rolled up the condensed report, and sealed it with wax. Leaving his office, he walked the short distance across the control room to Sen's office.

Compared to his own, Sen's office was spacious and well-appointed. A large desk dominated the center of Sen's office, surrounded by several chairs. Crelian placed the rolled parchment on the desk and noticed a report sitting off to one side. He then glanced around the room. As usual, Sen and the rest of the locals had already retired for the evening.

Crelian quickly returned to Sen's desk and retrieved the parchment. Sen was engrossed in his report to Deleon, clearly irritated by Crelian's team working so closely with his own. He was still perplexed by the need for such detailed information and planned to consult Deleon about their future once the work was complete. It was an intriguing question— what to do with them? For Crelian, the answer was simple: let them leave and continue on their way. With that thought, he left the office and walked slowly back to his house, lost in contemplation.

The night air was warm and still. An owl glided silently overhead, and the millions of stars sparkled brightly against the clear, cloudless sky. Crelian paused and gazed upward, watching a shooting star streak across the darkness. As he marveled at the celestial display, another shooting star appeared, but instead of vanishing, it halted in mid-air before swooping down toward the earth. Crelian's eyes remained fixed on the spot where the enigmatic star had disappeared. A short time later, the star ascended from the Earth and soared back into the inky night sky. A smile crept onto Crelian's face as the realization dawned on him. He finally understood the source of the mysterious liquid. He hurried back to his house with renewed urgency to share the breakthrough with Cret.

The house was silent except for the gentle crackle of the fire in the cooking pit. Crelian presumed everyone was still at the ceremony. He walked over to the fire and added a few more logs, causing the flames to leap higher and cast a warm, inviting glow around the room. As he prepared some tea, adding water to a pot hanging above the fire, Cret walked in just as he settled down beside the flames.

"Everything is cleaned out and ready for testing in the morning," Cret reported as he entered the house.

"Good. Let's hope it's finally fixed." Crelian poured the near-boiling water into two clay mugs, adding a few mint leaves to each. He handed one to Cret. "Have you noticed the number of shooting stars lately?"

"Yes, I was meaning to talk to you about that."

"Tonight, I saw one that stopped midair, then fell sharply to the ground. A moment later, it took off again."

"It departed? Are you sure?" Cret asked, raising an eyebrow.

"Very sure. The liquid the Locals are storing is fuel waste from starships."

"So, the Locals are letting who knows who dump their fuel waste on this planet?"

"It appears so. At least now I know what to do with the sludge if the bulge pumps don't work tomorrow."

"What will become of all that waste decades from now?" Cret asked, concern evident in his voice.

"I'm not sure. If it mixes with any of the substances native to this planet, who knows what it will become," Crelian said, shaking his head, troubled by the implications.

"I'm going to retire. I'll see you in the morning," Cret said.

Crelian nodded, watching as Cret left. He lingered by the fire for a while longer, slowly sipping his tea and contemplating the future. The warmth of the fire and the soothing aroma of mint helped calm his thoughts. Eventually, he stood, finished his tea, and retired for the night, ready to face the following day's challenges.

Crelian and Cret arrived at the plant early the following morning to test the bulge pumps.

Cret sighed. "Let's hope this works." He signaled the burro handler to start the pumps. A loud chime echoed through the complex, followed by a series of pops as the pumps gradually roared to life.

A large fountain of sludge erupted into the air. The oily black liquid began to swirl, and the level in the tank slowly decreased. Crelian and Cret held their breath as the swirling sludge was steadily sucked out of the holding tank. Once most of the sludge was removed, several locals climbed into the tank to sweep the remaining residue toward the pump openings.

When all the sludge was removed, and the personnel had exited the tanks, a second, louder chime rang. The bulge pumps were shut down, and the entry pumps started up, filling the tanks with a new batch of liquid. Crelian's team began the process anew, adjusting the composition of the liquid to ensure it would pass through the holding tanks effectively. The locals observed intently, meticulously recording every detail of the procedure. The mixing process would occupy the better part of the day. Crelian left Cret in charge of overseeing the work and headed off to speak with Sen about their impending departure.

"The pumps are working already? They haven't been here that long. We've been trying to repair them for months, and now these outsiders with their so-called advanced technology fix them in just over a month?" Sen's sneering voice echoed down the deserted hallway.

Crelian stopped just short of the door, his ear catching the conversation.

"Yes, Sir," the man responded.

"Find Crelian and have him report to me immediately. I need to come up with something else for them to do until I hear back from Deleon."

Crelian darted around the corner, careful to stay out of sight. Adamos's footsteps echoed in the corridor as he walked away. Crelian waited until the sounds faded before he crept closer to Sen's office. He needed to hear more to understand what Sen was planning.

He pressed his ear against the door, trying to catch any additional conversation. Adamos walked by without noticing him, allowing Crelian to remain hidden. *What does Deleon intend to do with us?* Crelian wondered, frustration bubbling up at the constant secrets and mysteries surrounding the locals. He shook his head, hoping the rest of their group had made it safely to Atlantis. After a brief pause to steady his thoughts, he stepped into Sen's office.

"I have good news, sir," Crelian announced as he entered the spacious office. "All the pumps appear to be functioning. We should have a clearer picture tomorrow after a few cycles."

Sen's eyes widened briefly before he quickly composed himself. "It's about time," he muttered, shifting his gaze back to the desk. He feigned interest in the report Crelian had submitted the previous day, pretending to read as if he hadn't been caught off guard.

"Did you see Adamos before coming here?" Sen asked.

"I saw him in the distance, but we didn't speak. Do you need me to fetch him?"

"No, that won't be necessary. Just report back after you've completed five runs through the pumps."

"Five, sir?" Crelian hesitated. "I was hoping we could leave in a day or two. We're eager to reunite with the rest of our party."

"Let me remind you that your stay here is at our discretion," Sen said, his tone cold and measured. "You'll be released when we no longer require your services and not a moment before. You'll leave soon enough, but I want to ensure those pumps remain operational. I'd hate to summon you back for more repairs."

"That sounds reasonable. I'll inform my crew," Crelian replied, keeping his tone neutral. "Anything else, Sir?"

"No, you may go." Sen dismissed him with a curt wave, signaling the end of the conversation.

Crelian left Sen's office with a grim expression. *Five runs!* Each run took nearly a full day, meaning they'd be stuck here longer than he'd hoped. He resolved silently that they would be ready to leave as soon as the fifth run was complete— no delays. By then, Deleon's response would have arrived, but what would it say? What decision would he make regarding them?

Crelian's thoughts churned as he returned to the pump room. When he delivered the news to Cret and the team, their shared frustration was palpable, expressed in a collective groan.

"Make sure your wives have your belongings packed and the animals ready," Crelian instructed, his tone firm. "We're leaving as soon as the fifth run is complete."

"In the dark?" Georgios asked, eyebrows raised in surprise.

"Yes, in the dark," Crelian confirmed, a note of urgency in his voice. "I have a feeling that Deleon and Sen will try to delay us—or worse."

"I want us out of here as soon as possible, even if that means sneaking away in the dead of night," Crelian said, his voice low and determined. "Pack in secret—don't even tell your servants if you can avoid it. I'll have my wife secure extra food under the pretense of celebrating a job well done. The rest of you gather what you can without raising suspicion."

The days dragged on as they conducted repeated tests on the pumps. Everything appeared to be functioning properly. Meanwhile, Sephi and Camtis gathered enough provisions to either host a well-earned celebration or sustain them for several weeks. Crelian hoped this stockpile would be sufficient to get them a significant distance away and closer to another village. From the last letter he received from Neiluios, he had a rough idea of the direction the rest of their group had taken. They might never catch up with the others if they veered off that path before reaching a settlement. Crelian shook his head, trying to push away the unsettling thoughts. *No point in dwelling on what-ifs right now,* he told himself. *We need to leave here as quickly as possible.*

Crelian was seated at his desk, penning his nightly report to Sen, when the door swung open abruptly. Japster stormed in, a dark scowl etched on his face.

"Back so soon, Japster?" Crelian said, his tone neutral.

"Why did you send me to Deleon with a letter that simply said, 'Hello, Deleon; Hope all is well'? What was the point of that?"

Crelian's gaze hardened. "I needed to get you out of The Plant while we finished the repairs. You've been sabotaging our efforts for some time now."

"How dare you accuse me of that?" Japster's voice was filled with indignation.

"I couldn't prove it until you left and your son was given the day off. With the repairs complete, I hoped we would be gone before you returned," Crelian replied calmly.

"So, you planned to abandon me and my family here?" Japster sneered, his anger palpable.

"You've made it clear that you care more about what the Locals think than about us. I don't understand why Addident ever sent you on this mission. When the Locals say it's time to leave, you'd better be ready. We'll depart with or without you."

Japster's sneer deepened. "If you had the choice, what would you do?"

"Without you," Crelian replied flatly.

"You might get your wish," Japster shot back, his voice thick with anger. He stormed out of the room, leaving Crelian to watch through the crack of the door. Japster's furious stride led him directly to Sen's office, pausing only once to cast a fierce glare back at Crelian's door. Crelian quickly ducked back inside, his heart racing, hoping Japster hadn't seen him.

"Sen, they're planning to leave with or without me," Japster said, his voice edged with desperation. Sen looked up from his paperwork, his expression darkening.

"Then you must do everything in your power to stay with them," Sen replied, his tone cold and commanding. "If you want to secure a place of rank for yourself and your son, you'll need to prevent the others from reaching Atlantis. Do whatever it takes to keep them from their goal."

"You still haven't explained why it's crucial that they don't reach Atlantis," Japster said. "How can I trust you'll help me secure a higher rank if you keep secrets?"

Sen met Japster's gaze and sighed. "All right, here's the truth. I'm part of a group called the Society. We're descendants of those sent from Romota to replace Poseidie and his followers. They witnessed the damage Poseidie caused and vowed to end it. Poseidie abused the powers granted to him by the Gods and it now falls on our shoulders to fix the problems they allowed. The Gods do not truly care what happens to us. We are on our own," Sen scoffed. "Our main objective is to locate and destroy any remaining Romotian technology."

Japster considered Sen's words carefully and pondered the man's belief that Poseidie was granted god-like powers. "And what about those from whom you take this technology? Aren't they upset?"

"Some are, but most come to understand that what we offer is far superior," Sen replied. "Our society operates on the principle of equality—there are no rich or poor, no divisions. Everyone contributes and benefits equally. It creates a community without jealousy or disparity."

Japster frowned. "But if everyone is supposed to be the same, how do you justify having leaders like you and Deleon?"

Sen leaned forward, his expression serious. "Equality doesn't mean anarchy. We need leaders to maintain balance, ensure fairness, and protect the system from corruption. Deleon and I oversee resource distribution and make sure everyone has what they need. In places like Atlantis, the ruling family hoards wealth and power, leaving the people to suffer. We're offering something better—a system where people are freed from their oppressors and join us willingly because they see the benefits of our way. When we enter a village, the people recognize this and rise up with us, removing the greedy rulers who have kept them down."

"Yes, I can see that your way is better." Japster nodded. "I wish to stay with you and contribute all I can."

"In time, you shall," came the response. "But for now, I need you to stay with the others and make sure they don't reach Atlantis. The Society is growing stronger, and soon we'll have the resources to bring that evil city down. If they reach Atlantis with their technological knowledge, it will set us back years—years we can't afford to lose for the sake of everyone on this planet."

Japster's brow furrowed. "And Addident? What happened to him and the others who stayed behind at Camp Roma?"

"Does it matter? Addident is just a reflection of the corrupt rulers we've overthrown. I've heard about how he treated you. Why are you concerned about what happened to him?"

"It's not Addident I'm worried about. My son is friends with one of the guards' sons. That's the only reason I'm asking, Sir."

"Your son should choose his friends more wisely. Forget them—they're no longer a concern. Go now and prepare your family to leave with the others. I'll send further instructions later."

"Yes, Sir." Japster left the Plant and walked home to his family. A smile slowly spread across his face. Neiluios and Addident were likely dead, and soon, Crelian would join them. Hepluosis would be relieved to hear that Cret was no longer a threat. Japster would ensure that Sen and Deleon placed him in a high position to advance the Society. He would rise to greatness and power. He would see to it.

∞ 33 ∞
ATTACK

"**WE** will complete the final test tomorrow, Sir," Crelian said, his gaze fixed on the swirling liquid in the holding tank below from his vantage point on the catwalk. Sen approached quietly, his movements careful and deliberate. When Crelian spoke, Sen froze, caught off guard.

"Good, good," Sen replied. He joined Crelian at the railing, peering down into the tank with a shared, contemplative silence.

"Any additional problems?" Sen asked.

"None, Sir. My crew is planning a celebration for tomorrow night after the final test. You and your men are welcome to join us if you wish."

Sen grunted thoughtfully. "I'll let my men know. Where is this to take place?"

"We thought the conference hall would be the best location."

"That will be fine." Sen's mind raced. The conference hall was situated far from the main gates. With everyone gathered in one place at the rear of the camp, they'd have no easy escape. It was the perfect setup.

Crelian glanced at Sen, his sinister grin faltering when he met Crelian's gaze. His expression quickly turned impassive. "Report to me after the test tomorrow, before your celebration."

"Yes, Sir."

Sen took one last look at the tank before turning to leave the catwalk.

"What did he want?" Georgios asked, emerging from the other side of the catwalk.

"Nothing unusual," Crelian replied. "Is everyone ready to leave?"

"Yes, Sir. The women and children are prepared to move at a moment's notice. When do we depart?"

"I told Sen we're holding a celebration tomorrow evening after the final test. He'll assume we'll all be at the conference hall at the camp's rear. I want all children older than five to be outside the walls with some of the servants disguised as part of a nature lesson," Crelian instructed.

"Have all the servants go to the conference hall early to set up the celebration to get them out of the way. All the women and children should be in their houses, ready to leave at a moment's notice. Make sure all the animals are packed and prepared for the move. I'm scheduled to meet with Sen right after the final test. Everyone should head toward the gates as soon as that meeting is over. If I don't make it out, keep moving—don't wait for me."

"What do you think Sen might try to do?" Georgios asked.

"I don't know, and I don't plan to find out," Crelian replied. "Let's just hope we manage to get away from here and reach Atlantis safely."

Georgios nodded in agreement. Crelian reassuringly gripped his shoulder and led him off the catwalk.

Cret sprinted up to his father, coming to an abrupt halt. "Father, did Japster tell you what happened at Camp Roma?" Cret panted, struggling to catch his breath.

"Slow down, Son. What are you talking about?"

"I overheard Hepluosis talking to a Local about an attack on Camp Roma from about half a month ago," Cret said between gasps. "He mentioned that the same people have been spotted heading this way."

"Japster didn't mention that," Crelian said, his expression darkening. "Thanks for the information." He headed off to bed early that night, the weight of the news heavy on his mind. Despite his worries about the following day, sleep came quickly.

Cret was jolted awake by the sound of screaming. He fumbled to light the candle by his pallet in the darkness and hurried to the window. The camp was engulfed in flames. Hooded figures moved through the chaos, using torches to set fire to anything flammable. Locals struggled to contain the fires, but their efforts were overwhelmed by the onslaught.

Suddenly, the front door of their house was thrown open with a deafening crack. Several hooded men stormed inside. Cret raced to the main room, where he found his father already there, ready to face the impending danger.

"What's the meaning of this?" Crelian demanded, his voice cutting through the chaos.

"Gather what you can and follow us. You're in danger," one of the intruders replied urgently.

"Son, help your mother and sister," Crelian instructed. "Camtis, get the animals ready. We're leaving tonight."

Amid the chaos of the burning camp and the hooded figures wreaking havoc, Crelian's men and their families slipped away unnoticed. They traveled through the night and into the next day, driven by the constant fear of being pursued. Though no one spoke of it, the anxiety in the group was palpable, keeping them moving swiftly. It wasn't until dusk that the hooded men finally allowed them to rest.

Crelian approached the man who seemed to be the leader of the hooded figures. "Who are you?" he demanded.

After a moment, the man turned to face him and pulled back his hood. The others followed suit, revealing their faces. Crelian, half expecting them to look markedly different, was taken aback to see they were similar to himself.

"We call ourselves the Loyals," the leader said. "We are dedicated to Atlantis and saved your life last night. I must admit, I'm impressed with how swiftly you managed to gather all your belongings and animals."

"We were planning to leave this evening," Crelian said. "Over the past several days, we packed everything in secret. What brought you to us yesterday?"

The leader responded, "We have spies at the Plant and at the place you called Camp Roma. We learned that you were scheduled to be executed tonight." Several people gasped in shock. "Even though you planned to leave, you wouldn't have made it out in time. We decided it was best to act swiftly before Deleon could ensure your complete eradication."

"Thank you for saving us," Crelian said. "I'm Crelian. And you are?"

"I'm Simos," the leader replied.

"Why would Deleon want us killed? We're no threat to him," Crelian asked, puzzled.

Simos explained, "Deleon's hostility stems from a long-standing issue. It's rooted in the story of Poseidie and the replacements sent by Romota." As Simos detailed the background, Crelian listened closely, his mind racing. He shook his head, reflecting on how most people were easily swayed by whoever promised them security. It seemed the Society would face little opposition on this planet.

"How much further until we reach Atlantis?" Cret interrupted, breaking Crelian's thoughts.

"Several months of hard travel," Simos answered. "We'll need to stop for the winter and continue in the Growing Months."

"Several months!" several voices exclaimed in disbelief.

Crelian glanced around as people huddled closer, their concern growing.

"What happened to Addident and Neiluios?" a woman's voice called out from within the crowd.

"Their guide, appointed by Deleon, is one of ours," Simos explained. "They're on their way to Atlantis and will likely arrive a month ahead of us. Our route is more direct, and we have access to technology that the Society hasn't destroyed yet. But for now, everyone must rest. We have a long journey ahead, and you'll need your strength."

From the back of the crowd, Japster and Hepluosis glared at their rescuers. "I'll ensure we never reach Atlantis," Japster said quietly. "And you'll assist my son."

Hepluosis grinned at his father. "Whatever you say, Father. I'll do as instructed."

TO BE CONTINUED...

Thank you for reading *The Beginning of the End*.
I hope you continue to join Neiaphi and Cret on the next
leg of their journey in Book #2, *The Journey Continues*, and
Book #3, *The End of Atlantis*

Join my email list to be notified when the next book
becomes available.

Thanks again, and May the Gods Smile on You!

NeiaphisAtlantis@gmail.com

Sarah M Wasson

Within the shimmering embrace of Las Vegas, Nevada, I dwell with my beloved husband and son. My heart is imbued with the spirit of enterprise, juggling my pursuits as a pet groomer, amateur golfer, horse whisperer, falconer, and devotee of the fantastical realms of sci-fi.

Fantastical Realm Publishing

www.FantasticalRealm.com
FantasticalRealmPublishing@gmail.com

www.ingramcontent.com/pod-product-compliance
Lightning Source LLC
Chambersburg PA
CBHW020549120726
47903CB00001B/192